The Paradox of Imagination

E.M.Attridge

ISBN: 9781070514574

Imprint: Independently published

Cover Illustration Copyright © 2019 E.M.Attridge

Cover design by Terry Gallivan

Editing by Bex Stafferton

Acknowledgments

Many thanks as ever go to my daughter, Kierra. Without your vivid imagination, this story would never have seen the light of day!

Jiya, you were born during the making of this book. For you, I would like to give thanks for all the sleepless nights and the beautiful artwork drawn across my laptop.

For support and encouragement, I would like to give thanks to my darling wife, Anupreet. I know me writing this book has driven you a bit crazy, but hey it was worth it, don't you think?

Bex, for your amazing editing skills and impeccable attention to detail, I thank you for transforming this book into an even more wonderful story.

Terry Gallivan, for your amazing artwork! Keep up the hard work!

Russell, for your input and incredible ideas when I got the dreaded writers block!

And finally, all the wonderful contributors on my Facebook group page who have continued to support me over the past year.

Here are the top contributors from the T.P.o.I. Group Page:

Shaun O'Malley, Shaun McCombie, Sarah Henderson, Gwilym Roberts, Darren Radcliffe, Nathan Sandiford, Anthony Walker, Michael Watson, Sarah O'Malley, Christopher Allan, Julie Sanderson, Susie Langdon, Andrew Johnson, Kylie Longmuir, Simmo Richards, Lizzie Hibbard, Stephen Wilson, Helen Attfield, Lloyd Lewis, Terry O'Malley, Robert Little, James Lee Ritchings, Teresa Evans & Stephen Murphy.

For my dearest father, Peter

Part 1

"Everything you can imagine is real."

Pablo Picasso.

Chapter 1

December 22nd 2017. Bristol, England.

5 days to termination…

This was the worst time of year for Michelle. Life was increasingly hectic living in Bristol during the run up to Christmas; everyone was in a rush and the busy, bustling streets were so tightly crammed with shoppers. She absolutely despised Christmas shoppers and would often imagine them as hordes of headless chickens, aimlessly wandering around blindly searching out that last minute present. Of course, when customers came up to her in the shop she would smile politely, but deep down she was annoyed. She'd had thoughts about throwing in the towel and walking out on more than one occasion, but she couldn't; it was her only source of income and her lazy boyfriend Shaun certainly wouldn't get off his arse to help her out. To make matters worse she couldn't stand her boss Trudy; a thoroughly evil woman, who people often likened to a witch, or as Michelle liked to put it, "the next Anti-Christ". Trudy was a large woman, who was renowned for eating at every given opportunity -

doughnuts being her preferred food of choice. She had grey, thinning hair, wrinkles that charted their way across her face like a London Underground map, and her teeth were yellow from years of heavy smoking. As for her dress sense…well, it was simply awful. Her daily 'uniform' consisted of a brown dress that looked as though it had stepped straight out of an eighties catalogue and those scratchy, woollen knee high socks that school girls wore and made her look like a very fat, very old, head girl. The ironic thing was, the store she owned was a fashion shop.

"Michelle, I'm going to need you to work through your break today, we're far too busy for you to put your feet up," said Trudy spitefully.

"But Trudy, I've been on my feet since eight A.M., it's two thirty now and I'm knackered. Can't I just go and grab a quick cuppa?" begged Michelle.

"No, you can't. And don't question me, I'm your boss, just do it!" shouted the large woman with an angry frown, "You know we struggle when Dawn's away."

Dawn was Trudy's favourite, but only because she never questioned her authority like Michelle did. Dawn had zero personality and she was weak, that's why Trudy favoured her. She simply did as she was told and that was that. Trudy liked compliance and that's exactly what she got with Dawn.

Wearing an unconvincing smile, Michelle slogged it out for the rest of the day, exhausted and irritated by the relentless stream of desperate scrabbling customers. Six o'clock eventually arrived and it was finally time to close the shop. She sat down and sighed, placing her head in her hands. She'd never enjoyed working in the shop. The harsh glare of the spotlights and the endless walls of mirrors meant she could never escape

2

her reflection and she would often catch a glimpse of herself, revolted by the image that stared back at her. She always looked tired these days, with dark bags under her eyes, and her mousey, bleached hair never quite went the way she wanted it to. As for her saggy breasts and broad, bulky shoulders, Michelle hated them. She'd never really had much confidence in her appearance, even though complete strangers regularly complimented her on how good she looked.

She left the shop without saying goodbye to Trudy and walked hurriedly home. All she wanted to do was flop on the sofa and forget all about how crappy her life was. Things had never been the same since her husband Peter had died. It was nine years and she still thought of him with longing and heartbreak. He had been a confident, charming man and she missed him terribly. A tiny tear rolled down her cheek and the all too familiar feelings of utter sadness and loss washed over her. To this day no one knew how he had died. It had happened under extremely strange circumstances and it was something that had haunted her for some time now. She also carried with her the heavy burden of guilt knowing that her daughter Rose had never got to know him properly; he had died shortly after her fifth birthday.

Michelle arrived home twenty minutes later, naively hoping that Shaun had cooked something, or at the very least had done some housework. But, as she'd expected, he hadn't. He just sitting, with his feet up, watching the TV.

"You've done fuck all!" Michelle yelled accusingly.

"Nice to see you too!" replied Shaun sarcastically, looking at her with a sly sideways glance, but then quickly returning his gaze to the TV.

"Where's Rose? Did you remember to collect her from Jackie's?"

"I thought you were collecting her?"

"How could I Shaun? I've been working since early this morning. You're the one who's been sitting there doing nothing all day!"

Michelle walked back out the front door, slamming it behind her in anger. She was completely at the end of her tether with him.

The streets were empty only with a few street lamps providing a warm welcoming glow. It was an icy cold night, and a frosty mist covered the air like a grey blanket flecked with the dim light from the ghostly yellow street lamps. Michelle hugged herself in a vain attempt to conserve what little body heat she had left. It only took her ten minutes to get to Jackie's house, but it seemed like an eternity. Walking up the front path she shivered as she knocked on the front door and jumped as it was opened almost immediately. Jackie was an old friend of hers; a petite, rather round woman with short black hair, rosy cheeks and a kind face, although the look on her face wasn't particularly kind at the moment. She wasn't married and was someone who could be described as 'unlucky in love'. Men would use her for sex, and then she'd never hear from them again. She often joked to Michelle about taking a vow of celibacy and that she'd be better off becoming a nun. Michelle and Jackie had gone to college together, spent holidays together and were once very good friends, but things had changed since Peter's death. She'd become distant, less friendly, and although she'd still look after Rose to help Michelle out, even that was becoming strained.

"Where have you been?"

"I'm so sorry Jackie. Shaun was meant to pick her up."

"I don't know why you waste your time with that man. He's no good for you."

Michelle ignored her. She knew she was right, but she really didn't have the energy to argue about it with her again tonight. And anyway, she was fed up of having to justify his behaviour all the time. She couldn't, no she wouldn't, defend him anymore, even if she was terrified of his controlling and abusive ways.

Rose popped her head up in the background and walked out to join Michelle. She was a pretty girl with striking blue eyes, a beautiful radiant smile and blonde hair that she'd tied up neatly in a ponytail today. And she was extremely intelligent for a fourteen year old; sometimes she'd come out with words that Michelle hadn't even heard of. Michelle had tried on numerous occasions to get her into a private school, but she couldn't afford the extortionate fees and they had all refused to offer her a scholarship. They'd told Michelle that, *"she doesn't concentrate"*, *"she's too much of a dreamer"*, and that *"she's impossible to teach"*.

Rose was wearing her school uniform; a green jumper with a yellow tie and black skirt. Michelle had never liked it. She thought it looked too green and made her daughter look like some kind of garish, animated frog.

"Hi mum," Rose said, smiling.

Michelle gave a little smile back and gently wrapped her arms around her daughter's slim shoulders, before ushering her out into the cold air.

"You need to look after her, I don't trust that Shaun one little bit," said Jackie.

Michelle nodded, thanked her and headed off, choosing to ignore her friend's concerns yet again.

"How was your day?" Michelle asked.

"I saw Chloe in the corridors at break and… she hit me."

"Oh, come on Rose, I'm sure she didn't mean it. It was probably just an accident, you know how busy it gets at breaktime. Whenever I've seen her she's always been ever so polite."

No mum, I'm not making it up. They think I'm strange, they all do, they call me a dopey dreamer. It's happened loads mum, I just haven't always told you. You don't understand. You're just annoyed that I can't stay in one school and be happy there. I hate it mum, I don't want to go back. I don't want to go to any school!"

Although Rose was a bright girl, she did have a habit of daydreaming and would often drift off into her own little world, before being brought back to earth with a bump by an understandably irritated teacher. Yet, this was the first time Michelle had heard anything about bullying. It had happened in her previous schools, but Michelle genuinely thought she was happy at this one.

"I'll sort it out, don't you worry. I'll speak to your teacher and see what we can do about it. Look, it's nearly Christmas and we can spend some quality time together, then perhaps, if the teachers don't do anything, we can look at changing schools. Get you into a better one, how's about that?"

Rose nodded unconvincingly. She knew it wouldn't make any difference whatsoever which school she went to. This had been the third one and none of them were any different. It was as if she had a sign written across her forehead saying, *"Bully me"*.

They walked on in silence, bracing themselves against the bitter cold, until eventually they arrived back home. Michelle dreaded seeing Shaun again. She knew there'd be more trouble and she knew how upsetting it was for Rose to see them argue. They both walked through the door in nervous trepidation about what would be waiting for them inside. Rose walked into the living room first and sat down in Shaun's favourite chair. She wouldn't normally dare sit there, but seeing as he didn't appear to be in, she figured it wouldn't harm. She felt a sudden surge of rebellion course its way through her veins. He was probably up at the Winterbourne pub getting drunk; he was always in there these days. Anyway, this chair was much closer to the TV and sitting anywhere else would obscure her view. It was nice to get prime position for a change. She found the remote squashed down the side of the chair and retched as she removed a sticky mass of hair from the buttons. Switching the TV on, she changed the channel from the sports to *Mucky games for mucky kids;* a game show where kids had to get as mucky as they could to win prizes and be crowned the filthiest child.

"Why do you watch that rubbish?" called Michelle from the kitchen, "They should be handing out prizes for the tidiest, not the dirtiest!"

Rose grinned and gave a little snigger before returning her attention back to the TV show. However, her amusement didn't last long. She heard the front door bang and Shaun pounded into the living room. He was a scruffy character, with a wispy unkempt beard and his belly stuck out like some grotesque heavily pregnant beast. But that wasn't the worst of it, his body odour, made up of a mixture of sweat and alcohol, created a rancid stink that overpowered the room as he walked towards Rose. He hadn't been to the pub at all; he'd been sleeping.

"Get the fuck out of my chair! And why've you put that shit on?" he demanded.

Rose stared up at him, her heart pounding. She jumped abruptly out of his chair, quivering as she handed him over the TV remote.

"Don't talk to her like that!" screamed Michelle, hastily rushing in from the kitchen to defend and protect her vulnerable child.

"This is *my* TV and this is *my* chair," he replied angrily, "Get the fuck out of my way woman!"

He pushed Michelle to the floor and her head thumped against the wooden chair. She tried getting up, but couldn't and Shaun placed a foot on her weakened body, pushing down hard with his heavy boot and grinning sinisterly.

"Don't hurt her!" cried Rose, as she attempted to push his leg from off of her mum. Shaun grabbed Rose's ponytail and pulled her to one side, dropping her to the floor like a rag doll. She crawled away sobbing and grabbed the phone on her way out of the living room. Frantically dialling the number for the police, she held it to her ear and waited.

"Which service do you require?" came a calm voice at the other end of the phone.

"Police!" cried Rose.

"Can you tell me your name, please?"

"It's Rose."

"OK Rose, what's happening?"

"My mum's boyfriend is hurting her, please you've got to hurry!"

"It's OK, calm down love. Where do you live?"

"49 Havanock Square."

"Right Rose, an officer will be with you shortly," the operator reassured her. *"Stay on the phone, tell me where you are? Where is your mum now?"*

"He's hurting her… I can hear him… he's hitting her… she's in the living room… please hurry!"

"OK Rose, now listen. Where are you? I want you to get somewhere safe, can you do that for me, Rose?"

"Yes, I'm in the bathroom. I don't think he knows I'm in here."

"OK that's good. Now, lock the door and wait for the police, they'll be there soon."

Rose sat with her back against the bathroom door, desperately waiting for the police to arrive. It could only have been a few minutes, but to Rose it felt like an eternity. Eventually however, there came the sound of loud banging from the front door.

"POLICE, OPEN THE DOOR!"

Shaun didn't respond to the demand and continued hitting Michelle, who was now lying bloodied, swollen and unconscious on the floor. Rose heard the sounds of the door being kicked down and then the police rushing in. They heaved Shaun off of Michelle and he pushed and punched them as they struggled to restrain him. Then suddenly, he stopped, his body going rigid from the voltage that passed through him. The room fell silent with only the sound of the Taser ticking uncontrollably. Rose ran out from the bathroom and rushed over to her mum. She grimaced at the unrecognisable sight of her mum lying on the blood-stained carpet. Sobbing, Rose cradled Michelle, as if she were the mother figure in this relationship. She held onto her tightly, feeling the rage beginning to manifest itself inside her. She wanted him dead. She wanted him to go and never come back.

You evil man.

I'll make you pay for this.

Chapter 2

Rose had never liked hospitals. She had bad memories of being here when her father died; all that smell of antiseptic, it brought vomit up to the back of her throat. She could remember so vividly watching the doctors rushing around and most of all she remembered, and could still feel the devastation it had left after his death. Even though Rose had only been five at the time, she'd always somehow felt responsible, especially after her mum had gone through several nervous breakdowns. But Michelle had always reassured her there was nothing she could have done and that she shouldn't blame herself. She walked alongside Jackie, tightly clasping her hand as they entered the ward, dreading seeing the damage that wretched man had caused. Rose's anxiety was worse than it had ever been and no matter how hard she tried not to think about it all she could hear was her mother's screams as each of Shaun's punches broke yet another bone in her body. A female doctor appeared and gave Rose a comforting smile.

"Hello, you must be Rose. I'm Doctor Oakley. Your mum's doing well, but we need to keep a close eye on her for a bit longer. I must warn you that she has lots of tubes attached to her and there's lots of machines in there with her, but please don't worry, she's in good hands."

Doctor Oakley turned her head and nodded at Jackie in acknowledgment.

"So, how's she doing Doctor?"

"She's doing well, better than we expected. We've taken several X-rays, which show she has a fracture in her left eye socket as well as some areas of substantial bruising around both her cheekbones. She's still unconscious at the moment, but she's an extremely lucky lady. We're going to need to operate on her sometime this evening to help repair the fracture. Here, follow me and I'll take you to her."

Rose and Jackie trailed after the Doctor. It was eerily quiet in the room, the silence interrupted only by the occasional beep from the monitoring equipment.

"I'll leave you with her. Please don't hesitate to ask if you have any questions, I'll just be outside," said the doctor kindly.

Jackie gave the doctor a teary smile. Rose sat down next to her mum and held her limp hand, staring down at her battered face. It was terrible. She couldn't understand how anyone could do this to another human, let alone her mum who wouldn't even hurt a fly.

Jackie raised her hands to her mouth in shock at the sight of Michelle's injuries. Rose would need all the support she could get right now. She put a comforting arm around her and softly told her,

"Don't worry Rose, she's a strong woman your mum, she'll pull through. You can stay with me until she gets better."

They sat there in silence, tears filling their eyes as they watched Michelle. Time ticked by and they continued sitting there for what felt like hours, until they were kindly asked to leave by the ward nurse.

The drive back was sombre and Jackie turned the radio on to try and fill the silence. Rose couldn't help but replay the haunting sound of her mother's cries for help over and over in her head and it filled her with an intense rage.

"I think I'm going to go straight up to bed Jackie. I want to be on my own for a little bit," Rose said as they both entered the hallway.

Jackie nodded and kissed her lightly on the forehead.

"Yes, that's fine love, you go on up, you've been through a lot today. There's a bed made up in the spare room and you can find a towel in the airing cupboard if you need one. Just call me if you need anything OK and remember, I'm right here."

Rose forced a smile and headed up the narrow staircase. Making her way to the spare room, she clambered onto the bed and lay there, gazing up at the Artexed ceiling. She went over what had happened that night, the pain of her mother continually playing over and over like a stuck video tape. It was all still so vivid. She began to shake, her anger overwhelming her. *That monster*, she thought, *how could he do that to her?* Beads of sweat formed on her forehead and she wiped them away with the back of her hand.

His face, all she could see was his face.

That horrible, evil man.

She closed her eyes and imagined him in terrible agony. She thought about him slowly burning, his skin peeling away in layers, and watching his panic-stricken face, as the fat dripped from his roasting body. There was so much pleasure in watching him suffer and she laughed at his inability to escape. Smiling to herself she thought, 'now you can suffer and now you will die'.

She held onto that last image of Shaun burnt to a crisp in her mind and sensed a feeling of complete satisfaction. As the image slowly faded, she turned onto her side and slowly drifted off into a deep, relaxing sleep...

Chapter 3

4 days until termination…

The following morning Rose awoke to the sound of laughter and shouting. She climbed out of bed and wandered over to the window to see where it was coming from. She was met by the sight of a group of school children gleefully playing together in the lightly snow dusted street. They were attempting to build snowmen, throwing snowballs at one another and looking as though they were having the time of their lives. She stared down at them with a feeling of sadness, wondering what it would be like to have friends to play with. She felt so lonely. Gazing up at the beautiful morning sky, she noticed how every now and again thin wispy clouds broke up the vibrant blue and how the glaring sun cast its blinding rays leaving her mesmerised, almost trance-like, before the spell was broken and she was abruptly snapped back to reality. With her feet firmly back on planet earth, she thought about what she'd do over the course of the day. *Perhaps have breakfast and then help Jackie with some errands.* She liked helping Jackie out and sometimes would even be rewarded with a bit of money in return, plus it would help keep her mind off things. *Then, in the afternoon I could go into town and buy some get well gifts for mum, and if I have enough time I could go to the library.* Rose loved going to the library; it was a space in which she could dream and fantasise as much as she wanted and not be interrupted. Not having to control her thoughts made her feel free, leaving her to go wherever she wanted. No one could stop her.

She got dressed, putting on the same clothes as the previous day. She knew she'd have to return home eventually to pick up her belongings, but she was dreading it. She didn't want to go back; the memory was too painful, it was still too recent. As she descended the stairs, she was greeted with a warm hug from Jackie.

"Morning Rose, how are you today?"

"I'm OK thanks Jackie, a little upset still, but I'll be fine."

Jackie gave a little smile and leant over and kissed her on the forehead.

"That's my girl. I've made pancakes, I know how much you like them, so go on in and have your breakfast. You'll have to excuse me a minute though, I need to put the bins out."

Rose sat down and began tucking in to the steaming stack of pancakes on her plate. She watched as Jackie left the room clutching two bulging sacks of rubbish. Casually looking around, Rose noticed the large collection of pewter mugs that were stacked neatly on Jackie's large pine display cabinet. Some were large, some were tiny, some looked old, and some looked new, but in her mind she couldn't understand what the fascination was with them. *I mean, they're just mugs!* She turned her attention towards the TV. *Boring,* she thought, *the news.* She carried on eating her pancakes, mopping up the syrup with her fingers and chewing each mouthful with joy. But then something caught her attention and she paused mid-bite, listening carefully to what the news correspondent had just said...

'*A man believed to be in his late thirties has been discovered in a car park near the Winterbourne pub. Police have stated that he has suffered horrific burns and died at the scene.*'

'*Inspector Caroline Taylor of the Avon and Somerset Constabulary has stated:*

'*At this stage we do not know the identity of the man in the vehicle and will be identifying the individual through dental records. After reviewing the CCTV footage we have found what appears to be another person present, a black male, approximately six foot two inches, wearing only his underwear. The man, believed to be in his early twenties, is seen behaving erratically and is clearly in a lot of distress. As of yet we do not know who this individual is and we urgently request that if anyone knows this person, or if you believe you may have seen him in the area, to please contact the Avon and Somerset Constabulary, or to contact Crime Stoppers.*'

Rose was in shock! S*urely I couldn't have done that, surely not, it can't be Shaun...it can't be?* Her stomach twisted and she began to feel a wave of nausea sweep over her. Jackie returned from putting the bins out, singing a happy little song to herself as a slightly half-hearted attempt at taking her mind off of the horrific events from the previous night and to try and help lighten the atmosphere between her and Rose. However, when she spotted Rose's shocked expression she stopped singing and asked,

"What's wrong, Rose? Are you feeling OK love? You look terribly pale."

Rose stood up, pushing her chair out from behind her, and then turned abruptly and ran off in a panic. Picking up her coat, she opened the door and ran out, failing to hear the fading voice of Jackie calling out from behind her. The children in the street watched as Rose struggled to keep her balance on the slippery path, but once she'd found her feet she started to run. Tired and out of breath, she gradually slowed her pace and walked the rest of the way. She was near her mum's work place, and she really didn't want to go near there; she might bump into that horrid woman her mum moaned about all the time. Instead, she decided to take a different route; it would take longer, but at least she'd avoid any unnecessary confrontations.

The library was busy, but even so, the only sound that could be heard was the soft swish of pages being turned. Rose sat down in the most secluded area she could find and thought about what she'd just heard on the news. She couldn't understand how this could have happened. Shaun spent most of his life at the Winterbourne pub, *what if it was him? Had she killed him?* She shook her head in disbelief and picked out a random book from the shelves. It was a thick dusty hardback entitled, '*Finding your God, by Dr. E.M.A*', not her usual choice but she wasn't interested in reading, she just wanted to blend in and not draw attention to herself as she sat and gathered her thoughts. *What if I try it again?* she thought. She glanced around the library searching for a suitable Guinea pig among the quiet readers and students, to test her theory out on. Her gaze stopped on an old woman, who was sat in the corner staring closely at a computer screen. She was wearing what Rose would describe as 'old people's clothes'; a sort of mustardy tartan look with a matching wheeled tartan shopping bag. *OK* she thought; *let's try it on her.*

Rose closed her eyes and imagined the old lady as she sat there quietly minding her own business looking closely at the computer screen. She pictured the room with the signs that said 'Quiet please' and 'Check out our latest DVD range'. She imagined the distinctive blue carpet, the wooden beams that stretched from the ground up and the long line of computers leading up to the unsuspecting lady. She made it all so clear and vivid in her mind. She then visualised the old lady lifting up out of her chair and levitating helplessly in mid-air. Her wheeled shopping bag was dragged off by an unseen force; its contents flung out haphazardly in all directions. She saw the group of startled students jump out of their chairs and run for cover, their petrified screams and shouts piercing her eardrums.

Rose opened her eyes to see if anything had happened, but as she'd suspected…nothing. *See, it can't have been me; it must have been that naked man after all.* She sighed with relief at the proof of her innocence and cradled her head in her hands, before closing her eyes and this time flying off into her own magical world…

She was in a bright, vibrant land where the trees, flowers, people and buildings were all so colourful. She was flying way above everything, looking down at the spectrum of colours below her. She was able to soar and swoop and land wherever she wanted to and it filled her with a sense of freedom that she so lacked in reality. She imagined having friends, friends that would play with her, friends that didn't care who she was or what she was like, that liked her for being her. She felt happy here and this made her feel calm, her anxieties now reducing down into a deep sense of tranquillity.

However, as was always the case, these happy visions never lasted for long.

The land became dark, the colours fading to shades of grey, the bright trees and people becoming distorted as the light rapidly faded. Rose was now in almost complete darkness with just a dim spotlight illuminating a small area of space. A shadowy creature slowly approached her, but she couldn't make it out properly and she had no idea what it wanted. It wasn't a person, or an animal, but more like an entity. An entity with no logical shape, a dark shadowy being with strange metallic eyes and its movements flowed like liquid water. It hovered in the distance, completely stationary, staring at Rose through its haunting eyes, before swiftly approaching and screaming loudly;

"CHATTI CARTOM DESTRUCT ORMATI!"

"Excuse me," a voice interrupted. "Excuse me, we're about to close the library."

Rose opened her eyes, disorientated and unsure for a moment of where she was.

"I think you've been asleep my dear," said the librarian.

"What time is it?" Rose muttered, embarrassed at having been caught.

"It's one thirty, we close early today."

"Oh gosh, I'm so sorry I didn't realise. I'll go."

Rose stood up, leaving the book on the table and made a hasty exit out of the library. She couldn't understand how the time had passed so quickly. And that creature... what was that creature? Her heart thumped erratically as panic surged through her body and she felt the familiar sensation of anxiety grip her body. She took some long, slow deep breaths and started to feel her body relax back down. The bitterness of the cold winter breeze felt sharp against her skin and she wrapped her arms around herself to try and keep herself warm. She looked at the beautiful evergreen Christmas decorations hanging from the shop windows to try and distract her from her thoughts and to try and inject a sense of normality back into her life.

"Rose!" called an unfamiliar voice. "Are you Rose?"

Rose turned around to see a large, rather masculine looking woman, wearing a brown skirt, knee high socks and a tight fitting brown jumper waddling towards her.

"Yes," said Rose with a confused look.

"Hello there, it's good to finally meet you, how's your mum doing?"

"Um, she's doing OK thanks," she replied cautiously.

"Sorry, you don't know me very well. Your mum used to bring you into the shop when you were a toddler. I thought I recognised you, you're the absolute spit of her. Oh sorry, where's my manners, I didn't introduce myself. My name's Trudy; I'm your mum's manager."

Rose went rigid.

"Oh yes, yes I do know of you, mums mentioned you… a lot."

Trudy drew closer to Rose and smiled, her yellow teeth grinning menacingly at her.

"Your mum should be working, why's she not at the shop? I haven't heard from her and I've been trying to call her."

"She's in hospital. She was involved in an argument with her boyfriend… and… and she has some bad injuries to her face." said Rose, retracting back as Trudy leaned further forward.

"Yeah just like your mum you are, a lying little shit. Your mum probably deserved it, that good-for-nothing scumbag. You tell her to get her arse down to the shop pronto or she'll no longer have a job to come back to."

Trudy barged past Rose, pushing her against the wall. Rose was shaking with fear, but she couldn't quite believe what that woman had said about her mum. *Mum was right, she is horrid. How could she be so nasty to me, she doesn't even know me. And mum can't help being in hospital. It's all Shaun's fault.* She repeated Trudy's unkind, slanderous words over and over in her mind just as she had with Shaun's and as she did so she began to feel the rage bubbling deep within her. *That evil woman deserves to suffer. She deserves a taste of her own medicine.* She sat down on a bench, shaking uncontrollably from the adrenaline rushing through her body.

She closed her eyes and pictured Trudy walking back to the shop, visualising the hordes of shoppers rushing past her and the long line of taxis waiting to take them home. She imagined Trudy tripping on a loose paving slab, her huge body dropping heavily to the ground like a stone in water and her screams echoing out against the concrete buildings. Rose felt her excitement increase as she watched Trudy's body slam against the solid road, before picturing a perfectly timed bus passing by; its wheels crushing Trudy's head. Like a balloon popping, her brain and cranial fluid exploded out over the road, spraying several unfortunate passers-by. The bus screeched to a halt, skidding as the crushed head left trails of blood and fragments of skull behind it. Rose smiled to herself, "that's what you deserve you evil woman."

She opened her eyes. Her anxiety had reduced and she felt a wave of relief wash over her. Taking a deep breath, she continued her walk back to Jackie's house. Christmas was less than a week away and with the realisation that her mum was unlikely to be out of hospital in time, Rose felt deep sadness. Tears streamed down her face as she thought of spending it without her and she looked with bitter envy at the carol singers and Christmas shoppers passing her in the street, oblivious to her pain. She turned her thoughts to what presents she could give her mum. *Flowers were a must and she liked books, so maybe a nice romantic novel would be a good idea. And she was obsessed with marshmallows, so she'd get her some of those as well, that would definitely cheer her up.*

Just then she noticed some commotion. There were police cars, ambulances and a large crowd of people gathered in the distance. She drew closer, casually passing by, wondering what all the fuss was about. As the crowd dispersed, Rose caught a glimpse of what had happened… A bus, she saw a bus, just like the one she'd imagined! She stared in bewilderment trying to convince herself that it was just a coincidence, it must be something else entirely. *Yes*, she thought, *it must be a car that's hit the bus, surely that's it.* But then she overheard two men talking to each other.

"Apparently, a woman fell into the road and a bus ran over her," said the man.

"Jesus! That's terrible, what a way to go," replied the other man.

"I know! I don't think she survived either, well you wouldn't would you!"

Rose staggered to the side of road, vomit bubbling up from her stomach, causing her to retch and double over. Wiping her mouth, she pushed her way through the crowd and hastily made her way back to Jackie's.

When Rose got back to Jackie's, she sat down and switched on the TV, desperate to know what had happened. *Was it Trudy? Had she really caused her death?*

Jackie poked her head around the corner of the door before walking in and sitting beside her.

"What happened this morning Rose, why'd you run off like that?"

"I guess I was just upset about the whole situation with mum and stuff," she lied.

"Listen, I know it's hard, but at least now that evil bastard will be out of your life for good. I expect he'll be facing a long stretch in prison for what he did to your mum. But seriously Rose, you mustn't run off like that, I was so worried about you. I was this close to calling the police, I was that worried about you."

Rose looked up at her sheepishly.

"Yes, I know, I'm sorry for running off like that. And yes, you're right, he won't be bothering us for a long time," Rose said with a mysterious smile.

"That's the spirit love," said Jackie placing an arm around her. "Now, let me make you a cup of tea, I've got some of those yummy biscuits you like."

Rose nodded her head approvingly and watched as Jackie left the room. Even though she was 14, it seemed as if Jackie still thought of her as a kid. Deep down it really annoyed her all that patronising talk and the nicey nice act, but if it meant Jackie leaving her alone, then it was worth playing along with it. She curled up on the sofa and flicked through the channels, hoping there'd be some information about Trudy. She remained on the sofa for most of the afternoon, worried that if she left she'd miss the news she was after. Jackie kept checking in on her from time to time and she was getting noticeably more stressed about Rose's increasingly strange behaviour.

"You don't normally watch the news Rose, why don't we put something else on, something a bit more positive, yeah? I'm sure there's something way more interesting and far less depressing than what you'll see on there," said Jackie as she went to change the channel.

"No, no it's OK, I'm not really in the mood for movies or soaps. Leave it on the news, I'm watching it," snapped Rose.

"OK, OK," replied Jackie with an odd look, "whatever makes you happy. I've got a few things to get on with anyway, so let me know if you need anything. And listen, don't worry about the shopping OK, we can do that tomorrow."

Rose nodded without really acknowledging what Jackie had said, her eyes staying firmly fixed on the TV. Suddenly the latest breaking news story filled the screen.

'*Woman dies in tragic accident when crossing the road.*'

Rose's heart started pounding and she sat up.

'*A woman died after being struck by a bus on Gloucester Road at approximately one forty this afternoon. One witness claims that the woman tripped over a loose paving slab and collided with the number two bus, which was en route to the city centre. Witnesses claim she was walking back to the clothing shop she owned after visiting the post office. The woman is believed to be fifty three year old Trudy Merchant, the owner of Trudy's fashion shop. Although confirmed identity has not yet taken place, there are reports that a driving licence belonging to Trudy Merchant was found in a handbag at the scene. At this time police are not treating the incident as suspicious, but merely a tragic accident. Our thoughts go out to her family and friends during this sad and tragic time.'*

Rose switched off the TV and stared at the blank screen. Had she managed to cause Trudy's death simply by imagining it? She felt scared. *This was crazy, was she going mad?* She couldn't help but think about Shaun too, *was it him, had she murdered him too? Was it even murder? Can it really be murder if you've only thought it?* It was far too complicated for her to understand and anyway, who would possibly believe her? The phone rang, disrupting her from her thoughts. She jumped and listened out as Jackie answered it.

"Hello?" said Jackie wedging the phone between her shoulder and her ear as she carried on drying a cup with a tea towel.

There was a pause.

"Oh my, that's wonderful news, I'll tell her now. Thanks, bye."

She put the phone down and looked at Rose.

"Rose that was the hospital, it's good news! Your mum's regained consciousness, and although she's still a bit weak and a little confused the doctors are impressed with her recovery and have said she's up for visitors. Would you like to go and see her?"

Rose jumped up and hugged Jackie tightly.

"Careful!" said Jackie laughing, "I nearly dropped the cup! I'll take that as a yes then, come on let's go and see your mum."

They were met by the familiar smell of hospitals and the sight of doctors and nurses rushing about trying to deal with the latest emergency. Noticing Jackie and Rose, Doctor Oakley approached them both with a hopeful smile.

"How are you, Rose?" she asked.

"I'm OK thanks Doctor Oakley."

"That's good to hear," the doctor smiled. "Your mum's awake, but she's finding it incredibly difficult to remember exactly what happened to her. She has something we call post-traumatic amnesia, it's something that can happen after a head injury. She's also very weak still and she may find it hard to talk. But I assure you Rose, she can hear everything you say to her."

For once Rose felt happy. It was such a relief to know that her mum would be OK and that now they could think about starting over again and building a new life together without that evil man. She walked into the room with Jackie and they both looked down in sympathy at the battered woman lying on the bed.

"Hey Rose," said Michelle with a weak smile.

Rose held her hand and began crying.

"Oh sweetheart, don't cry. I'll be OK," mumbled Michelle reassuringly.

"It's good to see you're doing OK Mich," said Jackie warmly. "Rose has been staying with me, but we still need to go over to the house and collect her belongings, so I'll need to get the keys off you at some point if that's alright?"

"Yes, yes of course, and thank you so much for looking after her. I think they've got my belongings up at the nurse's station," Michelle replied with a grimace.

"Look, don't talk just rest. I'll go and find the keys, don't you worry yourself" said Jackie and she left the room to go and collect the keys.

"How you doing Rose?" asked Michelle weakly.

"Mum, some strange things have been happening and I don't know what to do about it."

"Oh Rose, a lot's happened recently, it's to be expected that you'll be feeling a bit out of sorts."

"No, you don't understand mum…"

"Got them!" Jackie called out, as she walked back in dangling the keys. "Now, I don't want you overexerting yourself, so stop the chitter chatter for now and get some rest, doctors orders," she said with a wink.

An hour passed by with little conversation, but that didn't matter to Rose, she was just glad to have her mum back and she felt almost relieved that she didn't have to explain the events that had happened. It would be too much for her mum to take in, especially in her current delicate state. It was getting late, so they decided to head home. They stood up to say their good byes and then walked out hand in hand, past the nurse's station, down the long corridor and out into the car park until they eventually got to Jackie's car. It was an old Citroen Dolly, which Jackie absolutely adored, even though it was horribly slow, especially up hills. It was a kind of grubby mustard yellow colour, with burgundy wheel arches and two protruding lights at the front resembling two googly eyes. They climbed in and made a vain attempt at warming their hands up on the pathetically slow blowing fans.

On the drive back Rose asked,

"Jackie?"

"Yes Rose."

"Can I ask you a question?"

"Of course you can sweetheart."

"Do you think it's possible to do things with your mind?"

"I don't understand, what do you mean exactly?" Jackie replied casting a puzzled look at Rose.

"I mean, you know like Matilda, you know in the Roald Dahl book I've got."

"Yes, I know the one."

"Well, do you think it can happen in real life?"

"Um... well I'm not sure love. Why'd you ask?"

"No reason, just interested I guess."

They fell into silence again. Rose could feel her anxiety levels rising as they approached the house and all the memories of her mother being beaten combined with her sinister thoughts about Shaun and Trudy's death came into her mind once more. Rose was certain she'd never intentionally hurt someone, well not physically, she was only fourteen years old and not particularly strong after all. But there was still a nagging doubt playing in her mind. They drove on until arriving at the house.

"Do you want me to get your things?" asked Jackie, noticing Rose's obvious discomfort.

"Yes please, if you don't mind," replied Rose with a sigh of relief.

Jackie smiled at her and got out the car. Rose sat and waited and thought about how she could possibly try to explain her situation to her mum. *Surely I can't just say... Oh, by the way mum I killed your boyfriend and your boss. Oh yeah and I did it with my imagination!* She sighed and turned the volume up on the radio. *'Dreams'* by Gabrielle blasted out from the speakers. *How ironic,* thought Rose.

'Another true classic by the wonderful Gabrielle and her beautiful song 'Dreams'. Join us again for some more amazing hits from the nineties after the latest news...'

'Police investigating the death of the man at the Winterbourne pub have released details of his identity.'

Rose held her breath,

'Thirty nine year old Shaun McCombie, a former war veteran who served in Iraq and Afghanistan, and who was recently released on bail for a domestic violence charge was found burnt to death in his van on Thursday evening. The police are interested in seeking a man who was seen in the vicinity at the time and would encourage him to come forward. Avon and Somerset Constabulary have released CCTV footage of what appears to be a black male, in his early twenties, with a height of approximately six foot two inches. He is pictured naked with only his underwear and appears to be in a lot of distress. The police are convinced that the offender knew Mr McCombie and are currently carrying out an extensive search of the surrounding area. If you see this man, please do not approach him, he is considered extremely dangerous. Once again we would like to encourage people to come forward if they have any new information.'

Rose shook with fear. *What if they find evidence that I did it?* Her heart thumped erratically as her anxiety increased once more. *What if they arrest me? And who's that naked man they keep going on about? I didn't see him when I was dreaming of Shaun's death? Maybe it was him. Maybe it was just a coincidence that I thought of it?*

Rose squirmed in her seat. She didn't feel like talking to Jackie when she came back, her negative thoughts were dominating her mind way too much to concentrate on anything else. She sat deep in her own thoughts for the remainder of the journey, occasionally replying to Jackie's questions with a blunt one word answer. She was so frightened about what was happening to her. *When will this nightmare end?* she worried.

But, unbeknownst to Rose, this was only the beginning of a much bigger nightmare …

Chapter 4

3 Days to termination…

The doorbell rang and Rose stirred from her slumber. She looked at her watch whilst rubbing the sleepy dust from out of the corners of her eyes; it was 8:30am. *Bit early for visitors*, she thought and then sat up and stretched her arms up as high as she could. She smiled as the rush of endorphins surged satisfyingly through her body.

"Rose love, you awake?" Jackie yelled out from downstairs.

"Yeah, I'm just getting dressed," Rose replied stifling a yawn.

"OK well make it snappy, there's some people here who'd like to talk to you."

Rose quickly bunged on her jeans and a baggy jumper that was lying on the floor from the day before and then slowly made her way downstairs. She walked into the living room, where there was a tall uniformed police officer stood over by the TV. His face was giving nothing away as to what this could be about, however when he spotted Rose he gave a small smile and gestured for them both to sit down. Sat on the other chair was a smartly dressed woman in a grey suit. She had a pair of round wire framed glasses perched on the end of her nose and was clutching onto a clipboard and pen. The woman turned to face Rose and gave her a gleaming smile, revealing a perfect set of pearly white teeth. Rose gulped nervously, desperately trying to hold it together as best she could.

"Hello Rose," said the woman, "don't look so worried. We've just got a couple of questions we'd like to ask you about Shaun McCombie."

Rose looked over to Jackie, who was sat perched on the armrest.

"My name is Inspector Taylor and this is Sergeant Fitch."

Sergeant Fitch gave Rose another one of his smiles and raised his hand in acknowledgment.

"Now Rose, I don't want you to be frightened and I know how hard it will be for you to talk about this, but it's really important you explain exactly what happened on the evening your mum was hurt. I don't know whether you know or not about the incident Shaun was involved in?"

Rose nodded cautiously and said, "Yes, I saw something on the news about him."

Jackie shot a confused look at the Inspector and exclaimed, "Why? What's happened to him?"

"Mr McCombie was found dead in his van. The van had been set alight, but we don't yet have any information on how it was started, or by whom. We may have one possible lead; a man was seen on the CCTV camera adjacent to Mr McCombie's vehicle. We have put out an appeal on the local news, however as yet we haven't had any significant response."

"But… but why didn't you tell me Rose? When you saw it on the news, why didn't you tell me? I don't understand…excuse me Inspector… I need to just take a moment."

Jackie stood up shakily, clearly unsettled by the news, and walked past the Inspector and out into the kitchen.

"We haven't spoken to your mother yet Rose, as we appreciate she's still in a bad way and don't want to impact her recovery, but we do need to talk to you if that's OK? Can you tell me in as much detail as possible what happened that evening?"

Rose explained the events of the evening as best she could, telling them all about how her mum had collected her from Jackie's and how she'd made the now regrettable choice to sit in Shaun's seat. She explained how he'd relentlessly beaten her mum and that how nothing she did would make him stop.

"Thank you Rose that's really helpful, you're doing great. I know it's hard for you to remember absolutely everything that happened that night, but as I said before it's of vital importance understand the events leading up to his death. So, if there is anything, anything at all, that you can think of you need to let us know OK?"

Rose nodded.

"Do you know of anyone that my may have wanted to hurt Mr McCombie in any way? Perhaps someone who was close to your mum or maybe someone who has something against him? Can you think of anyone who may have had reason to do this to him?"

Rose hesitated and then stuttered, "No…no…not that I can think of, I mean he knew a lot of people at the pub, but I'm not sure whether any of them had issues with him. And I don't know who that naked man is on the CCTV either…I've never seen him before."

Rose trembled. She felt as though she should to say something about her own concerns, but how could she; it sounded ridiculous. Tears rolled down her flushed cheeks and she started to sob uncontrollably.

Jackie rushed to her side and put an arm around her shoulders.

"Oh Rose, it's OK love."

"It's all my fault," Rose cried. "All of it's my fault!"

Inspector Taylor looked at her sympathetically and said, "How can it be, Rose, none of this is your fault, please don't go blaming yourself. No one should ever be beaten up for sitting in a chair!" She tapped her pen on the clipboard a couple of times and then stood up. "I think we will resume this another time. Jackie, can we talk in the other room please?"

Jackie released Rose from her embrace and gently caressed her cheeks, wiping the tears away with both thumbs.

"I'll be right back," she reassured her and walked out with the two officers.

"Jackie, we understand that Rose has been through a very traumatic experience and in situations like hers we'd suggest she gets some professional help," Inspector Taylor said and passed Jackie a business card. "This is Dr Anu Sharma; she is a very good Psychiatrist and one we've used a lot in instances like this. She works with children who have experienced domestic violence and other traumatic events. As her intermediate guardian I would strongly suggest that you consider this for Rose."

Jackie took the card and thanked the officers.

"If Rose tells you anything more about what happened with Mr McCombie, please contact us as soon as you can," she added.

The two police officers said their goodbyes and Jackie showed them to the door, before returning to check on Rose.

"Oh lovey, I know it's been hard for you these past couple of days, but why didn't you tell me about Shaun?"

"I wanted to, but I was too scared," Rose whimpered, sniffing and wiping her tears away. "It's all my fault. I killed them. I killed them both."

"What do you mean you killed them both, course you didn't lovey, why on earth would you say such a thing?"

"The other night I was lying in bed dreaming... I was dreaming about Shaun being burnt in that car. I wanted it to happen. I wanted him to suffer. I wanted him to die!" She choked on her tears as she desperately tried to explain herself.

"Oh lovey, come on now, that's ridiculous. You've been through a tough time and after what that man's done to your mum, it's only natural you'd feel like that. Of course you'd want something bad to happen to him! Look at me," Jackie said, pulling Rose in front of her and looking deep into her eyes. "It's OK to be angry. And anyway, what's all this talk about 'both'?"

"No, no you don't understand Jackie," Rose said, shaking herself free from Jackie's hold, "I'm not making this up, it was me who killed Shaun and I killed my mum's boss Trudy too. I killed them both Jackie!"

"Trudy? What do you mean, what's happened to her?"

"She's dead too, she fell and got run over by a bus. It wasn't an accident, it was me. I did it. I got angry with her after she started bad mouthing mum and so I imagined her tripping and falling under a bus. I saw her die in my head before it had even happened. I don't know what's wrong with me, Jackie. I'm so scared."

Jackie desperately wanted to believe Rose, she really did, but these claims of hers were just so wild. *The girl must be in shock,* she thought.

"When did you see Trudy?"

"After I ran off to the library the other day. She came up to me and asked why mum wasn't at work. She was awful to me Jackie and she said all these horrible things about mum. I couldn't help myself, I just felt so angry and I wanted to make her suffer, to pay her back for what she'd said." Rose sobbed even louder as the realisation of what had happened finally hit her.

Jackie hugged her gently and gave her a kiss on the cheek.

"Please Rose, don't do this to yourself, you really aren't to blame. It sounds to me as if Trudy's death was just one of those unfortunate things, pure coincidence. Listen, perhaps we shouldn't mention this to your mum just yet. She's way too fragile at the moment and to be honest I doubt she even knows about Shaun yet either. I suggest we keep it that way for the moment and concentrate on getting her better."

Rose exhaled deeply. Deep down she'd always suspected no one would take her seriously, but she'd still clung on to the tiny glimmer of hope that they'd maybe believe some of what she was saying.

"I know," said Jackie, trying to change the subject, "let's get your mum those presents you were after. What was it again…flowers, chocolates, marshmallows, oh and a book wasn't it? Come on that'll help take your mind off stuff for a bit."

The shops were absolutely manic! Excited children were running around, cyclists whizzed past on the pavements outside and the joyful festive harmony coming from the Salvation Army band was enough to make even the biggest Scrooge give in to the festive spirit. Under any other circumstances, Rose fully embraced this time of year. She had such fond memories of the last Christmas she'd spent with her dad before he'd died. She remembered him dancing that funny dance he used to do and playing tricks on her with a napkin and a coin. It always filled her with such happiness when she thought about her dad and she'd always felt as though he was watching over her and protecting her. It was the one thing left that gave her any comfort these days.

Rose and Jackie weaved their way through the maze of street traders who were out selling their festive produce until they reached Trudy's fashion shop. Rose's heart started pounding and she felt the panic rise up and erupt inside her. The shop looked closed, which was not a good sign this close to Christmas, especially as everywhere else was so busy. Then it hit her, now Trudy was dead and with her mum in hospital there was no one left to open the shop.

"Earth to Rose, come in, is there anybody in there," Jackie called, waving her hand in front of Rose's face to break her out of her trance. "Are you alright lovey? Look, I promise I'll tell your mum when she's better OK? But seriously, I really don't think it's a good idea her knowing about Trudy right now."

She enticed Rose away from Trudy's shop with the offer of a cream cake and a can of cola from the quaint little café opposite. They sat near the window, so that Jackie could people watch. Rose absentmindedly picked crumbs from her cake; she wasn't in the mood to eat anything.

Setting her teacup back down onto the saucer, Jackie tried making conversation to help break the awkward silence.

"I phoned your school today Rose, they said they're keen for you to go back."

Rose shook her head frantically.

"Don't worry, I explained everything and they completely understand. They've said you can come back after the Christmas break if you like."

Rose felt a sense of relief wash over her. She couldn't imagine going back to school after everything that had happened and she definitely didn't want to have to deal with Chloe and her evil posse of hangers on. She nibbled the edge of her cake and then slurped the dregs of the cola from the can.

Feeling refreshed, they left the café to head to the supermarket in search of gifts for Michelle. Scanning the shelves for any special offers, Rose spotted her mum's favourite chocolate and a bunch of beautiful, bright flowers. "This should cheer mum up," said Rose to herself with a little smile.

Jackie was over by the book section, looking through the limited stock that was on display.

"Hey, E.R. Rivers, your mum likes him, doesn't she? Looks like this is his new one. 'Love Lust' sounds right up your mum's street," she said reading the blurb on the back of the book.

"Yes, she does, but I think you'll find the author's a woman Jackie. Her name's Anne Rice. Female authors used to change their names all the time, because publishers thought the books wouldn't sell if people thought they'd been written by women. I guess maybe it's a tradition that's continued, to kind of create an air of mystery if you like."

Jackie looked at Rose in awe, clearly impressed by the young girl's knowledge,

"Well there you go, you learn something new everyday, don't you?"

"I'm fairly sure she hasn't read this one yet, so let's get it," Rose said heading off to the tills with slightly more of a spring in her step.

They arrived at the hospital at about 10:30 am and having spent so much time here recently they were beginning to feel more at home in the sterile white corridors that smelt of strange medicinal chemicals. When they reached Michelle's ward they were relieved to see her sat up in bed looking much better. She was clearly still in a great deal of pain, however the morphine seemed to be doing its job. Michelle glanced up and smiled lovingly at the sight of two women.

"Hey you two, how are you both?"

"Don't worry about us, we're good," replied Jackie.

"how are you mum? You seem more awake, I'm just so relieved you're OK," Rose said, sitting down in the chair next to the bed.

"Thanks sweetheart. And guess what? They said I might be able to go home tonight, isn't that great? They have to do a few more tests, but they're really impressed with my recovery so far and they've said that as long as I rest and don't do anything too strenuous then I should be back on my feet in no time. Once I'm back we can start afresh and move on with our lives." She smiled and held her hand out to Rose. "Have either of you heard from Shaun? Did the police get him? Is he going to prison? We'll have to move away Rose, I don't want him finding us. We need to get as far away from him as possible. I won't let him hurt you Rose, I promise."

Rose squeezed her mum's hand reassuringly and said, "Mum, there's something you should know." She coughed nervously, trying to think of how to break the news to her mum, but the words dried up and she realised there was no easy way of explaining any of this.

Jackie cleared her throat and jumped in,

"Shaun's dead Michelle. His body was found in his van at the Winterbourne pub on Thursday evening."

"What, but how?"

"Someone set fire to his van and he didn't get out in time. The police don't know who did it yet. They've had some leads, but no one's been arrested."

Michelle stared blankly at them both, shocked by the news. She didn't know whether to feel upset or relieved.

"I'm so sorry Michelle. I'm afraid that's not all, your boss, Trudy… well she's dead too. She got run over by a bus on the Gloucester Road."

Michelle lay back on the bed, deep in shock as Jackie explained everything in greater detail. She told her about the police visit and about the potential suspect who'd been spotted lurking near the van and about the strange circumstances of Trudy's death. Rose listened in silence. She knew she couldn't tell her mum about her visions yet, she'd had to deal with far too much already and the last thing she wanted was to upset her even more.

They travelled back to Jackie's house in silence, as was mostly the case these days. Rose didn't feel like talking. Her depression and anxiety had taken control of her thoughts and the last thing she felt like doing was making idle chit chat. She was happy her mum was better, but somehow she felt as though this wasn't the end of their troubles.

"Rose love, so we both know you've been through a tough time of late, more than anyone should ever have to go through. And well the thing is I've been given a contact number for a very good therapist who can help you feel better about yourself," said Jackie.

"Is that what you think Jackie, that I need a therapist? Do you honestly think I'm crazy?"

"No, no, of course not, I just think it will help matters if you're able to get it all out of your system. Then afterwards we can go see your mum again, you never know, she might be well enough to come home. Maybe it was wrong of me, but I've already spoken to the psychiatrist and she said that if you're up for it we pop in later this afternoon. What do you reckon?"

Rose reluctantly agreed. It was worth it just to keep Jackie off her back for a while and the therapist might even actually listen to her. Plus, she was absolutely desperate for her mum to come home; it would certainly make Christmas so much easier to deal with if she had one parent there with her.

The practice was in a tall three-storey terraced building that Rose guessed was Victorian or somewhere round that era. It had two empty flower baskets hanging from either side of its large, green oak door and a moss-covered statue of what looked like a dog, tucked into the corner of the entranceway. The door creaked as Jackie pushed it open, revealing an impressive entrance hall adorned with old, crooked beams and antique carved wood panelling. The air was filled with the stifling scent of lavender, but it made Rose feel calm and she relaxed her shoulders in response. The receptionist was a young girl with long blonde hair that reached down to her waist and she wore a cornflower blue polka dot dress that fitted her hourglass figure as if it had been purpose made for her. A delicate gold pendant hung from her neck and she kept self-consciously touching it every time someone spoke to her. Her face lit up as Jackie and Rose approached the desk.

"Hello," she said in a well-spoken accent, "how can I help?"

"I have an appointment booked for Rose Herkes with Dr Anu Sharma. My name's Jackie Dawson, I called yesterday."

"Just a minute, I'll check for you," replied the receptionist.

She tapped away at her keyboard.

"Ah yes of course, I remember, I'll let Dr Sharma know you're here. She'll be with you shortly. Please take a seat." She gestured to a row of green velvet chairs.

A few minutes passed and just as Jackie was about to pick up a magazine from the table a voice called out Rose's name. They stood up and taking Rose's hand for reassurance, Jackie led the girl towards the smartly dressed therapist. She was a naturally beautiful woman with long straight hair, tanned skin and a friendly picture perfect smile. The subtle scent of sweet, floral perfume filled the air around her.

"Hello, it's lovely to meet you. I'm Doctor Sharma. You must be Rose, and I'm guessing you must be Jackie?"

They both nodded.

"Would you both like to come through?"

"No… um… do you mind if I go in on my own?" Rose asked Jackie with an insistent look.

Jackie hesitantly agreed before returning to her seat in the waiting area.

"Please take a seat. Now Rose, how have you been feeling over the last week?"

Rose felt the words pour out of her, like a dam bursting its banks; once she started she couldn't stop. She explained in great detail the events that had taken place: Shaun beating her mum up, how she was terrified that her mum was going to die, about Trudy and her unfortunate death and the fact that her death now meant her mum no longer had a job to go back to.

"I want you to understand that when traumatic things happen to us it's perfectly natural to fear the worst. Our brains can do funny things when we're under a lot of stress and anxiety. So, we need to teach ourselves coping mechanisms to help deal with this. What do you do to keep yourself calm, Rose?"

"Well, I daydream quite a bit, it helps me escape. I love going to the library because it's so nice and quiet and it means I can think about anything I want without anybody interrupting me. Usually they're really lovely calm dreams, but sometimes they get interrupted by these strange dreams that creep into my mind and take over. Dreams of evil spirits, well that's the best way I can think to describe them, and they scream at me. That's when I wake up. I find it really difficult to relax. I spend most of my time feeling frightened and I ..." she hesitated, unsure whether to open up to this stranger.

"Go on Rose, carry on, what were you going to say?"

"I have these thoughts, these horrid thoughts. When Shaun did what he did to my mum I felt so angry..."

She paused.

"It's OK Rose, everything you say in this room is completely confidential, I promise. You can tell me anything."

"I thought about Shaun dying in that van, I mean before it actually happened. I wanted him to suffer like he'd made my mum suffer. I wanted him to die. It was me that set fire to his van. I did it in my mind and I did the same to Trudy. I wanted her dead, she was horrible to me and she was even worse to my mum. I imagined her getting run over by that bus and then it happened."

The doctor looked at Rose questioningly.

"I see, so you blame yourself for their deaths?"

Rose slowly nodded, her bottom lip trembling.

"Rose, when we experience a traumatic event such as this, it can leave an imprint in your mind, a bit like a photograph. When you think about the event, or something reminds you of it, the photograph reappears and the body releases lots of chemicals in the brain. It often happens when we get angry and it's what makes our thoughts become irrational."

"But I'm telling you the truth," Rose whispered desperately.

"What you are experiencing is perfectly normal for someone who has suffered like you have. Our brains interpret information in a much more negative way when we have experienced trauma. What I need to help you do is come up with a way of coping with them to help break the negative thought cycle that is driving these thoughts."

"I told you, I'm telling the truth," Rose shouted with frustration, "I killed them and no one believes me. No one believes me!"

Her body started shaking and she fixed her eyes on the ground to try and gain control over the anger rising up within her.

"It's OK Rose, calm yourself, take a deep breath and try and relax. No one's saying you're lying, we're just trying to help you."

Rose averted her gaze and looked up at Dr Sharma, taking deep, slow breaths to bring herself back to a state of calm.

"Tell me about your mum Rose, how are things between you?"

"My mum works so hard, she'd do anything for me. She's always tried so hard to protect me from Shaun, but he was a horrible man. My mum was far too good for him. I wish my dad was still here then my mum would never have met that evil man."

"Tell me about your dad Rose, what was he like?"

"I don't really remember him that well. I remember bits, like I know he was funny and he made me laugh all the time. He'd do this funny dance and sing in a high-pitched voice and I remember him doing magic tricks and giving me cuddles, always giving me cuddles. Mum really misses him, I can tell, she talks about him all the time. We never found out how he died. I just wish I could remember more about him."

"It's difficult to remember things when you're very young, you see there's a time in our lives between birth and about the age of five that we struggle to remember things in detail. It's known as the 'childhood amnesia' stage. Most people can't recall much before the age of five, as the brain and neural networks are still developing and it's hard for information to be stored."

Doctor Sharma stopped writing in her notebook and put her pen down. "Rose, if you're willing to come and see me again I think it's worth trying some hypnosis, perhaps we can help you that way. Your fears may have started as a result of your father dying and your anxiety can be controlled if we can find the root-cause of it. The visions you are experiencing may well be the result of your past experiences."

"Why won't you believe me?" Rose said restlessly. "What if it happens again? What if I kill someone else?"

"Rose, please listen to me, I can assure you that you haven't killed anyone! Your brain is simply trying to make sense of everything. Your brain might believe that you've killed them, but you haven't."

"So how exactly do you explain how I managed to visualise their deaths in exactly the same way they then went on to happen? You can't blame that on coincidence."

Dr Sharma paused, thinking about how best to explain the intricacies of the brain to a child that was clearly delusional.

"It's possible that when you heard about their deaths your brain somehow interpreted that information as you being the perpetrator. You haven't really killed them; you've convinced yourself that you have. This is common after a traumatic experience. I'm very sorry Rose, but I'm afraid we've reached the end of our session today. We can arrange another appointment after Christmas, if you'd like to come back and see me?"

Rose stood up and shrugged. She felt deflated and let down by the whole thing.

She closed the door and headed over to where Jackie was sat.

"So, how did it go?" Jackie asked.

"OK, I guess," Rose replied sullenly.

Doctor Sharma walked over and spoke directly to Jackie, "It's going to take time, these things don't get better overnight, but she did well for her first session."

Jackie smiled.

"Thank you for your help doctor, I've got complete faith in you. She'll be feeling back to normal in no time."

"I've booked you in for the Monday Rose. The quicker we deal with these issues, the sooner you'll start feeling like yourself again. Until then please try to stay calm, do some activities to take your mind off of things. I find listening to calming music really helps, so have a go at making a relaxing playlist you can listen to when things feel like they're getting on top of you."

"Thank you, Dr Sharma, I'll make sure I look after her," Jackie said.

"It's my pleasure. Have a wonderful Christmas and I'll see you again soon."

They left the practice with mixed emotions; Jackie felt relieved knowing that Rose was seeing someone who would be able to help overcome her demons, yet Rose felt more alone than ever. Sitting in the car, impatiently waiting for the decrepit heater to start blowing out hot air, Rose drew comfort from the thought of being reunited with her mum.

"I really hope they'll let mum out in time for Christmas," she said sadly.

"Well, the doctor did say that if she's improved enough it's a possibility, so all we can do is keep our fingers crossed."

The car pulled up at the hospital thirty minutes later, and as they entered the busy ward, they clung on to the hope of good news.

"Hi mum."

"Hello sweetheart, how are you?" Michelle said giving Rose a tight squeeze.

"I'm fine. So, are you allowed to come home?" Rose asked excitedly.

"Well look, my bags are all packed, so I guess that means I can!"

Rose squealed with joy, launching herself at her mum.

Jackie hung back in the doorway, taking in the happy sight before her.

"That's wonderful news Michelle, I'm so pleased for you both. Finally, you can get back to some sort of normality. Obviously, you're both more than welcome to stay at mine until you decide what to do with your house."

"Thanks Jackie, I really don't know what I'd do without you."

This was the happiest Rose had felt in ages. This was their chance to rebuild their lives without that horrid man and even though it was Rose who'd killed him, she didn't care anymore. She was happy he was dead. It meant he'd never be able to hurt her mum again.

Doctor Oakley appeared at the doorway.

"Hello," she said giving a tired smile. "I'm presuming from all the squeals you've heard the good news? It should be fine for you to go home. However you must take it easy. No heavy lifting, no strenuous exercise and plenty of rest. Most important of all, have a good Christmas, doctor's orders," she said with a wink. "Any problems, no matter how small, you get straight on that phone, OK?"

Michelle nodded and smiled, wincing through the pain of her sore face. She was so glad to be finally leaving, although the thought of going back to the scene of the crime sent shivers down her spine. And what about her job, what was she going to do about money? How could she afford Christmas now? *I mustn't worry about it, I'll find a way. I should just be grateful I'm still alive,* she thought.

When they got to Jackie's house, Michelle struggled out of the car, groaning and grimacing with every step she made towards the front door.

"I've made you a bed up downstairs in the lounge so you don't have to keep going up and down."

"Thanks Jackie, you're such a great friend. I know we've had our differences in the past, but I want you to know I'm ever so grateful for all your support, over these past few days."

"Don't be daft Michelle, that's what friends are for."

The women embraced one another and then Michelle carefully made herself comfortable on the sofa. Jackie walked out to the kitchen to begin prepping the turkey for Christmas day. She enjoyed cooking; it certainly helped take her mind off how lonely her life was. She gave a huge sigh as she rubbed oil over the skin of the bird. *Will I ever find love again?* she wondered. Her past boyfriends had been useless, well, all but one of them. He'd been so kind and so loving; she missed him so much.

As she mixed the herbs and spices together she called out,

"I've nearly finished in here. We can put that programme on, you know the *Royle Family Christmas Special*, you always loved that one Michelle."

"Sounds like a good idea," Rose called back.

Rose and Michelle sat cuddled up on the sofa together, enjoying being in each other's company again. But as much as Rose loved having her mum back home she couldn't shake off that gnawing feeling that she was to blame for two people's deaths.

"Mum?"

"Yes dear."

"I need to tell you something and I'm not sure how you're going to take it?"

Michelle looked at her daughter and said, "Go on love, you know you can tell me anything."

"I have horrible thoughts mum, really horrible thoughts. I thought about Shaun and Trudy dying before any of it happened. I wanted them both dead so badly and it came true mum. They both died because of me. There's something wrong with me and I don't know what to do?"

Michelle paused, looking over at her daughter with confusion.

"I don't understand Rose," she said nervously. "No one can kill people with their minds. I'm so sorry my love, I hadn't realised this was affecting you so badly. We'll get you some more help OK? We'll go and see that doctor lady again, yeah?"

"No mum listen, they died exactly as I had imagined it. My mind made it happen, it was my mind that caused their deaths, I just know it."

"But Rose love, that's not possible, it's your mind playing tricks on you. Please don't talk like this, you're making me worry."

"It's true mum, I promise. Why will no one believe me?" She rested her head against her mum's shoulder and started crying.

Michelle gave her a squeeze, instantly feeling bad for not believing her daughter, but also worrying about how she could help her move on from this.

"I'm so sorry Rose, I didn't mean to get annoyed. Jackie told me you went to see a therapist today, how did it go?"

"She wouldn't believe me either, same as you and Jackie."

"Hey it's OK sweetheart, I know you're upset. Come on let's try and forget about what's happened for a bit and concentrate on enjoying Christmas together."

She looked down and smiled lovingly at Rose hoping this would put an end to all this crazy talk. Rose wiped the tears away with the back of her sleeve and took a deep breath. Her mum was right, it had been such an awful start to the Christmas period, but it would be different now that

Shaun was out of the picture. She'd try her best to move on from this, for her mum's sake. But there was still something negative lurking inside her, a nagging doubt that things weren't quite right. It was a dark, oppressive feeling, something hiding away in the back of her mind, waiting to emerge. A gut feeling that something terrible was about to happen…

Chapter 5

3 Hours to termination

C hristmas came and went and it wasn't at all what any of them had hoped for. Rose had spent most of the last few days alone in her bedroom, hiding away from the rest of the world. She didn't care about Christmas, she didn't even particularly care about any of the presents she'd received. She just wanted to be by herself, in her room, alone with her thoughts. With the end of the holidays looming, her thoughts turned to going back to school, and it filled her with dread. She enjoyed learning, in fact she was incredibly intelligent when she put her mind to it, but that was just it, she struggled to concentrate. Her mind was always wandering off to the same strange fantasy land and the teacher, when spotting her, would clap his hands sharply and yell, *"Rose, are you with us?"* The rest of the class would laugh at her, anyone unusual or acting differently was prime target to the cruelness of secondary school kids.

It made her feel so anxious.

So alone.

So different.

She hated it.

She shook her head as if trying to shake out the negative thoughts and thought instead about her therapy. She wasn't exactly keen on that either, but for the sake of her mum she knew she should persevere with it.

"Are you ready?" her mum called out.

"Yes mum, just coming."

Rose wandered sullenly into the kitchen. She was wearing a knee length blue denim dress and her hair was tied up in a messy ponytail. Her face was pale and drawn and she looked exhausted.

"I wish you wouldn't spend so much time in your room Rose, I'm really worried about you. It's not healthy to be spending all that time on your own." Michelle said, her back to her daughter as she carried on washing the dishes.

When there was no reply, Michelle turned to look at her and was shocked at how awful she looked.

"Are you OK Rose?" Michelle asked with concern.

"I'll be fine," replied Rose. But she didn't feel fine, she felt sick. Her mind felt so chaotic, as though there were a million different words, pictures and feelings all rushing around her head bumping into one other, like London commuters during rush hour. It wasn't helped by the fact that no one understood what she was going through, not properly. No one was willing to take the time to really listen to her and this made it so much worse.

Michelle turned back to the dishes and gave a small sigh. She felt so helpless. The psychological implications of what had happened to Rose was too much for her to cope with and if she wouldn't open up to her and talk about things, there was nothing more she could do. At least she had agreed to see the therapist again, hopefully that would help.

Jackie dropped Rose and Michelle off at the practice and they waved her off before walking into the building. The receptionist glanced up at them both, a welcoming smile plastered across her flawless face.

"Hello, we have an appointment with Dr Sharma at 2pm."

"Can I take your name please?" she asked politely.

"Rose. Rose Herkes."

The receptionist tapped out the name on her keyboard and said,

"I've let Dr Sharma know, she should be with you in a couple of minutes. Please take a seat."

Rose sat on one of the chairs, slouching herself down into it and crossing her arms in a defensive way. "This is so pointless, she'll just say it's all in my mind and that I'm basically going crazy," she muttered to herself.

Michelle eased herself into the chair next to Rose with a slight groan. Her face still showed signs of dark bruising and her body ached all over, but despite her injuries she was going to make absolutely certain that Rose got all the support she needed. Michelle had hardened up over the years; she'd had to, after putting up with the levels of abuse she'd suffered from Shaun. If nothing else it had made her strong, both in spirit and in mind. She remembered one time when he'd beaten her with a fire poker. It was the most pain she'd ever experienced in her life, worse than childbirth, and she'd ended up covered in cuts and bruises all the way up her arms from trying to defend herself. She'd never told anyone about it. She was too scared, too ashamed and she certainly didn't want to give him any more reasons to be angry with her.

But when he went after Rose, well she wouldn't put up with that, she wouldn't let him get anywhere near Rose. Over her dead body, and it had been close on many occasions. Several times she'd been beaten for protecting her daughter, but it had been worth every punch, every kick, to know she'd spared her the same torture. She could count on both hands the number of times she thought she was going to die at the hands of that monster and she was lucky to have survived this last attack. The memories and scars would stay with her forever, but no matter how horrific each attack had been, she wasn't going to let this man ruin their lives.

"Rose Herkes," called Dr Sharma.

Michelle and Rose stood up and walked across to Dr Sharma. Her smile was warm and welcoming and she looked like a woman who was passionate about her job, as though she genuinely cared and wanted to help. But Rose was still annoyed that the doctor hadn't listened to her properly during her first visit.

"You must be Rose's mother, it's so lovely to finally meet you," Dr Sharma said putting her hand out to Michelle.

Michelle shook the doctor's hand and said,

"It's lovely to meet you too Dr Sharma and thank you so much for your help."

Doctor Sharma smiled and motioned for them to sit.

"Please take a seat. Now, how are you both getting on?"

"It's been a tough few days doctor, but my face is a lot better than it was, thank you. Enough about me though, I'm concerned about Rose. She's quieter than normal and has become really withdrawn. I want to help her, but I just don't know how."

"I understand, It's OK Michelle, I'm here to help and the first step is that you're both here."

Rose looked at the floor. She might as well just let the adults talk, after all they seemed to know more about her than she did herself, or at least they thought they did. *They know nothing,* she thought.

"Rose, so tell me, how are you? What's been going on since I last saw you? How was Christmas?"

Rose rudely ignored the doctor and carried on picking at the edges of her fingernails.

Doctor Sharma looked back at Michelle and smiled.

"Don't worry, these symptoms are quite common Michelle, it will take time for her to recover from the psychological trauma. When I last spoke to Rose, she was complaining about experiencing visions, hallucinations if you like, of Shaun and Trudy dying. Does she still mention whether she's having these images?"

"Yes, she's told me about some of them, about how she thinks she killed Shaun and Trudy. Doctor, is there a chance it could be genetic? I've got a history of depression and schizophrenia and I worry that it could be something I've passed on."

"Well yes, it's a possibility, but in Rose's case I think there's more to it than that. Rose believes that Shaun and Trudy's deaths are somehow connected to her thoughts. She has convinced herself that she is the one responsible for their deaths. There are lots of reasons why she's doing this and I've spent a lot of time thinking about it, but the most reasonable answer is something known as, "Fantasy Prone Disorder." People who suffer from this condition are prone to interpreting their dreams as real life events. Their brain struggles to differentiate between imagination and reality. They experience delusions and paranoia and it's as if they're living in a fantasy world, often going in and out of a trance. From what I can gather Rose is experiencing all of these symptoms. My opinion is that all of this stems from the time her father died and it's slowly been building up and getting worse. It's of vital importance that we try and get her to open up about how she was feeling back then and whether there was anything else that happened during that time that we aren't yet aware of."

"I see," said Michelle. "So, how can we do that? I can barely get her out of her room, let alone get her to talk to me."

"If you agree, I'd like to use hypnosis on Rose to help unearth some of her memories that she might have locked away. I want to be able to dig deep into her subconscious and find out where all this started."

Michelle looked at Dr Sharma with concern. All this talk of hypnosis was a bit too much for her. She'd only ever seen it on TV before, and that had been on some game show where the contestants were made to believe they were naked, or that they were chickens, or that they were in love with the host. It had seemed incredibly humiliating and she couldn't see how on earth it would help Rose. But what other choice did she have? She needed help and Dr Sharma seemed to know what she was talking about.

"Is it safe?"

"Yes. Hypnosis is perfectly safe, in fact it is one of the most natural phenomena we possess. It's essentially like daydreaming. When we daydream, we open up other parts of the brain and this allows a person to be more susceptible to suggestion and compliance. Imagine the brain as a giant computer that has lots of files stored away. Normally we find it consciously hard to retrieve them, however what is really clever is that the subconscious part can retrieve these lost files; it acts as a kind of secretary for your memories if you like. When we use hypnosis, we can help open up the subconscious and retrieve any information that may be causing distress. So, what do you think Michelle, would you be happy for Rose to follow a course of hypnotherapy?"

"Yes," she replied, albeit slightly reluctantly.

"And are you OK with this Rose?"

Rose shrugged her shoulders, still avoiding eye contact with the doctor.

"That's great. As Rose is under the age of 18, I will need you to sign the consent form to say that you agree to her being put under hypnosis."

Dr Sharma passed the consent form and a pen to Michelle, who quickly scanned the small print before signing her name at the bottom.

"Right, now we've got the formalities out of the way, Rose I'll need you to go and lie down on the couch, please. Michelle, I need you to be really quiet."

Rose dragged herself over to the couch, scuffing her feet along the carpet as she went. Michelle shifted uncomfortably in her chair. It was worrying and disheartening for a mum to see her daughter behave in this way, especially when she'd always been such a happy and polite girl.

"Rose, I want you to ignore any sounds you might hear, the sounds of cars outside, any creaks of the floor or furniture, and any other sounds in and around the building. I want you to focus on my voice and only my voice. I just want you to lie down and try to relax. Relax each and every muscle in your body. Your scalp, your head and face, your neck and shoulder muscles, your arms, chest, your back and stomach, and down towards your legs and feet. Imagine all of your muscles beautifully relaxed and easy, feeling very lazy.

"Rose I want you to imagine you are on a beach. The sun is shining, you can feel the warmth all over you - it's not too hot, just comfortable. You can see birds flying above you and as you look around you can see a beautiful sandy beach and crystal clear water in front of you. I want you to make it very clear in your mind. You look across to the other side of the beach and notice a flight of stairs. There are ten broad steps leading down to your own special garden. You wander over and begin to descend the steps counting as you put each foot down. And when you reach zero I want you to feel as relaxed as you can in your own very special garden."

"10... Take the first step down, relaxing and letting go.

9... Feeling more and more relaxed.

8... Your body becoming lighter and lighter.

7... Feeling really comfortable.

6... You're doing really well.

5... No need to hurry, plenty of time.

4... You can almost smell the flowers in that beautiful garden.

3... You're starting to feel lighter, so light you feel yourself starting to float.

2... Getting closer now, time to let go.

1... All the way down now to...

0."

"I want to take you back to when your father was alive. I want you to tell me about him. Tell me about a time when you remember being with him."

The look of constant worry had disappeared from Rose's face and she looked more relaxed than Michelle had seen her in a long time.

She could see her father, he was playing with her, and she was laughing so much. She was so happy, the happiest she'd ever been.

"I'm with him now."

"OK, good, what are you doing with him?"

"We're playing a game; we're playing 'Guess Who'."

"Are you happy?"

"Yes, I'm so happy."

"Where is your mother?"

"She's at work. It's just me and dad, he's making me laugh... but wait...there's someone at the door. Dad's going to see who it is."

"Who is it Rose?"

"It's Jackie."

"What's happening now Rose?"

"She's coming in.

"OK good Rose, what are they doing now?"

"Dad's talking to me, he's putting a DVD on for me. It's 'Beauty and the Beast'. He's telling me to stay here while he shows Jackie the secret Christmas present he's got for mum upstairs."

"That's great Rose, carry on."

"But I'm not doing what he tells me. I'm following them up the stairs. They can't see me because I'm hiding behind the door."

"What are they doing Rose?"

"They're on the bed. They're kissing, they're touching each other."

Michelle jumped out of her chair, her face a mixture of emotions, *that bastard,* she thought, *that bitch!* She bit her tongue, struggling to contain her outrage. Dr Sharma shifted awkwardly in her chair, looking at Michelle with sympathy.

"How does it make you feel Rose?"

Rose started to become agitated, her body shook and tensed and her hands gripped onto the side of the couch.

"It's making me angry. I don't want my dad to do that to her. What about mum? He should be doing that to mum. I want them to stop. In my head, I'm saying 'stop it, stop it!'"

"Then what happens, Rose?"

"I want him gone, I want him to feel the pain that mum will feel when she finds out. He shouldn't be doing that with her. Jackie's not my mum. I'll make him suffer for this. I hate him. I HATE HIM!"

"What's happening now?"

"I hate him so much. I want him dead. Die! DIE!"

"What's your dad doing Rose, tell me what's happening?"

"He's grabbing his head, he's screaming in pain."

"Why is he screaming in pain Rose?"

"Because I told him to die... wait... there's someone else in the room."

"Who's in the room Rose?"

"I don't know, I can't see who it is. It's black and it's got silver eyes. It's moving like water. It's coming towards me... it's coming towards me! It's screaming. Make it stop, it hurts my ears! It's talking, it's saying something to me!"

"What's it saying Rose?"

Her body went rigid and she started shaking violently.

"CHATTI CARTOM DESTRUCT ORMATI!"

Rose opened her eyes abruptly and with a glazed look turned around to stare at the doctor. Her mouth opened wide and she screamed,

"CHATTI CARTOM DESTRUCT ORMATI!" before closing her eyes and lying flat on her back as though nothing had happened.

"Who's saying that? Who's talking Rose?"

"I don't know. I can't see it, it's gone now."

Rose's breathing slowed and her body became limp.

"My friend is here, he's scared it away."

"Who's your friend Rose?"

"His name is John, he is kind to me."

Rose gave a strange little laugh.

"He talks funny."

Michelle rushed over to her daughter, her maternal instincts kicking in as she desperately tried to protect her daughter from whatever was happening.

"Stop it, stop it please! I can't hear anymore, I can't bear to see her like this!" she wailed.

The doctor nodded in agreement.

"Rose I want you to come back to me. After five I want you to come back to the room, feeling relaxed and alert. 5…4...3…2…1…"

"What happened? What did I say?" Rose asked looking at how distressed her mum was and seeing the shock on Dr Sharma's face.

"Are you OK mum?"

"I'll be fine," replied Michelle, avoiding eye contact with Rose and nervously fiddling with the ends of her hair.

Doctor Sharma looked over at Michelle with an anxious expression.

"I understand this has come as a big shock to you. I too am a little perplexed by this I'll admit. But I am sure there's a logical explanation for Rose's behaviour during the hypnosis."

"I don't understand? What did I say?" Rose shrieked, the worry rising up in her.

"Rose, you said that you saw your father with Jackie, they were getting close to each other and that they were kissing. You said that you wanted him dead and that you thought about him dying..." The doctor hesitated, before speaking again. "You spoke in another language too Rose, a language I do not recognise. Do you speak any other languages? You also mentioned a friend called John. Do you know anyone called John?

"No, I don't speak any other languages. And I don't know anyone called John."

Doctor Sharma looked puzzled.

"I don't think we should read into this too much. It's entirely possible that you misunderstood what they were doing, it could have been perfectly innocent. And you must realise that it's not possible to kill someone using your mind," she said reassuringly. "It is possible that Rose has produced a false memory of her father. She may have picked up this language watching television or reading a book and then over dramatized events in her own life. The brain has an amazing ability to store unusual information and it's not uncommon for children to have imaginary friends either, which is what I think this John character must be."

Michelle was fed up with being fobbed off with a load more psycho mumbo-jumbo, she'd had enough. Her anger burst out in a tirade of emotion.

"This is bollocks!' she exclaimed. 'This is meant to be helping my daughter not making her worse."

"I'm sorry you feel that way," replied Dr Sharma calmly. "I'm simply giving you my expert opinion based on the information Rose has just told us. This obviously goes way deeper than I first thought and I would strongly suggest Rose comes back for more sessions on her own."

Michelle marched over to Rose and grabbed her hand.

"Let's get out of here," she hissed. Rose was too frightened to argue. She'd only seen her mum this angry on very few occasions and she knew it was best to stay quiet. Michelle made her way hastily out of the door, dragging Rose behind her and ignoring the curious stares of the receptionist and other patients.

They caught the next bus back to Jackie's. Both sat deep in thought, unable to comprehend what they had just experienced.

Michelle thought about what Rose had said…

She couldn't understand how her husband could do this to her? And her best friend, how could Jackie be so deceitful? She'd confront Jackie later. She needed answers and she'd make sure she got them straight from the horse's mouth. That bitch! I'm going to kill that bitch! Then it dawned on her, Jackie's behaviour, it all made sense now. Why Jackie had become distant when Peter had died It was because they'd been having an affair. How could they, how could they do that to her?

Rose was struggling to make sense of her thoughts as well, but then that was nothing new…

She didn't know what to say to her mum. Had she really killed her dad? Did she really see dad and Jackie together? And why was she talking in another language? And who the hell was John? She felt confused. A deep sense of panic bubbled deep within her.

What was mum going to do to Jackie?

Chapter 6

10 Minutes to termination…

Michelle was desperate to confront Jackie and her hands shook maniacally as she fumbled about with the key in the lock of door. She finally managed to get the door open, then burst in and headed straight to the kitchen, startling Jackie who was pouring herself a cup of tea.

"My God you scared the life out of me!" Jackie said, placing a hand on her heart. She smiled cheerfully at them, but her smile quickly faded when she noticed the enraged look on Michelle's face.

"You bitch! Tell me what you were doing with Peter. Go on, I want to hear you say it. What filthy things were you doing?" shouted Michelle.

Jackie's hands started trembling. She put down her cup of tea and took a deep breath, trying to keep calm and act as though she didn't have a clue what Michelle was on about.

"What?" she said with a nervous chuckle, "I don't understand, what are you going on about?"

"You were having an affair with him,weren't you? The man I loved and you, my supposed best friend! How could you do that to me?!'

"It was only the once, I promise!" Jackie cried guiltily. "It didn't mean anything. He loved you, Michelle. You were always the one. He talked about you all the time. I was just jealous and he was such a great man and… " Jackie paused and then burst into tears.

Michelle was fed up of people lying to her and no longer able to control her anger, she picked up a kitchen knife that was lying on the side. With all rational thought gone, she lunged violently at Jackie with the knife.

"Mum! Put the knife down!" cried Rose.

"Michelle! You're not thinking straight, come on put the knife down. Put it down and we can talk about this," Jackie said, putting her hands out in a defensive stance. "I know you're upset. Just put the knife down and then we can sit down like adults and talk about this calmly. I know you don't really want to hurt anyone. Please, it won't bring Peter back, there's no point."

Michelle took a deep breath, her face seemingly crumpling with sadness and regret at her actions. She dropped her hands to her side, but kept hold of the knife. Jackie carefully inched closer to her, drawing the sobbing woman into her arms.

"I'm so sorry Michelle. There's not a day goes by that I don't feel guilty for what happened that day. There was nothing I could do. He died so quickly. I'm so sorry he died Michelle and I'm sorry for what I did. It should never have happened."

During all of this, Rose had hidden herself away in the corner. Without realising she had been holding her breath the whole time and only now did she release it with a loud gasp. She cautiously emerged from the shadows and walked towards the two women.

Michelle lifted her head from Jackie's shoulder and gave Rose a strange smile, before bursting from Jackie's embrace.

"You bitch! I hate you!" she screamed wildly.

She grabbed Jackie and plunged the knife deep into her neck. Blood immediately started pumping out of her jugular and Jackie instinctively clutched her hands to her throat, terror written across her face.

"You can join that bastard in hell, you fucking whore."

Michelle retracted the blade and stabbed at Jackie again. With each cut, more and more blood gushed out of the gaping wounds, covering the living room in a mist of crimson. Jackie tried to speak, but her voice came out in a guttural cough, splattering blood in Michelle's face. She fell to the ground and lay helplessly clutching onto life. As her breathing became increasingly laboured, Michelle stood over her convulsing body and viciously spat in her face. "You're no friend of mine," she sneered. Jackie stared up at the ceiling. Life was draining out of her and as she took one last dramatic gasp she mouthed the word 'sorry' at Michelle before closing her eyes forever.

Rose looked on in disbelief. What had just happened? She hit the side of her head with her hand to make sure she wasn't having one of her visions.

"Mum, what have you done?" she whimpered.

Michelle turned to Rose, a crazed look in her eyes.

"You knew about this you little shit, didn't you? You knew what they were up too all this time!"

"I didn't mum, I swear I didn't! I would have told you if I knew, I promise. Mum, please put the knife down."

Michelle started slowly walking towards Rose, her clothes and face splattered with Jackie's blood. She was holding the knife above her shoulder and had a look of intense evil in her eyes. Rose backed herself up against the wall.

"Mum don't do this, please. I love you mum, please don't hurt me!" Rose begged.

Michelle grabbed Rose by the hair and swung the blood-soaked blade, digging it deep into her daughter's arm. Rose screamed in pain as she tore her arm away. This made Michelle lose her grip and gave Rose her chance to escape. Rose frantically rushed upstairs to the bathroom, hastily locking the door behind her and collapsed to the floor. Shivering with fear, she loosened the saturated, bloodstained sleeve of her top. She winced in pain as she inspected the cut on her arm. Grabbing a towel from the side of the bath, she wrapped it around the deep wound in a desperate attempt to stop the bleeding. She propped herself up against the bath and listened out in terror to the sound of her mum creeping up the stairs.

"Rose, where are you? It's mummy. I promise I won't hurt you. Come on out Rose. Don't be frightened."

Rose stifled her yelps of fear, desperately trying to calm her breathing and trying as hard as possible to come up with a plan to get her out of this horrific situation. There was nothing else she could do, *she had no choice* she thought as she covered her face with her hands and took the image in her mind.

She imagined her mum being pulled backwards by a powerful force. Losing her balance, she wobbled at the top of the stairs before falling backwards, her arms flailing wildly. The pictures on the wall fell in perfect symmetry with her mum who was desperately trying to grab on to something, anything, as she fell. Rose imagined the sound of her deafening scream as her head thumped against the bottom step, her neck twisting from the impact. She pictured her mum lying there, lifeless, her eyes staring blankly at the wall. Her mum was dead.

There was silence.

Rose sat there for a few minutes longer, listening out for any sounds of movement, any tiny sound that would give her mum away. After a few more minutes of silence she slowly gained the courage to unlock the door. Stepping out of the bathroom, she mentally prepared herself to deal with the sight of her mum's body. She peered hesitantly around the banisters, anticipating the terrible sight that had only minutes ago been in her mind. There she was lying there, just as Rose had pictured it! Rose's mothers head was twisted freakishly facing the wrong direction and her terror stricken eyes stared blankly up at Rose. Rose sat on the top the step, staring down at her mum with mixed emotions. She'd known for a while now that her thoughts were dangerous. It was as if she was cursed by an evil force that was slowly destroying everyone she had ever loved. Everything in her whole life had been turned upside down. She stayed sitting there for what felt like ages, her thoughts turning more and more erratic as the realisation hit her that she had killed her own Mother! *What's the point of carrying on? I've got no one left in my life that I care about. No one will even know I've gone. I might as well not be here any more.*

She stood up on shaky legs and walked back into the bathroom. Opening up the cabinet on the wall, she peered at the multitude of pillboxes and medicine bottles. Without further thought, she opened bottle after bottle swallowing the contents of everything she could find. Staggering back to the staircase, she descended the stairs carefully stepping over the fallen pictures and clutching at the bannisters to steady her rapidly weakening body. She stood over her mum's body, tears streaming down her face. Lying down next to her, she stared into her glazed eyes and as the poison began to take hold, she softly whispered,

"I love you mum."

Termination complete.

Part 2

"If we shadows have offended, think but this and all is mended, that you have but slumber'd here, while these visions did appear. And this weak and idle theme, no more yielding but a dream."

William Shakespeare

Chapter 7

August 10th, 1599. Colchester, Essex, England

30 hours to termination…

It was a sight not worthy to be seen by any man.

Rotting.

Putrid.

Unbearable.

Jack looked down at his last remaining cow. The beast had stiffened with rigor mortis, its bulging grey eyes staring lifelessly into the distance and its legs stretched out rigidly before it. Its jaw had been removed. Cut cleanly away, but there was no indication of a blade having been used. The tongue had been perfectly sliced, yet there was no sign of any blood. He gave a heavy sigh; he'd had enough of this. It was the tenth cow he'd found like this and still there was no logical explanation. Jack could only think that it must be someone who held a grudge against him, but how they were doing it was a mystery to him. His neighbour, Andrew stood beside him, looking as equally baffled by the precision of the cuts on the carcass. No man was capable of such clean craftsmanship on an animal, not even the finest butchers in town could achieve such levels of skill. He looked at Jack,

"This maketh nay sense Jack. What man or creature hath done this?"

"'Tis nay doubt the work of the Devil himself or if't be not that beast, it must be the work of the Sheriff. T'was mine very last cow, we hath but nothing left."

"Fear ye not Jack, I hast some food for thee. I shall sendeth some over with the twins later this evening. I hast not much, for the drought hath ruined mine crops, but t'will feed thee and thy family for a while."

This was a terrible time for the majority of the people in the country. There had been no rain for several weeks now and the crops were all failing. Only the rich could afford to survive. Unfortunately for Jack and his family, he was by no means considered prosperous.

Jack nodded, reluctantly accepting the kind offer from his friend. He hated charity of any kind and Andrew had already helped him out on countless occasions, including saving his life.

Andrew Fleming had once been a wealthy Merchant and several years earlier had managed to bribe the authorities after Jack had deserted the war against the Spanish. Both Jack and Andrew knew it wasn't because of cowardice; it was simply down to the fact Jack couldn't bear the possibility of his children having to live without him in their lives. Jack had seen many a good man die on the battlefield and he wasn't prepared to make that sacrifice; his family meant more to him than any allegiance to his country did. He had left his barracks and returned home, only to be caught several months later and then placed in the stocks for two whole days. Above his head hung a sign emblazoned with the words

"Behold the deserter, Jack Potter."

73

Jack had been left with extensive bruising to the face from the objects that had been thrown at him and when the two days was up he was then sentenced to death by hanging. Fortunately for Jack, Andrew had stepped in at just the right moment and offered an undisclosed amount for Jacks release. This didn't go down well with the Sheriff and the townsfolk. Deserters were seen as scum and as a result of Jack's lucky escape, and in order to make him pay for this deed, the Sheriff made sure he suffered in other ways. His taxes were higher than anyone else's in town and the Sheriff's men would frequently visit, unannounced, with orders to take whatever they could from Jack's home. And then of course there was the drought; someone needed to be blamed for that. Jack and his family were easy scapegoats.

"Andrew, I can taketh no more from thee. We shall survive without charity."

"Playeth not the fool Jack, I will not see thee and thy family struggle. Maketh sure thee doth hide it away, I knoweth what the Sheriff beest like. Please taketh what I offer thee, for the sake of Mary, Jane and John. Thee cannot alloweth those folk to starve. I hath oft thought thy pride shall destroyeth thee Jack."

Jack stared at the fly ridden carcass, his mind filled with fear and worry. Deep down he knew Andrew was right and that he had no other choice. He looked at his friend gratefully and said,

"I thank thee kindly good sir, I art forever in thy debt. If ever thou needeth me, I shall beest there, I give thee mine honest word."

Andrew smiled and patted him on the shoulder.

"Good fellow, now helpeth me with this beast."

Chapter 8

25 hours to termination

The sun began to set and much to the relief of the town the temperature had reduced to a much more bearable level. Yet despite the heat and the increasing risk of death from starvation, many of the people had to carry on as best as they could. Chores still had to be done; no excuses.

John and his sister, Jane, sat on the piles of dry hay that they had just finished sweeping from the stable floor of their beloved horse, Copper. They'd had to deal with a lot since their father had been arrested for desertion and although John was too young to remember it himself, he'd only been five at the time, everyone in the town made sure he was reminded of his father's deed. He'd been kicked in the face by a horse as a toddler and it had caused quite some concern for the family. The townsfolk would look at his crooked nose in pity and mutter "poor lad" whenever they saw him. However, when their pity changed to whispered insults and he became known as "the deserter's son" it upset him deeply. John was a kind and quiet boy, a deep thinker who always thought of others before himself. He hid himself away behind his mop of big bushy hair, observing the world through a protective shield with the philosophy that as long as people were nice to him he would always be nice to them. Jane was the complete opposite to John, so much so that you would never have guessed they were related. She had long, luscious blonde locks and big blue eyes and had it not been for the stigma of her father she would have had every young man in town vying for her attention. She was two years older than John and so remembered her father's arrest vividly. Their mother, Mary, had tried to comfort her, but strongly believed she had a right to know the truth and Jane remembered her telling her, "Father may never returneth, we must prepareth to live without that gent." Jane had cried herself to sleep every night, cradling her younger brother in her arms, while praying for her father's return. And when he did return it was as if an immense weight had been lifted from her shoulders, such was the relief. Since then she had developed a strong and ruthless personality as a means of protecting her family, especially her brother, against the hatred of the town. If nothing else, it had strengthened her bond with her brother and now they were inseparable.

Sitting alongside them were their friends, the Fleming twins, Arthur and Abigail. They'd known each other ever since the twin's father had moved into the dwelling close by. Their mother had passed away several years earlier from an unknown illness and Andrew had taken on the role of being chief carer to his children.

The four of them huddled together in the stable, lazing in the comfortable silence that only comes from years of close friendship. John sat cross-legged, twirling a strand of hay between his fingers. He knew the twins would break the silence first, asking him the same old questions they always asked. But he didn't mind, so long as there was no mention of those darker, scarier secrets.

As if on cue, Arthur said, "Tell us more about thy dreams, John." His eyelids twitched excitedly and both John and Jane fought the urge to laugh; Arthur tended to twitch a lot when he got excited. He was a short boy, much smaller than other children his age, and he looked almost angelic with his blonde curls and striking blue eyes. He stared up at John, twitching with anticipation.

John laughed and indulged his friends with more tales of his dreams. "Folk in later years than ours doth wear colourful robes of fine material, much finer than ours. And those gents doth travel by horseless carriages that doth move by themselves. The buildings art most wondrous, some art taller than our tallest spire."

John had a reputation for being a bit of a daydreamer and was known for coming out with strange things. In spite of this, even if what he said was purely imaginary, Jane and the twins loved listening to him. He talked about travelling forwards in time and seeing some of the most amazing things.

"Dost thou talketh to the folk there John?" Abigail asked, tucking her long blonde hair behind her ear and batting her eyelashes at John. She'd always had a secret crush on John and although she made it very obvious, not once had it been spoken about between them. Arthur would joke about it with her, but Abigail would always deny it.

"I hast a friend there, but the lady doth see nor hear me no more. I knoweth not wherefore, for at each moment we did much talking. I bethink it did change at which hour her father died."

"By what name doth she go?" asked Abigail jealously.

"Rose, her name is Rose. The lady is so lovely and kind, but she doth hath a horrid gent in her life and her mother doth suffer also."

"John, telleth them about what else thee hath seen," said Jane.

John looked at her nervously and said, "No, I wish not to speaketh of that."

"Please John, please telleth us," pleaded the twins.

John hesitated. The thought of the things he had seen sent shivers down his spine and he never really spoke of it, except to Jane. But he hated disappointing people and he could see how desperate they were to hear more. He took a deep breath and began to explain the darker side of his visions.

"I hath seen much darkness, like demons, monsters that doth come at night when I sleep. They hath metallic eyes. They moveth like water and they maketh a noise like a beast screaming in agonising pain. I knoweth not what those gents art saying for they doth speak in a language most strange. 'Tis most frightful."

John dipped his head. These visions had affected him greatly and he felt a confused mix of relief and embarrassment at having finally revealed these thoughts to someone other than his sister. He knew he could trust the twins, but if anyone else found out about it there was a chance they may report him and have him tried as a witch. People didn't need any more reasons to hate him and his family and with the recent drought the Sheriff was looking for anyone to blame. Sorcery was a hanging offence and if John's visions were heard by the wrong ears, he would almost certainly be hanged. With this playing on his mind, John said,

"I wish not to speaketh about this anymore."

The twins could see John was uncomfortable talking about it and not wanting to cause him any upset they stood up to go home.

"Here is the food from our father," said Abigail, passing a small sack over to him.

John took it from her with thanks. They all hugged each other and then recited the vow they said every time they left each other; the vow never to speak of anything they had talked about.

"Our secrets doth remain entrusted to ourselves alone. If any folk doth breaketh this vow, our friendship shall beest banished to hell."

The twins left to go home and Jane turned to face John, a guilty look spread across her face. She knew he didn't like talking about it and perhaps she shouldn't push him, but she genuinely thought it might help him if he did.

"I am most sorry John, I should not hath bringeth up the subject. I bethought 'twould help thee, mine brother."

John nodded with a wry smile. He couldn't be angry with her, after all it wasn't her fault he kept having these visions, he just wished he had some answers. Why was he experiencing it? What did it all mean?

They were about to leave for home when a voice called out from the doorway of the stable. Jane flinched, recognising the voice straightaway. It was Christopher, the boy from the neighbouring dwelling. He was a short and ugly boy of fifteen and he walked with a distinguished limp. His skin was covered in pustule filled boils and although he hadn't been officially diagnosed, Jane suspected he had leprosy. He would often hang around outside their house, staring at them from a distance, but not saying anything. Jane detested him; he was an untrustworthy nuisance and it made her cringe to think that a boy such as Christopher should be so infatuated with her.

"What dost thou want Christopher?" she said with a sigh.

Christopher leaned against the entrance pillar, a smirk on his spotty face.

"I hath heard all about thy conversation, 'tis most interesting. Thou knoweth I could hath thee for witchcraft, dost thou think I should inform the Sheriff?"

"Nay, please Christopher," begged John, "please thou must telleth nay man."

Christopher's grin widened in malice.

"I will keepeth what I know to mine self for now. John, leaveth me to speak to thy sister, I hath many words I should like to sayeth to her," he said, looking over at Jane and licking his lips.

Jane shuddered and turned to John. As much as she couldn't bear the thought of being stuck in a room alone with this hideous boy, she knew she had to protect her brother at all costs. "Aye John, leaveth us be, I will beest fine. Waiteth for me outside the house, I will return anon."

John hated leaving her there, but he knew how stubborn Jane was once she'd made her mind up about something and he also knew they didn't have much choice if there was any hope of Christopher keeping his mouth shut. He gave Christopher a threatening look as if to say 'don't you dare do anything to my sister', before slowly backing out of the stable. He walked a few steps before ducking behind a bush and strained to hear what Christopher was saying to Jane.

"My father hath said that I must prove to be a real sir. Taketh off thy robes, Jane, let me prove it to thee," said Christopher, who was already undressing her with his eyes.

"In thy dreams boy, mine robes are staying put. Thou art nothing but a horrid knave and if mine father findeth out what thee hath done, he will killeth thou himself."

"Ha, thee maketh me laugh mine lady. Do thee bethink anyone wouldst believeth thee? A deserter's daughter no less? I can hath thy whole family hanged and thee knoweth it. Now make haste, taketh off thy robes."

Her bottom lip quivered as she realised she didn't have a choice. Christopher was right, no one would believe her and she couldn't risk her family being arrested. Reluctantly she undid the ties of her apron and began unfastening her kirtle. Tears streamed down her face as she stared up at his disgusting face. He placed his hand on her right breast and leaned forward, forcing his weight on her. Losing their balance, they fell to the ground and Christopher landed heavily on top of her with a grunt. She closed her eyes to try and block out what was happening, but nothing could hide her disgust as Christopher began to lick her neck. From his hiding place outside John could hear everything. He crept over to the stable and carefully peered around the corner of the doorway. When he saw Christopher groping his sister, anger boiled deep within him and he knew he had to put a stop to it.

That gent should not beest doing that to mine sister. Taketh thy hands off her.

Suddenly he felt something come over him, as if something had taken over his mind. It was a presence he had felt before, except this time it felt stronger.

He thought about his horse, Copper and visualised him snorting and pacing around the stable, getting more and more worked up. He pictured the horse rearing his legs and kicking the door to his enclosure, kicking at the wood over and over again with his hooves.

John saw Christopher look back at the horse, startled by the sudden loud bangs and then suddenly the stable door smashed open. The infuriated horse charged towards Christopher, who was trying unsuccessfully to stand and move out of the way. Jane saw her chance to escape and pulling her clothes around her she ran to safety in the far corner of the stable. The horse raised itself onto its hind legs and gave an almighty neigh as its front legs struck the ground. Terrified, Christopher backed away from the beast before turning and limping as fast as he could outside into the darkness.

Jane fastened her kirtle with trembling fingers and then fell to her knees sobbing loudly. John rushed straight over and crouched beside her, placing his arm around her shoulders.

"What happened, John? Wherefore didst Copper beest like that? That horse didst saveth me, Copper hast saveth me from that awful boy!" she wailed.

John pulled her in to his shoulder to try and comfort her. He felt confused by what had happened, it was as if he had somehow been able to control the horse with his mind. Similar things had happened before, but he put it down to coincidence, too afraid to believe it could be anything else for concern over what the consequences might be. But this confirmed everything he had ever feared. He couldn't tell Jane, he couldn't tell anyone; it sounded crazy.

Grabbing Jane's hands, he helped pull her up to standing.

"John, thou must not telleth father about this. Giveth mine own word, please."

"But what if that gent doth try this once more?"

82

"John please, please giveth mine thy word. For that gent can get thee arrested for witchcraft and then we will all beest hanged. Please John, bethink of our family."

John nodded reluctantly. He hated Christopher more than anyone he'd ever known, but he respected his sister and he knew she was right.

Jane sighed with relief. Wiping her eyes with the hem of her kirtle she said, "John, taketh the food the twins left us and I shall calm Copper."

John looked around nervously, still shaken by what had happened. "But what if 't be true and Christopher doth return?"

"Didst thou see his face? Why that gent 'twas petrified," Jane laughed, "that gent will not beest back, not while Copper is here."

And although they were correct about Christopher, he would certainly not return that same night; they could never have imagined what else was watching them, observing their every movement,

Something ominous

Something Sinister

Something utterly terrifying

Chapter 9

23 hours to termination

Nervously tapping his fingers on the table, Jack absentmindedly watched his wife as she scrubbed at the dirty clothes. The crops were failing and his cattle had all perished, the future of the family farm was looking bleak. Under normal circumstances, Jack would perhaps have accepted the effects of the drought more easily, but the mutilated bodies of his cattle played heavily on his mind and he knew there was more to it than that. He gave a long drawn out sigh and said,

"We doth work tirelessly and for such little reward. The crops art failing and we hast lost another cow to the same fate. I knoweth not what is happening for it maketh nay sense."

Mary paused mid-scrub and looked at him sympathetically. She was a kind hearted, very intuitive woman who was hard working like her husband. Jack would often tell her how beautiful she was and with her long, blonde curly hair it was clear which parent the children took after.

She'd had to cope with Jack's low moods on many occasions and she knew he found it particularly difficult dealing with his hard work going to waste. He'd worked so hard to build up the farm, saving his money in order to buy and keep his beloved cows, and now in the space of just a few weeks they were all dead.

"How hath we lost more, Jack? 'Tis the townsfolk, 'tis not? Those gents doth blame us for the drought, yet they art responsible for our losses, are they not?"

She blinked away her tears.

"Please Jack, we must remaineth stout, for the children's sake. We hast survived before, we shall survive once more."

She paused and then spoke again,

"Jack, when thou were out with Andrew, some of the Sheriff's guards did visit; those gents doth wish to talk to thee."

"Aye, 'twill beest the taxes. Those gents will beest back anon, thee wait."

"Doth we hast anything to giveth those folk?"

"Nothing," replied Jack anxiously, "I am most fearful those gents may taketh us to the prisons and put us in the stocks."

He placed his head in his hands, defeated. He had tried so hard to support his family during this oppressive time and he knew that because he was a deserter it only served to make matters worse.

Mary put down the clothes and dried her hands on her apron. She walked over to Jack and placed her arms around him, embracing him tightly.

"What art we to doth, Jack?

"We hath to leaveth, Mary. We must taketh whatever we can and receiveth far away from here. We shall leaveth before those gents returneth for the taxes. Wherefore art the children, Mary?"

"They art with the Fleming twins, they shall beest home anon." Jack held onto his wife, drawing comfort from her embrace. In the past, Jack had been able to give the guards some of his crops as payment, but there was barely enough left to feed his family and he would not see them starve.

There was a subdued silence in the house that evening. Mary made herself busy with chores in an effort to hide her distress from the children, and Jane and John were keen to keep a low profile after what had happened with Christopher earlier. Jack sat with a worried expression on his face, stirring his soup, deep in thought. When the children had finished their supper, they stacked their bowls and got dressed into their smocks.

"Sleep well thee two, we hast a busy day tomorrow and we shalt beest up with the larks," Mary said, kissing them both on the forehead.

Jane looked up at her mother inquisitively and said,

"Mother?"

"Aye, Jane?"

"Is father well? That gent looks most worried."

"Thy father worketh so hard and 'tis true he is worried my child. He doth long for the rain 'tis all."

Jane sensed there was more to it than that, but knew there was no point asking any more questions; her mother was just as stubborn as she was.

Mary left the room and joined Jack in their own bedchamber, which consisted of nothing more than a straw bed that was riddled with tiny insects that bit and crawled over their bodies throughout the night. They knew they needed to get as much rest as they could, despite the uncomfortable humidity and the nagging concerns over what tomorrow would bring.

Chapter 10

15 hours to termination

The sun cast a beautiful orange haze across the fields, marking the dawn of a new day. Jack looked at the beautiful image with disappointment; still no rain. If it would rain even just a little he would be able to hold off the Sheriff's tax demands for a few more weeks, but it was wishful thinking.

He tore off some bread and had a sip of ale, before making his way to the stable to prepare Copper for their departure. The Sheriff's guards would be here soon and he needed to make sure they were long gone before they arrived.

"Waketh up we hast to wend!" he called into the house.

Groaning noises came from the bedchambers as the rest of the family sluggishly dragged themselves up from their beds. They knew all to well that if Jack wanted you to do something you did it, no questions asked. Jane dressed herself in a green kirtle and laced bodice and tied a brown apron around her waist. Still half asleep, John wobbled as he put each leg into his brown long hose and then pulled his loose breeches over the top. He grabbed his white shirt and went to meet with the rest of the family, who were sat eating their breakfast of bread and ale.

"Consume up, we hath a long journey ahead of us and we must wend now."

"Wherefore art we going father? Why must we make haste?" asked Jane.

"I shall bid thee on the way, there is nay time to waste." replied Jack.

Jack and John gathered bags and ale carriers as Mary and Jane prepared and filled them with bread and jars of honey. They were just about to head out of the door when a loud knocking stopped them in their tracks.

Jack looked at Mary.

It couldn't be the tax guards; they had their own very distinct knock. This was different, more frantic, louder; more desperate. The knock came again and Jack grabbed the handle and pulled the door open. Andrew was stood there, looking pale and worried.

"Andrew! What art thee doing here at this hour?" asked Jack.

"The twins, hast thee seen them? They hath not returneth home and I am most fearful. Hast thee seen them?"

Jack turned to John and Jane, knowing they were the last people to have seen them.

John shook his head and said,

"Father, we hast to behold for those folk. They art our friends, Andrew is thy friend, we must searcheth for them."

"Aye, aye we shall all wend. Hangeth the bags on the cart and we shall searcheth for the twins," agreed Jack.

The five of them ran to the cart to hang the bags up, before splitting up to search for Arthur and Abigail. Even though Andrew was a kind man, he could be very strict with his children and for that reason it was very unlike them to not return home on time.

After only a few minutes of searching there came a piercing scream from behind the house.

It was Mary.

Andrew, Jack and the children ran over and found her holding her face and shaking hysterically. When she saw the others she pointed to the large oak tree that towered over the house.

"The twins, the twins art there, over yonder!"

Jack and Andrew stepped closer to where Mary was pointing and gasped in unison. Two naked bodies lay next to each other, unmoving. Horrified, Andrew moved closer, praying to God that it wasn't his children, but there was no doubt that it was Abigail and Arthur. He dropped to his knees and Jack ran to catch him, stopping in his tracks as he took in the gruesome sight of the bodies. Their eyes and ears had been removed, but there was no sign of blood, no indication of struggle, just hollow sockets and flattened ear canals. The genitalia of both children had also been removed, but again no blood had been shed, just exposed flesh showing where their parts had once been. This was the work of the same person who had murdered Jack's cows.

Andrew screamed hysterically, sweeping their limp bodies up into his arms and cradling them like babies.

Jack knew he couldn't let his own children see their friends like this; the sight would haunt them forever. With the help of Mary, he grabbed their arms and ushered them back into the house, leaving Andrew to grieve alone.

Once inside, Jack sat down and took a long drink of ale. Despite what had happened, he knew that staying here was now even less of an option. Standing up against the Sheriff's men was one thing, but there was a killer among them and he needed to protect his children, before they became its next victims.

"We must maketh haste," Jack instructed.

"But what about Andrew, we cannot leaveth that gent," pleaded Mary. "He hath no one and he is in no fine state to be left alone."

"We must think of our own Mary, he must knoweth not of our plans, there art too much at stake. The cart is loaded, we must wend, quick make haste!" shouted Jack

John and Jane stood in shock, numb to the chaos that was going on around them. No one had explained to them why it was they had to leave and now that the twins were dead it made the situation even more terrifying. They'd never seen their father as anxious and upset as this before; he wasn't a man easily scared, but fear was etched in every detail of his face.

Jack lunged forwards and grabbed them both, pulling them towards the door; there was no time to lose. They made their way over to the horse and cart and climbed in. Jack grabbed the reins, squinting in the bright light of the early morning sunshine. In the distance he could just make out the shape of horses moving towards them and as they drew closer he knew exactly what it was.

It was the Sheriff's guards.

There wasn't enough time to turn the cart around and there were too many men to consider charging through them, they would have to seek refuge in the house.

"Jane, taketh thy brother and receiveth in the house now!" Jack shouted, jumping off the cart and then offering his hand to Mary to help her.

Noticing their intended escape, the guards increased their pace.

Jack removed his sword from its sheaf and stood his ground, preparing to fight and protect his family.

"RECEIVETH IN THE HOUSE!" he screamed, glancing back to make sure his wife and children were doing as they'd been told. Mary fumbled with the locks, her eyes nervously flitting over to Jack, worried for her husband, but mindful she must get her children inside. The door burst open and the three of them rushed in. Mary locked it behind them and they stood with their ears pinned to the door listening to what was happening outside. There was lots of shouting and the sounds of horses' hooves, then silence, before the sound of a guard speaking.

"Mr Potter, or shouldst that be, deserter," he chuckled maliciously.

"Thou leaveth mine family be, they hath done no wrong!" Jack shouted.

"There art two dead children over yonder, dost thou knoweth anything about that, deserter?"

Jack walked slowly backwards towards the house until his back hit the door. They had blamed him for a lot of things, but never murder; this was a new low. The guards dismounted their horses and walked threateningly towards him.

"Thou stayeth hence from here, thee hast nay right to beest here. "

"On the contrary deserter, we not only hath the right to beest here, but we hath the right to arrest thee for murder."

Jack swung his sword in front of him in anger and the blade brushed against the arm of the guard stood nearest to him. The guard yelped in shock and pulled his arm back protectively. Blood trickled out of the graze. The two other guards unsheathed their swords and lunged at Jack, as he attempted to hold them off with his own weapon. One of the swords struck his wrist, slicing effortlessly through flesh and bone and Jack screamed in agony as his entire hand fell to the ground. His head spinning, Jack twisted his body round and tried to open the door with his other hand, but it was too late. Seizing his chance, one of the guards raised his sword and thrust it into the side of Jack's head. His body shuddered, as he whispered through the door to his family, "I doth love thee all," and then he fell heavily to the ground.

Dead.

On the other side of the door, Mary and the children were oblivious to what had happened. The door was made of thick, heavy oak and aside from some shouting they had not been able to make out what was going on. Without warning the door swung violently open, throwing the three of them across the room, and the three guards entered. They grabbed Mary and pulled her up from the floor. Jane and John jumped up and tried to push the men off her, clawing at their arms and kicking at their legs, but it had little impact. These men were strong and they had fought tougher battles than this. Mary struggled against them, but then stopped when she felt a cold blade against her neck. A sharp pain spread deeply across her throat and she gurgled helplessly as blood bubbled out from the gaping wound. John and Jane screamed in terror and watched as their mother slumped forwards and the guards dropped her, leaving her to bleed to death.

For fear of their own safety, they ran to the corner clutching each other in desperation.

"Prithee hurteth us not," they pleaded, as one of the guards grabbed Jane and threw her across the room. He turned and looked at John, their enraged eyes meeting in deadlock.

John's anger boiled inside him, churning and rising up into an eruption of hatred that coursed throughout his body. As this anger intensified, his body started to shake uncontrollably and he closed his eyes in preparation.

He wanted them dead. He wanted them to suffer. Imagining each guard being grabbed by force, he watched as the startled men were dragged across the stone floor of the kitchen. Out through the door, out to the front of the house, where slowly their bodies rose in the air and hung there levitating weightlessly. He visualised them being pulled limb from limb. Their arms and legs being slowly plucked from their bodies and their heads pulled away from their necks. Bones cracked and splintered as they slowly dislocated and ligaments stretched like rubber bands until they violently snapped. Harrowing screams filled the air and a smile spread across John's face as he slowly opened his eyes

Receiveth up, receiveth up!" shouted Jane.

John shook his head and blinked.

"What hath happened?" he said in confusion.

She grabbed his hands, pulling him up forcefully, and dragged him towards their mother, even though it was clear she was dead. John swayed unsteadily, his whole body disorientated by what had happened. None of this felt real. If he could just find somewhere to lie down and sleep he'd be able to wake up and none of this would have happened. His parents would still be alive and life could carry on as normal. Jane shook him, trying to make him see sense, and then pulled him outside to check on their father. They crouched over his body, prodding and poking him, desperately trying to wake him up. But it was no use, like their mother he too was dead. They fell into each other's arms, sobbing loudly.

Blinking her tears away, Jane peered bleary eyed at the horrific sight looming in front of her. Neither of them had noticed it at first, their sight had been confined only to their father, but now here it was like a scene from a war-ravaged battlefield. Gasping in terror as the memory of what John had done came flooding back to her, she gently pushed John away and sat back on her heels. John had done something, something terrible to those guards, and yet he hadn't lifted a finger. It must be some kind of sorcery. She stared at John and pointed in the direction of the dismembered corpses lying on the ground.

"Behold, John!"

John turned to look where Jane was pointing. Without saying a word, he slowly started to walk towards the bodies and then stopped and rubbed his eyes in disbelief. Blood covered the ground and body parts lay scattered like discarded puppets across the parched grass. His heart thumped against his chest as the realisation of what he had done began to dawn on him.

"What didst thee doth John, what didst thee doth?"

"I knoweth not," John replied, shakily, "I bethought about those folk dying. I bethought them being torn apart by mine anger. I knoweth not how, but mine dream hath come true, Jane!"

It had all happened so quickly, Jane was unsure as to what part John had in it all. He hadn't touched any of the guards, she'd watched him, he had been stood still the whole time. But she had seen it with her own eyes, those men had been ripped to pieces. How was it possible?

Unsure what to do, they ran back to the house and crouched next to their mother. John held her cold, limp hand and looked to Jane. Despite being a girl, she was the eldest and he always looked to her to figure things out. She looked back at him with watery eyes and said,

"John, we hast to receiveth out of hither. The Sheriff will findeth out his men have returneth not and those gents shall beest hunting us down."

"What about mother and father, we cannot leaveth those folk here."

"We must burneth the house down. We must maketh those gents believeth we art dead too. Gather up the body parts and we shall burneth those folk in the house. Those gents can knoweth not what thou hast done, John," she said, hurrying outside.

John grabbed the lit candle from the table and headed outside. He touched the flame against the thatched roof and it caught instantly, spreading its fiery blaze across the house. The drought had turned the thatch into the perfect kindling and it wasn't long before the entire house was ablaze; transformed into a burning inferno. The children gathered together the bloodied body parts, retching as they heaved them across the ground and flung them into the flames.

"John, make haste. Helpeth me with these bodies, they art too heavy for me."

He ran over and grabbed the tattered thigh stumps of a mutilated torso as Jane held onto the shoulders. Blood gushed out of the open wounds, covering them both with its scarlet stain.

They worked tirelessly, clearing the mess, clearing away the evidence and were just about to throw the final body on the fire, when Jane spotted movement from the corner of her eye. Instinctively she turned to see a familiar figure watching them.

It was Christopher.

Jumping in panic, she dropped the torso to the ground, and John looked at her strangely.

"Mine God, 'tis Christopher!" she whispered.

Without thought, John spied the glint of a sword on the ground and he rushed over to pick it up. He could barely lift it, it was so heavy, but gathering all his strength he raised it up and waving it amateurishly at Christopher.

"What art thee doing?" Christopher called out. "Wherefore could I heareth screaming? And wherefore art thee burning thy house down?"

He limped over to them, unperturbed by John's attempt to scare him off. Sniffing the air, he retched as his nostrils caught the scent of burning flesh and his eyes widened as he noticed the burning bodies at the base of the house. He clutched his stomach and vomited on the ground, then looked up at Jane and John, his face pale with disgust and horror.

"What hast thee done? Art those guards?" he questioned. "Whither art thee parents?"

He hesitated looked over to the entrance of the burning house.

"Is that thy father?" he said, noticing Jack's body.

Jane looked at John in despair, who looked back at her blankly.

Seizing the opportunity, Christopher tried grabbing the sword from John and the two boys wrestled to gain ownership of the weapon. Christopher eventually prized it from John's hands and they stood there waiting to see what his next move would be.

Christopher edged forward, jabbing the blade towards John. But then suddenly, a strange humming sound vibrated in the distance, like a swarm of bees buzzing above their heads. The three of them looked up, but there was nothing but clear blue skies.

Turning his attention back to John, Christopher yelled,

"'Tis witchcraft. Thou art both hags!"

"We art no hags Christopher!" Jane shouted at him above the rising humming sound.

"How doth thee explaineth this? Who hath murdered thy father and wherefore art the Sheriff's guards in pieces?"

Jane's lip quivered. She didn't know the answer, there was no answer, but she was certain if they were handed in to the Sheriff they would almost certainly be hanged. The humming sound became louder and an intense bright light radiated from the sky. Jane felt the hairs on the back of her neck stand up and she shivered in response. Shielding her eyes against the light, she reached for John's hand and screamed,

"RUN!"

Chapter 11

13 Hours to termination…

Jane ran haphazardly through the forest with John following closely behind her. Thick brambles scratched at their skin as the thorns tore through their clothes, but it wasn't enough to stop them. Adrenaline and fear shielded them from the pain, driving them forwards. Confused and out of breath, Jane slowed to a walk before stopping. She pressed her palms against a nearby tree and bowed her head attempting to make sense of everything she had witnessed. John collapsed in a heap next to her, gasping for air. It was hard to work out how far they had run exactly, but it must have been at least half a mile. Jane gathered herself and looked at John.

"John whate'er didst happen with Christopher, might it be that it wast some folk that wanteth to help us? Might it be that mother and father art looking down upon us and protecting us from the grave. 'Tis the only explanation I can bethink."

Still out of breath, John ignored his sister and concentrated instead on wiping the sweat from his forehead.

"John," snapped Jane in frustration, "I needeth thee to focus, will thee please open they ears to me. We hast to worketh together if we art to receiveth out of this alive."

John stared solemnly at the ground, his face streaked with the marks of sweat and tears. He would never get to see his parents again, never be able to hold them, touch them, laugh with them, be with them. How could life go on without them?

Jane looked on in sympathy. She understood that he was upset about mother and father, she was too, but she also knew that her father wouldn't want to see them this way. He had raised them to be strong individuals who fought for their survival and looked after their own. She was the eldest; it was up to her to take charge.

"John, listen to thy sister. Our mother and father art gone. 'Tis a hundred times more melancholy than e'er we can imagine, but there art nowt we can changeth. We hath but each other. Dost thou understandeth me John? I needeth thee to be strong"

He knew she was right, she always was. He looked up at her and nodded his head, wiping his nose on the back of his sleeve. Jane eased herself down next to him and wrapped her arms around him. She would make a good mother one day, and despite having lost so much John knew that he should be grateful that he still had his sister.

"John, we can walketh to Andrew's house this way. That gent shall helpeth us I am most certain."

She stood and grabbed both of his hands, heaving him up to standing. Her words of encouragement filled John with some degree of hope and with one hand still firmly clasping hers, he followed her in the direction of Andrew's house.

Chapter 12

10 Hours to termination…

Christopher arrived at the town hall with his father, Philip, in tow. Both men were feeling anxious; they knew what the sheriff could be like if he decided his time was being wasted. They looked up at the large stone structure looming ominously in front of them and the seemingly endless flight of steps leading up to a set of dark heavyset oak doors. Philip turned to his son and said sternly, "Thou must not beest affeared mine knave. Mindest thou doth not play the part of a mistress."

Phillip was a well-known and generally well-respected figure in the community. He had once come first in the towns' annual 'Horseshoe' event; a game that involved throwing a horseshoe as far as you could, and for this reason alone he was still regarded as a hero to this day. He was a large and somewhat burly man and his entire body was covered in a thick blanket of dark hair. His face was framed by a bushy unkempt beard that looked like a twisted and tangled thorn bush, which was rather apt because if you ever got on the wrong side of him you would certainly not escape unscathed. Most of the townsfolk had witnessed him beating Christopher at one time or another. It was a common, if not daily, occurrence. Phillip considered his son as weak, as a black mark on their reputable family name and had even branded him as a homosexual, something which was very much frowned upon. Indeed, it was Philip who had encouraged Christopher to rape Jane, telling him that if he had sex with her it would prove his manliness. But that was something else his pathetic son had failed at. Christopher nodded apprehensively, as they hastened through the massive doors. Glancing around the large open room, they saw a man dressed in black sat in one of the corners. His balding head was hunched over a scroll and he was scribbling his quill with great concentration. As the pair approached the man, the light of a nearby candle cast a dark shadow onto the wall, displaying the sinister silhouette of a devilish male figure with a sharp pointed beard and a large fanned collar that encircled his thick tree trunk of a neck.

It was the Sheriff.

Philip pushed Christopher forward and the Sheriff looked at him with a stern expression.

"What doth thee wanteth knave?"

"I believeth I hast witnessed witchcraft sir… The Potter family sir… Thee knoweth, the deserter?" Christopher stuttered.

The Sheriff placed his quill on the desk and rolled up the scroll.

"I see. And doth thou hast any proof of this lad?"

"Thy guard's sir… those gents art dead… those gents hast been killed in the most brutal of ways sir. I didst see their arms and legs pulled off yond folk my good sir, 'tis sorcery of the darkest kind. John, the deserter's son, didst hath a sword and when I confronted that gent I didst see their father wast dead. But at which hour I didst try to taketh the sword from that gent, a bright light shineth down upon me, blinding me. Those folk hath used sorcery, they art hags sir, I am most certain."

The Sheriff stood abruptly, pushing the chair away with his feet. He'd been searching for an opportunity like this for some time now. The townsfolk were getting restless, they were asking too many questions, demanding too much from him. He needed an explanation for this terrible drought and this was perfect. He grinned at the news of the deserter's death, it had been a long time coming, but those children needed to be found. They were trouble and he couldn't have murderers running around; it would be bad for his reputation.

He grabbed Christopher by the shoulders and ordered,

"Showeth me knave, I must see this with mine own eyes."

John and Jane made their way through the woodland, jumping with every leaf that rustled, every twig that snapped underfoot. They knew the Sheriff and his men would be out searching for them by now and so hadn't stopped even just once. If they were caught, they would be made to stand up in court and the sentence would almost certainly entail torture and death. Irregardless of your age, witches were shown no mercy, and their father's reputation would do nothing to help their plight.

John stopped suddenly in his tracks. He was exhausted. Sensing that her brother was no longer following her, Jane turned and headed back to check on him.

"Art thee well brother?"

"I needeth to stand ho for a moment."

"We shouldst keep moving. Andrew's house 'tis not much further hence." She anxiously looked around, keeping an eye out for any movement or sounds from the bushes.

"Didst thou heareth that Jane?" John whispered, his eyes wide with fear.

Jane cocked her head to listen and whispered back, "What John, what can thou heareth?"

They both held their breath, straining to hear.

"John, I heareth not a thing," Jane said, noisily releasing her breath, "thou art hearing things. Be not affeared, cometh let us move on from here."

"It doth soundeth like the voice of a mistress, but her language 'tis not like ours."

"What madness art thee speaking, John? Cometh now." She went to grab his hand, but John pushed her gently to one side and made his way through the thicket.

The voice sounded louder now and John was able to make out the words.

"The time has come. There is no escape. There is no escape. THERE IS NO ESCAPE!"

"Jane didst thou heareth that?"

"Nay John, I heareth not a peep!"

John moved cautiously in the direction of where the voice seemed to be coming from, but there was nothing to be seen. Just that loud, unnerving voice repeating the same mantra over and over. Then suddenly she was there, right in front of him, the vision of an old lady. He blinked his eyes in disbelief and noticed that the woman had no legs; her upper body was simply floating across the ground as if being blown by a gentle breeze. He stared in shock, not sure what to make of this vision and then, voice trembling, he whispered to Jane.

"Canst thou seeth her?"

Jane looked over John's shoulder, squinting through the bushes, trying to make out what it was that John had seen.

"Art nowt but trees, John. Thou art seeing things."

John remained transfixed by the strange levitating woman. Her hair was grey and she wore clothing that he had never seen before. Ignoring Jane, he tried calling out to the woman.

"Hello."

The old lady paused and tilted her head to one side before slowly turning to face him. Her piercing eyes stared chillingly at John, sending cold shivers down his spine. He shuddered and subconsciously began taking small steps backwards. In response to this she floated towards him and then spoke once again in that strange form of English he had heard her speak before.

"The time has come. There is no escape. There is no escape. THERE IS NO ESCAPE!"

"I understandeth not fair maiden," said John politely, "What dost thou mean?"

Jane looked on in confusion. Feeling concerned by her brother's strange display she grabbed him by both shoulders and shook him hard.

"John, 'tis enough, stop at once."

But John remained steadfast and called out to the lady again.

"What dost thou mean? Wherefore art there nay escape?"

Without warning the old woman harrowingly screamed, *"Nobody lives. Nobody lives. We all die. WE ALL DIE!"*

An intense flash of light and a strong wave of energy passed through John knocking him off his feet and hurling him to the ground. John opened his eyes and groaned with pain. Gently easing himself up, he looked back in the direction of where the woman had been, but she was no longer there. Still feeling shaken and confused, he now looked for Jane, checking to make sure she was OK, but she too had vanished.

"Jane!" he shouted, "Jane, wherefore art thee?"

No response.

He tried again, this time his voice cracking with concern and angst, "Jane!"

Looking down he noticed two indents from where her feet had stood.

"JANE!" he screamed.

The sound of his frenzied outburst echoed around the canopies, sending a flock of birds fluttering up into the sky. He called again and then listened intently for a response.

Nothing.

Jane would not leaveth me so. Wherefore art thou? Could she be scared per chance? Could she be in yonder bushes hiding? Perhaps she hath runneth to Andrew's house, aye 'tis true, that wilt beest it.

Taking comfort in this thought, John hurried on in the direction of Andrew's house, searching for signs of his sister along the way. However, with each step he took the doubt began to creep into his head. What if he should have stayed where he was? How had she disappeared so quickly? Would she really have run away without him? Deep down he knew the answers to these questions that were plaguing his mind and it filled him with a deep sense of dread. Tears welled up in his eyes and he screamed out again in desperation, "JANE!"

Chapter 13

8 Hours to termination

Christopher held his head high, as he led the way alongside his father, the Sheriff, twenty guards and the Sheriff's assistant, Joseph to the scene of the crime. When they arrived at Jack's house, Christopher pointed towards the dismembered bodies, but kept his eyes averted so as not to have to witness the horror for a second time.

The Sheriff looked over, blinked and then turned to look back at Christopher.

"And where didst the witches runneth too?" he calmly asked.

"Over yonder sir, past the house in yonder direction, by the dwelling of Andrew Fleming, sir."

"Well done knave," the Sheriff said patting Christopher firmly on the back, "thou hath done the town most proud. Witches such as these shouldst not be living amongst us gentlefolk for they bring much damage to our livelihood. I shall make certain thou art rewarded for this. For now, thou must returneth home to rest and my men will call on thee for the court hearing anon. Good day"

Having been dismissed, Christopher and his father left to go home.

The Sheriff beckoned to his men to follow him and he strode across to get a better look at the mess before him. It was as bad as Christopher had described. Limbs had been strewn haphazardly across the field and decapitated heads lay dotted around the blood-stained grass, like abandoned balls in some macabre game of boules.

"'Tis sorcery," shouted the Sheriff angrily. He turned to Joseph and said, "There can be no other explanation. What think'st thou?"

Joseph looked nervous. He'd never seen anything quite like this before, apart from on the battlefields of course. But this had happened outside of someone's house, without any weapons by the look of things, and the damage was by far the most brutal he had ever seen. Something wasn't right.

Joseph was normally a strong-minded man. He had fought and survived every battle he had been sent to and working for the Sheriff had certainly toughened him up over the years. And although his thin, gaunt appearance would have you question his ability on the battlefield, he was both agile and fast and when asked would boast of having killed two hundred men. He was the Sheriff's most favoured ally and the Sheriff respected his opinion on such matters as these. However, the sight that lay before them was proving too much, even for Joseph and he shuddered with a deep-rooted terror as he drew closer to the corpses to inspect them in more detail. He turned them over, one by one, with the side of his boot, searching for clues and examining the injuries.

"No sword hath been used sir. The arms and legs hath been pulled off with a force most strong. There art no ropes to beest seen and there art no marks on the bodies. Whate'er hath done this most hideous act is neither man nor beast."

The soldiers, who up until now had been cautiously milling around the edges of the field, reluctant to get too close for fear they too would be struck down by whatever evil power had done this, walked hesitantly over to the collapsed building in the search for clues.

"Sir there are two bodies hither," called one of the guards. "I believe 'tis that of the deserter, sir. Both bodies doth look to be whole, they hath limbs aplenty and their heads art joined to their necks."

The Sheriff looked up from his conversation with Joseph. They had been talking in hushed tones, trying to ascertain what may have happened, but they had yet to reach a conclusion other than that of witchcraft.

"Those witches hath shown no mercy, they hath killed their own parents as well as our guards," muttered the Sheriff with disdain.

"We hath found footsteps this way sir," said a different guard pointing towards a patch of trampled grass and broken twigs.

"We must make haste," ordered the Sheriff, "If these hags art callous enough to kill their own parents, then there is no knowing what they might do. Men, we must make haste to Mr Fleming's house. They must be stopped!"

Chapter 14

7 Hours to termination

The trees towered above him, engulfing him, swallowing him up with each step he took further into the forest. He could just about make out Andrew's house through the dense undergrowth and he prayed that Andrew and Jane would be there, waiting for him and that then this nightmare would all be over. The house was a large, solid bricked building with aged wooden beams criss-crossing from each side. Ivy covered most of the walls, partially covering the windows and doors and surrounding the house was a moat of murky, stagnant water. His mind wandering with thoughts of being reunited with his sister, he stumbled slightly as his foot caught on something. He looked down and saw a pile of clothing.

It looked like Jane's.

He hastily picked up the clothes and drew them up to his nose, inhaling the scent. Yes, it was definitely hers. Clutching the garments to his chest he looked around and cautiously walked on, stopping every now and again to look behind him in paranoia. He carried on in this way until he saw a figure sitting by a tree.

It was a girl.

Running towards her, John excitedly exclaimed,

"JANE! JANE, I HATH FOUND THEE!"

But as he got closer, his excitement turned to horror as he realised that although the figure was indeed his sister, something wasn't right. Her eyes, ears and lower jaw had all been removed and her genitals had been sliced off with clean precision.

There was no blood.

No chunks of hacked flesh.

No sign of struggle.

Just the empty, dead shell of his sister.

In that split second his whole life came crashing down on him. What monster had done this? He dropped to his knees and violently vomited over the forest floor. This was too much; he had to get away from here. Unable to look at his sister's mutilated face, he looked away and blindly threw the pile of clothes over her head. He vomited again and then ran shakily away, continuing on his mission to make it safely inside Andrew's house. Andrew would help him, he was sure of it.

There was a bridge over the moat around the other side of the house, but in his confused state he jumped carelessly into the water. The fetid sludge rose to his waist and he waded wearily through the tangle of weeds over to the embankment. He clambered out and rolled onto his back gasping with exhaustion. Despite having seen it with his own eyes, he refused to believe that his sister was dead.

It had to be a dream.

Any moment now he'd open his eyes and he'd see her smiling face.

And everything would be alright again.

He lay there for a few more minutes, praying with all his might, believing that if he just prayed hard enough it would be true. Slowly he opened his eyes and stared up at the empty sky above him.

He eased himself up and squeezed the water from his clothes. They were still wet and he smelt terrible, but it would have to do. Banging loudly with his fist on the door he waited for Andrew to answer.

There was no response and after trying again, this time banging harder, he tried the handle and to his relief found that it was unlocked.

The room smelt of burning candles. John smiled to himself. This was good news; it meant that someone was in. He closed the door behind him and then stopped. The sound of sobbing was coming from another room. The floorboards creaked as John tiptoed past a row of neatly lined up leather boots over to the door on the far side of the room. Pressing his body against the wall, John took a deep breath before gaining the courage to peer around the corner. The kitchen was a mess. Remnants of half-eaten bread and empty bottles of wine had been thrown across the floor and broken plates and mugs lay in pieces around the room. John slowly ventured into the room and spotted Andrew crouched in the corner, kneeling with his head in his hands. On the table opposite lay the bodies of Arthur and Abigail. John put his hand to his mouth in shock. Not the twins as well!

"Mr Fleming?" John finally asked, looking at the distraught man.

Andrew removed his hands from his head and looked blankly at John, his eyes glazed and distant. There were several half empty bottles of wine surrounding him; he had clearly been drinking. Unresponsive to John's concern, Andrew put his head back in his hands and carried on crying, whispering incoherently between each sob.

John tried again,

"Mr Fleming, mine own mother and father art dead. And Jane, mine beloved sister hath suffered the same fate," he said, gulping hard. "Mr Fleming, I knoweth not what I must do. The guards art searching for me and I am but alone in this world. Please I needeth thy help kind sir!"

Andrew turned to face John again, his face marked with the dirty tracks of his tears. He stood shakily and shuffled precariously over to John. John nervously fiddled with a loose thread on his sleeve, unsure of what Andrew was intending to do, unsure of how he was going to react to him. He stopped, mere millimetres from John's face, so close that John could feel the warmth of his breath, smell the stale potent fumes of the alcohol. Andrew grabbed John towards him and embraced him tightly, almost collapsing into him, relying on John for support.

No words were spoken.

None were needed.

Silence said it all.

After a while, Andrew slowly released his grip on John and breathed deeply. He had heard every one of John's words, but his mind had refused to let them register. Shock does that to a man.

Wiping his nose on his arm and clearing his throat, he spoke.

"John, thee shouldst beest with thy family, wherefore art thou hither?"

"Didst thou not heareth me, Mr Fleming, those folk art dead!"

Andrew looked at John, his eyes wide with shock.

"Thou must be mistaken. What hath befallen?"

"The Sheriff's guards hath murdered mine very own mother and father. And Jane, Jane hath met the same fate as that of Arthur and Abigail. I knoweth not by what means or by whom. She was with me and then she was gone, it didst happen in the blink of mine eye. I didst find her thenceforth, outside of thy house, with nowt on but the skin she was born with."

Andrew stepped back in panic as the realisation of what John was telling him began to sink in.

Something was out there

Hunting them down.

And it wasn't the guards.

He couldn't let the boy back out there on his own. He owed it to his friend to protect him from whatever was doing this.

He took a deep breath and said,

"John, I hath lost mine own children. The pain of which I would inflict upon no man. I hast nowt to liveth for. But thine father was a good man and I giveth thee mine very own word that I shall careth for thee as good as mine own. Thou will beest safe hither and thou can stay until 'tis safe for thou to moveth on. I hath not much room and 'tis nowt fancy, but thou can sleep in mine cellar, 'tis safe down there. The Sheriff will be here in due course, that I am most certain, but I will beest here and I will keepeth thee from harm."

Unable to contain his emotions, Andrew started to cry once more. He was a broken man; a shell of his former self. His very heart had been ripped from his chest and torn to pieces. His children were his world and without them he was nothing.

Choking back the tears he said,

"I must first bury mine own children. John, prithee leaveth me with those folk, I must beest by mineself for a while."

John thanked him for his kind offer of help and bowed his head in respect, before climbing through the hatch that led down to the cellar.

The air inside the cellar was cold and damp and John shivered as he realised his clothes were still wet from the moat. He looked around in the hope of finding something to wear, but there was nothing other than a dusty old sheet that was draped over some furniture. It would have to do. He took off his wet clothes and pulled the sheet around his shoulders, shivering and coughing as the dust particles filled his throat. Small rays of light filtered through the gaps in the wooden slats of the walls, but it wouldn't stay light for long and John knew that with the darkness there would come loneliness and grief. Visions of Jane and her mutilated face consumed his mind and he had no doubt that the memory of this would haunt him for the rest of his life.

How will I ever live without thee Jane, I miss thee.
I miss thee so much.

Chapter 15

4 hours to termination

*T*he wind felt cold against his skin, as if winter had come early. He shivered as he tried to keep warm, but it was useless.

All around him was white.

Everywhere.

White.

Great swathes of white blanketed the ground and encased him in a ghostly mist.

Obscuring his vision.

Clouding his mind.

The houses were different to what he was used to; more symmetrical, more perfect and less real looking. And the horseless carriages shot by at speeds incomprehensible to him. Light came from poles high above the ground, but it wasn't from candles, this was a brighter, static light. It was all so beautiful yet so alien and unfamiliar to him at the same time. He floated down to ground level, masterfully

navigating his way through the streets. An unexplainable energy was
pulling him, drawing him towards a central point, a doorway. He didn't
know what he was doing here, or what lay behind the door, but it felt
right. Reaching out his hand to open the door, he gasped in surprise as
it passed through the solid matter with ease. Floating forwards his
whole body drifted through as though the door were made of air. He
moved up the staircase, staring in wonder at the material that covered
each step; a finer, coloured sheep's wool. The corridor at the top of the
stairs led into a room in which peculiar candles hung from the ceiling
and there were pictures of people, pictures that looked more detailed
and more realistic than he had even seen, hanging from the walls. Sat in
a chair in the corner of the room was Rose.

"Rose? Rose, can thou heareth me?"

There was no reply.

He tried again, "Rose, 'tis me, John!"

Hearing the sound of heavy footsteps approaching, he turned to see
the man he had seen before with Rose and Rose's mother. He was a
large, bulky man with a delicate wispy beard that looked out of place on
his hardened face. The man bellowed profanities at Rose,

"Get the fuck out of my chair! And why've you put that shit on?" he
demanded.

John saw Rose staring up at him, fear etched across her face. She
jumped abruptly out of his chair, quivering as she handed him over,
what seemed to be a rectangular black box.

"Don't talk to her like that!" screamed Roses Mother, hastily
rushing in from the kitchen to defend and protect her vulnerable child.

The man pushed Rose's mother to the floor and her head thumped
against the wooden chair. She tried getting up, but couldn't and the

horrid brute placed a foot on her weakened body, pushing down hard with his heavy boot and grinning sinisterly.

"Don't hurt her!" cried Rose, as she attempted to push his leg from off of her mum. The man grabbed Rose's ponytail and pulled her to one side, dropping her to the floor like a rag doll.

"Rose, receiveth out! Make haste, hide!" screamed John

The light of the room started to fade out, as if something was sucking it away, distorting it into a million tiny fragments and extracting itself from John's sight.

And then the darkness.

It came with such frightening force, a presence filled with negativity and a dark, deep oppression.

And there, there it was. The shape he had feared all his life. The entity that had haunted his every thought. There before him, hovering like suspended water, its hollow silvery eyes penetrating his very soul. Without any warning, the shape rushed forwards screaming the words,

"CHATTI CARTOM DESTRUCT ORMATI!"

Chapter 16

2 hours to termination

John awoke to the sounds of banging from the floor above him. It was so loud that the vibrations travelled all the way across the ceiling and down through the walls. He flinched in terror as the intensity of the banging increased. *It must be the Sheriff*, thought John. He carefully inched his way closer to the staircase, collecting his clothes along the way. Silently, he dressed himself, shivering as he struggled to pull his arms through the damp sleeves. He could hear Andrew shouting obscenities at whoever it was outside, followed by a loud crash, as if a door had been smashed from its hinges. There was more shouting and then the sound of a fight breaking out.

John listened in fright.

"Where art the children!" shouted a voice.

"Thou knoweth where they art, they hath been murdered, killed by the hands of thy very own guards. Thee art cowards the lot of thee, killing a family. I doth know how much pain thou hast made for those folk. Thee disgust me, thee impertinent levereter"

"I shall not beest spoken to in that manner. Thou art nowt but a blinking idiot! Guards, restrain that gent!

John heard more scuffling and cries of pain from the floor above. He could only begin to imagine what they must be doing to Andrew up there and he would not stand by and let it continue any longer. This was his father's friend, he must help him. Taking a deep breath, he released the latch and gently lifted the wooden cover, peering through the gap to see what was going on. Andrew was sat on one of the wooden chairs, being held down by two of the guards.

"Holdeth that gent," barked the Sheriff, who was pacing around Andrew like a lion stalking its prey.

He grabbed the closest candle from the small table next to him and proceeded to wave it underneath Andrew's chin. The smell of burning hair filled the kitchen and Andrew's agonising cries prompted John to crawl out of the hatch and shout,

"Release that gent, I am here, 'tis me thou art looking for."

The Sheriff turned and grinned, rubbing his hands together in glee. His guards stepped forwards and John stood with his arms out, ready for them to escort him away.

But at that moment, a loud humming sound came from outside. It was the same sound John had heard with his sister earlier that day; the sound of a thousand swarming bees. Everyone stood still, feeling confused and disoriented by the droning buzz, which seemed to be getting louder and closer. Suddenly a blinding light penetrated through the windows, causing the guards to release their grip on John so that they could shield their eyes. Squinting against the intense brightness, John tried to make his way over to Andrew in a bid to release him from his shackles, but stopped when he saw what was happening to him.

Andrew's body had gone completely rigid, his arms and legs stretching out like stiffened wooden rods. His mouth dropped open and out came a terrifying unearthly scream. Slowly, his body lifted up from the chair, throwing off the ropes as if they were thin lengths of string. The Sheriff, Joseph and the guards watched in horror, then turned and fled to the hallway, their faces conveying their panic of the events unveiling before them. John remained in the room, fearfully watching as Andrew's clothes were violently ripped from his body in one swift motion. Red lines began to appear around his eyes and mouth. Deepening and widening as though incisions were being made in the surface of his skin. But there was no blade. No knife. Nothing physical that could be seen to be making these marks. His ears began separating from the side of his head, hanging and then flapping down like pieces of loose material. His mouth and eyes met the same fate as his ears. Both features sliced and removed, leaving behind gaping bloodless holes in his face and an eerie, gurgling noise rising up from the vocal cords. John watched helplessly as the skin on Andrew's chest became etched with the words,

Takila nen t Dna. Takila en t Ema

Consumed with fear and knowing that Andrew was beyond his help, John barged his way past the Sheriff and his men and made his way outside. The piercing light was still there, casting its bright white glow across the landscape and obstructing his field of vision. He staggered around, trying to feel his way through, but he was lost. Blinded by the thick static energy that was cutting through and pulsating in his retinas, he tripped over something and tumbled down an embankment, the stagnant water of the moat breaking his fall. His arms thrashed wildly in panic and then his body relaxed as it sank to the bottom of the moat. Images of his mother and father, his sister and the twins flashed in his

121

mind. It was as though his whole life was replaying out in front of him. A pleasant sensation of nostalgia washed over him and he smiled as he felt his mind slip away into darkness.

He wasn't frightened.

He was ready.

To face death.

From nowhere, he felt a hand grab him by the shoulder and then an arm wrapping itself around his neck, pulling him out of the murky depths. Coughing and spluttering he opened his eyes to see a tall man towering above him. It was Joseph.

"What hast thou done?" Joseph screamed.

Still struggling for breath, John eyed the man with caution. He was just as baffled as he was. Joseph kicked him in the ribs, angered by the boy's lack of response. John groaned in pain.

"Dead. All of them. What hast thou done?" repeated Joseph. "The Sheriff and his men hath been defaced, akin to that of Mr Fleming. 'Twas thee. Thee and thine evil sorcery. Thou art a witch!"

Before John could defend himself, a large rock came hurtling towards him, striking him in the head. It hit with such force that it was as if the rock had passed right through his skull and out the other side. Blood trickled down his face as the shadow of unconsciousness swept over him.

Chapter 17

10 Minutes to termination

John awoke with a start. The sound of taunted cheers and booing made his head throb with discomfort and he instinctively went to move his hands to try and soothe the pain away. However, his hands were firmly restrained in something solid, something wooden and he realised he had been put in the stocks. The cheering grew louder as the crowd noticed that he had come to and people began calling out to him.

"The deserter's son is awake!" they cheered in unison.

John strained to look up from his awkward position and found himself surrounded by various rotten vegetables and broken eggshells. The foul smell hit his nostrils, making him retch. The baying crowd started to throw more vegetables at him, some of which landed at his feet, others hitting him on his arms and face. Out of the corner of his eye he saw someone he didn't recognise running towards him. The stranger stopped in front of John and forcefully pushed a handful of overripe tomatoes into his eyes, the sweet juice squirting up his nose and running down his face. Blinking away the tomato juice he noticed Christopher standing in line, waiting to humiliate him. When it came to his turn, he strode up to John and maliciously hissed,

"'Tis but the beginning, witch!"

Grabbing a handful of putrid vegetables from the basket at the side of the stocks, Christopher joyously smeared it across John's face, laughing with sick glee at finally getting some form of revenge. Tears streamed down John's face, but they were not tears of humiliation, nor were they tears of hurt or shame, they were tears of sadness and regret. Sadness for the loss of his family; regret at not having died with them.

Joseph stood before the angry mob. Since the death of the Sheriff he had taken on the position and he was keen to make it clear that he was now in charge. In his new role as Sheriff, he would be the judge and would be the one to decide John's fate. He called out to his citizens, bellowing loudly above the roar of the rapturous cheers.

"Silence everyone, silence! Thee seeth before thee, the deserter's son, the witch whom hast brought much destruction to our town and community. This hag is guilty of acts against God and our fellow men. This hag hast dried up our lands, he hast butchered our Sheriff, killed our guards, murdered innocent people, including his very own family. There is nay question this witch deserves the harshest of punishments. I sentence him to death."

With the decision made, Joseph ordered his men to release John from the stocks. Two of the townsfolk stepped forward and unfastened the restraints. Stretching his arms out in relief, John groaned with pleasure as the blood rushed back into his limbs and he felt the stiffness ease. He was happy to accept his fate. Finally, he would be reunited with his parents and sister and they would be a happy family once more, safe in the house of God.

He was escorted over to the hanging platform, which had already been prepared for his public execution. The thick rope swung in the breeze as if taunting him. Joseph grasped it in one hand and slipped the noose over John's head. It settled around John's neck and he gave a slight shiver in trepidation.

"Dost thou hath aught to say, witch?"

John looked out at the crowd, feeling the force of their hatred and disgust towards him. How could these people be so unforgiving? These people that he lived among, some of whom were once his friends, these people that could so easily find themselves in the same position as him one day. Looking back towards the ground he weakly nodded his head in acceptance of his fate and patiently waited for death to greet him.

"This hag thee seeth here before thee, hast nay words. This hag doth not seeketh forgiveness from God, for he is a product of the Devil and shall burneth in the realms of hell!"

And with that, Joseph kicked the stool out from under John's feet, leaving him hanging there like a carcass in an abattoir. The rope strained against his weight, choking him and cutting off his oxygen supply. John struggled, an instinctive reaction to fight for his life, his body twitching and twisting. For a moment, John felt an intense, unbearable pain, but then it dispersed, almost as if something had taken it from him. He felt relief, at peace with the world, and although he could still hear everything around him; the cheering and cursing, the sounds of laughter and joy, he felt as though he had been transported to another realm. The light filtered away into darkness and he felt a light breeze blowing against his face. And with it there came something wet, something refreshing, something familiar.

One spot, one tiny dot, and then a splash.

Rain.

Termination complete.

Part 3

"There is only one dream I can guarantee...my death."

Stephen Evans

Chapter 18

*W*hat's that noise?

His breath grew faster as the adrenaline consumed him. The room was dark, aside from a small sliver of light that was squeezing its way through the thin wooden slats.

"Who's there?" he shouted, and then froze waiting for a response from a presence that he could feel so strongly.

The only answer that came was the rapid beat of his heart, which was pounding rhythmically in his ears. He slowly edged his way across the timber wall, the splintered wood digging painfully into his hands, until suddenly he heard a voice.

"CHATTI CARTOM DESTRUCT ORMATI!"

It was a voice so piercing, so terrifying, it made him instinctively recoil in fear. The unnerving sounds became louder and louder.

He peered around the corner, holding his breath, attempting to see who, or what, was talking in this strange language. Two entities stood illuminated by a single ray of light, but they had no obvious shape to them and they appeared to be talking to someone.

It looked like a boy.

As he stood there taking in the two strange, unearthly figures, watching as their silhouettes hovered side by side, he couldn't quite believe what he was seeing. Beads of sweat ran down his face and he struggled to keep his ragged breath under control. He swallowed hard as both creatures turned to face him in unison, their watery forms moulding and transforming into a more recognisable body like structure.

The entities screamed at him, "CHATTI CARTOM DESTRUCT ORMATI!" and glided closer. Panicking he ran blindly in the opposite direction, desperately trying to escape this nightmare vision. The darkness engulfed him and he staggered on, arms outstretched trying to feel his way out of the room. But in the space before him two shapes appeared in front of his face and he let out a fearful shriek.

"CHATTI CARTOM DESTRUCT ORMATI!"

Chapter 19

10 hours to termination

Apex woke abruptly, frantically punching his arms at the empty air; feeling everything, yet hitting nothing. The building was shaking and the pictures and his neatly arranged action figures fell from the shelves onto the ground, like defeated soldiers struck down by bullets on the battlefield. He sat up shivering, his clothes and bed covers drenched in sweat. "Oh shit that was terrible!" he muttered to himself. "And another fucking earthquake too!" He thought back to his dream. He'd had a lot of vivid dreams lately and he couldn't work out what they meant. The clock was flashing 9:15 am, he was going to be late again, but the prospect of going to college didn't excite him in the slightest. He'd much rather go round to his bro's for a smoke; it was far more interesting. He reached over and pushed the button that moved the automated covers away, then slumped his feet down onto the soft carpeted floor. Standing up and stretching out his arms, he gazed disapprovingly at his reflection in the mirror. The dark black bags under his eyes made him look permanently stoned, but then in truth he *was* always stoned, and the night terrors weren't helping matters. They were getting worse, disrupting his sleep patterns, often making him feel as though he was getting no sleep at all. Yet, his mum regularly complained about how his snoring kept waking her up, so he must be getting some sleep.

He pressed the button on the mirror and a robotic voice spoke,

"Face and head analysis in progress… face and head analysis in progress… A total of seventy hair follicles have been destroyed over the last twenty-four hour period. Your hair percentage is approximately twenty three percent hair loss. No further wrinkles of the skin found. Skin quality acceptable. Dark circling of the eyes… requires attention… Carbon monoxide levels high… Reduce smoking to increase oxygen levels…"

"R.E.M. sleep analysis commencing… please wait… more sleep required…Estimated R.E.M. sleep percentage…eight percent…"

"Overall assessment… below acceptable… recommended daily activity… reduce smoking, increase rest periods and avoid strenuous exercise…

"Printing report… please wait… please wait…

"Piece of fucking junk, 'below acceptable'!" he shouted back at his reflection.

Deep down he knew it was right though; he *did* smoke a lot. Every night he'd be round his bro's getting totally stoned, but in his defence it was the only thing that helped take his mind off of his depressing life. Even his own family treated him like an outcast, bullying him about his weight and his premature hair loss. He was only nineteen, yet he was losing his hair already and looked far older than his years. But on the plus side, he did have a good face and he was what you would call a good-looking guy. He certainly hadn't had a shortage of girlfriends, even though most of them had been heavily overweight. He lived with his mum and grandmother, and despite the death of his father not long after he'd been born, judging by the photos his mum had dotted around it was clear his looks came from him. Relations with his family had never been great and his grandmother in particular would curse him for not doing anything about his weight or moaning at him for not spending enough time with the family. She had very old fashion views and took great pleasure in telling him that, "*men were never like that in my day.*" She talked endlessly about the Third World War, telling him about how the men were so much nicer back then, especially the Russians after they'd invaded; they were very charming and great in bed! She was always telling Apex to take more pride in his traditional African roots, but he never took any notice of her.

He pulled up his smart self-zipping trousers, before putting on his self-buttoning shirt and self-tying tie; this particular accessory was new and was the very latest in state of the art technology clothing. It could be used as a phone, a camera, you could pay for your food with it, you could scan anything at the college including all the E-libraries data, and you could even project holographic movies, but of course the college frowned upon this particular function being used on site. This was standard clothing for college and if you weren't smartly dressed you'd be sent home with a strict warning that should it happen again you would be kicked out. Two strikes and you're out.

He rushed downstairs, grabbing a melty bomb cheese roll from the side on his way through and hastily opened the front door.

"See ya Mom!" he shouted.

"Hey, wait Apex! What about your lunch? Are you not taking it?" she called back.

"Nah, it's OK Mom, I ain't got time."

He reached the conveyor-pave and got his five dollars out. In his opinion the conveyor-pave was the best way to get around, because although there was the option to take the conveyer cars, they were far too expensive for his meagre student budget, and the conveyor-pave would still get him to college in half the time. He looked around at the crowds of fat people and wondered what on earth this country had come too. Almost ninety percent of the country was obese and that statistic was continually growing. He was the unusual one in this society. People would stare at him as if he were the freak for being a relatively fit, slim guy. He couldn't understand where the country had gone wrong. For years the country had been warned about an epidemic, but nobody in America had taken any notice. Other countries around the world had banned all meat and fast-food products. They were all strictly vegetarian now and if you were caught eating meat or junk food there were harsh punishments. He desperately wanted to get away from the U.S. and would always talk to his bro Chaz about leaving, but there were tight restrictions, education being one of them. Before even attempting to leave, he would need to get through college.

Apex arrived at the tall white domed building that was the college. It had been built after the war to honour the men, women and children who had died. That was sixty-five years ago now, but still the memory lived on. Two statues protruded from the sides of the building; one of Carle Barker and the other of Ivon Marks; the undisputed heroes of the war. They had negotiated a truce with the Russians and North Koreans, something that had never been achieved in the entire ten years of war. No one knew exactly what had been said, but it had obviously worked!

He strode through the entrance and waited to be scanned, impatiently tapping his foot as the lasers moved up and down emitting their distinctive hum.

"Welcome Apex Mensah, you are exactly twenty five minutes and thirty one seconds late, you will receive three marks on your attendance record."

"Fuck you!" he shouted raising three fingers at the machine in defiance.

Walking past the reception he noticed a group of fat ladies eating their sausage platters, the grease dripping down from their grotesque mouths. *Gross,* he thought and turned away in disgust. He got into the lift, pressed the button to take him up to the twentieth floor, and braced himself for the inevitable lecture about not being in on time.

"Nice of you to join us Mr Mensah, sit down and I'll talk to you later," said Mr Coval. Mr Coval was a large man who was today wearing a rather unflattering black suit that showed off all of his unsightly bulges and a self-buttoning shirt that threatened to burst at any moment. His hair was a greasy, grimy kind of grey that showered flakes of skin whenever he moved, leaving behind a disgusting trail of dandruff wherever he went. Mr Coval turned to face the class, which consisted of a mix of fat teens and advanced robots. Robots were required to learn too and were treated just like human pupils. Technology had advanced so much that their appearance and speech was pretty good and it was often difficult to tell if they were human or not. Apex sat in his usual place by the window. It looked out towards the Great Bridge, so named because it had been barraged in the nuclear attack seventy years ago, but had somehow still managed to stay standing.

"Listen please… Class, can I have your attention, please!" Mr Coval bellowed.

The class fell silent.

"Now, because of the sudden increase in the unusual and unpredictable earthquake activity recently, we will require all of you to stay at home for the next couple of weeks."

The class erupted into cheers and laughter.

"Quiet please!" yelled Mr Coval.

The students fell silent again.

"As you know, these buildings are not affected by the earthquakes themselves however, college policy dictates that all students must remain off college premises if there is a sudden increase in the earth's tectonic plate movements. But, what that does *not* mean is that you won't have any work to do. You are all fully aware that we are in the last few months of your studies and although we have covered topics such as the ban on the automotive industry in 2100, the great famine of Europe in 2045, and the ancient Egyptians and the great Mayans artefacts, we still need to cover the Tudor age in England. Some of you may find this interesting and some of you may not, but you must all complete this module in order to graduate, so you might as well quit your moaning and get it done. Do you understand?" The class nodded and Mr Coval continued. "You will be required to research the Elizabethan period; their beliefs and values. Now, there is a huge selection of information on this subject, most of which can be found in the E-library. I'll give you one month to complete it and I want your best work please. Right, when you've filed all your material you can leave." The students made their way out of the classroom, groaning in unison at the task ahead of them.

Apex sighed. He was so close to finishing college, but he absolutely detested history; it was something that had never interested him. He'd only just about scraped through all the other topics and now he had to try and feign interest in something that had happened seven hundred years ago.

"Apex, can you come here please?" Mr Coval called out.

Apex reluctantly turned and walked back to his tutor.

"What's wrong with you Apex? You turn up late looking like you've been up all night, doing God knows what! I wish you'd take your education seriously. You've nearly finished your studies and I don't want you to fail at this last stage. You need to sort your life out and really focus on this last module. Seriously Apex, what on earth will you do with yourself if you fail?"

Apex nodded in agreement. Mr Coval had a point, but at that moment he just wanted him to shut up. He picked up his bag and left the room, heading towards the E-library. As expected, it was packed with students sitting, talking, laughing and eating. He lowered himself lethargically into a chair and gave an exasperated sigh as he stared at the hordes of overweight kids. Frowning in utter disgust at the sight of their morbid frames, their rolls of fat drooping towards the ground, he listened in on a group of girls who were boasting about how much they had consumed the night before.

"Hi Apex," said a familiar voice.

It was Olive.

"Hey, what's happening?" he replied.

"Oh God you wouldn't believe the morning I've had! It's been insane. You know that skinny girl Jessy? She got beaten up in class by the twins."

"Shit!" said Apex in surprise.

"I know! They were teasing her for being so skinny and knocked her clean out. I felt so bad for her. They were calling her 'veggie lover' and telling her to get out of the country! She stood her ground, but there was no way she would have won against those two fatties."

Apex shook his head. "What the fuck's going on? It's getting beyond a joke now," he said angrily.

"I know! That's been the fifth attack this week Apex, you should watch yourself. Those earthquakes too, did you feel them? I mean I've felt them before, but not as often as this. It's getting pretty scary, don't you think?"

"I know it's crazy, isn't it. Some serious shit is going down, I can feel it. Just be safe, OK Olive."

"I will. Hey, what you doing tonight, fancy coming over to study?" she asked.

"Nah, I'm off to Chaz's for a smoke. You fancy joining me?"

"I might do… I'll call you," she said then gave a flirty smile and walked off.

He liked Olive; she wasn't like the other girls. Other girls were lazy, they were permanently eating, and they'd forever criticise how skinny he was, but not Olive. Olive was cool, she was thoughtful and most of all, she was hot!

He smiled to himself as he watched Olive walk off, then turned his attention to the desk in front of him. His thoughts returned to the horrific dream he'd had last night. *The strange entities, the way they'd changed shape, what they'd said to him, if only he knew what they were saying*, he thought. It wasn't the first time he'd had dreams about these dark, oppressive creatures. In fact he'd been having the same dream, with the same people for at least three times a week for as long as he could remember. He dreamt about men being torn apart at the arms and legs, their limbs being effortlessly ripped away from their bodies. He'd see a boy running away into the woods... and then it would just end. It would always end in that same place and he'd never been able to work out what was going on. Sometimes there'd be a girl in the dream too. She was always crying, always in despair and it was both scary and saddening to see her like it and not be able to help her. Her hands would cover her face, but she'd never take them away and he never got to know why she was upset. He'd tried to ask her, but she never responded. It was as though she couldn't hear him. The dream last night though, well that had been crazy! He'd seen these entities before, but never this close and this time it had felt as though they were trying to communicate with him. As though they were trying to tell him something, but what? They had been getting closer and closer with each dream, almost to the point where he felt as if they might grab him and take him somewhere. And that boy, who was he? Thinking about it was draining and it had left him feeling scared and confused. He forced the thoughts from his mind and instead turned his attention to this evening. *As soon as I get out of here I'm going straight to Chaz's house. God how I could do with a bong.*

"Apex Mensah!" called a voice loudly.

Apex turned towards the direction of the voice with a startled look on his face.

"There's no point daydreaming, that work's not going to do it by itself!"

"Sorry Mr Coval," Apex sighed.

"I want to see you do some work, come on crack on boy"

Apex pulled his tie up to his mouth and spoke,

"Can I have all your information on the Elizabethan period?"

He sighed, "Please!"

The E-Librarian replied in her robotic voice,

"Manners cost nothing Mr Mensah… Searching for all historical journals from the Elizabethan period… please wait… please wait… please wait… The search has produced seven thousand nine hundred and fifty four journals…"

Apex sighed again.

"I think you need to be more specific Apex," said Mr Coval sarcastically.

He put the tie up to his mouth and spoke again,

"Can I have all records of values and beliefs in the Elizabethan period…please?"

"Searching for all values and beliefs in the Elizabethan period…searching…please wait … please wait… The search has produced five hundred and sixty journals… would you like to save and view these?"

"Yes," replied Apex.

"Oh for fuck sake… Please!"

"Files downloading… please wait…please wait… All files have been stored on your tie."

Apex pressed his tie against the E-table and the holographic journals appeared before him. He started to read, but he wasn't in the slightest bit interested, so he skimmed through, turning page after page, thinking about life and dreaming of living in a country that accepted people no matter what they looked like. A country that hadn't annexed itself off from the rest of the world, a life where he could walk around without constantly seeing overweight people and being met with their disapproving looks. He continued to mindlessly turn the pages, when his attention was caught by a page that read:

'*Elizabethan witch trials 1550-1600'.*

Witches, he thought, *this could be interesting.* He wasn't sure why exactly, but he felt somehow drawn to it and continued to flick through the pages. Each one had its own journal on individual witch trials and witch hunts. He paused at a page that read,

<u>*Witch hunt, case 510: the case of John Potter, 1599, Essex, England.*</u>

We discovered the bodies of three of our guards on the present day, all of whom hadst experienced a most horrid death. Their bodies hadst been dismembered by what can only beest described as an unknown force. We didst discover the bodies of Jack Potter and his wife, Mary Potter, the parents of John and Jane. We believeth they hath all been murdered by these two witches. The event apace cameth to our attention at the hour in which Christopher Pratt hath explained what he hadst witnessed. That gent toldeth us that the two Potter children wast responsible for the deaths of the guards and of their own mother and father. He didst say that the children hadst escaped in to the woodlands…

Apex's heart thumped. It sounded exactly like the dreams he'd been having. Shutting off the E-table, he sat back in his chair and nervously chuckled to himself about just how ridiculous that was. It was surely just coincidental.

"Mr. Coval?"

"Yes Apex."

"I've found some information on the Elizabethan period that I think could be pretty interesting, it's about witchcraft. Um… so…can I go now?"

"Apex, you have to promise me you'll take this seriously, I don't want you to fail. 16th Century witchcraft is a fascinating subject, something I know a little about myself, but a word of warning: witches were never burnt at the stake in England, even though a lot of historians may lead you to believe that was the case. They were hanged, so trust me, I *will* know if you're trying to pull a fast one. Just make sure you research it fully and remember to ask me if you need any help, you can always call me on your E-tie. OK yes, you can go, but I want you to promise me you'll sort yourself out, get to bed early and stay off the drugs. Oh and one last thing, make sure you protect yourself from these earthquakes."

Apex smiled and gave him a friendly pat on the shoulder, before discretely brushing the flakes of dandruff off of his hand onto his uniform. He wasn't such a bad fellow after all, well apart from the dandruff of course.

"That's cookie sir, I'll make you proud, don't you worry."

Mr Coval smiled back at Apex, he'd always had a bit of a soft spot for him and there was no doubt the boy was smart, he just needed to sort out his concentration levels.

Apex walked away, glad to be finally getting out of this place. He knew he'd finish the module, but there was no way he was going to quit the weed and he definitely wasn't scared of any stupid earthquakes. He made his way over to the lift and squeezed himself in between the obese bodies of a group of college students. He gagged in repulsion of their grotesque frames, heavy breathing and the horrid smell of greasy sweat. They looked him up and down, as though he was some kind of circus freak, as if they'd never seen a slim person before. He shifted awkwardly from foot to foot for the duration of the descent, feeling the uncomfortable gaze of their stares and inwardly hoping they'd be getting off before he reached the bottom. Hostility towards slim people was becoming increasingly common in the community and he felt unsafe wherever he went. Racism wasn't an issue at all these days; it was slimism that made him nervous. The hardest thing for him to come to terms with was that even his own family were becoming like all those other bigoted people. They told him to put weight on. They made excuses for not inviting him out when there was a family event, or when they were going out in public. They told everyone that he had a condition that made him thin, that even if he ate the same amount as everybody else he still wouldn't put on weight. It was all lies. He just wanted to be healthy and there was no way he was going to be like everybody else and get fat. As a consequence, he tried his utmost to keep away from his folks whenever he could and he always tried to make sure he got home once they were asleep.

The lift ground to a halt and the large people rushed to get out before Apex, jostling him out of the way with their podgy elbows. They looked down at him in disgust, their noses held high in the air in an authoritative manner. Apex took no notice and merely continued towards the scanning system.

*"Scanning in progress… scanning in progress… Hello Mr
Mensah… Do you have permission to leave?"*

"Yes Mr Coval said I could go."

*"Checking Authorisation… Please wait… Please wait…
Authorisation granted. Have a nice day. Apex, I have a message from
Mr. Coval, he asks you to…Sort your life out…"*

Apex sniggered and made his way out of the scanner.

He thought about going home first, he didn't feel well at all and
could do with going to bed. All the sleepless nights were catching up
with him, but he was too frightened to sleep, the dreams were getting
way too intense. Instead, he started making his way to Chaz's.
Although the conveyor-pave was just a few minutes' walk away, it was
too expensive to make use of it all of the time, plus it would only take
him twenty minutes by foot and it would help keep him fit. He couldn't
justify spending five dollars to save ten minutes of walking. A voice
caught his attention and he glanced over to see a scruffy man wearing
tatty, ripped clothing pacing up and down the sidewalk preaching loudly
to anyone that would listen. Apex had seen him a few times before,
usually preaching about the threat of a new type of war, but this time it
was different…

"Men, women and children tell us your names? Tell us where he is?
Tell us so we may find him… Tell us now and you may be spared…"

Apex watched as the man's behaviour became increasingly more
aggressive. He started grabbing at startled passers-by, asking them odd
questions, staring into the very depth of their souls. Suddenly the man
approached Apex, grabbed his shoulders and glared at him manically.

"Tell me your name…?" he spat angrily.

Feeling unsettled, Apex stared back at the man, open mouthed and confused as to what to do.

"What the fuck, what you doing man?" Apex shouted, pushing the man away from him and then hastily walking off. It wasn't long and he heard the sound of sirens approaching. They'd arrest the madman and probably send him to the asylum, *fucking freak,* he thought. "What the fuck, what you doing man?" Apex shouted, pushing the man away from him and then hastily walking off. A large crowd had gathered behind Apex, watching as the crazed man was dragged away by the police-bots. It was normal practice to use police-bots these days as human officers were far too overweight and unfit to be capable of doing their job properly. Apex sniggered to himself and went to turn away. But then the corners of his mouth dropped and a serious look came over his face when he noticed that the man was staring him in the eyes. No one else, just Apex. Suddenly, those haunting words he had heard so many times before, came from the man's mouth. The hairs on the back of his neck stood on end as he heard the broken but recognisable whispering.

"CHA…TTI CART…OM DES…TRUCT ORM…ATI!"

Chapter 20

8 hours to termination

A pex stood outside Chaz's front door, shaken by what had
happened. Although the door had been finished in a
welcoming bright red colour, it was virtually impenetrable.
After last time, Chaz had made sure that if he was ever robbed again the
doors would only be wide enough for him and Apex, or anyone else
slim enough to get through. The rest of the city's inhabitants would
never fit; they were way too fat. Apex thought it was a bit stupid, but he
had to admit it was working. He waited to be scanned…

*"Scanning in progress… Scanning in progress, welcome Apex…
How are you today?"*

"I'm just cookie Sitara."

"I'm pleased to hear that."

The door opened and Apex was immediately confronted by a thick
cloud of smoke.

"Shit man, I can't see anything!"

"Hey man, good to see you!" called a voice from the corner of the room. "I've just smoked one; I'll get another one loaded up for you now."

Chaz was also a slim guy. His body was etched with tattoos of dragons and mythical beasts and his perfectly toned physique was proof of how much he worked out. He was proud of his appearance and couldn't understand why others wouldn't want a physique like his. Despite being fit, he was a heavy hash smoker and made his living from selling it. Sometimes he'd make up to six thousand dollars in just one day, but it was fine because it was all completely legal and above board. In fact the local council positively encouraged smoking it, as they said it was "beneficial to public health". Which was certainly true, scientists had backed it up with years of research, but Apex and Chaz knew the real reason the drug had been legalised. They were convinced the government wanted people to smoke so that they would eat more fast food, which would consequently help fund other organisations. Apex wasn't too bothered though, as the drug had never made him want to eat any of that shit anyway.

"Cheers Chaz," said Apex eagerly rubbing his hands together in anticipation.

He sat down and as the smoke slowly evaporated it revealed the small box-shaped room. There were pictures everywhere, mostly of other countries, which Apex and Chaz would spend hour after hour looking at and dreaming of the day when they could both live somewhere else. There were also pictures of slim, healthy, semi-naked women; a rare sight in America these days.

"So what's up then bro?" Chaz asked.

"Just came from college bro. Man, I hate it there!"

"Don't blame you bro. I don't even know how you can even stand going outside, let alone college. You've got balls I'll give you that," said Chaz lighting the bong. "Here, take a chuff on this."

He passed the tube over to Apex and lit it for him. Apex inhaled taking in a huge lungful of the burning fumes, then coughing and spluttering as the stream of thick smoke exited his lungs.

"Oh… That's some good shit!" Apex exclaimed, flopping back into the chair looking relaxed and happy.

Chaz grinned. There was nothing more pleasurable to him than getting his bro well and truly stoned.

"Some weird shit has been happening bro, some really weird shit," said Apex after a while.

"What do you mean bro?"

"I've been having some fucked up dreams bro and I've been reading some stuff that's really freaked me out too. I keep dreaming about the same things, like bodies being ripped apart and there's this boy. But the really crazy thing is I read some report from seven hundred years ago in the library at college today that describes the exact dream I've been having!"

"What the fuck you talking about? Man, you need to chill out on the weed bro, it's fucking with your brain. Shit, I'm a bad influence aren't I? I won't give you any more."

"Chaz, it ain't the weed, I really think some weird shit is going down. I can't explain it, but something ain't right man."

Chaz stared at Apex unsure whether to take him seriously or if it was the weed doing the talking.

"Here, let me get you a beer. Sitara, can I have two beers please?"

"Beer coming up Chaz, I hope you enjoy it. I got you "smoking barrels". It is apparently the best lager import from the UK. It took me some time, but I think you will like it."

"Thanks Sitara, I don't know what I'd do without you," Chaz replied gratefully.

The table in the centre of the room made a low humming noise and two bottles of beer rose up from an opening in the middle of the tabletop. They picked the bottles up, clunked them together and said "Cookie" before swigging and touching fists.

"It does sound a bit messed up bro, but I wouldn't worry about it. We both have a lot going on, sounds to me like you're letting it get to you. This country is messed up bro, it's no wonder you feel like you do. Why'd you think I sell marijuana? It's so I don't have to leave the apartment. I do all my shopping through Sitara and get it delivered."

Apex nodded.

"You OK man, you look a bit pale?"

"I'll be alright bro, just need more sleep."

"So anyway what's happening with you and Olive bro? Man she's got the hots for you!"

"You think so?"

"You're all she talks about! I'm serious bro, she wants you bad."

Apex chuckled.

"Bro seriously though, why would she want a fucked up guy like me?"

Chaz grinned.

"Hey, fancy a game of work out zombie legend?"

"Nah bro, don't really think I can concentrate, and anyway you always win."

"Yeah good point, OK I'll put the news on instead. Have you been seeing all this shit with the earthquakes? Man, there's some weird stuff happening, no one's got a clue what's causing it."

"Can you put ARK News on please?" Chaz ordered Sitara.

A holographic image of two smartly dressed newsreaders appeared before them.

"Tremors have been felt in several other countries, but appear to be much stronger over Western Europe, with readings of up to seven on the Richter scale. Scientists all over the world are baffled by this phenomenon, but have stressed that there is no cause for alarm. William Maude-Roxby, a Professor of Seismology in the UK, said this earlier today."

"We have never experienced earthquakes of this scale in the UK and we cannot predict if there will be any more. At this point we are still unsure as to the cause of this unusual activity. However, we have some of the best and well-respected scientists working together as we speak. One theory suggests that climate change within the atmosphere combined with the build-up of pollution from previous years has interfered with the planets plates, causing them to move erratically, or more so than usual. The other theory states that the earth's inner-core is somehow strained, which is generating an increased gravitational pull. Despite the earthquakes, we believe that it will pass and are keen to stress that any environmental damage caused by our forefathers is under control and will continue to improve. Please be patient while we continue our research on this. I will return later today to provide further updates."

Chaz turned to Apex excitedly and said,

"See man, I told you some crazy shit's happening. I thought we had it bad here, but it looks like the whole world is shaking. I've never known anything like it!"

"Yeah, that's some crazy shit!" replied Apex, easing himself up out of the chair. "Look bro, I ain't feeling too good. I need to get some sleep; I'm so tired. I'm gonna head home."

"Bro are you serious? You never go home at this sort of time. Things must be bad!"

Apex walked unsteadily towards the exit and turned round to give a half-hearted wave to Chaz.

"Hey bro, take it easy and if you feel better tomorrow come over, bring Olive too."

Apex nodded and headed outside, grateful for some fresh air. He breathed in heavily and instantly began feeling better.

"Apex! Apex!" called a voice.

He turned to see a beaming Olive running towards him.

"I tried calling you, but I left my calling chip at home and then I tried using my E-tie, but it blocked me. I know we can't use our ties outside of college, but I always like to give it a go. Anyway, I thought I'd just come over instead on the off chance I'd see you. How come you're leaving Chaz's so soon?'

"I felt sick, so I decided to go home; I'm pretty tired."

"You want me to come with you?" Olive asked with concern.

He thought for a second, before nodding his head and said,

"Sure, I'm feeling a little better now, but it would be nice to have some company."

It didn't take them long to get back to Apex's house. He hesitated at the door. He didn't particularly want to invite her in, as his family would be there and they'd only make some snide comment, or complain about how skinny she is. He definitely wasn't in the mood for dealing with that right now.

"Listen, I'd ask you to come in, but I'm worried what my folks will say to you."

"Hey, I don't mind, I'm used to hearing it from my own family. I mean, I presume you're talking about my weight?"

He grinned. He'd always known they had a lot in common and the fact it included family problems attracted him to her even more.

"Alright, come on in then. Welcome to my humble abode," he said waving his arm in the air and bowing.

He unlocked the door and motioned for Olive to go in first.

"Aww, such a gentleman," she said smiling.

"Mom! Gran! You in?"

His relief was clearly visible when there was no reply. *Must be out,* he thought. They headed up to Apex's bedroom. Olive had been to his house once before for Apex's sixteenth birthday and his bedroom hadn't changed at all. She wandered around inquisitively, looking at the collection of pictures on his wall.

"Did you draw these?" she asked.

"Yep, I sure did. Well, actually I used the dream catcher program, because I keep having these weird dreams."

"What's the dream catcher program?"

"Oh man, it's so cool. Basically you put these sensors on your temples like this…" he put them on demonstrating to Olive. "Then you simply go to sleep. When you dream, the images are printed onto the computer. It's so awesome!"

"This one's a bit freaky. What is it?" she asked pointing.

"Oh that one... Well that one...um... It's a little hard to explain, because...well, I can't explain it. It's like this weird ghost creature that I see a lot. It fucking scares the shit out of me. It's all I ever think about Olive; it's driving me up the wall."

Olive looked at him in concern.

"Do you think dreams actually mean something?"

Apex thought for a second.

"Here, let me show you something."

He pulled out one of the dream catcher images.

"Look at this one... What do you see?"

She instantly recoiled in disgust.

"Oh my God, what's happening to those men? Are their arms and legs being ripped off? And look at their heads, it's terrible!"

"Yep, they sure are. Right, look at this one." He pulled out another dream catcher image. "OK, what can you see in this picture?"

"Well, it looks like a boy running away to me. So what does that one mean?" she asked with growing interest.

"OK, wait... Look at this."

He pulled the E-tie up to his mouth and spoke,

"Can I please have the document of John and Jane Potter, 1599"

"Searching... Searching... Document found... Please scan your tie on your E-table..."

He put his tie onto the E-Table and a holographic document appeared in front of them.

"Right, now read this."

Witch hunt, case 510: the case of John Potter, 1599, Essex, England.

Olive read through the article that Apex had found in the library earlier that day.

"OK yeah that's pretty weird Apex, but surely you don't think it's your dream do you?"

He shrugged uncertainly.

"Have you read any more?" she asked.

"Nah, I shut it off, it freaked me right out."

She read on.

"We hath followed a trail to findeth these hags and doth suspect John and Jane Potter didst seeketh the assistance of Mr Fleming, who we kneweth wast a valorous friend of Mr Potter the deserter. Mr Fleming hath lived several miles from the Potter family and as we didst gain entrance to his house our suspicions hath been confirmed. We hath questioned Mr Fleming and John Potter didst at that time appeareth and relent to the Sheriff. We hath been aware of John's sorcery but hadst not expected t to befall on us. The Sheriff, Mr Fleming and twenty of our personal guards hath been murdered before mine very own eyes. I wast fortunate to escapeth after John hadst ranneth from the house. I discovered anon that gent near to death after falling into the river. I hath drawn out what I bethinkst to hath occurred. Having seen with mine own eyes the most terrible deaths of that of Mr Fleming, the Sheriff and the soldiers who art with us, it seemeth to mine mind that the two incidents art connected. John wast nowt but a beldams and possessed a most heinous threat to our community. I didst capture the hag and returneth him to the town where that foul gent wast found guilty of sorcery and wast executed anon."

Joseph Oakley, 1599.

Olive looked closely at the illustration that accompanied the report. It showed three guards levitating in mid-air, having their arms, legs and heads ripped apart from their bodies.

"Apex," she whispered, "I think you need to see this."

She pointed at the picture.

"Oh my God!" said Apex comparing the two pictures. The drawing looked almost identical to his dream catcher image.

"How's that possible?" he said shakily.

"I don't know Apex, it's really weird. How could you dream about something that happened nearly seven hundred years ago? Surely it's not possible?"

"I don't know, but I think John is the boy I've been dreaming about. He's the one running into the woods and I think I've seen him being confronted by the entities too."

"How do you mean?" she asked.

"I mean, I think I was the one that scared them away from that boy. Last night I dreamt I was in a wooden house. It was dark and I couldn't see anything, because there was only a tiny bit of light, but I could hear these really creepy voices. They were talking in another language. When I checked to see what it was I saw two shapes screaming at the boy. I'm pretty sure it was John. When they saw me, they left him alone and came after me instead. It's really freaked me out."

Olive shook her head in disbelief.

"It's not possible; surely it has to be a coincidence."

"I know it sounds crazy Olive, but so many strange things have been happening recently. My fucked up dreams and these crazy earthquakes means I've been getting hardly any sleep and I'm exhausted Olive. I went to see a doctor, to see if he could give me anything to help me sleep, but all he suggested was that I eat more and put on weight. Waste of fucking time!" He put his head in his hands. "I can't make sense of any of it."

They sat in silence for a few seconds before Apex spoke again.

"Hey, sorry where are my manners, let me get you a drink. What do you fancy?"

"Water's fine," she replied smiling sweetly.

He stood up and left the room to get the drinks, leaving Olive to look through the piles of dream catcher pictures. There were some really odd ones in there that made her feel uneasy just looking at them. For instance, there was one image of a man with no eyes or ears, but then this would be in a pile mixed up with a perfectly normal image of a woman in old-fashioned clothing holding a baby. She picked up the image of the weird entities that Apex had mentioned and studied it in more detail. The liquid shapes and hollow metallic eyes made her shiver causing her to drop one of the pictures from the stack onto the floor. She picked it up only half glancing at what was on it, doing a double take when she realised what it was. The image was of her, completely naked and having sex with Apex. Hearing Apex's approaching footsteps, she hurriedly hid the picture underneath her and nervously cleared her throat.

"Here you are," he said passing her a glass of water and sitting down next to her.

"Apex, can I ask you something?"

"Sure."

"Do you think of me?"

"Uh, what do you mean?" he asked, a confused look on his face.

155

"I mean do you think about me in a certain way?"

"What do you mean?"

"OK, look I found this picture." She pulled it out to show him.
"We're having sex Apex, look!"

"Oh my God…um…shit… You weren't meant to see that!"

He snatched the picture from her in embarrassment.

"I'll throw it away, I promise. Look, I'll rip it up now."

"It's OK Apex, I don't mind. It's actually quite nice you think of me
in that way."

 She drank her water and then kissed him on the cheek.

"I've got to go now Apex, but will I see you tomorrow?"

"Um… yeah sure, I'd like that." He gave her an awkward smile and
followed her down to the front door.

"How about you come over to mine and we can talk more about
your dreams," she said flirtatiously flicking her hair from her shoulders.

"OK," said Apex giving an excited chuckle, "sure, that would be
great."

He watched until Olive was out of sight and then closed the front
door and went back up to his bedroom, grinning to himself. *Man she's
amazing* he thought. Pleasant thoughts of Olive didn't last for long
however and his mind quickly turned back to his crazy dreams. The
thought of sleep frightened him; he was absolutely terrified of seeing
those entities again, but he was so tired. He got undressed and climbed
into bed, lying there looking into space and trying to clear his mind. He
lay there for what felt like hours, before eventually closing his eyes and
drifting off to sle

Chapter 21

4 hours to termination…

*H*e *desperately tried to kick the window open, but the flames were too intense.*

"Help me! Help me!" screamed a desperate voice.

"Oh shit! I can't get you out, it's too hot! It's burning, it's too hot!

Apex helplessly stood and stared in horror as the burning man clawed at the window trying to escape the scorching inferno from within. The man's harrowing screams continued to echo their way through Apex's mind and as he stood back, wiping the sweat away from his face with the back of his hand, he took one final glance before the scene blurred and changed…

It was the girl. Her hands were covering her face, but it was definitely her, and she was sobbing loudly.

"What's wrong?" he asked, "Please, tell me what's wrong?"

She took her hands away and pointed. Apex looked in the direction she was indicating, squinting his eyes to make sense of the hovering liquid form he could just make out in the distance. However as it drew closer, making that familiar and distinctive scream, Apex started to panic. He turned and ran, feeling the figure's energy rising up behind him, but as he glanced back, he realised it had gone. There was a foreboding sense that something was about to happen and it was quiet. Deathly silence, a silence so eerie and so still it made Apex feel sick to his very core. He turned his head to take a second glance and as he did so, the entity was right there, in front of his face, it's empty silvery eyes staring at him.

"CHATTI CARTOM DESTRUCT ORMATI!" it screamed and forcefully grabbed Apex's shoulders.

"CHATTI CARTOM DESTRUCT ORMATI!" it repeated, followed by a terrifying scream.

Apex sat up screaming, shaking with fear, "Why me, what have done to deserve this," he shouted. He took a deep breath and closed his eyes, desperately trying to replace the nightmares with more positive thoughts, "Think about Olive, yeah think about her and you'll have better dreams, it must be all the shit going on in my life, that's what it is," he said reassuringly to himself. He tossed and turned from his back to his side, but no matter what position he lay in he just couldn't get comfortable. He let out a sigh of frustration and opened his eyes, staring blankly up at the ceiling, like he had done the day before and the day before that. There was a soft tap on the door and then the deep gravelly voice of his mum.

"Apex, you in there?"

"Yes Mom."

"Did you feel the earthquake?"

"No Mom, I must have slept through it."

"Aren't you supposed to be at college? And what's that smell? Is that perfume?"

"I didn't feel well, so I came home. A friend came back with me," he said in a monotonous tone, he was exhausted by the conversation already.

"You want some food? I've got some of that fried chicken."

"Nah, I don't feel like eating."

"No wonder you feel ill Apex, you never eat! You really must start eating more. People are starting to talk; it doesn't look good. Oh and by the way, I saw your Aunt Poppy earlier, she asked me to pass on a message."

"Yeah? What is it?"

"CHATTI CARTOM DESTRUCT ORMATI!"

Apex woke abruptly, his heart pounding.

"Oh shit," he gasped, trying to regain his composure. The lines between dream world and reality were becoming more and more blurred and he wasn't sure how much more he could take of this.

"Apex, you in there?" a voice called from outside his door.

"Yes Mom."

"Did you feel the earthquake?"

"No Mom, I must have slept through it," replied Apex, sensing that something wasn't right. He began to shake, the fear rising up and consuming his body. It was if he knew what she was going to say, like he'd heard it before. He mouthed the words as his mum asked,

"Aren't you supposed to be at college? And what's that smell? Is that perf…"

He sat up sharply and cut her off mid-sentence,

"Mom…"

"What?"

"Did you see Aunt Poppy today?"

"Yes, I've just come back from hers. Why?"

"Did she have a message for me?"

"Yes she did as it happens. She said that you hadn't been to see her for quite some time now and that she misses you Apex."

Apex let out the breath he had been holding. It had just been a dream after all. He lay back down on his bed and stared up at the ceiling, listening to the deep sigh coming from the other side of the door as his mum walked off down the corridor. His extreme tiredness, the exhaustion of trying to stay awake night after night was too great. He blinked his eyes, desperately trying to keep them open, but the more he fought it, the harder it became…

Everywhere was dark, nothing there but an eerie silence and a static energy. His hairs stood up. He could sense a presence but couldn't tell where it was coming from. Then out of nowhere he could feel himself travel, it was such a strange sensation, the feeling of movement, except he had no visual reference of where he was going. A small slither of light was now visible in the distance and it was gradually getting closer to him. He eventually realised he was at college, in his class room. He was stood at the back and everyone facing away from him. He could see Olive too, she was sat at the front. He knew it was her, he could tell from the long hair and slim figure. It was strange because she was

never in the same class, in fact she studied something completely
different. He called her name,

"Hey Olive!"

But there was no response. In fact all the students remained in their
seats, unmoving like statues. Then the door of the classroom opened and
in walked Mr Coval. His head was lowered, his face hidden from view.
He stood in front of the class but did not make a sound. Apex called out
again,

"Mr Coval, is everything ok?"

But there was no response.

"Mr Coval?"

Then without any warning, Mr Coval lifted his head and to Apex's
horror his face was coated in blood. His eyes were removed and his
ears and nose had also gone. Apex screamed as he tried to escape, but
the wall behind prevented him. The rest of the class, including Olive
turned their heads freakishly, their necks snapping a they turned a clear
180 degrees. Then all at once they spoke the same words,

"CHATTI CARTOM DESTRUCT ORMATI!"

Apex woke up, sweat dripping from every pore of his body.

It had happened again.

Chapter 22

2 hours to termination

Apex's eyes shot open.

"What the fuck's going on!" he screamed hysterically.

Clawing at his covers, he finally found the button to remove them, got up and put his gown on, before racing to the bathroom. Shaking wildly, he turned the tap on and splashed his face with cold water. He no longer recognised the face staring back at him in the mirror.

What's happening to me? Why me? What's wrong with me?!

He was interrupted by the sound of groaning noises followed by hushed whisperings coming from downstairs. *What's that?* he thought and cautiously started creeping his way down, still feeling spooked from his dreams. When he reached the entrance to the living room he was shocked to see his mum standing in the corner. She was facing the wall and her arms were hanging loosely by her side.

"Mom, are you alright? What are you doing?"

She didn't reply, so he edged closer until he realised,

"Mom, is that a knife? Why are you holding a knife? Mom, what are you doing?" He reached out to grab her, but as he did so his feet slipped on something and he looked down to see a large pool of dark red liquid. His eyes followed the trail...

"What the fuck!"

It was his gran. She was on the ground, surrounded by her own blood, barely recognisable. Her eyes had been gouged out and her nose and ears had each been cut off and thrown across the room. Trying to stop himself from retching, Apex looked back over towards his mum, who was still facing the wall.

"Mom what have you done?"

Her large frame stiffened, almost as if she had no control over her own bodily functions. She spoke in a mechanical, inhuman tone,

"What is your name?"

"What the fuck are you talking about Mom? It's me, Apex."

"You are not him, are you?"

"I don't know what you mean Mom? What have you done to Gran?"

"Because she was not him. Tell me where he is?"

"Who Mom? Who are you talking about?"

"Ema."

"Who on earth's Ema?"

She turned to look at him, her face void of all emotion and her skin pale and corpse-like. She moved jerkily towards him and Apex instantly started to back off, terrified by what was happening. It had to be a dream, he had to make himself wake up, but he couldn't. Out of the corner of his eye he suddenly noticed that his gran had risen from the floor and was standing rigidly, blindly looking in his direction. With her mutilated, expressionless face she stared at him before hoarsely ordering,

"Tell me your name?"

Unable to take any more, he quickly turned away and ran towards the front door, his fingers fumbling manically with the lock. He finally managed to open it before sprinting out in to the open air, heading to the only safe place he knew.

Chaz's house.

It was dark, but for some reason the streets were filled with people walking around. Something wasn't right. It was 3am, there shouldn't be this many people around, especially considering it was a weeknight. But the strangest thing was that there were people scattered on the ground, lying motionless. Apex carefully picked his way through, taking care not to step on anyone at the same time as looking around to try and work out what was going on. Groups of people were fighting, some were using metal pipes and rocks as weapons and some had knives. All of them were screaming manically, it was like a scene from a horror movie. He noticed a bruised and battered looking person sat on the sidewalk.

"What's going on?" he asked.

The man looked up at Apex with the same empty, expressionless look his mum had given him earlier. Like his gran, this man also had no nose or ears and there were no eyes either, just deep gaping holes.

"What is your name?" the man yelled, "Where is he, where is Ema?"

"What the hell's going on?" Apex yelled back, the noise alerting the big crowd of brawling men, women and children. Some continued to fight, but others broke off and started spasmodically running towards Apex, screaming and shouting.

"TELL US YOUR NAME! TELL US WHERE HE IS?"

Panicking, Apex turned and ran in the opposite direction, away from the hordes of crazy fat people. Their sluggishness was no match for his athletic sprint and he was able to easily shake them off. In his head he worked out another, longer route; it would add a few more minutes to his journey, but at least he'd be safe from those maniacs. He carried on running as fast as he could until he reached Chaz's house and impatiently waited to be scanned.

"Scanning in progress… please wait… please wait… Good morning Apex… unfortunately Chaz is sleeping. You will have to return later when he is awake… Have a great morning!"

"OPEN THE FUCKING DOOR NOW!"

"Negative… Chaz is sleeping… please return at a more convenient time…"

Apex kicked at the door, banging it as hard as he could.

"If you don't step away from the door I will be forced to call the authorities."

"Call them then! This is a fucking emergency!"

With that, the alarms kicked in, sending deafening high-pitched wails screeching into the night.

"Emergency… Emergency… Emergency…"

Apex covered his ears and looked around. In the distance he spotted a large group of people staring in his direction, obviously alerted by the ear-piercing sounds of the alarm. They started to approach, their fat bodies walking with that same fitful movement, increasing in speed the closer they got. It was as if they were being controlled by an unknown force, something out of control and absolutely terrifying.

Apex banged louder, his body now slamming against the door, desperately trying to force his way in.

"CHAZ, OPEN THE FUCKING DOOR NOW!"

The door swung abruptly open, causing Apex to fall sharply to the ground. Chaz stood there looking half asleep and confused.

"What the fuck is going on?" he said rubbing his eyes. "Why have the alarms gone off?"

He tapped at a keypad on the side and as the peals of the alarm stopped, Apex stood up and screamed,

"CLOSE THE FUCKING DOOR NOW!"

"Alright, alright! Keep your hair on!" Chaz exclaimed as he shut the door, "Bro, it's 3am, why on earth are you here? And why the hell have you got your dressing gown on?"

Apex staggered into the small box room and sat down in a chair. He was shaking uncontrollably and kept twitching his head around like a restless owl. He stood up again to look out of the window. Chaz wasn't used to seeing his friend behaving so erratically, something serious must have happened.

"Find a weapon, anything!" Apex said, his voice intensifying.

"Wait, calm down bro. What's happened?"

"My Mom murdered my Gran. She was all cut up bro, and her eyes and ears man… they'd been cut off! And outside… outside bro, there are people killing each other! They're stabbing each other. They came after me bro… it's… it's like a Zombie movie bro! Except… except this shit is real, we have to get somewhere safe!"

"You're kidding me right? Zombies? Haha, that's funny bro, you had me there. I mean it's funny when you joke around and all that, but at three in the morning? Anyway, even if there were "zombies" out there, we'd be safe in here, I've got three ounces of weed, that should last a bit of time and I've got loads of food, plus don't forget we've had loads of practice on that Zombie legend workout, they wouldn't stand a chance!"

"Chaz we need guns bro, real guns, we need grenades. It would take more than one bullet just to take down one obese zombie, but a few hundred... we don't stand a chance. We have to run... we have to find a military base... we need help bro!" Apex screamed.

"Bro, you're serious aren't you?"

"Totally serious Chaz, look out the window."

Chaz walked towards the window, straining his eyes to make out anything in the darkness.

"Bro I can't see anything there. You sure you're feeling OK? Look, let me go outside and see what's happening."

"Chaz, don't do it, they'll get you and they'll kill you. Don't do it!" Apex shouted.

"Shit man, there ain't no zombies out there, trust me."

Chaz got up and walked out to the large metal door. He stood outside for a few seconds, looked around and then returned to Apex with a confused look on his face.

"See I told you bro it's completely clear, no one out there."

He patted Apex on the shoulders before sitting down to load up his bong.

"Bro you should seriously cut out the weed, this shit is making you hallucinate."

"I don't want any weed, that shit isn't going to help!"

"Seriously Apex, there's no one out there."

Suddenly, Sitara announced,

"Scanning... scanning ... please wait... please wait... unknown males outside, would you like them to enter Chaz?"

Chaz stood up and nervously approached the holographic camera image.

"What the fuck!" he shouted, "Oh my God! He's got no eyes! Shit man, you were right... there's more of them... Oh my God, there's hundreds of 'em!"

"I fucking told you! What they doing out there?"

"They've got knives bro... Oh shit, they're stabbing each other. What the hell's going on? Sitara don't let them in! Call the police!"

"Calling the police... please wait... please wait... there is no response from the police... would you like me to try again...?"

"Yes, keep trying," Chaz demanded desperately.

Loud bangs started coming from the door, the metal creaked as the hordes of zombies pushed their grotesquely overweight bodies against it, hitting and stabbing each other at the same time.

"What's happened, why are they like this, why are they killing each other?"

"I don't know man, but they kept asking for my name and then asking me for someone called Ema. It's gone crazy out there bro. Put the news on, it's got to have something on there."

"Sitara put channel forty on," Chaz ordered.

"Channel forty news now on..."

"Where are the presenters? Oh shit, there they are!" shouted Chaz.

The presenters, like the zombies outside, were stiffly walking around, blood covering their faces and their eyes had been gouged out. They were hitting each other with any object available; chairs, desks, cameras, it was televisual carnage.

Both presenters, along with the camera crew and production team chanted,

"Tell me your name... where is he? Where is Ema?"

"Oh my God what's going on!" exclaimed Chaz. "This is widespread, we're talking a proper apocalypse bro. This station is based like fifty miles away!"

Apex sat in silence, watching the crazed news presenters, unsure what to do. All of a sudden something dawned on him,

"Shit, I've got to call Olive! I need to know she's OK."

"Ask Sitara, she'll call her for you."

"Sitara, call Olive now!" Apex demanded, his voice wavering.

It rang, but there was no answer. Apex ordered Sitara to try again, and thankfully this time she answered,

"Hello...? Chaz? It's late, why are you calling me?"

Apex exhaled with relief, she was safe... for now.

"Olive where are you? It's Apex."

"Oh hey Apex. Um, I'm in my room, where else would I be?" She sounded confused.

"Something bad's happening... I need to get you, now. We have to get out of here..."

"Slow down Apex what..."

She broke off.

"Olive!" shouted Apex.

He heard muffled talking.

"Mom... Dad... It's just Apex, go back to bed, I won't be long."

Apex strained his ear against the phone and heard a voice in the background say,

"Tell us your name... where is Ema?"

She screamed loudly before the phone went dead.

"Olive! Olive! Fuck sake… OLIVE!"

Termination error detected…Attempting emergency backup for termination…please wait…

A loud banging from the rear of the house startled them and Chaz got up to investigate. Apex frantically tried to call Olive again, tears filling his eyes.

The banging stopped.

Silence...

Emergency termination backup in progress, 93% complete… please wait…

"You OK? Chaz? Chaz, what's going on?" Apex called, his heart thumping wildly.

No response.

Apex flinched as he heard the sound of glass breaking. It sounded as if the window had been smashed. Terrified of what he might find, Apex walked cautiously towards the kitchen. He had a really bad feeling about this. Chaz was stood looking out of the broken window. His mouth was wide open and a dense black smoke was making its way into his body.

"Chaz…? You OK? Talk to me Chaz."

He began to make a deep throated, gargled groan and his body went rigid. He turned sluggishly towards Apex, gazing at him with an empty, washed out look. He fumbled with the glass that lay scattered over the kitchen surfaces. When he failed to get a grip on it he went for the next nearest item; a knife. Lifting the blade up towards his head, he slowly started to slice away at his ears. Blood splattered everywhere, but he continued to cut, now working on the other ear, then his nose, and finally his eyes. Hot red liquid oozed down his face and his empty sockets exposed optic nerves which fell down over his bloodied cheeks.

Apex screamed,

"No! Not you too! What are you doing Chaz? Put the knife down bro, it's me Apex…"

Chaz spoke, but it wasn't his normal voice. It came out in a croaky half strangled tone,

"You're not Ema… you're not Ema…"

He drew closer, forcing Apex back towards the front door. The blood soaked knife hung loosely at his side. He was cornered. There was no escape. He would have to barge past him. He tried to push Chaz away, but it was useless. Despite his horrific injuries and the debilitating way in which he was moving, Chaz swiftly swung the blade at Apex before he had a chance to move out of the way. The edge of the knife sliced through his neck with ease and Apex instinctively grabbed his throat. A warm crimson trickle ran through his hands. He coughed and spluttered, trying to resurface from the sea of blood that was drowning him. A wave of scarlet pulled him under and he collapsed onto his back, his eyes fixed upon his best friend, pleading for help. Suddenly, it was as if something was being pulled out of him, as though Chaz was consuming his very soul.

99% complete. Commencing emergency transition… error… error… transition interference… performing obstruction protocol… please wait…

Chaz's mouth opened in a slow mechanical movement and the same black substance that had earlier made its way into his body began to drift over towards Apex. It smothered his face, concealing his eyes and descending him in to darkness.

Obstruction protocol in progress... please wait... please wait...

Obstruction successful... termination complete...

Part 4

'The world of reality has its limits; the world of imagination is boundless.'

Jean-Jacques Rousseau

Chapter 23

Unknown location

R ose opened her eyes. It was pitch black.
No sound.
No movement.
Nothing.

Is this what happens when you die?

Slowly standing up, she reached her arms out in front of her, feeling around for anything, anything at all that might give her a clue as to where she might be. Yet still, nothing. She carefully took a few steps forward before tripping over something heavy on the floor.

What was that?

Pushing herself up, Rose crawled back over to the object and tentatively placed her hands on it to work out what it might be. Hair, ears, nose, arms and legs; it was a person.

"Hey, can you hear me? Are you OK?" she whispered, gently shaking the person to see if it got a reaction. She shook the body slightly harder and a tiny whimper came from one end and a stir of movement.

"Are you OK?" she repeated, "Who are you? Do you know where we are?"

The person made a few more garbled noises and then suddenly sat up sharply and said in a male voice,

"Whither art I? Wherefore is t so dark?"

"Sorry, what did you say?" Rose asked, confused by the strange use of language.

"Whither art I? Wherefore is t so dark?" he repeated.

"Why are you talking like that? You're obviously English, but it doesn't sound right?"

"Nay, 'tis thee that speaketh strange English. Canst thou helpeth a man up please?"

Rose gripped his hand; it felt dry and rough with callouses, and pulled him up so that he was now standing in front of her.

"Who art thee?" he asked her.

"My name's Rose. Who are you?"

"Thou shalt refer to me as John."

"Well, it's nice to meet you John, despite the circumstances. Look, I have no idea where we are, but I think we should stick together and try and find a way out of here."

Linking hands they guided their way through the darkness, carefully treading across the unknown landscape. Their echoing footsteps told them that wherever they were, it had to be somewhere with walls, somewhere confined.

"Hello? Is there anybody here?" Rose called out.

The pair froze in silence, holding their breaths and intently listened out for even the slightest of sounds.

Nothing.

Suddenly, a bright light consumed the darkness. A light so bright it made Rose and John flinch in pain, their eyes unaccustomed to this degree of brightness. Shielding their eyes with their hands, they saw that they were standing in a large dome-shaped room.

"Ah hello!" called a voice, *"You must be Rose and you must be John. Welcome. I do apologise for the darkness, but we generally keep the lights switched off when we can. It conserves the energy. We have to be very economical here to help make things run smoothly. Anyway, I'm afraid we're still waiting for one more of you, but I imagine he's still in transit. He shouldn't be too much longer."*

Rose and John looked up towards where the voice appeared to be coming from. There was nothing there. The walls and floor looked as if they were made of liquid; they had a graceful fluidity to them almost like liquid mercury, yet they were also solid and strong at the same time. It was unlike anything Rose or John had ever seen before.

"Um… hello?" Rose shouted up, "I can't see you? Who are you and why have you bought us here? What is this place?"

"Ah yes, of course, of course. I'll explain everything in much more detail when we have our other addition, he should be with us shortly. Now, I believe you two have met before?"

Rose looked over at John in confusion.

"No, I'm fairly certain I've never met him before."

John returned her gaze, looking at her properly for the first time, before exclaiming,

"Aye! Aye thou art Rose! I do knoweth thee, I hath seen thee before."

"No, I don't think so John, you must be mistaking me for someone else."

"Aye, 'tis thee. In mine dreams, I hast seen thee in mine dreams!" he shouted excitedly.

"Hang on, what was that? In your dreams John, I've been in your dreams? My therapist told me I had mentioned a boy during hypnosis. His name was John... that must be you! She said you'd helped me in some way. But no, surely this can't be real, you were just imaginary, something my mind made up to protect me. You can't be real!"

John nodded excitedly before replying,

"I saw that evil sir hurt thee. I wast trying to help thee. That gent wast hurting thee and thy mother."

Rose stared at him her mouth open wide in shock.

"You mean Shaun?"

"Aye, that evil man, Shaun if that beest his title"

"Rose and John, I understand that all of this may be a little strange for you, but I will explain everything to you soon," the voice said reassuringly. *"Ah, here he is now. Apex, hello! It's wonderful to have you here. We experienced a great deal of trouble removing you from your time zone, in fact I was slightly concerned we may have lost you altogether, but thankfully we got to you in time."*

Apex was lying on his back. Every now and then his body tensed and twitched as if he was fighting something off. His eyes slowly opened and then jolting back into consciousness he leapt up and yelled,

"What the fuck! Where am I? Oh my God! Where are they? Are they still here? Are they coming to get us?"

He hurtled towards the far wall, too caught up in his own distressed thoughts to notice that there were others in the room with him.

"Apex... Apex, it's OK. You're safe here."

Apex stopped in his tracks and turned to face in the direction of the voice.

"Who is that? Where's your voice coming from?" Frantically looking around, he noticed John and Rose. He gave them a quick look over before asking again, "Who are you? Where am I? Am I dead? Is this where you go when you die?"

"Apex calm down, I'll explain everything. Now that I have you all together I can tell you exactly why you are here, so it is very important that you listen carefully. But first let me introduce myself. My name is Calcus and I live here along with many others like myself. I am from a place that has been lost, far within a future time zone. In fact we are so far in the future we have no idea what date it actually is…but that is not really relevant for what I need to explain to you now."

Apex looked up angrily.

"Bullshit. This ain't right. What kind of sick joke is this? You can't just snatch people and feed them this bullshit. What's going on?"

"Apex I understand that you are confused, but I really would appreciate it if you wouldn't swear, it has no place in my domain. And in answer to one of your questions, no Apex, this is not a joke."

Apex paced erratically around the liquid flooring, muttering profanities under his breath.

"Why can't we see you?" asked Rose.

"I have no physical form, I am merely consciousness. In the future we have no need for a body; the mind does everything. We have discovered new ways of expressing emotion without visually sensing it and we have learnt how to use our senses without a physical body. However, we do not have what you have, but I will come on to that shortly. What I am about to tell you will be very difficult for you to

accept, but what I do tell you will be the absolute truth. Everyone who exists in our universe is born in their own time zone. Each one of you is from a different time zone. Let me demonstrate. John, where are you from?"

"Essex, in England sir."

"Good and what year is it?"

"Why 'tis 1599, sir."

Apex looked at him in astonishment.

"Oh my God, it's you! I've seen you in my dreams! You're the one that ran away in the woods! You're the man I read about in a report at collage. Shit, I can't take this anymore, it's gone beyond crazy now."

John looked at Apex.

"How doth thee knoweth me? I hast never seen thee before in mine life."

"Please don't worry John, I will explain everything you need to know in due course. Rose you next, where are you from?"

"I'm from Bristol in England."

"And what year is it?"

"Erm, well it's 2017 obviously," Rose giggled nervously.

Apex laughed.

"You gotta be shitting me!" he shouted shaking his head in disbelief.

"May I remind you to please mind your language Apex, now tell me, where are you from?"

"I'm from Southfield Detroit in the U.S., it's the year 2200. Everyone knows that time travel is impossible, so this is all a load of bull!"

"Apex, I never mentioned anything about time travel. All time zones co-exist, they are present all the time, running parallel with one

another. Napoleon is still fighting, Hitler is still invading Poland and the third, fourth and fifth world wars are still happening. You see, if time does not stop then there is no future or past, because they are all happening as we speak. Do you understand?"

Apex hesitantly nodded, clearly unconvinced.

"Wonderful. You see, what is so unique about living in our own time zones is that it gives us eternal life; we are all immortal. To put it simply... we cannot die."

"What do you mean eternal life?" Apex sniggered condescendingly.

"Exactly what I have just said: you are born, you live your life in varying degrees, then you die and after you die you are reborn again. Amazing, isn't it?"

"So what, you mean reincarnation?" Rose asked.

"Kind of, except you are not reborn in to something or someone else, but simply as the same person. You relive your life over and over again; there is never a beginning and never an end. Your life is relived infinitely. In short, you are never completely dead."

"OK, so if this is true then wouldn't life become a little boring if we relived the same things over and over again?" Apex said defiantly.

"Let me ask you this, how many times do you remember living the same life?"

"I dost not," answered John.

"Me neither" said Rose.

"That's because we have the ability to forget. Although, there are times when you may remember doing something before... déjà vu I believe it's called. You may also see other people walking around, people that don't match your own time zone. They may appear as apparitions or entities, they can be almost transparent or sometimes

180

even in solid form. It all depends on the strength of the energy they are emitting."

"You mean ghosts?" asked Rose.

"Yes, I suppose you could call them that. They are simply people reliving their lives in their own time zone; they are not dead at all. Their time zone has simply converged with yours."

The three of them stared in complete bewilderment. This information blew apart everything they had ever believed in, everything that their world, their life stood for. How could they possible begin to believe what Calcus was saying?

John spoke first,

"How dost this man Apex knoweth me and how doth I knoweth Rose?"

"Well you see, sometimes your time zones can interact, in the ways that I have just mentioned to you. They are attracted to each other and when this happens you end up experiencing a fraction of each other's time zone. The strength as to how you make contact greatly depends on how much energy you as a person emit. The three of you however, are special. You all have something in common, something that sets you apart form the average human being. Each one of you has the ability to use your imagination to affect reality. You are able to control and manipulate matter and this sometimes happens when you don't even realise, for example when you dream. This gift you have requires great practice, but when you master it you will all be able to achieve amazing things. Apex, you can see others in your dreams just like Rose and John can, but you have lost the ability to use your gift in the real world. This is likely due to technology and your smoking habit, it has quite literally fogged your imagination."

"How do you know all this? I mean, how can we trust what you're saying?" Rose asked.

"I know this because we are far more advanced than the time zones you have come from. We have discovered more about human existence than anyone else has. Our knowledge and understanding is extensive, however I will admit there is still a lot we cannot explain. Rose, John, Apex, it is important that you trust everything that I tell you. In order for our lives to continue in the way that they have been, it is imperative that you have faith in me."

"OK, OK so you've told us all this, you've told us we're special, what do you want exactly? Why have you bought us here?" demanded Apex.

"We have taken you out of your time zones because we need your help."

"Help? How can *we* help?" asked Rose.

"You each have a gift that no one else possesses. Out of the countless people who exist in this universe, you are the only ones who have this special ability. Rose and John you have both used this skill already when you used your imaginations to manipulate and destroy matter."

"Matter, what is this matter thou speaketh of?" John asked looking puzzled.

"Objects, people, animals, everything you can touch and feel are matter."

John scratched his head; he was finding it extremely difficult trying to keep up with this strange version of English, none of it made any sense to him.

"So at which hour I hath killed those guards, the Sheriff, Philip and Christopher I hath used this gift?"

"That's right John."

Apex looked at John, giving him the once over and properly taking him in for the first time. His clothes were dirty and torn and he looked as if he hadn't ever washed. *What is with that nose? It's well messed up,* he thought. *And that accent... that's gotta be acting, he must be putting it on.*

"So, I am not a witch?" John asked.

"No John, you are not a witch. We really don't know how or why each of you has this special gift. It is possible that you were given this ability by a higher intelligent life force, one we have not yet encountered. What we do know is that you were given this power for a reason, we're just not entirely sure why yet. Nevertheless, what you have is unique and special and I suppose in some respect you could almost liken it to the extraordinary talents of Shakespeare, or Einstein. Both are exceptional in their abilities and there are very few people who can compete, certainly no one from their own time zones. They have a special gift just like you three, however yours is far more special."

John nodded his head, trying to make it look as if he knew what Calcus was saying; he knew who Shakespeare was at least.

"It's the same for you too Rose. You used your imaginative ability on Shaun, Trudy and your mother to manipulate and destroy them. Please don't spend too much time worrying about it though, because they will simply be reborn and lead their lives again."

Rose looked down. Even though she'd been left with very little choice, she couldn't help but feel immense guilt at having killed her own mother. She started to cry.

"Rose, mine family hast gone too. I knoweth what doth feels like," said John putting his arm around her.

"OK, so we've apparently got this gift, what do we do with it and why do you need our help exactly?" Apex asked, a sarcastic tone creeping into his voice. He didn't believe a single word of any of it, but if he had any hope of getting out of here he would have to play along. He was just an average guy, of barely average intelligence, struggling to scrape his way through his studies and life. He was no more special than the next guy and he certainly didn't have any special gift.

"The time zones are in serious danger. Every living organism is in peril. The Greys want your ability in order for them to have eternal life. They have been trying to increase their knowledge of it for centuries and it is only now that they fully understand how it works."

"Hold on, hold on! Greys? What do you mean Greys?" asked Apex, "What, like little grey aliens or something?"

"Yes, they have travelled light years to get here from another time zone in another dimension. We do not know where this time zone is, or even which dimension, but we do know that they have discovered ours and they desperately want what we have."

"Oh my God this just gets better and better. I've had enough of this shit, can you please just tell me how to get out of here? I really need to get a smoke on and all this weird shit is doing my head in!" said Apex pacing restlessly across the floor. "And not only that, but I'm in my fricking dressing gown and underpants for God's sake!"

Rose looked over at him with tearful eyes and sniggered; he really did look quite a sight.

"Apex, please could you be serious, this is important!" ordered the voice.

Apex stopped pacing and sat down in a sulk.

"The Greys have been visiting ancient time zones for many thousands of years in an attempt to understand how the human race exists. They have tried the friendly approach, offering gifts and their knowledge to various ancient civilizations, the Egyptians and Mayans for example, and relations were good up until a certain point. The Greys have always had an underlying plan to understand our immortality, but it was a paradox for the Greys, even for their superior advanced knowledge and technology; they could not work out how we never died. Cattle mutilation, human mutilation, abductions to extract sperm and female reproductive organs, all these actions to find the answer to our immortality, and now they've finally worked it out. It isn't our genes at all; it's something else entirely different."

"So what is it then?" asked Rose.

"The Universe as we know it is governed by a 'God'. He is the creator, the maker of everything. Everything you do and say is governed by him, and the Greys have discovered that this God is responsible for everything, including your ability to have eternal life. The Greys do not possess this ability; they die and are never reborn. As a consequence, they envy every single one of you. They want what you all have and will do whatever it takes to get it. All of you will have seen these grey aliens before at some point."

"Listen bro, I have never seen a grey alien in my life, you're talking bull. Everyone knows aliens don't exist!"

"Trust me Apex, you have seen them."

"Oh really, so when did I see these little grey men huh? Go on tell me, this should be interesting." He looked at John and Rose with a smirk.

"In your dreams, Apex. They look like liquid water, their screams are enough to frighten even the most hardened of people, they are relentless and they have no mercy. Sound familiar?"

The three of them stood there, stunned. Visions of the horrifying dreams filled their minds and each one of them shuddered at the memory.

"Yes, I've seen that," said Apex shakily.

"They are trying to frighten you because they see you as a threat. They are aware of your gift and this is a huge problem to them."

"What language doth they spake?" asked John.

"They speak in their own ancient language. However they use telepathy and telekinesis to communicate and manipulate. I imagine you would have heard them say something like, "Chatti cartom destruct ormati". It translates as, "All dreamers will die."

They nodded in unison, each of them remembering the horror of hearing the phrase screamed st them night after night.

"They can enter and control any living organism, just like a puppet. However, they find it difficult to control you and this is because of your gift. They cannot get in your heads as easily as others, because you have the ability to fight back. The Greys fear you all, but Apex is the exception, as they are aware of your inability to use this gift. Don't worry though, as I am certain that will soon change."

"So, what are they planning?" asked Rose.

"They are planning a huge invasion to search for the creator, to search for the God that governs everything. If they find this God, they can alter their own destiny, which means they can attempt to control the God who controls our universe too. They are in their millions and they are heading towards your time zones. Only you three can stop them. Obviously, it is entirely unrealistic to believe that the three of you could possibly destroy them all; there are far too many of them. Instead, you must fight them off and buy yourself some time in order to find the God and warn him, before they reach him."

"OK, so when are these "Greys" going to attack and where do we go about finding this God?" asked Apex starting to take it all more seriously.

"We believe they already have Apex, in your time zone."

"Oh shit, of course! So, all those fat zombies were being controlled by the Greys? It all makes sense now!" shouted Apex, "All of them were going on about someone called 'Ema'."

"That's right Apex, the Greys call this God, 'Ema'. Unfortunately, we know very little about this God. We know this God exists in one of your time zones, however we do not know which one. The good news is that the Greys also do not know which time zone he is in. They are looking in each one as we speak and be in no doubt, they will search until they find him. If the Greys find him before us, then the human race will be in serious danger. If the Greys succeed in finding the God, they will force him to give them eternal life in exchange for human mortality."

"So, do we travel to the future or the past or… I'm confused, where would we even start to look? Are you saying that the God could be in Apex's time zone?" asked Rose.

"Fortunately, it appears not, as I am certain they would have found him by now. Our sources suggest they will be attacking John's time zone next and that is where you need to go now. It may still be some time before they do, but it is important that you two take the time to teach Apex how to use his ability. Mastering this skill will see you become a powerful force against the Greys, but you need to be able to control it."

"I knoweth I hast used this gift sir, but I knoweth not how I didst so," said John.

"You will know how to use it when you need to. Your fear and anxiety is what drives this energy. The more you practice your gift, the more powerful you will all become. And the more powerful you become, the less you will require your primitive emotions to control it."

John nodded, but he remained unconfident that he would be able to do it again and more to the point whether he wanted to. The thought of going through some of the traumatic things he had already been through scared him senseless.

"Do you have any more questions?"

"Aye, what about mine family?" John asked, "Art they alive?"

"Fear not John, your family are safe, they have simply been reborn. And when we defeat the Greys you will all go back to your families."

"Man, I don't want to go back!" exclaimed Apex, "I hate it so much!"

"Apex I'm sorry, unfortunately there's nothing I can do to change that. However, if you find the creator, then he may be able to help you. If the Greys find him though, we are all destined for extinction. Do you understand?"

They nodded.

"There is just one more thing I need to tell you before you go, so please listen very carefully. You must always stick together. Never allow yourselves to be separated, it would be disastrous."

John and Rose nodded again, but Apex stood there with his arms crossed defiantly.

"Man, I ain't going anywhere. There's no way you're getting me to go to John's shitty time zone. This sucks big time!"

"Apex, please listen to me. Without you we could be in serious danger, we need your help."

"Go on then tell me this, why can't you do it? You're from the future, you use telepathy, why can't you sort the fricking Grey's out?"

"Apex, I do not have what you have. We cannot go near the Greys. As soon as they find the creator they will get inside our minds. We cannot manipulate or destroy matter in the way that you can; we are depending on all of you Apex. I can't guarantee that you will have a better life when you return, but if you choose not to help I can guarantee things will get much worse. You must find Ema and you must leave now before it is too late.

Apex relaxed, his arms dropping to his sides, resigning himself to his fate. He sighed and then reluctantly agreed,

"OK, I'll do anything if it means I don't have to go back to my own shitty time zone."

"Excellent. Now please walk through the wall you see in front of you, this will transport you to John's time zone. Oh, and by the way Apex, try and keep the bad language down to a minimum, they're not so accepting in the sixteenth century. And you may want to find some clothes while you're there too. Good luck."

Apex scowled and started walking towards the gateway that had opened in front of them.

As the three of them stood together, the liquid wall opened revealing a giant black hole. As the nerves started to kick in, they instinctively stepped backwards, but it was impossible to escape. A powerful vacuum sucked them towards the hole and suddenly the blackness became a blinding light, which pulled them into the black abyss. But it wasn't frightening anymore; it was beautiful. Time zones whizzed past them at lightening speed, millions and millions of them smoothly gliding past like tiny bubbles infinitely expanding out in all directions. It was unlike anything any of them had ever seen before and this was only the beginning…

Chapter 24

August 10th, 1599. Somewhere in England

The three bodies floated gently down, emerging from the darkness of space into an intense blinding light. The atmosphere was overpoweringly humid and as they neared the ground, they saw a vast patchwork of fields sprawling out beneath them. Dotted with tiny doll like farmhouses, it really was a wondrous and breathtaking sight. But as they drew closer a terrible putrid stench hit them; the putrid stink of blood, disease and death. Something must have happened... something bad.

"Where the fuck are we? And what the hell's that gross smell?" Apex gagged, holding his hand over his nose.

"I have no idea where we are, but I know where that smell's coming from," said Rose, turning and pointing behind them.

The boys looked to where Rose was pointing and saw a field of bloodied grass filled with the rotting carcasses of hundreds of dead cows. The three of them staggered back in disgust, frantically swatting at a swarm of flies that had started to hover around them.

"Eurgh man! Let's get the fuck out of here!" said Apex. He motioned towards a clearing and started to head off.

Ignoring him, Rose turned to John and said,

"John, this is your time zone, do you know where we are?"

"Nay, I am most sorry. I knoweth not where we art?" he replied.

Realising the others hadn't followed Apex stomped angrily back over to them.

"Man, how did I end up here? This fucking sucks!" he raged, throwing his fist out in a fit of anger. "We don't know where we are, I'm in the sixteenth century *and* I'm wearing a dressing gown and underpants!"

Rose smiled, trying hard not to laugh. John looked blankly at him. He struggled to understand what this strangely dressed, dark skinned man was saying. He decided to keep quiet. He was glad to be here with Rose though, she felt familiar, as though he'd known her a long time. In fact, she reminded him of someone he knew. *Rose could beest like mine big sister, the lady can behold after me and I can behold after that lady,* he thought. The thought gave him comfort and he smiled happily to himself.

"Seriously, I must be tripping! This must be some bad LSD we've been given or something," Apex shouted, prodding Rose with his finger to check if she was real.

"Hey, what are you doing?" Rose yelped.

He poked her again.

"Ouch, stop it!" she cried.

"Come on, this can't be real. If this is a dream, then I should be able to do whatever I want!"

He prodded Rose again, harder this time.

"Ouch! Apex I mean it, that really hurt!"

"And if you're not real and this is a dream, then my finger should be able to go straight through your arm."

"Apex enough already, seriously stop it!"

Unsurprisingly, his finger failed to go through her arm and he pulled away, muttering guiltily,

"Sorry, I didn't mean to hurt you, I'm just finding it all a bit strange... you know, what with everything that's going on. I'm just trying to make sense of it all."

"'Tis strange for us too!" said John, giving Apex a threatening glare, "thou hurteth not that lady again!"

Apex bowed his head apologetically and put his fist out to John,

"You're an odd kid, but you got some balls talking to me like that. Hey, give me some cookie."

"I understandeth not?" John said in confusion.

"Here look, put your fist out like mine and touch them together."

The two of them touched fists. John remained puzzled.

"And what dost this mean? What is 'cookie'?"

"Shit, I forgot you're like seven hundred years older than me!"

"Actually, Calcus said that we live beside each other, so technically John is the same age as us," Rose said rubbing her bruised arm.

"I guess you're right, man this shit's well deep. John, a cookie is a form of respect, like shaking someone's hand, yeah?"

John nodded, looking uncertainly at Apex.

"Come on guys, we need to stop chatting and work out where we are, let's go," Rose interrupted.

They headed towards a large thatched farmhouse. Its walls were painted a bright white with beautiful crisscrossing dark wooden beams and there was a large stable attached to the side, but there were no horses to be seen. Apex ran over to one of the windows and peered inside, looking out for any signs of life.

"I can't see anything," he called back, "just furniture and a load of old ornaments. It looks empty to me, I don't reckon anyone's here."

A large oak door dominated the front of the building. Rose knocked, but there was no response.

"There's no one in, maybe we should find somewhere else, find some people we can ask about Ema," said Rose.

Apex shrugged, he wasn't sure what to think any more. Everything felt so surreal. He was irritated by the fact he had no decent clothes to change into and although he'd only been here a few minutes he was already missing the luxuries that were considered the norm in his own time zone.

"Just open the fucking door, will you."

"Apex, could you please stop swearing! And no, we can't just walk in. It's not right, no matter what time zone you're from."

"Rose is right, we can walketh not into a stranger's house, we could be hung for such an act."

"Man, I ain't gonna let you two talk to me like that! Who do you think you are? I'm like the oldest one here, so it's me who should be making the decisions. I'm fed up with…"

Apex stopped mid sentence, sensing a presence nearby. He glanced at the others, who had also fallen silent, and beckoned for them to come closer to him. A deep, growling sound was coming from behind them and as they turned to look they knew they were in trouble. In front of them was a snarling black dog baring its sharp fangs, drool dripping from either side of its mouth.

"Oh shit, I fucking hate dogs, you gotta do something guys," Apex whispered anxiously.

"Don't move, just stay still, or it'll go for us," Rose whispered back shakily.

"Try the door, is it unlocked?" said Apex.

John slowly moved his hand towards the handle. It turned a little, but not enough for the door to open.

"I cannot do't, 'tis too stiff."

The evil hound edged closer, growling deeply, before violently lurching at them.

"Shit! Fucking do something!" Apex shouted in panic.

John looked around for something to use to defend them against the dog. He noticed a long wooden hoe leaning against the wall. Grabbing it with both hands he wildly swung it in front of the dog, forcing it to retreat. Just as it looked as though the beast was giving up, suddenly more dogs began to appear from out of the shadows. There were six, seven, maybe eight, similar black, very vicious looking dogs. Without hesitating, Apex rattled the handle of the door. It was stiff, but his fear had given him a renewed strength and he managed to force it open.

"Quick, get the fuck inside!" he shouted, jumping over the threshold. Rose and John swiftly followed him in and he slammed the door shut behind them, breathing heavily as he leaned his weight against the door. "That was fucking scary. Where the fuck did they all come from?"

"We hast nay crops and the animals art diseased, 'tis not unusual to receiveth wild dogs around these parts, they art starving, just like everyfolk here," explained John.

"Shit, that's bad man. But wait, I thought you guys were magic or something, that's what that invisible guy said back there. Why the fuck didn't you use your magic? Or is it all bullshit, you can't really do anything, can you? Come on admit it, you're a couple of frauds."

"Apex, we're still learning, just like you. I don't know why it didn't work, maybe it's just that we need more practice," replied Rose.

"Yeah whatever, seems a bit convenient if you ask me," Apex huffed, pushing past them into the kitchen.

Rose looked at John, shaking her head. She'd not long met the boy and already she detested him. *Stupid idiot*, she thought. Taking John's hand, she cautiously followed Apex through the doorway of what appeared to be a workshop. There were saws and chains and large piles of sawdust covering the floor.

"Man, how the fuck do people live like this?" Apex sneered.

Continuing on, they came to a thin wooden staircase and treading carefully, so as not to make too much noise, they climbed the creaky steps until they came to the top floor. There were a few different sized rooms up there, but only one displayed any visible signs of life; a tidily made bed, a wooden table and a neat pile of meticulously arranged clothing. All the other rooms were completely empty. Satisfied that there was no one in, the three of them headed back down to the kitchen and sat at the large oak table.

"Looks like we have the place to ourselves," said Apex, grinning. "Look! Look at all those bottles over here."

He picked one up, blowing the dust off it and then pulled the cork out and took a long swig.

"Man, this shit ain't bad!" he said, before taking another gulp from the bottle.

"Apex, it's not a party, we're not here to get drunk!" Rose said with a frown.

Up until now John had kept quiet, but as he watched Apex he couldn't help but get angry. He couldn't understand how a person could so easily take someone else's possessions, "Thou is stealing Apex, 'tis not right for a man to stealeth from another," he muttered.

Apex ignored him and carried on drinking from the dusty bottle before wiping his mouth and saying, "OK, so if we're really what Calcus says we are, then you have to show me how to do it, because if the best you can do is swing a stick at a bunch of rabid dogs, then you're gonna need me to step it up a gear."

"Look Apex, I keep telling you, we don't know how it works!" Rose said glaring at him. "But I agree we need to do better, so let's have a go and see if we can do it." She looked around for something to experiment on. "There, let's try it on those bottles. Each of us has to try and pick the bottles up using only our imagination, you OK with that?"

John nodded.

"Oh man, this is going to be awesome! If you can seriously move those bottles I'll…" Apex thought for a moment, "I'll cover my face with that cow shit we saw outside."

Rose looked at him in disgust and said, "Gross, you'd do that?"

Apex nodded. He was confident they wouldn't be able to do it and he'd take great pleasure in mocking them when their stupid game didn't work.

"Come on John, you go first," said Rose encouragingly.

John closed his eyes and focused on the bottles. He pictured his surroundings: the stone wall, the silver ornaments placed neatly on the small table, that distinctive wooden musty smell. He tried to build up the anger and anxiety that he constantly battled with. And then finally, he placed the image of the bottles into his mind, slowly moving them out of their rack.

Rose and Apex watched intently for any signs of movement, but there was nothing.

John sighed, "I cannot do't."

"Try again," said Rose gently, "you can do it, I know you can."

Apex gave a smug smile, "You're wasting your fucking time and mine for that matter. It's a fucking joke."

John glared at Apex in annoyance, then concentrating with all his might he tried again. The sheer determination was clearly marked across his face, but it was no use, it still wasn't working. He exhaled deeply, disappointed in himself, but more so because he felt as though he had disappointed Rose.

"See, I fucking told you!" shouted Apex angrily. "You ain't no magic wizards, you can't do shit!"

John scowled at Apex, he felt so angry. *Shaking uncontrollably, his breathing rapidly increased and he imagined Apex levitating, his body being pulled upwards by an unseen force. The large oak door suddenly opened and slammed itself against the wall and Apex's body was forcefully pinned against it. His arms were pulled behind his back and his legs restrained together. John pictured Apex struggling to get free, terrified by what was happening to him. He imagined the bottles lifting out of their racks, floating side by side, as he lined them up ready to aim them at Apex's head.*

"John!" Rose cried, "don't do it! We need him!"

The bottles accelerated towards Apex and the oak door slammed shut causing ornaments to fly across the room and smash against the walls.

There was only one thing Rose could do to try and stop him.

She imagined the bottles stopping before they hit their target. They froze in midair, just hovering there, suspended in space, mere millimetres from Apex's frightened face.

John felt his body go limp. Overcome by exhaustion, he fell to the ground completely unaware of what he'd done. Both Apex and the bottles fell in perfect synchronisation with John. The glass shattered as it made contact with the hard floor and the liquid sprayed over Apex. The room fell silent. Apex got up and brushed the glass from his gown, clearly shaken by what had just happened to him.

"What the hell did you just do?" he shouted, backing away from the pair of them and cowering fearfully in the corner of the room.

"What didst I do?" asked John weakly.

"You nearly killed Apex, that's what!" cried Rose.

"Don't come near me, stay the fuck away, you're both freaks!" Apex.

John looked over with concern,

"My most humble apology Apex, I didst not mean to, t just happened."

"We really need to learn how to use this properly," Rose said. "We need to learn how to control it, so that we use it to our advantage, rather than to attack one another."

John nodded in agreement and cautiously edged closer to Apex, holding his fist out.

"Giveth me some cookie," he said smiling.

"Bro, you scared the shit out of me!" Apex said, shakily standing up and touching his fist against John's. "But bro, seriously I have to admit, that was fucking awesome! You gotta teach me how to do that!"

"Boys, this is serious," said Rose. "We have to learn how to do this properly and only use it if or when we really have to. We can't go around using it to play tricks on people. It's dangerous. We need to take it seriously. Please Apex, promise me you won't use this unless you really need to."

"OK, sure, I promise. As soon as I've learnt it, then I promise I will only ever use it if I have too," he grinned excitedly.

"So, come on then, tell me how you did it?"

"Wait did you hear that?" whispered Rose.

"What?" replied John.

"Horses, I can hear horses!"

Apex walked over to the window and looked out.

"Shit someone's coming! We have to hide somewhere, quick, upstairs!"

The three of them ran upstairs and darted into the first room they came too. Unfortunately, it was one of the empty ones. There was nowhere to hide.

Chapter 25

"Who the hell hath done this?" screamed an angry voice. "Eve cometh hither and see this"

"I'm coming, I'm coming," Eve called out, hastily entering the house to see what all the fuss was about. "Oh mine, what hath happened? Hath someone been in our house, hast they taken anything George? Oh, how could this befall? We hath lost all our cattle and now this. Oh George, what art we to doth?" she sobbed breathlessly. "Art they still hither George? What if the thieves art hiding in the house? Do something George, do something!"

George looked at her, his worried expression revealing the deep wrinkled crevasses of a man who had worked hard all his life.

"Passeth mine sword," he ordered.

She passed him the weapon and as he nervously grasped it between his frail aging hands he told his wife, "If those gents art still hither I am going to maketh sure those gents payeth for this."

Eve watched as George walked into the next room. He pointed the sword straight out in front of his scrawny torso and carefully peered around the corner.

"Oh, doth beest careful," whispered Eve putting her hands up to her face.

George slowly made his way up the stairs, the floorboards creaking with every step, forcing him to stop and listen out for any movement from the rooms above. When he reached the top of the staircase, he guided his shaky hand towards the door handle of the first room. Perspiration clung to the hairs on his face and as he slowly turned the heavy rusting handle he felt his heartbeat quicken. The door creaked as it slowly open and George took a startled jump backwards when he saw the three strangers staring back at him.

"What! Who art thee? Wherefore art thee in mine house? Thieves!"

He haphazardly waved the sword in the air, looking at them in confusion, trying to make sense of what he was seeing.

John spoke first. "Pray thee kind sir, we wast lost, we hath stolen nothing. Please putteth down thy sword sir. We wilt tidy the mess and we wilt leaveth. Thou needeth not to hurt us kind sir. "

Using the blade of the sword, George motioned for them to move towards the door.

"Moveth," he said, "and bethinkst thee not to runneth, I hast some very hungry dogs out yonder."

They sidestepped past him and walked down the stairs, their heads bowed in shame and their arms raised above their heads in submission. George followed closely behind, digging the sharp point of the sword into Apex's back.

"Shit, that hurts! Lay off it man!"

Startled by the strange language, George pulled the sword back and when they were all back in the kitchen he shouted,

"Sitteth thee down there. Eve, wend to the town council and asketh for the Sheriff. That gent canst deal with these trespassing thieves."

Eve absentmindedly nodded at her husband, fearfully gazing at the three strangers in her home.

"Wend Eve, leaveth now!"

She jumped and hastily made her way outside to the idle carriage.

"What art thee doing in mine house?" George growled.

They looked at one another with blank expressions. There was no logical explanation as to why they were there and they definitely couldn't tell him the truth.

"Sir we art travellers. We hast been walking for miles," John stammered.

"Wherefore wast thee in mine house?"

"We didst knock sir. We bethought no one lived hither sir. We art sorry and if thee alloweth us to wend, thee will not see us again."

Ignoring John's pleas, George continued his tirade,

"Wherefore art thee hither servant? Thee knoweth the blacks art not welcome. We barely hast enough to consume for our own in this drought, let alone thee black imports. Thee should beest sent back. Thee art no servant of our God, thee art not his follower, wend back to thine own country and practice thy religion there," he said, glaring at Apex.

"Hey! What the fuck you talking about man? I ain't religious and shit man. And what do you mean send me back? Mother fuc…"

"What mine cousin hither means is that we hast been sent to travel to… um… to Chelmsford in Essex sir. We art…um… messengers for the Queen's guards… and we must leaveth immediately!" John interrupted, in the hope of preventing Apex from getting them in even bigger trouble.

George however was not convinced.

"Why doth thee talketh like that?" he asked, looking at Apex with suspicion. "What sort of English doth thee speaketh? I hast never heard this strange tongue?"

Before waiting for an answer, he looked over to Rose and said,

"And wherefore art thee not speaking wench? Who art thee and wherefore art thee with this black servant?"

Rose gulped. She didn't know what to say to this terrifying old man with his warty face and his off-white beard that was stained from years of pipe smoking.

"Art thee mute wench? Speak up!"

"OK, OK," she said nervously, "We've been sent here from different time zones on a quest to find someone, a God..." She sighed. It was going to be impossible to explain to someone from a time zone four hundred years before hers and even more so to someone whose beliefs were so deeply rooted in religion.

"What art thee talking about wench?" George scoffed, closely inspecting his prisoners as he paced around the table. "Is this some kind of witchcraft? Or doth thee worketh for the Spanish? Art thee spies?"

"No sir, we art not spies," said John coming to Roses's rescue, "we art messengers. We art hither to behold for someone by the name of Ema. Doth thee knoweth that gent?"

"What kind of name is that for a sir? No! I hast never heard of that name."

"Look man I'm starting to get really pissed off," Apex moaned. "Let me make this simple for you. I'm from Southfield Detroit in a country called America. I'm from the year 2020 and I'm here in your shitty little time zone, wearing my fucking underpants and dressing gown. Now if you'd kindly let us leave, we'll be on our way!" He started to make his way over to the door, when George pointed the sword threateningly at him.

"How dare thee!" he shouted, enraged by the manner in which Apex had spoken to him. "How dare a black servant talk to me like that? Our God wilt banish thee for this, thee wilt beest sent to the realms of hell."

"Look man, I've had to deal with way bigger shit than from a crippled old man and his tiny little sword."

He made a grab for the sword and as both men struggled to take hold of it, the sharp blade cut into Apex's fingers.

"Let go, you stupid old man, let go of the fucking sword!"

"I will not servant!"

John and Rose looked on in horror as the two men fought wildly, turning in circles, tugging and pulling at the sharp weapon. Seizing his chance, Apex pulled his upper body back and then swung it violently forward, head butting the old man and breaking his nose upon impact. George collapsed to the floor, his blood splattering everywhere and he released his grip on the sword to support his injury.

"Let's get the fuck out of here!" Apex shouted, kicking the sword into the far corner of the room and running towards the door. He paused and then turned back to pick up an unbroken bottle of liquor.

"Right come on, lets go!" he shouted.

Rose and John followed Apex, who was running towards a stony road, but in their haste they had completely forgotten about the dogs.

"For fucks sake man!" shouted Apex.

As the dogs got closer, John closed his eyes.

He imagined the dogs lifting off of the ground, their legs wriggling helplessly. But something wasn't right.

He opened his eyes to see the dogs still there, growling at them with salivating jaws.

"Apex, maketh me angry, maketh me wanteth to hurt thee," he said.

"You gotta be shitting me. Make you angry? Last time I did that you nearly killed me."

"I know, but these beasts do not maketh me feel like that. If thou doest not maketh me angry, they will killeth us!" exclaimed John.

"OK, well…um… your nose looks like you've been in a food blender. It's ugly, you're ugly…you ugly nosed little boy."

"Apex, what art thee talking about? I said maketh me angry."

"Well, I don't fucking know!" Apex shouted back angrily.

"They're getting closer!" shouted Rose, huddling closer to Apex and John, "Do something!"

"This is all your fault John, in fact you're the reason your family died and now it's gonna be the same with us. You could have saved them if you weren't such a selfish little shit."

"How dare thee!" John screamed, "I could not helpeth those folk. I hath tried, you knoweth that. How can thee sayeth that?"

John felt his anxiety levels rising. He felt utterly distraught by what Apex had said. Closing his eyes, he pictured his family and saw their horrified faces as each one faced death. These visions had haunted him ever since that fateful day and the fact he'd never had a chance to say goodbye to Jane made his anger reach absolute boiling point. He moved his thoughts to Apex and pictured him levitating off the ground, restrained and frozen by that same unseen force as before. Suddenly something stopped him.

It was Rose.

She was talking to him in his mind, "John, you must channel your thoughts towards the dogs, use that energy on them, not Apex."

Realising what was happening, John dropped Apex and turned his focus on to the angry dogs instead. He visualised them being dragged away from Apex, who was currently lying helplessly on the ground trying to fend of the pack of angry hounds. He summoned the strength to grab their hind legs with his mind and forcing them away from Apex he threw them as far as he could possibly imagine.

Out of mind, out of sight.

Gasping for breath, John collapsed back onto the soft grass.

"You did it!" Rose shouted excitedly, "You threw them over those trees. I've never seen anything like it John, you sent them miles away!"

"Yeah well done bro, that was fucking close! Next time focus on the real enemy instead of me though, yeah?"

"It doesn't matter now, what matters is that we're safe. Come on, let's get out of here," Rose said, helping first John and then Apex up from the ground.

Not sure of where they were going, they walked aimlessly across the fields, searching for anything that would give them a clue as to where they were. It was an unbearably hot day and the glaring sun blasted its relentless heat down upon them. They were dirty, tired and thirsty and it wasn't long before they needed to stop for a rest.

"Man, that was some crazy shit! I don't ever want to see another fucking dog again!" Apex exclaimed, leaning against a rickety fence post. "One of those fuckers bit me too, did you see? I think I handled that old dude pretty well though, did you see his nose explode? Man, he got knocked the fuck out!" he said, chuckling at the memory.

"He was an old man Apex, hardly something to be proud of," retorted Rose. "And seriously, could you please cut down on the swearing?"

"OK, OK, I'll do my best," he replied, opening the bottle he'd stolen from earlier and swigging heartily. "Ah, that's some good stuff!"

"Oh yes, and aren't you forgetting something Apex?"

"What?" he asked, holding the bottle to his lips.

Rose grinned and pointed in the direction of the field.

"What? Why you pointing at the field?"

"Don't you remember?" she sniggered.

Apex closed his eyes and sighed.

"OK you were right, I was wrong. I guess a bet's a bet." he said, passing Rose the bottle of liquor.

Reluctantly, he walked over to a pile of cow dung, took a deep breath and dipped his hand in it to break the crusty surface. A thick, brown liquid oozed out and he looked in disgust at the mess covering his hand. The smell was vile and as he edged his hand closer to his face, both Rose and John started gagging at the thought of what he was about to do.

"Are you seriously going to do it?" asked Rose.

Apex rubbed his cheeks and forehead with the festering brown muck, until he could take the stench no longer and started to retch.

"I didn't think you'd do it!" giggled Rose.

"Oh mine, wherefore would thee doth that? And t doth smell awful!" said John, watching as Apex stood up and snatched the bottle back from Rose.

"You think *I* stink, John? Man, that's a joke, you should try smelling yourself!"

Confused, John sniffed at his clothes, before shrugging his shoulders. Rose intervened before things got too heated between the pair.

"You should do something about your hand Apex. That wound looks deep and the last thing we need is for it to get infected. As much as I respect you for following through on a bet and I really do appreciate your help back there, touching that dung wasn't the smartest thing you've ever done. We need to get it cleaned up."

John ripped off a piece of his already torn shirt and passed it to Apex.

"Here, wrap this around thy hand, t'will cease the bleeding."

"Man, that's kind of you and all, but it's a bit dirty."

"Apex you've just been touching cow poo, I'm fairly certain there are more germs in that than there is on John's shirt."

"Don't worry about it, I'll just use my gown. And anyway, I can't get infections. In my time zone, we're given injections when we're born that gives us immunity to pretty much anything."

With Apex's wound wrapped, the three of them continued on their way. The sun was fading and the temperature dropping and they still had yet to see a single person. Sitting on a patch of soft grass, they were grateful for the rest, but knew they still needed to come up with a plan.

"OK then you two, what are we going to do? Finding this Ema is like looking for a needle in a haystack, we can't just keep on aimlessly walking in the hope we'll find him."

"I knoweth not Rose," replied John. He thought for a moment, watching as Apex glugged down the last of the stolen wine. "Ho, what if... I mean... thee knoweth what Calcus hath said about being reborn?"

"Yes?"

"Mine mother, father and mine sister, those gents wilt all beest alive again. Oh mine! Can we wend there? Can we?"

"John, but what if… what if they aren't there?"

"Your meaning doth escape me Rose, but we wilt at least hast somewhere to wend."

"OK true, but first we need to know where we are. John you're from this time zone, so it makes sense for you to do the talking. Apex you just keep your mouth shut and pretend you're a servant, it's way easier than trying to explain about you being from a future time zone."

"Man, I ain't no fuc…" Apex started to retaliate, but paused when he noticed Rose's disapproving look. "I ain't no frickin servant," he muttered sheepishly.

"John, you go over to that house and ask them where we are."

John walked nervously over to the house and knocked at the rickety wooden door. After a few seconds, the door opened revealing an elderly friendly looking lady. She smiled at John. Having spotted this, Rose turned to Apex and said with relief,

"It's an old lady Apex, she seems happy enough. Are you watching? Apex?"

She turned around to see what he was doing and tutted to herself when she saw him drinking the dregs of the bottle. He threw the now empty bottle into the hedge and then sat down against a tree and burped loudly.

"He's coming back!"

John walked over to them, the smile on his face revealing there was good news at last.

"So go on then, where are we John?"

"We art quite far from mine house."

"How far exactly?" asked Apex.

"Well, we art in Aylesbury."

"OK, so where's that?" asked Apex getting frustrated.

"'Tis about thirty hours walketh yonder."

"OK, that's not so bad, plus it's the only plan we have at the moment. We can't just sit here and wait for the Greys to come," Rose said.

"If those fricking Greys come anywhere near me I'll be ready," slurred Apex.

"You're drunk! You're drunk, you idiot!" she snorted derisively at him.

"I ain't drunk," he replied, stumbling and putting his hands out against the tree to stop himself from falling.

Rose rolled her eyes and turned to speak to John.

"Which direction do we need to head in John?"

"East methinks."

"Which way is East?" Apex asked, spinning around and pointing his finger like he was some kind of human compass.

"Stop it Apex, this is serious!"

Rose thought for a moment.

"The sun rises in the east and sets in the west and the sun is nearly setting over there, so that must be east. We need to walk this way. And Apex, you need to sober yourself up somehow, we need you to be alert and on guard."

"Yeah, whatever," he burped and staggered after them.

Chapter 26

They had been walking for several hours now and the light was fading fast. They were all beginning to feel tired and the temperature had dropped.

"We should stop," said Rose. "Do either of you boys know how to make fire? It's getting a little chilly."

"I do," said Apex pulling out a lighter from his dressing gown pocket. "Man, it's a good job I smoke in my gown!"

"At least you're good for something!" said Rose sarcastically.

"What is that?" asked John excitedly pointing at the lighter in Apex's hand.

"Oh man, you got so much to learn. It's a lighter. What you do is push down on this button here and the flame appears, like this." Apex demonstrated how the lighter worked. He looked as proud as if he had invented it himself.

"It beest magic!" John whispered in awe.

"You'd think that being from a time zone so far in the future you'd have had the sense to stop smoking. And seriously, you're telling me lighters haven't changed in nearly two hundred years?" Rose scoffed.

"Smoking is perfectly fine, in fact it's encouraged. The weed is good for your lungs and a lighter's a lighter, it doesn't need to evolve!" he said with a smug grin.

"What is it like in thy time zone, Apex?" asked John, who was clearly entranced by all these new things.

"Jeez, where do I start? It's bad, really bad. Most of the population are vegetarian; all meat and fast food is illegal, except for in America. That's the unhealthiest country in the world and seriously everyone's fat, well except for me of course, and Chaz and Olive, we're the minority."

"I knew there was a problem, there is in my own time zone, but I never thought it would get so out of hand," said Rose in surprise.

"Fast food? Is that a cow that runneth fast? John naively asked.

"No man," Apex laughed, "fast food is food that's made real quick, but it's really bad for you and it's packed full of chemicals and shit. It makes you fat and causes all kinds of health problems. Of course in my country they want you to be fat, it's how they make their money. Anyway, how about your time zone Rose, what's it like there?"

"Pollution's a big issue and there are wars happening and loads of corruption. I don't really have much of a life in my time zone, it's actually quite depressing. The only good thing about my time zone is my mum, and of course my dad… well, when he was alive."

She went quiet and Apex shifted uncomfortably.

"Come on let's get this fire going," Rose said, breaking the silence and picking up some dry twigs.

Rose and Apex gathered sticks and dry leaves, passing them onto John who stacked them up. It wasn't long before they were all sat huddled together around a blazing fire, each one deep in their own thoughts.

"Hey, Rose."

"Yes Apex?"

"That Calcus, he said you killed your mom… what happened?"

She looked at him sadly.

"Oh… well… I killed Shaun, he's my mum's boyfriend, because he beat her up. I was so angry about it that when I went to bed I thought about him dying and the next thing I know, he actually died. He died exactly as I had imagined it. And then the next day, I killed my mum's boss. I'd had these really scary dreams…" she hesitated, frightened by the memory, "I dreamt of those liquid entities, the Greys, that Calcus was telling us about, and then it was like I went somewhere in my mind, like they'd taken me somewhere. I was gone for hours, but I don't know where I went, and I know I wasn't sleeping during that time. All I know is that I woke up at one thirty, I remember because it was lunchtime, and I just felt scared, so scared."

"But how did that end up in you killing your mom?"

"She found out my dad had been having an affair with her best friend. She went psycho when she found out. She killed Jackie and then she turned on me. I didn't want to kill her, I was defending myself, I had no choice."

Rose broke off, her eyes filled with tears.

"So if you killed your mom, how did you end up dying?"

"I killed myself."

"Shit man that's fucked up! I don't understand why people kill themselves, well not now anyway. You'll only go and get reborn and live the same shitty life again anyway, so what's the point!" Apex chuckled to himself, pleased with his apparent understanding of this new meaning of life that had been thrust upon them.

Rose stayed silent.

"So John, I couldn't help but notice your nose bro, what happened to it, I mean it's all a bit crooked isn't it?" Apex asked.

"I wast kicked by a horse at which hour I wast younger. I don't very much recall t, but mine mother said I nearly hath kicked the bucket. t doesn't bother me much, but I findeth t hard to breathe through t."

"That's rough man. I didn't know being kicked by a horse made you kick a bucket!"

"He means he nearly died Apex," said Rose with an exasperated sigh, "seriously do you not know anything?"

Apex looked confused, he couldn't get to grips with this stupid language. He shrugged his shoulders and carried on questioning John regardless.

"So go on then, why are you here, what's your story?

"The guard's hath killed mine family so I hath killed those folk with mine mind. I wanted those folk to suffer, so I ripped those folk apart. But then there wast Jane, mine sister and I hadst no one left in mine life, I just wanted to die, I hadst nothing left to liveth for." He began to sob loudly, "I misseth them... I misseth them so much."

"Shit man, I'm sorry," said Apex awkwardly patting him on the back.

Rose instantly took over, her empathy more in tune with John's and she batted Apex's hands away saying,

"Back off Apex, you've done enough damage already."

"Hey you know what, I lost my mom too! She got possessed by one of those fucking Greys. She had her face cut off and then tried to kill me for fucks sake, so don't you go thinking you're the only ones suffering here. I saw my gran get cut up, I lost my girl and my best bro, my best bro who fucking killed me. It was the most fucked up thing I have ever seen."

He stood up and turned and walked away, muttering to himself quietly.

"Where are you going?" Rose called out.

"I'm going for a shit if you must know, I've been holding it in for ages. Then I'm going to find something to clean this shit off my face, there's got to be water around here somewhere."

Rose pulled a face in disgust.

"Alright, but don't go too far, we don't want you getting lost!"

Apex waved his hand dismissively and walked off in to the darkness of the woods.

"Listen John, it's OK, we need to hold onto the fact that our families are still alive, they never really died. It's pretty comforting, don't you think?"

John nodded, his tears now subsiding. He sniffed and wiped his nose with the back of his tunic sleeve.

"Thee art kind Rose. What would I doeth without thee? Thee remind me of Jane, mine sister."

She smiled softly at him. She was flattered by John's heartfelt comments and even though they hadn't known each other long, she felt a sort of connection, almost like they'd been friends all their lives. They lay there staring up at the clear black sky, gazing in wonder at the infinite landscape of stars and faraway galaxies.

Apex meanwhile, was deep in thought.

Man how did I end up here? I can't believe I'm actually taking a shit in the fucking woods in the sixteenth fucking century. Apex chuckled to himself thinking about how ridiculous it sounded. *Man, when I use this power it's going to be awesome. I might even be able to fly!* Suddenly he heard a rustle coming from the bushes behind him. Too frightened to move in case he lost his balance and fell in his own mess, he remained crouched, underpants around his ankles, frozen to the spot waiting for something to happen.

And then... it did.

He felt a sharp pain on the back of his head and a wave of nausea and dizziness came over him. As he put a hand up to check if it was bleeding he felt another blow.

Then darkness...

Chapter 27

The young man was unconscious and there was blood coming from his head. *'Apex, is that you? Apex, talketh to me, where art thou? What hath happened to thee? Apex? Apex! They art taking that gent, helpeth me, they art taking that gent!"*

"John, wake up, it's OK, you're dreaming. Wake up!" shouted Rose, wildly shaking him from his slumber.

His eyes opened and he sat up abruptly, grabbing Rose by the wrists.

"Rose, they hath got Apex!"

"Who has?"

"I knoweth not, I could not see. In mine dream I saw a uniform, methinks it could be guards."

"Oh God no, what shall we do? How can we help him John, where is he?"

"Wait, I will try to see," John gasped and he closed his eyes, picturing Apex in his minds eye.

He visualised the Apex's dark features, his white, stained robe, and that annoying grin. He focused as hard as he could, putting all of his energy into that one vision. And then it came to him. An image that was weak, but clear enough for him to see that it was Apex and that he was in danger.

"Hold onto mine hand Rose. Bethink of Apex, think of that gent as hardeth as thou can," he instructed.

She held his hand and together they imagined Apex in as much detail as they could. It was working. The image started taking shape, gradually becoming clearer, until they could see Apex perfectly.

"I can see him John, I can see him!" shouted Rose excitedly.

John imagined the earth moving, the trees, roads, horses, houses, people, everything flying past them both at great speed. They could see the carriage Apex was being held in and they followed him until it stopped. A group of men pushed Apex forcefully out of the carriage and bundled him in through the doors of a building they didn't recognise.

John spoke to Rose in his mind,

"Rose we hast to wend there, imagine t now!"

Gripping each other's hands tightly, their mental strength intensified as they poured all of their energy into that one image. They could smell the earth, hear the sound of horses snorting and the stamping of their hooves against the dry ground, and the image slowly started to come into focus, moving out from the centre and reaching out to the very edges of their minds.

They opened their eyes and looked around in amazement. They'd actually done it… they'd travelled with their minds.

"John are we there, did we do it?"

"We hast Rose, we art hither!"

"Wow, this power really is special. I can't believe we just did that. Anyway, we better be quick, let's find a way in and rescue Apex!"

"We hast this power Rose, shouldst we not use it to enter?"

"John, we can't just storm in there and do magic. We'd have an entire army after us in seconds!"

He struggled to hide the look of disappointment on his face, but he knew she was right. He was finally getting used to this magic power of his and he was keen to use it as much as possible.

"Shouldst we behold around and see if we can findeth a way to receiveth in?"

"We need to be quick John, Apex could be in serious trouble. He hasn't learnt how to use his gift yet, and that worries me." She walked hastily towards the building, studying its structure and looking out for any possible entry points.

"What the fuck…where am I?" Apex screamed, looking helplessly around the dark dingy room. It was cold and there was a strong smell of body odour combined with the foul remnants of the cow dung that had now encrusted on his face. The pain in his head was unbearable. "Argh, my head, what the fuck is wrong with my head? It feels like I've been up all night drinking!" He cradled his head in his hands, wincing as he did so. A deep husky voice startled him, immediately distracting him from the pain.

"Thou art the servant who hath broken in to Mr Baxter's house. Thee assaulted that gent, he hath a broken nose. Doth not behold valorous, a black servant assaulting an elderly sir. I believeth that is pondered a harsh punishment."

"Hey man, who the fuck are you, get me out of this fucking chair!"

"What profanity am I hearing, such vulgar words from a mere servant. My name is Captain Sutherland, Commander of the Aylesbury unit. Wherefore art thou from servant? Wherefore wast thee in Mr Baxter's house? And whither art thy accomplices?"

"Man, you wouldn't believe me if I told you."

"Mr Baxter hath said thee speaketh strangely, whither hast thee learnt this lacking valour sounding English? And what strange robe is this? I hast never seen clothing like this before."

"Like I said, you'd never believe me."

The officer crossed his arms and studied this strange boy.

He looked across to the other side of the room and nodded at one of the four guards, before leaning in closer to Apex in the hope of intimidating him. Captain Sutherland was a young man with an extremely large moustache that pointed out sharply from either side of his face. There was a scar that ran down from the top of his forehead all the way down to the base of his neck.

"Hast thee ever heard of the rack, servant?"

"No, why would I?"

"Thou art not an easy one, art thee? Hast thee cometh with all the other Muslims? Hast thee travelled from Africa?"

"What are you on about man? No I'm not religious, religion doesn't even exist in my time and I'm from America, not Africa."

"What doth thee mean thou art not religious? If't be true thee embrace the Lord Jesus Christ then we may possibly spare thee, servant," said the man. He grinned sinisterly, his gaping mouth revealing an incomplete set of blackened teeth.

Apex pulled back in disgust.

"Man you need to see a fucking dentist! Back off, your breath fucking stinks!"

"Art thee playing with me servant? What is this dentist you talk of? And I wilt not beest spoken to in that tone! Telleth me who thee art, now!"

"Fuck you! You have no idea the shit you're getting yourself into. I have powers that can destroy your entire army, so you'd better watch yourself!"

Captain Sutherland and the guards laughed, it was highly amusing to watch someone admit to sorcery so easily.

"Thou art a courageous one, art thee not? Thou art admitting to witchcraft art thee?"

"I ain't no witch, what you talking about, everyone knows witches ain't real. Seriously, this time zone sucks ass! You suck ass!"

"What art thee talking about, servant? Talk in English."

"I am talking in English, I'm talking in English from a future time zone."

"Release that gent and taketh him to the rack, we wilt receiveth more answers that way," the Captain ordered.

The guards dragged Apex over to the rack and realising what was going on he screamed, "Take your fucking hands off me! You're all going to pay for this, you wait and see!"

Apex wriggled in a futile attempt to escape, but there were too many of them. They tied his arms to one end of the wooden contraption and then did the same to his legs at the other end.

"Are you for real? Are you seriously going to pull my arms and legs off? Man this is harsh. OK, OK, look I'll tell you the truth alright. Listen bro, your time zone is screwed. The Greys are coming and basically you're all screwed. We've got maybe a day, two at most, before they come. And from what I've heard, we're going to be in for some serious shit."

"What art thee talking about fool, what art these Greys?"

"They're about to invade and I'm going to take great pleasure in watching them

screw you over and making you their bitch. If you kill me they're going to destroy everyone."

Captain Sutherland looked perplexed. He couldn't understand half of what the boy was saying, but his tone and lack of respect angered him immensely. He screamed another order at the guards,

"That gent is a liar, turn t now!"

The guards turned the handles of the rack and the ropes started to tighten, stretching and creaking as the wheels slowly rotated. Apex's arms and legs began to pull away from each other.

"Man, this is actually quite nice you know, quite therapeutic," said Apex sarcastically, not wanting to reveal his true discomfort.

The wheels continued to rotate and the pain began to creep in.

"Argh man, stop! It's starting to hurt now, come on stop it. Hey, stop it! Shit!"

Outside, John and Rose could hear Apex's harrowing screams and they knew they had to find a way in fast.

"OK John, we've got no other choice, we're going to have to do it."

They held hands and their minds converged. They concentrated on visualising where Apex was, the image coming to them so clearly it was as if they were actually in the room with him. They could see him on the rack and they could see the overwhelming fear and excruciating agony on his face as the guards wound the cogs.

223

"Art thee ready Rose?"

"Yes John, I'm ready. Let's do this!"

They took a step forward and pressed their noses against the stonewall that faced them. Taking another step, the wall mutated into a vast liquid mass, its ripples expanding infinitely outwards, allowing them to walk effortlessly through to the other side.

"Release him now!" Rose shouted.

Startled, Captain Sutherland and the guards jumped as the two of them suddenly appeared in the room.

"Who art thee, how didst thee receiveth in?" Captain Sutherland shouted furiously. "Taketh those folks immediately."

The four guards charged at John and Rose, but John simply stood there and closed his eyes. Despite not knowing these particular guards, he had developed a severe hatred towards any soldier that worked for the Queen, since his family had been murdered in cold blood. His rage began to boil and explode from deep inside of him.

He imagined them being grabbed and their arms and legs forced tightly together.

The officer closest to John hesitated, confused as to why the boy wasn't trying to escape. Having noticed his slip up, Rose seized the opportunity to help.

She imagined the officer slamming against an invisible barrier, his body turning rigid. He then rose up with the rest of the guards and started levitating in a circular formation, each of them staring at one another with wide eyes. They tried screaming for help, but their mouths had been forced shut.

Realising what Rose was up to, John's confidence and strength began to increase and he took control.

He imagined the ropes around Apex slowly relaxing and loosening and as Apex's stretched body started to release, he saw the boy curl up and groan with pain as he tried to move his painful limbs. The ropes dropped to the floor and began to move as if they were alive. They hovered in the air before gracefully winding around the men's legs, pulling tightly with each twist, until they were all bound together. Concentrating harder, John pictured their bodies gradually drifting apart, floating further away from each other and as the cords stretched to their limit, John could hear the sound of the men's legs popping from out of their joints. Muffled screams filled the air, but this only served to make John more determined and he carried on inflicting great pain and torture upon the men. With the legs now dislocated, tendons and ligaments started to rip and pull apart from their bones. John smiled to himself and gave one final push. The legless torsos dropped to the ground and John collapsed, exhausted, beside them.

Rose opened her eyes and gasped in horror at the devastation that greeted her. The legless men were not quite dead and they groaned and writhed in agony on the floor around her. Fountains of blood pumped out of gory flesh torn stumps and she saw the white flash of exposed bone.

Captain Sutherland spoke first,

"Thee wilt payeth for this, the queen wilt sendeth a thousand men to findeth thee and at which hour those gents doth, thee wilt all beest torn to shreds for this."

Rose ignored him, he was no threat to them now, she had far more important things to be worried about, like Apex.

"Oh my God John, get up, we have to get Apex, quick!" she screamed. "Apex? Are you OK? Apex?"

Apex had passed out from the shock of the pain and he lay motionless on the rack.

"John get up, we have to get out of here!" she yelled in panic.

John slowly got to his feet and looked around in confusion.

Didst I very much doth that? he thought.

Mine lord," he cried, seeing Rose cradling Apex in her arms.

"John, how are we going to carry him? What can we do? We need to help him!"

"You can lift that gent Rose, useth thy mind to lift that gent."

She nodded and brought the image of Apex's limp body into her mind. She pictured him floating steadily in front of her, his body moving in unison with her direction.

"Doth we try going back through the wall?" John asked her in his mind.

"I'm not sure if it will work. I think we'll need Apex to imagine it too otherwise he might get stuck behind. Even if he knew how to use his power, he doesn't have the strength at the moment."

Carefully placing Apex onto the ground, she knelt down next to him and whispered in his ear,

"Apex, I don't know if you can hear me or not, but if you can you need to concentrate. You have to imagine we can walk through this wall. I know it sounds crazy, but you have to try because if you don't, then I don't think we're going to be able to get you out of here without being seen. Can you do that Apex?"

Apex mumbled something incoherent and moved his head ever so slightly.

He wasn't sure how to do it, but from the little experience he did have he knew he needed to feel some form of emotion for it to work. He

thought about his life before, how the people he loved had been taken
away from him and the anxiety and fear he had felt when the Greys had
attacked. He pictured his mom and grandma, Chaz and Olive, and felt
that deep sense of loss and heartbreaking grief that now came with it.
Focusing on his physical pain, he imagined his arms and legs were
healing, the muscles and ligaments returning to their original state. And
to his astonishment the pain actually started to ease. As he slowly
gathered strength, he imagined himself as being strong enough to stand.
He visualised the walls transforming from their solid state into an
expansive liquid mass and the three of them nervously edged forward
towards it. John passed through first, the liquid rippling outwards as he
walked with ease through to the other side. Rose stayed with Apex,
encouraging him to pass through the wall next. He edged closer, his
body still weak and unsteady, and as he passed through the wall he
collapsed on the ground at John's feet.

"Thee didst it Apex!" shouted John excitedly.

Finally, Rose appeared from the shimmering wall, relief washing
over her face when she saw that Apex had safely made it through.

"Quick we have to move, we have to get out of here!" she cried,
reaching for Apex's hands to pull him up. Together they supported
Apex on either side of his body and dragged him down a dusty path that
led in the direction of the town. If they could make it there, perhaps they
could find some who would help them.

Chapter 28

Essex House, Essex.
Residence of Robert Devereux, 2ⁿᵈ Earl of Essex

There was a slight shudder from the ground. Not particularly strong, but noticeable none the less. Small cracks started to appear, slowly spreading their way across the walls of Robert's grand mansion. Fragments of paint fell from the high ceilings, floating down like delicate snowflakes. Robert brushed the flakes from his hair and continued with his card game. The house had been falling apart for some time now, so he was used to it. Despite the unstable structure of the house, it was a truly magnificent building. From the outside it was nothing much to look at, with ivy covering most of the front and tiny windows peeping out from between the leaves. However, the interior of the house hosted a treasure trove of magnificent features and the gardens at the back of the house were immaculate. And it was these gardens there were Robert's greatest passion. So much time and careful attention to detail had been put into the impressive array of animal inspired topiary and he would spend hours just sitting in the window marvelling at their beauty. There were two statues on the wide expanse of land leading up to the house, one of himself and one of his predecessor. He had never liked his one, complaining that it made him look fat and ugly. There were noticeable dents in the bronze, from where he'd hit it with his sword in a fit of rage one time.

Today, he was sat in his favourite chair in a small room next to the front entrance. Although he was a tall man; he towered over most people, he liked small spaces. They made him feel safe and after everything he'd been through with the massacre and his humiliating defeat, he felt the constant need to feel reassured by the safety of his surroundings and his precious home comforts. He was regarded as quite the handsome man, with his long brown wavy hair and his pointy beard, both of which he would meticulously groom throughout the day. Not even one tiny hair was ever out of place.

He stared off in to the distance, a tankard of wine in one hand and a deck of cards in the other. Gulping down the last of his drink, he turned to his friend Paul and said with an irritable tone, "Passeth me more wine Paul."

"Robert, do not thee bethink thou hath hadst enough? And at which hour doth thee bethink the house wilt beest repaired, I feeleth not safe staying in hither"

Robert and Paul had been good friends for many years and the pair had an unbreakable bond. Paul had been a great leader and Robert had travelled alongside and fought with him in many a battle. Today however, Paul was just like any other middle-aged man. His hair had turned grey, his middle had expanded and the only thing that distinguished him from any other man of his age was a large birthmark that covered his left eye. Paul knew Robert better than anyone else and the trust they had built up between them ran deep. He had noticed recently how more and more depressed Robert was becoming. Both men had a mutual hatred towards the Queen and they spent endless hours discussing her assassination. Paul blamed her for Robert's increasingly negative state of mind, but on this day in particular Robert seemed even more distressed than normal and this worried Paul immensely. His friend had become but a shadow of his former self and would turn aggressive at virtually anything that was said or asked of him.

Robert slammed the cup down spilling droplets of wine onto the table and snarled at Paul,

"How dare thee question me, Paul! Passeth the wine now! And doth thee bethink that Queen is in any fit state to fix this decrepit house? The lady hates me Paul, the lady would rather t collapsed and hath killed me. I understandeth not what hath becometh of our friendship."

Robert had once been a close friend of the Queen and had been very fond of her. They used to play games together and talked for hours on end, so much so that many people believed they were romantically entwined. The Queen had adored him and made sure that as her trusted friend he was always well looked after. She had given him the income from the wine trade, which was a very profitable trade indeed. However, with things taking a turn for the worse when he had lost the battle against the Irish, this grave dishonour had lost him this friendship.

"Robert, thee must not alloweth thy defeat to receiveth thee, we wast low on men, we hadst nay choice but to retreat," Paul replied, picking the bottle up and filling Robert's cup.

"They madeth a fool of me! The Queen thinkest I hast failed that lady. I should never hast taken on the Irish, I wast nay more brain than stone." He clumsily swigged from the cup, clearly enraged by the subject. "I wast so close, so close to victory. Wherefore didst the Queen sendeth me such cowards?"

He leaned back in his chair and tapped the top of the deck of cards with shaky fingers. He had never forgiven the Queen, not since she'd clipped him around the ears that time. Even if she were a Queen, how dare a woman treat a well-respected man in such a manner, especially after everything he'd done for her. He had felt betrayed, embarrassed and more than anything else completely humiliated by it. He had been so close to withdrawing his sword and striking the monarch there and then.

"What must people thinketh of me Paul? Robert Devereux, the Earl, defeated by the Irish. The Earl who wast boxed by the Queen. The Earl who wast humiliated in front of her majesty's council. What utter humiliation!"

He sighed, dropping his head in his hands, before continuing with his deranged tirade,

"I despise that Queen. Oh how I long to removeth that lady from power. For too long we hast been ruled by this mistress, 'tis time for change Paul, 'tis time for change!"

"The lady is not getting any younger sir, she is old, we must simply wait. I giveth that lady several more years at most, nay more, and then thither wilt beest the changeth thou desires sir. "

"What, and alloweth that clotpole James to taketh over? Thee understandeth not Paul. I wanteth that power, I wanteth to beest the one who rules this country!"

A loud banging on the door startled the men and a voice from outside called,

"SIR, SIR!"

"See who 'tis Paul, telleth those folk to wend, I wanteth not to see anyone."

Paul walked over to the door and opened it to reveal a young looking man in uniform. His cheeks were bright red and he panted breathlessly, "I must speaketh with the Earl, sir."

"The Earl doth not wish to speaketh with anyone. Kindly leaveth, soldier. "

"Sir 'tis urgent, I must speaketh with that gent immediately."

Paul paused, before turning to face the Earl.

"Sir, the soldier wishes to talk with thee, that gent claims 'tis of the utmost urgency."

Robert looked up and drunkenly slurred, "Sendeth that gent in." He belched loudly and returned his attention to his drink.

The soldier apprehensively entered the room; he had heard the rumours of the Earl's erratic behaviour.

"Come over hither soldier."

"Thank thee, sir."

"What is thy name?"

"Arthur, sir."

"Come hither, Arthur."

Arthur approached the Earl with trepidation, keen to avoid angering the man.

"Come closer," Robert growled impatiently and he grabbed the soldier by the collar and pulled him in towards his angry face.

"At which hour I doth sayeth I wanteth not to see nay man, doth meaneth I wanteth not to see nay man. Art thou a fool?"

"Sir, the ground wast shaking, thither hath been destruction of buildings, many hath perished sir."

"Ah so it was not mine house?" muttered the Earl to himself.

"Sir, we believeth the shaking hast been caused by God. That sacred gent is angered by the trio of witches who art wandering our lands. Captain Sutherland and his guards hath been murdered by these witches. There art a servant of colour and two children; a knave and a girl. But they hath escaped our sights, sir. The priest hath said the hags must beest ceased. He sayeth they art a danger to our people and our army. He sayeth they hath infuriated God, and he is now taking t out on our lands and people."

The Earl released his grip on the soldier and took another swig of his drink. He stroked his beard thoughtfully and said,

"Witches, thee sayeth. How dost thou know they art witches?"

"Sir, one of our men… one of the men who wast murdered… he…"

"Go on, speaketh up boy."

"He hath said those witches didst walketh through walls, sir. And their legs… the murdered men's legs hadst been removed. I hast the bodies outside, sir. Thee must look sir, thee must see with thine own eyes."

Robert and Paul rushed to the door and peered outside. A carriage with four horses sat stationary in the courtyard. On the back was a mound of dead corpses that had been covered by a rug that wasn't quite large enough to fully hide the horror that lay beneath. Robert staggered over to the cart and slowly lifted a corner of the rug to confirm the nightmare for himself. The gruesome sight that met him made him gag

233

instantly. Fresh blood still trickled from the severed stumps, dripping onto the ground and splashing his boots. He stood there in silence, horrified but unable to tear his eyes away. After a while, he shook his head as if coming out of a trance and turned to the soldier.

"Where art those witches now?"

"They art hiding in the town sir and the troops from the barracks art searching. They hast not found those folk yet though, sir."

"Who else knoweth soldier?"

"Only thee, sir."

"Good, telleth no man. Paul, we must go, we must telleth the Queen. Leave good soldier, go bury these bodies, I hath to talk alone."

The soldier saluted and marched back to the carriage. Robert watched as the carriage trundled out through the gates, leaving a trail of blood in its wake.

"Paul, doth thee knoweth what this means?" said the Earl excitedly.

"Nay sir?"

"We hast a way to receiveth rid of this Queen. The Queen dost not killeth witches, the lady learneth from them."

"Sir, what dost thee imply?"

"We telleth the Queen of these witches. The lady wilt wanteth those folk alive for her own wicked uses, but I wilt gain their trust and persuade those folk to killeth the Queen. This could beest our chance Paul. This could beest our chance to triumph. Once the Queen is dead and we killeth those witches we can pray to God for forgiveness. God wilt be on our side, good wilt conquer all evil. We must leaveth now!"

Without waiting for a response from his friend, Robert ran to the house, grabbed his coat, gloves and leather cap and ran back outside. He mounted his horse and charged off through the gates. He would find these witches… no matter what it took.

Chapter 29

Aylesbury, Buckinghamshire

Apex, John and Rose had been walking for several hours now and their tiredness was starting to show. As they passed through the town they stumbled over objects hidden by the darkness of night. Despite feeling weary, their senses were on high alert and they listened intently for any sounds that might indicate trouble. Without warning, the ground suddenly started to shake with terrific force and the trees and houses creaked dangerously beside them. The three fugitives held on to each other tightly. This was a sign that the Greys were getting closer. With no clear idea of what it was they would eventually encounter, they all felt overwhelmed by a deep sense of impending doom. The tremor gradually died down and with it so too did the noise. For a split second an eerie silence filled the air before being broken by the barking of frightened dogs and the cries of terrified townsfolk.

"My God, did you feel that earthquake?" Rose trembled.

"You call that an earthquake?" Apex mocked. "That wasn't an earthquake. I've felt way worse than that. And you better get used to it, because according to that Calcus dude, the quakes are only going to get worse. Look, we need to decide whether we stay outside and risk being seen or if we try and find shelter. But I'm telling you if we do find somewhere we need to make sure we can get out quickly, because if these quakes get any worse I don't want to get fucking crushed. The way I see it is we're screwed either way, so what's it going to be?"

John sighed. He was still in shock at what had happened to the guards earlier and now with the earthquakes the enormity of the daunting task ahead of them only added to his anxiety. The one thing keeping him going was the thought of seeing his family again. Shaking all of his negative thoughts away, John turned his attention back to the memory of Apex walking through the wall.

"Apex thee didst t, thee passed through that wall, we all didst!" John whispered excitedly. "We canst do most anything now."

"Yeah man, that was crazy!" Apex said, absentmindedly striking his lighter. "Shit, we all walked through a solid wall! Man this is awesome, I'm ready for anything now. If those soldiers even dare think of coming anywhere near us, they're going to wish they'd never been born. Ha, those jackasses have no idea what's coming to them."

"Apex, we're here to kill the Greys and find Ema. We promised we'd only defend ourselves, we didn't set out to cause unnecessary harm," Rose chided.

"Yeah, yeah I know, but do you really think those guards are going to give a shit about us? It's either kill or be killed in this fucking time zone. John I don't envy you one little bit coming from here, it's…" he paused mid sentence, a look of confusion sweeping across his face.

"Hang on a minute, how did you manage to find me? You weren't even there when those soldiers pounced on me. And more to the point how did we get here? I mean I know I walked through that wall and everything, which is pretty awesome, but seriously what's going on?"

"We imagined it Apex. We imagined you and that we could see where you were. It's like we were connected to you in some way and that deep connection allowed us to travel to where you were being held captive. It was so unbelievably fast Apex, you would have loved it," Rose smiled.

"Woah guys, this is frickin' awesome! Oh man I wish I'd been there with you, you know seen it for myself like. Hey listen, thanks so much for helping me, it's nice to know you care," he said with a grin, placing his arms around the pair of them.

"We wast not worried about thee at all," John replied in jest.

"No, we weren't worried about you Apex, we were just worried that we wouldn't be able to use your lighter for the fires any more," Rose laughed.

"Yeah whatever, I saw your face Rose, you were concerned about me big time."

Rose smiled and was about to respond when the sound of hurried footsteps nearby made them freeze in terror.

Out of the shadows, a figure came in to view.

"Ho! What art thee doing hither? Art thee lost?"

"Um, aye, of sorts," John stammered, peering into the darkness to try and make out who the voice belonged to. He couldn't see a thing, but the voice told him it was coming from a girl.

"You should not beest hither, it be dangerous. If mine master findeth thee hither, that gent wilt surely kill you."

"Can thee help us?"

"I do not knoweth thee, what art thee doing here?"

"We will not beest any trouble, you hath my word," pleaded John. "We needeth some place to rest for a while."

There was silence as the girl thought about it for a moment.

"Can thee payeth me? If thou can, I can put thee in the cellar. The master doth never go down thither, but t'will cometh at a cost. And thee must promise thee wilt maketh no hurtling, for if my master suspects, he will surely killeth thou and me both," she answered.

"We hast no money on our persons," said John, "but please kind lady we will cause nay trouble. And I giveth you my solemn word we wilt payeth thee anon."

"Aye go on, but I wilt needeth money by the morrow. One of thee can wend and findeth a way to payeth me. The other two must stay locked in the cellar."

"Thank you, thee hath showed great kindness," replied John gratefully.

The three of them staggered after the dark figure, holding their hands out in front of them to feel the way. She stopped in front of a dimly lit building and beckoned them in. The comforting smell of freshly baked bread hit them as they entered and their empty stomachs rumbled in response. The girl gave a gasp as she took in the devastation that had been caused by the earthquake. Plates and cups had been smashed, tiny fragments of earthenware scattered across the floor, and a large oak table lay on its side. She fell to her knees and started sobbing.

"That gent wilt punish me for this. What am I to doth?" she wailed.

Apex and Rose stood in awkward silence, unsure of what to say or do. John however, stepped forward and spoke softly to the girl.

"Art thee well fair maiden?"

She turned to look at the three of them and slowly rose to her feet, blotting at her

eyes with the corner of her apron. She was a beautiful, slim-waisted young girl with long blonde hair that was tied up in a messy ponytail. She was wearing a white kirtle and brown apron and on her back was a round bundle tied securely to her shoulders.

"Oh!" she exclaimed, "who art thee? Art thee a black servant? Wherefore art thee with these children?"

Apex stared at her, his mouth gaping open gormlessly. She was the most beautiful woman he'd seen in a long time.

"Damn girl, you are seriously hot!" he spluttered.

"Excuse me? Wherefore would thee sayeth such a vulgar word?" the girl replied, offended by Apex's lack of respect.

"Apex that is a word lacking in valour, do not sayeth the 'D' word!" exclaimed John, who was equally shocked.

"Oh shit, sorry I mean, God you are so fit!"

The girl raised her eyebrows in disgust. She didn't fully understand what he was saying, but she could tell from the tone of his voice and his mannerisms that it was disrespectful.

"Apex, thou must not useth the Lord's name in vain!" John reprimanded.

"Oh, um, OK, I mean… you're very beautiful." Apex blushed and then curtseyed and held his hand out to the girl.

Rose giggled and John rolled his eyes and said,

"Please excuseth mine servant, he hath problems speaking."

Apex dropped his hand and glared at John.

The girl shook her head and started to unfasten the straps around her shoulders. Taking the bundle off of her back, she carefully placed it into her arms.

"What robes art thee wearing? They dost not behold like normal robes. And thy accent soundeth strange, servant. Wherefore art thou from?"

Apex opened his mouth to speak, but John quickly interrupted,

"He is mine servant. We hath escapeth from mine house in the next town. And this is mine cousin, Rose, she doth liveth with me."

Rose nodded uneasily. She was finding the whole situation very unnerving and felt reluctant to give anything away to a stranger, even if she was helping them.

"So, what's your name then honey?" asked Apex flirtatiously.

The woman stared at Apex.

"My name is Sarah, but that is nay matter. We must hurry before mine master returns. I needeth to tidy this lodging up or I wilt beest punished. And Jake is becoming restless, the child dost needeth a feed."

"Oh," said Apex disappointedly, "you have a baby? You should have said. Where's the dad then?"

"Excuse me? What doth this word "dad" mean?"

"I mean father, where's the father of your baby?"

She frowned at him. The subject of the baby's father was something she didn't like to talk about.

"Let me findeth thee some blankets, it can get very cold down thither."

As she left the room, Apex gazed after her perfectly formed body, licking his lips and smiling, then he turned to John and snapped,

"Fucking servant? What the hell! I'm not your fucking servant!"

241

Rose giggled.

"I hadst to sayeth something Apex," John said, stifling his laughter and holding his hands out in mock defence.

"Look Apex, you've got to stop telling people that we're from different time zones. They'll think we're crazy," said Rose. "And from what I've seen, they don't take too kindly to 'strange' people."

Apex rolled his eyes and muttered, "Fucking servant," under his breath.

With Sarah now out of the room, they took the opportunity to study the large kitchen in greater detail. A loaf of freshly baked bread sat on top of the stove and bunches of heather hung loosely above their heads. The wooden floor was uneven and rough with splinters, which had tried to be covered up by a piece of tatty old red carpet.

Sarah returned carrying a pile of ragged blankets. She carefully stepped over the fragments of broken bottles and passed the blankets to Rose.

"Here, taketh these blankets. They art a bit filthy, but wilt keepeth thee warm."

"Excuse me my lady, do you have any water I could clean my face with? And whilst you're at it, I don't suppose you have anything to drink as well, do you?" asked Apex in his politest voice.

"As thee well knoweth, there hast been a drought so water is hard to cometh by. And thee cannot drinketh the water, t maketh thee very ill. Mine master hath cider but that is all I can giveth for now. Thee art lucky I am not giving thee to the barracks. And because thee have not yet payeth me for helping thee, methinks thee shouldst not asketh for anything else - but yet hither thee art."

She passed Apex a bottle of cider, which he immediately uncorked and drank thirstily.

"Thanks my lady," he said with a wink and continued drinking until the bottle was empty.

Sarah brushed the broken fragments aside with her feet and lifted up the dusty carpet. Underneath there was a wooden hatch. She pulled the rusty handle and the hatch opened with a noisy creak. She turned to them and said,

"There art a number of things down thither so beest careful not to knocketh anything. Thee must be very quiet, mine master is not the most kindeth of people."

They nodded and started making their way down the steps into the dark and musty cellar, carefully avoiding the stacks of tools and other miscellaneous objects. Apex took his lighter from out of his pocket and pressed the button. The flickering flame lit the room, revealing more clutter and destruction caused by the earthquake. Rose pushed things to the side with her feet in an attempt to make a pathway for them. Brushing some cobwebs away, she managed to find an empty space in the corner of the cellar, just below a small window. "It's so cold down here," she gasped, sitting down on the hard floor and wrapping her arms across her body to keep warm.

"We need a better plan," she said to the boys. "We haven't made any progress in finding Ema and look John, I understand how much you want to see your family, but I'm sorry I just can't see how finding them will help us find this God. It feels like we're wasting time, time we haven't got."

John looked crestfallen, but nodded. Deep down he knew Rose was right. Their main priority was to find Ema, yet in the back of his mind he couldn't help but feel this was something he needed to do. Rose smiled sympathetically at him and felt a pang of guilt. She knew full well that if she were given even half the chance to see her mum again, she would do everything in her power to make sure it happened. She put her arm around him and looked over to Apex, wondering why he was being so unusually quiet. He was sat cross-legged with a sleazy smile on his face. Rose huffed and said,

"Apex, are you listening? We need to get smart, think of something else we can do. Oi, Apex! Earth to Apex!"

"Hey? Oh yeah, sorry - she is fit though, isn't she?" he said dreamily.

"Apex please, we have to concentrate on our objectives. You must stop being so distracted, and anyway, what makes you think she would be interested in you? I mean look at you wearing that dirty old dressing gown and you smell awful. Forget about her, and any other ladies for that matter, and focus on the task in hand."

Apex opened another bottle of cider he'd grabbed on his way down into the cellar and said,

"As if it matters that I smell bad, everyone in this time zone smells bad."

"Apex, this really isn't helping. I suggest you keep your mouth shut until you have something productive to say."

He took another large gulp of cider and said,

"So there's a Queen, right?"

John nodded.

"What's your point Apex? So what if there's a Queen?" Rose replied with annoyance. She was fed up with his silly questions and childish behaviour.

"Right OK, so it's simple. We find the Queen, tell her that danger is coming and ask her to send a message out to everyone asking if they know a guy called Ema."

"You know what Apex, that could actually work!" Rose said, standing up. "That's the best idea you've had since I met you!"

"See I am good for some things," he grinned and held the bottle of cider out in front of Rose and John. "Come on, you've got to drink something. I haven't seen you drink anything yet. I know it's cider and you guys are young and everything, but seriously you'll dehydrate if you don't drink something."

Both of them shook their heads. Apex withdrew the bottle and took another swig, "Oh well, your loss."

"So tomorrow we head towards the palace or castle or…" she hesitated, "John, where does the Queen live?"

"I bethink the lady spendeth most of her time at Richmond Palace, that is what mine father hath said. He said that the lady wast very much old and she hath a preference for Richmond Palace. 'Tis thought the lady is very ill and requests to kicketh the bucket thither."

"OK, well we don't have any other choice really, so that sounds like a good starting point," said Rose. "Now we need to get some rest. John, you can lay next to me. Apex you lay over there, the smell of that cow poo is making me feel sick."

"Ha! And you think lying next to John is better than me? He stinks way more than I do! Fine, I didn't want to lie next to you anyway." He tipped the remaining cider over his head

and scrubbed at his face. "There, better?" he said sniffing his armpits in jest. Man, you're right I seriously need a shower."

"What is a shower?" asked John.

"It's a bit like a stand up bath," Rose explained, "water sprays down from the ceiling and cleans you."

"That doth sound like magic!" said John. "I cannot recall when I last didst bathe?"

"That's gross," Apex said turning his nose up in disgust, "but I ain't surprised, based on what I've seen of this place so far."

"That is how 'tis hither," said John. "Tis only the rich that hast such luxuries."

"Bro, when we see that Queenie of yours, I'm dragging you and me both straight up to her bathroom. Man, I'll scrub you myself!"

"Apex, it's the Queen. You call her 'Queenie' and she'll chop your head off! You have to try and be polite and whatever you do, please don't swear!"

"OK, OK mom I'll be good," Apex said sarcastically, quickly dodging out of the way as Rose went to clip him round the ear. He gave a big yawn, "Man, I'm tired, I need sleep."

The three of them lay down on the hard, cold floor. They tossed and turned trying to find a comfortable position. After several minutes of this, Rose drifted off to sleep, closely followed by Apex, but John's mind was still filled with thoughts of his family. He so desperately wanted to see them again, to hold his sister and mother once more. Tears welled up in his eyes. He closed them and tried to clear his mind.

He imagined the walls of the cellar turning to liquid, the watery mass rippling out in all directions. He passed effortlessly through, taking several small steps until he was now on the other side of the wall. He visualised his house; a small wooden building with a thatched roof and dense woodland positioned on either side. He imagined the horses in the stable, chewing and snorting as they munched on the hay. He saw

246

buildings, trees, animals and people rush past him until he came to an abrupt stop.

He was there.

Chapter 30

Colchester, Essex

J ohn opened his eyes and was greeted with the familiar sight of the
building he had lived in all his life. A wave of nostalgia washed
over him and he grew excited at the thought of seeing his family
again. He couldn't wait to tell Jane all about Rose and prove to her that
his dreams weren't just dreams, that she was actually a real person. But
most of all, he was desperate to warn them about the impending
invasion from the Greys and about his quest to find Ema.

He took a deep breath and made his way to the front door. It was
late, but he knew his father and mother would still be awake, for they
were hard working people. He opened the door and stepped in to the
warm kitchen. There was a golden haze radiating from the burning
candles and as expected his mother was still up. She was sat at the table,
her back towards him, her head bowed over a piece of intricate
embroidery.

Hearing the door open, she spoke without turning to see who it was.

"I am glad thou hast returneth Jack. That Sheriff cameth to visit with three guards. I knoweth not what for, but those gents wanteth to speaketh to thee, methinks 'tis important."

John watched his mother for a while before softly speaking. "Mother."

Mary turned sharply. John had expected her to rush over and embrace him, to be happy at the very least, but instead she looked fearful.

"Who art thee, wherefore art thee in mine house?" she shouted, jumping up out of her chair and backing towards the far wall. "Get out of mine house, knave! Jane, Jane, help, cometh hither! We hast an intruder, bringeth thine father's dagger!"

John was confused. How could his own mother not recognise him?

"Mother 'tis I, John, your son."

"I hast nay son, why art thee saying those words?"

She scrabbled against the wall, trying to get as far away from John as possible. Despite her cries for help, Jane was still nowhere to be seen.

"Jane! Waketh up, bringeth thine father's dagger quickly!"

Jane appeared at the entrance to the kitchen, sleepy eyed and confused as to what all the fuss was about. She glanced at John without any signs of recognition and then looked over at her mother, who was now shaking and crying in the corner. She was holding her father's dagger loosely by her side.

"What is this, mother?" she asked and then turned to John and said, "Who art thee?"

"Why 'tis I, John, thy brother."

"Brother? I hast nay brother!"

John felt the panic flare up inside him. Why did neither of them recognise him? How could they not know it was him? He stood there trembling, unsure what to do next.

"Get out of mine house, knave," screamed Mary, grabbing the sharp blade from Jane and violently thrusting it at John. "We hast never met thee before and thou art not welcome here!" She swung the dagger in front of her, and even though the weapon wasn't the slightest bit close to striking John, the crazed look of intent on his mother's face made him scream and charge towards the entrance. The door swung open before he could escape and in walked his father.

"Jack hurry, we hast a trespasser!" Mary cried.

Jack looked at John, then lunged at him and grabbed him violently by the ear.

"Argh, that hurts!" John cried out in pain.

"Who art thee lad? What doth thee wanteth from us?"

"Father, 'tis me, John. Why doth none of thee know who I am?"

"We hath nay son, thou art mistaken. I shall take pity on thee this time, kindly leaveth and go back to where thou hath come from. We wanteth nay…"

The house suddenly started shaking. It was only very light, but it continued to build up until it reached a point where it felt as though a strong wind was rattling the very bones of the house. The group remained silent, waiting for the quake to pass, but instead it intensified and the wooden walls began to buckle making cups and plates fall from the shelves and smash to the ground. Chairs slammed against the wall, missing John by mere inches, but the force of it made him stumble and fall to the floor with a cry. Jack made his way over to Mary and Jane, dodging the falling debris and stepping over the broken crockery. He grasped them protectively around the shoulders and drew them into his body.

"What is happening Jack?" screamed Mary.

"I knoweth not. Keepeth hold of me."

Mary and Jane desperately clutched onto his shirt, nestling their faces into his body, trying to block out what was happening.

And then it stopped.

Everything was still.

Ever the one to seek blame, Jack turned to John and angrily roared,

"Do thee knoweth anything about this knave? Doth thee knoweth wherefore the house shaketh so?"

John stared blankly at his family. Even if they didn't seem to know who he was, he had a responsibility to warn them of the impending danger.

"'Tis the Greys, I thinketh they art here…

Chapter 31

Aylesbury, Buckinghamshire

The small house shook violently and the metal tools and crockery adorning the walls fell with a crash. A large wardrobe toppled over, landing next to where Rose and Apex were sleeping. Rose woke with a start, just as the tremor stopped and the only evidence of a quake was the carnage surrounding them. Instinctively she went to shake John.

"John, wake up! Did you feel that?" She reached her hands out and felt around next to her. "John, where are you?" Receiving no response, she shouted louder, "John where are you? Apex wake up, John's gone!"

Apex groaned and sat up, scratching his head in a daze. He had experienced many earthquakes in his time and was used to sleeping through even the most violent of tremors.

"What are you going on about? Why'd you have to go and wake me man, I need more sleep." He lay back down, but as it dawned on him what Rose had said he sat back up again with a start. "Hang on, what do you mean John's gone? How could he have gone?"

Before Rose was able to answer, a loud male voice boomed down from above.

"Who is down thither? I can heareth voices! Sarah receiveth now, who is down thither? Who art thee hiding in my house?"

Loud bangs came from overhead as the owner of the voice stomped angrily across the wooden hatch.

Apex sighed, rubbing his temples in frustration.

"Why can't we just have one night when shit doesn't happen? It's starting to freak me out, it's like one of those stupid old Hollywood movies, you know where things keep happening like people thought it would, you know like all clichéd and bullshit," he whispered to Rose.

"What on earth are you talking about, Apex?"

"I don't know, but his voice sounds kind of familiar, like I've heard it before. Seriously Rose, some bad shit is going down and I don't think it's the Greys this time."

"Oh Apex please, you're talking nonsense. Come on this really isn't the time for your silly games!"

They held their breaths and waited, hoping the man would give up and go back to bed. It was wishful thinking. They heard the sound of the latch being unlocked and Sarah's desperate pleas.

"Wend thee not down thither master. Thee wilt only hurt thy back again, sir."

"Get thy hands off me wench, or I will giveth thee another whipping!" the man yelled.

Apex and Rose crouched anxiously together, listening to the commotion, waiting to be discovered. In between the loud crashes, they could hear the sound of a baby crying and Sarah sobbing, "Please sir, do not hurt Jake."

This was too much for Rose. She'd seen her own mother go through too much suffering at the hands of Shaun to just sit there and do nothing.

"Apex, we have to help her…"

Apex was up on his feet before she'd even finished. Kicking his way past the fallen objects, he made his way up the narrow staircase towards the hatch. He fumbled furiously with the lock, but it was old and rusty and easily fell apart in his hands. Lifting the hatch door, he glanced up to see a short, fat man, dressed in a smock.

"Oi, get the fuck off her!" Apex shouted.

"What, who art thee? A servant, a black servant…IN MINE HOUSE!"

Apex clambered out of the hatch and towered over the little man. Spurred on by his newly discovered powers, Apex reveled in his role as knight in shining armour.

"Look man, I'm getting really pissed off with the people in this time zone calling me a fucking servant. I'm not from your time, I'm from a time far more advanced than here, a place that is still shit granted, but not as shit as this fucking time zone. I've been attacked by an old man, kidnapped and tortured on some fucking brutal rack thing and now this. I could crush you like an ant under my foot if I wanted to, so I would advise you take your fucking hands off her now!"

The man released the frightened girl and she rushed over to her baby, who was crying and lying helplessly among the rubble on the floor. But the man hadn't given up entirely. He fronted up to Apex, his fists raised, and he started punching into thin air.

"Man, you seriously think you can take *me* on?" scoffed Apex. Rather than scare the man off, it only served to infuriate him further. He

254

ran to the main door and returned with a wheel lock pistol. He held it out in front of him and pointed it at Apex.

"Apex, watch out, he's got a gun!" yelled Rose.

"Ha! You think that rusty old piece of shit is a gun? Seriously, you should see the kinda shit we have in my time zone, that ain't no fucking gun," he laughed and walked towards the man. He lunged to grab the gun from him, but missed and fell to the floor, landing sharply on his shoulder. Undeterred, he jumped to his feet and tried again. Seeing Apex heading towards him, the man panicked and started frantically fumbling with the trigger of the gun. Suddenly, there was a loud bang and a plume of smoke filled the room. The kitchen fell silent and the acrid smell of gunpowder hung in the air.

"Shit man! What the fuck!" Apex yelled at the man, "Rose, we need to get out of here, he's mental, we need to get out of here and go and find John." He turned to look at her. She stood, her mouth open in shock, holding onto her stomach. A deep crimson stain slowly spread across the material of her t-shirt. Stumbling forwards, she reached out her trembling blood soaked fingers to Apex, before falling to her knees with a cry of pain.

"Rose, shit! Are you OK? Rose!" Apex cried, reaching forward to try and catch her as she fell. He crouched down beside her and wrapped his arms around her quivering body, but it was too late. She gave a small whimper and passed out from the pain. Slowly easing her limp body down onto the floor, Apex stood up and glared at the man.

He closed his eyes and imagined the man's round, bearded face and how his eyebrows knitted together in such a way that it made him look permanently angry. He visualised him desperately trying to reload his gun, frantically trying to pour the gunpowder in. Apex continued to stare at the man, watching as his body went rigid, his arms and legs restrained by that now familiar force. Next he turned his focus to the gun, imagining it levitating in front of the helpless man, hovering for a few seconds then dropping and smashing to the floor. "Like an ant," he messaged to the man in his mind. Finally, Apex mentally pushed the man downwards with an intense force, the pressure causing his legs to buckle at the knees and then bend outwards with an eye-watering crunch. Apex continued to push until the man's thighs shattered, sending blood spraying out in all directions his pelvis began splitting in two.

Apex slowly opened his eyes and looked down at the man squirming around on the ground. His broken body was slipping and sliding in a pool of blood as he desperately tried to get away from Apex. But it was no use, his movements lessened and as he reached the threshold of the doorway his head lowered and he gave a final groan before collapsing.

Apex shook his head and ran back to Rose. Cradling her in his arms he whispered gently,

"Rose, are you OK? Wake up Rose, wake up!"

He ran his fingers over her neck attempting to find a pulse, but there was nothing.

"Shit man! Come on Rose, wake the fuck up! You can't leave me here on my own!" he screamed.

Sarah stood silently watching from the side of the room. She couldn't believe what had just happened.

"What hath happened? How didst thee doth that?"

"Don't worry about that now. Quick, help me with Rose!"

She hesitated, unsure whether to trust a man who had killed someone in such an inhumane way. And he'd done it without so much as even lifting a finger! But he had saved her from the master, so perhaps he was worth putting some trust in after all. She placed Jake softly down into the makeshift crib and grasped Rose's legs.

"Lift her onto the table," Apex instructed, hoisting her up by her arms.

Once she was on the table, Apex placed his hands on her chest and pressed hard, squeezing the air out of her mouth, then releasing and allowing her chest to rise up. He repeated this several times, but it was no good.

Rose was dead.

"What do we do now?" cried Apex, putting his hands up to his head. "She's fucking dead man, she's dead!"

"I am most sorry about your friend," Sarah said, "I didst warneth thou mine master hath a temper."

Apex sat on the cold floor, his head in his hands, sobbing loudly.

"This is so fucked up. Why me? Why is this shit happening to me?"

"Why art thee hither?" asked Sarah softly. "And how didst thee doth that? How didst thee crush that gent like that? 'Tis like witchcraft. Art thee a witch?"

Apex sniffed and wiped his eyes. He didn't feel like explaining anything right now, but what choice did he have, he needed as much help as possible at the moment.

"I'm from the future." He paused. "I mean, I'm from a future time zone. And Rose here, well she was from a different time zone to me. And John, who seems to have vanished into thin air, well he's from this time zone. Look, I don't expect you to understand. I know it sounds crazy; I wouldn't have believed it myself."

"I understandeth not, 'tis true. Thee mean thou art from another time, hast thee been resurrected? Art thee Jesus? Hast thee been sent from the heavens?"

"Um… well… not really…" He paused and thought about what it was he had been sent here to do. In some ways he guessed he could be likened to God, after all he did possess some amazing Godlike powers. However, now that he was on his own, and the job of finding Ema rested entirely with him, he wasn't feeling quite as powerful as he had been. But after experiencing just how powerful his new skill was and especially now that Rose was dead he knew he would do everything within his power to stop the Greys. He owed it to Rose.

Composing himself he looked up at Sarah and said,

"Actually, do you know what, yes I am, I am the almighty powerful one and I have been sent from the heavens to rescue this planet from destruction!"

All her life Sarah had been told that the saviour would one day be resurrected and she felt humbled that it was happening now, in her house.

"Oh my, thee art the saviour, thee art the lord himself!" she walked over to Apex and knelt down to touch his feet. "I am at thine service dear lord, asketh me and I will do."

Having never been in the situation where a girl was willing to do anything for him before, Apex fought off the urge to ask for a kiss and for once in his life thought sensibly. Desperate times called for desperate measures and he had to get to the Queen somehow or other.

"You really mean you'll do *anything*?"

"Aye my lord, thee art mine new master."

"OK then, so I'll need another bottle of that cider for starters, and I could definitely do with some new clothes," he said looking at his robe in disgust, "and I'll need you to come with me to show me how to get to Richmond palace."

"The Queen, thee needeth to see the Queen?"

"Yes, that's right, the Queen, can you do that?"

"Methinks I knoweth how to receiveth thither, but how wilt thee receiveth into the palace to see the Queen? Thee can not just walketh in and see that lady!"

"I'll find a way don't you worry. The Greys are coming and when they do, they'll kill us all. Finding your Queen is my last, my only, chance."

"I understandeth not, what doth thee mean by 'the Greys'?"

"They're from another dimension and they're on their way here, right now. They're going to invade your land and when they do all hell's going to break loose."

"Invade! Ha, those gents cannot invade; we hast the best navy in the world. We defeated the Spanish, I am sure those gents will not receiveth to our shores," said Sarah laughing confidently.

"Sarah, they're not coming here by boat, they come from the skies, from space."

"I understandeth not. What is space? How can they cometh from the skies? Art they like birds?"

"Look, don't worry about it now, we haven't got time. All you need to know is that if I don't find Ema soon then we're all screwed."

Sarah went quiet. These farfetched stories he was telling her seemed like madness, but after what she had just witnessed, she had very little choice but to obey him.

"Take off thy robe and I wilt receiveth thee some of the masters garments. They may not fit thee, but we can tryeth."

Apex nodded and started untying his robe, revealing a perfectly toned body underneath. Sarah looked at him in awe, running her eyes up and down his muscular frame. Apex held his gown out to Sarah, completely oblivious of her admiring glances.

"Are you going to take it then?" asked Apex.

"Oh, aye, aye of course mine lord," she said, blushing and hastily taking the gown from Apex. As she did so she noticed blood seeping from his torso, "Oh mine, thou is hurt. I bethink the bearing hath grazed thee, we should crisp t up."

Apex looked down at the wound and covered it with his hands. He hadn't realised he'd been hit, the adrenaline must have masked the pain, but he could feel it now starting to burn.

"Argh, shit man, that really hurts!" He clutched his chest then glanced over at Rose's body and realised there was no time for him to worry about a mere scratch. Standing up, he walked over to her, knelt down and brushed her hair away from her face and whispered,

"Don't worry Rose, I'll fix this. I'll find Ema for you, and for John, and when I do I'll make sure those Greys go back to wherever they come from. I don't know how I'll do it, but I promise…I will."

Chapter 32

Richmond Palace, Greater London, the Queen's residence

The streets of Richmond were manic. People were frantically searching for somewhere safe to hide, dodging falling debris as the buildings crumbled around them. The earthquakes were increasing both in frequency and in their intensity, shaking the earth deep within its core. More and more houses were collapsing and as they did great clouds of dust billowed out onto the streets, making it difficult to breathe. People lay trapped under collapsed doorframes, screaming and desperately reaching out for help, but people were too scared and worried for their own safety to stop and offer assistance. Startled horses and farm cattle charged into the frenzied crowds, crushing and injuring anyone that got in their way.

While all the chaos was going on outside, the Queen remained calm in the safety of her palace. An extravagant, overly ornate and grandiose structure, the palace, like it's inhabitant, had a way of looking down upon the town it reigned over. However, like every other building in the town, it hadn't managed to escape the destructive force of the earthquake. One of the eastern towers had collapsed and now exposed the tired looking room inside. Despite this, the Queen remained calm and collected as she sat in her chair by the fireplace. She was too old to worry about such trivial matters, after all she'd been ill for so many years now, it was only a matter of time before she would leave this earth for higher plains.

Her life had felt more or less worthless since her trusted attendant and closest friend Blanche Parry had died. In fact most of her close friends had passed on and now all she could do was wait for her own inevitable fate. Her maids often kept watch over her, making sure she didn't do anything silly and although she was very much humbled by their concern, she knew her age was against her and that it was time for someone else to take charge. And then there was that oaf of a man, Robert, oh how she detested him with all her heart. Yet with this intense hatred came a deep sadness too, because at one point she had liked him dearly, truly cherished his company. Until she had seen through his façade and spotted his true intentions that is. He was certainly no friend of hers any more.

"Your highness, thou hast the Earl of Essex hither to see thee," said her butler, Henry, as he entered the room.

"What dost that clotpole wanteth?" she sighed, "That gent should know I doth not wish to see him. And Henry, what wast that shaking? I wast lighting mine pipe whence I didst fall. Now mine cannabis is all over the floor and mine damned back is so painful. Would thee kindly gather up and refilleth mine pipe for me?"

The Queen's health had deteriorated rapidly over the years and she had become a lot frailer. A passing visitor had suggested she try the medicinal plant and although it made her feel strange and lightheaded, it eased her pain and discomfort immensely.

"I knoweth not what 'twas thy majesty," said Henry getting down onto his hands and knees to collect the scattered weed from the floor, "but the people of

London art very frightened. Many hath been killed by the falling buildings. The Priest doth say that God is angry; he says we must pray for his forgiveness. Thither wast a collapse in the east wing of the Palace thy majesty, the masons art fixing t as we speak."

He stuffed the pipe with the weed he had collected from the floor and handed it back to the Queen. She took it from him and he bowed and slowly backed out of the room. Deep in thought, the Queen twirled the pipe through her fingers, spilling the weed that Henry had just picked up for her. She didn't have the energy to talk to Robert; he'd had his chance on more than one occasion. Suddenly, the door swung violently open and in strode Robert. He removed his cap before bowing gracefully at her feet.

"How dare thee enter! Wast thee not told that thee must not attendeth me? I should hast thee arrested for this!"

"Your majesty I whole heartedly apologise, but I hath news that is of the upmost importance."

"I am not in the humour for idle talking, so this hadst better beest important."

"Your Highness we hath receiveth a message from our barracks in Aylesbury."

"What news? What news doth thee bringeth me?" the Queen asked impatiently.

"We hath a report of murder within our ranks my lady, five of our soldiers art dead."

"Who art the culprits of such a heinous crime?"

"My lady we hast reports 'tis the work of a runaway servant and two children."

"A servant and some children didst this?" the Queen laughed, "How can this be?"

"Your Highness we hast a witness that claims those folks could walketh through solid walls. Witchcraft is at work my lady, witchcraft."

"And who made these absurd claims, Robert?"

"It wast one of the unfortunate soldiers, God rest his soul, he didst die shortly after giving his story. That gent didst say those folk art witches and they hath used sorcery to removeth their limbs. All five dead soldiers art without legs, including Captain Sutherland."

"This news disturbs me greatly and I will standeth not for such actions towards mine own army. Whither art those folk now Robert?"

"We doth think they art hiding in the town of Aylesbury."

"Send more men hither at once, but they must not killeth those folk. I want to see these witches for mine self."

"Aye your Majesty."

He turned to leave, but the Queen called out,

"Robert, in recent times I hast becometh rather distant from thee. Our friendship hath becometh, shallt we say, strained. Thou hast failed me in battle with the Irish, which hath brought shame and humiliation to mine house. However, I am willing to giveth thee one final chance to proveth thine worth and humble servility. Thou must capture these witches alive, canst thou do this deed for me Robert?"

Robert nodded solemnly.

"But I warneth thee Robert, if thou faileth this task then I wilt hast little choice but to strip thee of thy title and sendeth thee out to exile. Dost thou understand? If't be true what thee sayeth is correct, that these wicked children and this servant can walketh through walls and didst slay five of our finest soldiers, then we may beest able to useth those folk. Thee wilt needeth help, Robert. Captain Peters is on his monthly visit, he can assist thee with his army."

"My lady, I giveth thee mine word, I wilt not disappoint. God is on mine side for he hath sent me a sign through the earth itself. His anger has been shown through the tremblings we hath felt and in the name of God himself I wilt find those folk and I wilt bringeth those folk to thee anon."

Chapter 33

Colchester, Essex.

The sun began to rise, casting an orange haze across the endless forest of trees that surrounded Jack's house. Light reflected off of the early morning dew, filtering in through the windows and revealing the extent of the damage. A wall had collapsed at the far end of the building, destroying both bedrooms and taking out most of Jacks tools with it. Most of the crockery had smashed and the little food that they'd had stored away, had been crushed by a fallen beam. This had been the worst earthquake yet, and they all knew the house wouldn't be capable of standing up to another. Mary and Jane wandered around the house, collecting anything that was still salvageable and placed the items in the corner of the kitchen. Jack just stood and watched, waiting impatiently for the women to finish gathering up their belongings so that they could search for shelter elsewhere. Even if they had to live in the stable for a few weeks, it was safer than staying where they were. Feeling the anger rising up within him, he shoved John with his elbow and spun around to face him.

"So telleth me knave, who art thee and whither hast thee cometh from? Why wast the ground shaking? And Greys? What art these Greys thou speaketh of?" His mind emptied itself of the questions it had been filled with since John had arrived.

John nervously stared at this man who he knew to be his father, or at least who had been once, in one time zone, some when.

"I hath nay words to explain, I understandeth very little myself. I wast hither before, I hath lived hither in another life, the same life in fact. But, I understandeth not how thee cannot knoweth me. The Greys art coming and they art in their millions. Those gents art going to invade our land and killeth us all. Thee must believeth me, I beg of thee, for thou hast to receiveth hence from hither and wend deep into the woods. Findeth the caves thee once took us to, stayeth thither as long as thee can and do not cometh out unless thou hast to."

John inhaled loudly and said with a deep, threatening growl, "Telleth me nay falsehoods knave. Thou taketh me but for a fool."

"Father," Jane interrupted, "let me speak with him."

"If't be true that thou art mine brother then thee would knoweth a gross amount about me, would thee not? Telleth me something that only I would knoweth."

John thought for a moment and then said,

"Thee wast attacked by Christopher, that gent didst try to taketh off thy robes but he wast frightened off by Copper, our horse. Thou didst say I should ne'er mention it again or that gent might telleth the Council. I saw it Jane, 'twas last night, in the stable yonder."

Mary and Jack looked at Jane waiting for confirmation from her that what this strange boy was saying was nothing more than a made up story. Their daughter would have told them if something as shameful as this had happened to her. Jane however, looked shocked. How could a stranger know something so deep and personal about her? Her lips began to quiver and she slowly stepped away from John, her eyes flitting nervously between the faces of her mother and father.

"How didst thee knoweth about Christopher?" she stammered.

"Jane, is this true? Didst that boy do those things to thee?" her father yelled. "Telleth me Jane, didst that disgusting knave do this to thee?"

Jane looked at the ground, her cheeks flushed with shame and her eyes welling up with tears. She glanced up at her father and sobbed,

"Aye that gent didst, that gent tooketh mine robes off and didst something to me. He hurteth me father, that gent hurteth me between mine legs. I wast on mine own, I wast afraid."

"I will killeth that knave!" Jack screamed and he snatched his axe from the side. Anger glowered in his eyes; he would kill any man who had caused harm to his family.

"Father thou must not!" exclaimed John.

"Father? I am not thy father! Wend witch, wend!"

"Calm down Jack," Mary said, stepping between the two men and wrapping an arm around her husband. "Calm thyself Jack. Sit thee down and we can speaketh more."

Jack took Mary's arm from his waist and started pacing angrily up and down the length of the kitchen. He picked up one of the wooden chairs and slammed it down, making splinters of wood fly out, adding to the pile of mess on the floor. Slumping down in the chair he gripped the axe tightly in his hand and growled,

268

"Passeth me the cider. God knows I needeth something. Passeth me t now!"

Mary quickly grabbed a bottle of cider and passed it to her husband. He snatched it from her and immediately drank its contents.

John remained silent. Everything he had lived for, understood and experienced, wasn't there anymore and it was a strange feeling. He knew there was no point feeling melancholy, not at the moment anyway, he had to try and push his feelings aside and concentrate on convincing them that what he was saying was true. If he didn't, he dreaded to think what would happen to them in the invasion.

He looked at Jack and said,

"There art more, father. The twins, the Fleming twins, those gents wast with thee that night, were they not Jane?" He turned to now look at Jane. "They wast helping thee in the stable. Their father came to the house looking for them and he asked wherefore those gents had not cometh home. That gent wast filled with worry. He will return in the morning, before the guards cometh for the taxes."

"Jack, methinks the knave beest telling the truth," Mary interrupted. "Three guards didst come yesterday eventide and those gents didst ask for thee. They sayeth not what 'twas about, but it be true that they art returning tomorrow."

"I speaketh nay lies," John said, "The guards art coming and they wilt killeth thee father. They wilt killeth first thee, father and then they wilt slit the throat of mine mother."

Jack put the empty bottle of cider down and turned his attention to John. These stories were far-fetched, yet some of what this boy was saying rang true. Perhaps it was worth hearing more of what he had to say.

"And what about the twins lad? Where art those folk?"

"Father, those gents art dead, they hath been murdered."

Jack jumped up out of his chair and with his axe still firmly gripped in one hand he grabbed John by the other hand and dragged him towards the door.

"Where art those gents knave, showeth me whither those gents art. If't beest true what thou sayeth then those gents should beest thither now. Showeth me knave, leadeth me to those folk. "

"Father, I cannot stayeth hither, I hast to wend, but thee can findeth those folk for thyself. Those gents art by the large oak tree, the one that towers above the others. They art thither naked, but beest warned they art without limbs. 'Tis the work of the Greys, those gents didst this evil deed. They hast worked their evil on most all folk in town and now those gents hast what they doth need. They art coming."

John strode confidently out of the house and headed to the woodland. He had done all he could do for the moment. It was time to go back.

He cleared his mind of all emotional attachments to his family and allowed the image of the safe haven to fill the space instead. But there wasn't enough detail. He couldn't remember where the house was exactly, or any of the small details of the room they'd found refuge in. He switched his focus to Rose and tried to capture the image of her beautiful blonde hair, the way her smile lit up her entire face and that distinct sweet feminine smell that followed here everywhere. He called out to her in his mind to try and make contact. "Rose can thee heareth me? I need to findeth mine way back, Rose art thee thither?"

He waited in the hope of a response. A sign. Anything at all to show his friend had heard him. That she could help him. But nothing came.

Feeling deflated, he looked towards the dense thicket of the forest. The light was fading fast, he should get moving. He would keep trying to get hold of Rose or Apex, but in the meantime he needed to try and make his way back on his own.

Suddenly he heard a voice calling out to him,

"Lad wait, wait!"

He looked in the direction of the voice and saw his family pushing their way through the undergrowth. They were out of breath and red faced from trying to catch up with him. When they got closer he noticed the relief on their faces and it filled him with deep joy knowing that they were concerned about him after all. Jack had a large satchel hanging from his shoulder. It was bursting from the seams with their salvaged possessions. His axe hung from his waist. Mary and Jane were also carrying bags and he could see the tops of bottles of beer and cider poking out from the top of them.

"Wherefore hast thee followed me?" John asked.

"Lad, we knoweth not what is going on, but thee talketh some sense. We saw whither thou wast walking and bethought it best to cometh with thee. I hath found the twins lad, and like thee hath said, those gents wast in a bad state. I hast never before seen sights such as these, 'tis most strange and we art willing to trust in thee."

John felt torn. On the one hand he felt so much relief that his family had finally seen sense and yet he couldn't let them to go with him, it was far too dangerous.

"I am most sorry father, but thee cannot cometh with me. 'Tis far too dangerous for thee. I hath lost you once, I willt not loseth thee for a second time. Wend and findeth some place to hide and be sure to stayeth thither."

"Thee hath said things that nay man would knoweth. And if't be true what thou speaks of, that these 'Greys' shall invade anon, then 'tis best we follow thee."

"Thou understandeth not father, I hast to receiveth back to the other two, those gents need mine help. I should ne'er hast cometh to see thee."

"We beest nay trouble, I give thee mine word. I hath fought in many a battle, so I know…"

His sentence was cut off as the ground began to shudder once more. The tremors felt different this time though, almost as if the vibrations were passing through their very souls. They clung desperately onto each other trying to stabilize themselves as the vibrations grew more violent, but they were too powerful. One by one they lost their balance and fell to the ground, screaming out as the trees began bending wildly, like a bow being pulled back before releasing its arrow. Flocks of startled birds flew up into the darkening sky, their terrified squawks adding to the ominous atmosphere that was brewing. Loud cracking noises and eerie high pitched creaking sounds filled the air as tree trunks started splitting in two and their earth covered roots emerged from the ground like corpses rising from the dead.

"Make haste, we have to moveth!" John cried, motioning to his family to join arms and hold on to one another. "It doth look much safer over yonder in that clearing, quick we must wend!"

They held onto each other's hands and ran, frantically dodging and ducking out of the way of swinging branches and flying debris, until they made it to the large open field.

"There art nay trees hither, we should beest safe," John gasped. He felt certain this was the Greys, it was almost as if he could sense their presence. Shielding his eyes with his hand, he squinted up at the ring of light that was shining faintly through the orange haze of the sun and there it was. It looked like liquid, a strange watery like substance that rippled, as if someone had thrown a stone across the surface of a lake, its rings expanding infinitely outwards.

"Something is wrong," said John, "Something is happening."

"Shh! I can heareth something," said Jane, putting a finger to her lips.

They held their breaths, anticipating something bad, waiting for the possibility of an invasion.

"Hark, doth sound like thunder," Jane whispered, as an eerie rumbling sound filled the air. They glanced nervously around the edges of the field, straining to see into the devastated copse and trying to work out where the source of the noise was coming from.

"Over thither!" Jack shouted pointing his finger at an adjacent field. "Look, over thither!" Approximately two hundred metres from where they stood were a collection of shapes that seemed to be moving together.

"It doth look like stags and deer, hundreds of the beasts! Behold, there art bulls too! Mine lord, behold the birds, there art thousands of those folk also!" Jack exclaimed.

The rumbling sound had now grown so loud that they could barely hear each other and as the raging stampede of animals intensified and the dark mass of birds gathered overhead, John was convinced he could make out the name 'Ema' in among the squawking. Suddenly the flock of birds swooped down upon the group, screaming 'Ema' so loudly it made them drop to the ground, clutching at their ears in pain. The birds seized the opportunity and launched themselves at the family pecking and scratching at their bodies and faces. Jack desperately tried to reach for his axe whilst at the same time batting away the beaks of the crazed birds. But it was no use, there were far too many of them.

"Receiveth these beasts off of me!" Jane and Mary both screamed, frantically waving their arms around in a futile attempt to stop the birds from attacking them.

As his parents and sister struggled to fend off the birds, John crouched nearby, completely unharmed. Strangely, the birds weren't attacking him. It was almost as if they were afraid, as if they knew he had powers and were purposefully avoiding him. Rather than physically fighting off the birds, he concentrated on using his mental strength to protect his family.

He closed his eyes and allowed his mind to be consumed with birds. Hundreds, thousands, millions of them swooped in and he visualised grabbing them with force and hurling them towards the charging animals. Like bullets, he fired each one at the advancing herd, striking and then penetrating the bulls and stags. The force of the blows struck the beasts down dead on impact, their bodies exploding and sending showers of fresh blood and flesh across the parched field.

John opened his eyes to see what he had done and although it had helped, it wasn't enough. They were still coming. He shouted to his family to follow him, but they just stood there, their faces devoid of expression. They were covered in blood and he realised that their eyes and ears had been removed. He lurched forward and vomited on the ground.

He sat up and wiped his mouth. The three of them slowly walked towards him addressing him with a harrowing monotone wail,

"All dreamers wilt beest killed, thee cannot terminate us. We wilt findeth Ema and at which hour we doth, thee wilt all beest destroyed."

John immediately jumped up and started running away from them. He had no idea what was happening, but he knew he needed to get away from them. They were no longer the family he knew and loved. Without looking back, he ran haphazardly through the forest, stumbling over the fallen trees. When he had reached a safe distance he risked looking back to make sure that he had lost them. As he did so he ran straight into a thick branch, striking his head and knocking him unconscious.

The snow covered everything in a beautiful blanket of white, but it was cold, so very cold. He didn't know where he was. It looked oddly familiar, yet entirely alien at the same time. He looked around, slowly adjusting to his surroundings, when he saw a girl that looked like Rose. She was with a lady, who he presumed must be her mother. They were walking towards a house. Wherefore hast I seen this before? he thought, furiously racking his brains in search of the memory. He realised with a jolt of fear what was about to happen and desperately tried to get her attention.

"Rose, Rose thee must not wend home, that gent wilt hurt thee and thy mother!"

He hurried after them, entering the house and going through to the lounge.

"Nay Rose, sitteth not thither! That gent wilt hurt thee both. He is coming, make haste and get thee off that chair."

John saw the stocky outline of Shaun enter the room and the story that Rose had told him began to unfold before his eyes.

"Receiveth off that lady, thou art evil, taketh thy hands off that lady! Rose, Rose hide someplace or that gent wilt receiveth thee – aye go in that chamber, thou will beest safe in thither - lock the door!"

The vision of Rose began to fade, turning into a dark oppressive feeling and he felt an unsettling presence in his midst. In the distance he could just make out a small area of light, it was only faint, but he could see something approaching.

As it got closer John's heartbeat increased in intensity, sensing the evil that was about to strike.

"Who art thou? Thou stayeth away from me," he shouted.

A slick liquid substance slid its way up to John and stared at him with haunting expressionless eyes.

John felt the thing trying to penetrate his thoughts, delving deep within his soul and there was nothing he could do to stop it.

It began to chant in his mind,

"CHATTI CARTOM DESTRUCT ORMATI!"

John awoke from his concussion with a shudder. He felt confused and disorientated and his head throbbed with pain. He carefully eased himself up to stand, using the trunk of a tree as support. The blood rushed to his head and a dizzying sense of panic surged through him as he remembered what had happened. Despite the early morning light, shadows lurked in the trees and he could hear the rumbling again. It was growing perilously closer and the bushes and trees around him began to shudder and shake. Although he knew what was coming he needed to look ahead so that he could work out a way to escape.

He closed his eyes and envisaged a small bush in the distance. The bush started flickering and all of a sudden it was on fire. The dry twigs caught almost immediately and the flames licked their way over to the bush next to it. It wasn't long before a large section of the woodland was ablaze with firelight.

Thousands and thousands of animals; deer, bulls, rabbits and foxes started leaping, trotting and walking towards him. But their movements were disjointed and rigid, as if they were mechanical. Some were scratching and biting each other, whereas others continued heading towards John, undeterred by the raging fire that consumed them on their way. John set to work immediately. He didn't have long. He imagined recklessly flinging them away from him, their blazing fur creating beastly comets across the sky. But it still wasn't enough to stop them in their pursuit. If anything, their pace and persistence only increased. He forced his mind to imagine as many beasts as he could, their bodies tossed into trees and then slamming to the ground. There were still too many of them. He couldn't fight this battle on his own. John screamed with a frustration and fear. Backing away from the mass of advancing animals, he focused his thoughts in a last ditch attempt to save himself from certain death. Using all his power he ordered his mind to grab one of the deer and he hurled it a herd of rabid bulls. They tumbled and rolled into one another, like a ball striking the pins in a bowling alley. He heard their crazed moans as they somehow managed to right themselves and continued to advance. They leapt onto him, smothering and engulfing his whole being. All he could do was protect his face with his arms and wait for the inevitable. He screamed as the pain of a thousand heavy weights pressed down on him. And then suddenly he felt a pull from behind. A strong force was tearing him away from the horror, ripping him from the animals. The landscape started rippling and his field of vision became distorted. The animals slowly started to blur and fade out at the edges, their bestial cries ebbing away, until there was nothing was left.

Chapter 34

Aylesbury

The room was small. It contained a dirty unmade bed and a wooden side cabinet, which had a bible placed on top. In the centre of the room was an enormous wooden table that dominated the cramped space, making it feel even smaller. On the top of the table was a quill, a cracked porcelain bowl containing some rotting fruit, a large mirror and a collection of very strange looking dolls. Apex turned the dolls around so that they faced the other way; they gave him the creeps. He sat down on one of the wooden chairs and stared at his reflection in the mirror, wondering how on earth he had got here. Despite already meticulously touching the table and dolls, squeezing the soft, fetid fruit between his fingers, and even fondling Sarah, he still wasn't convinced that this was real. However, real or not, it didn't change anything. Rose was still dead and John was still nowhere to be found. He was alone, in a different century, challenged with saving the world. It was shit.

Sarah was humming to herself as she sorted through a pile of clothes.

"It fits thee sir, 'tis a little tight but it willt do for now. Thee never knoweth, the Queen may dress thee in something much finer," she said with a smile.

"Man, I look like a frilly pansy! This is really embarrassing. Are you sure guys actually dress like this?" he said tugging at the sleeves.

"Sir, only the wealthy wear robes made of the finest cotton such as these."

Apex raised his eyebrows in mock surprise.

"Listen, you don't need to call me sir, or master, or whatever, just call me Apex OK?"

"But, thou art the lord, thou art the saviour," Sarah responded, kneeling down before him.

"You don't need to kneel either. Just talk to me like a normal person."

She remained on her knees and rested her hands lightly on the tops of his feet. She muttered a short prayer to herself, before standing to adjust his attire a little more.

"I still can't believe Rose is dead", he said sadly, "I need to bury her, I can't just leave her like this. She deserves a proper burial."

"Aye my lord. Thou art not to blame, 'twas but bad fortune thy friend wast shot. That gent ne'er had a valorous aim with a pistol. Mine master hath a shovel in the kitchen."

Apex stood up from the chair to get a better look at what he was wearing in the mirror. The outfit was black and it had a stiff white collar that encircled his neck. It was so tight he felt as if he could barely breathe and he tried to loosen it with his fingers. The long hose were just as tight; they felt as if they were going to cut his blood circulation off at any moment. No matter how much he adjusted, pulled and twisted, the clothes didn't feel right, but this was not the time to be worried about what he looked like. He needed to focus on burying Rose and then getting to the Queen's Palace. Apex ushered Sarah out of the room and they walked back to the kitchen.

"Man, I can hardly walk in these, let alone run!" he said with a grimace. As he got to the entrance of the kitchen he paused, staring in bewilderment at the empty table.

"What the fuck! Where's she gone? We left her body on the table, where's Rose gone?"

Before Sarah had a chance to reply, the building began to violently shudder and the beams
above their heads started to crack and splinter. Instinctively, they shielded their heads with their hands to protect themselves from the huge chunks of stone that were falling from the ceiling.

"Quick! We've got to get out of here before it crushes us," Apex spluttered, as he choked on the dust from the falling debris. "Quickly, grab Jake, we have to get out."

Sarah quickly picked up her baby and followed Apex outside. As she did so, her foot caught on the threshold of the door making her lose her balance and she stumbled across the garden. The earth continued to wildly shake and the roof tiles and parts of the chimney fell to the ground, smashing and narrowly missing them. The building gave one last almighty cracking sound, before collapsing into a pile of rubble, sending a huge mushroom cloud of dust shooting up into the sky. Standing from a safe distance, Sarah clutched her baby protectively to her chest. Apex laughed.

"Tell me sir, what doth amuse thou so?" Sarah asked angrily. Considering they'd escaped death by mere seconds, she found it very strange that he was taking it so lightheartedly.

"The irony of it, the fucking irony!" Apex said, shaking his head. "It just keeps fucking happening, doesn't it."

"I understandeth not."

"Clichéd and utter bullshit, that's what it is. I mean seriously, this shit only happens in the movies, not actual fucking real life! Anyway, we're safe that's the main thing. But what I really want to know is, where the fuck is Rose?"

Chapter 35

Robert, Paul, Captain Peters, and his army of men arrived at the Aylesbury barracks. Under the Earl's strict orders, they had not stopped to rest on their journey and fatigue was starting to set in. Regardless of this, Robert marched powerfully towards the main entrance. He was greeted by a rather pathetic looking soldier, who spoke with a stammering lisp, made worse by his nervousness at speaking to a man of such authority and with such a reputation.

"Whither hast thee looked?" Robert brusquely demanded, dismounting his horse and straightening his jacket.

"Um… w-w-well, we h-h-hasth been th-th-thearching thir… b-b-b-but..." the soldier stuttered.

"But what? Make haste soldier, spitteth thine words out!"

"The g-g-guard th thir; those g-g-genth do not w-w-wanteth to befall to thith w-w-witchcraft. They art f-f-frightened thir, those gents art afraid."

"Frightened? Thou telleth them that any man whom doth not help find these witches, wilt see the hangman's noose anon. Dost thou understand?"

The soldier nodded gingerly and muttered "Aye thir." He saluted and then quickly marched into the barracks.

"What art thee thinking sir?" asked Paul hesitantly.

"That we must search every household until we findeth these witches. And whence we findeth them, we shallt tell them that the Queen is too old and that she is a danger to our empire. We will offer up great riches as a reward for them killing the Queen. They will beest powerless to resist, such is the nature of these evil beings. And once the Queen is dead, we can seize power Paul. We can rule this country and make t most wondrous again!"

"Dost thou really believe thou can take power with such ease my lord?" Captain Peters asked. "The palace is guarded by hundreds of men, all fighting to protect their Queen. 'Twill be nay easy fight sir."

"Thou art entitled to your opinion Captain, but as your Commander I order thee to obey me. Thy soldiers and these dimwits from Aylesbury art to cometh with me and seize power from the Queen. Dost thou understand?"

The Earl glared at Captain Peters. He reminded him of someone he had once known, someone close to him, but he couldn't quite put his finger on who it was. He looked at this tall, slender man, taking in the detail of his bright blue, gold tasselled jacket and the impeccable stitching on the seams of his neatly pressed trousers. His long pointed nose, goatee and huge moustache that curled up at the ends were all so distinctive and it frustrated him that he couldn't place whereabouts he knew him from.

Captain Peters nodded reluctantly and turned to look at the doors of the barracks, out of which came a long line of terrified looking men.

"Good, I am glad thee hath all seen sense. There is nay room for cowards in the Queen's army," said Robert, as he looked each soldier up and down. He randomly pointed at one of them and barked,

"Thee lad, cometh hither."

The young soldier in question looked startled at being picked out by the Earl and he turned to his comrades thinking that perhaps he had made a mistake.

"Aye thee, make haste, cometh hither."

The soldier composed himself and brushed his blue uniform down with his hand. He cleared his throat and nervously stepped forward.

"What art thee afraid of lad? What art so terrifying about these witches, pray tell?"

"Methinks 'tis the powers sir, those gents can rip thee apart with their minds. Captain Sutherland is a stout sir, he doth not wend down easily, but thee hath heard what hast becometh of him."

The Earl rubbed his chin and then clapped his hands together sharply. "Men, I wanteth all thy attention. Hither is a lad who doth allow his fear of witches to control his mind. I wilt now showeth you who thee should really beest frightened of…"

He turned his back on the soldiers and took a small mirror out of the satchel that hung from his saddle. He stared lovingly at himself, smoothing his eyebrows and straightening his beard, before shifting his gaze so that the soldiers could see his reflection in the mirror. With his spare hand, he withdrew his pistol from its holster, turned and pointed it directly at the young soldiers head, before pulling the trigger. The soldier fell to the ground and a loud gasp rang out from the soldiers.

Robert looked at them sternly and they immediately straightened themselves up. They knew better than to question his actions. If he could shoot one soldier, he wouldn't hesitate to execute any one of them too.

"Let that be a lesson to thee all. If any of thee dare to disobey me or try to flee, thee wilt end up like this sorry excuse of a soldier. Dost thee understand?"

"Aye sir!" the men replied in chorus.

"There art approximately three hundred of us men and thither art five hundred dwellings. I wanteth thee to travel in groups of three and if't thee discover these witches thee must sendeth those folk to me. I wilt giveth the group of soldiers who findeth the witches mine very own cellar of wine, is that understood?"

"Aye sir!"

Robert headed towards the houses and the soldiers marched behind. They barged their way into any house that was still standing, violently kicking the doors open. The residents screamed in terror as the soldiers ransacked their homes. After searching for several hours, a soldier spotted two figures in the distance, one of whom matched the description of the fugitive.

"Over thither sir, t looks like the black servant!" he called out to the Earl. "That gent appeareth to beest with a mistress sir."

"Flank them, they cannot get away!" shouted Robert excitedly.

The small army split in to three groups, two of which promptly diverted on either side of Apex. Robert and the remaining group meanwhile, gathered in the centre until they were close enough to block Apex and Sarah's route.

"Oh for fucks sake man!" Apex yelled angrily, "Why can I not just do something without these dumb asses getting in the way all the time?" He looked at the small army in front of him and then looked left and right. They were completely surrounded.

The Earl marched forward, a triumphant grin plastered across his face.

"I am most pleased to hath found thee at last. Tell me servant, wherefore art thy fellow wiches?"

"Look, I ain't no fucking servant and I ain't no witch either, what the fuck are you on about?"

Apex turned to Sarah and muttered, "I'm seriously gonna punch someone if they keep calling me servant." He turned back to the Earl and said, "My, as you put it, 'fellow witches' are either missing or dead."

Robert stared at Apex with a perplexed expression.

"What language art thee speaking servant? It doth sound like English, yet 'tis not the normal English of our land."

"Look bro, I'm getting pretty tired of having to explain myself, so spare me the time please. And seriously can you stop calling me servant. My name is Apex, alright?"

"Aye, of course, Apex and please accept mine sympathies with regard to thine comrades. However, my men and I hath heard all about thee and what thee can do and I hast some valorous news for thee."

"Oh really, what 'valorous' news could you possibly have? I take it by 'valorous' you mean good news? Shit, good news doesn't exist in this fucking time zone, so I can't wait to hear this," Apex responded sarcastically. "Actually bro, I ain't got time for this shit. I've got way bigger problems to deal with right now, so could you please just let me get on with what I was sent here to do?"

"I wilt alloweth thee to wend freely Apex, but thee must first doth something for me."

"What could you possibly want from me?"

The Earl dismounted his horse and walked over to Apex. He leaned in close and in a hushed tone whispered in Apex's ear,

"The Queen doth request a meeting with thee servant, sorry I mean Apex. She hath heard all about thy powers and desires to understandeth how thee do't. The Queen hath long hadst a fascination with all things magic and witchcraft and she is very excited about meeting with thee."

"Well actually that's pretty handy, because I need to see the Queen anyway," he paused, "but what do *you* want from me?"

"The Queen hath been around for some time now, Apex. She is, well… how do I putteth this… the lady is getting old and her decision making hath become, shall I sayeth, erratic."

"Right, so what exactly are you asking me to do?"

"I can giveth thee mine entire possessions, thee wilt hast thy freedom and beest a wealthy gent in the process. I may even giveth thee an officer's title, what sayest thou?"

"Yeah that all sounds good, but you haven't answered my question yet, what the actual fuck do you want me to do?"

"All I ask of thee is to killeth that lady."

"Are you shitting me? You want me to kill your Queen? And what happens if I don't? What happens if I let her know about your little plot to kill her off eh, what then?"

"Then I wilt returneth to the Queen myself and I shall explain to her that this wast thy feeble attempt at escape. The lady is more likely to trust her good, loyal and trusted friend over some black servant she hath never met before. And if the lady is in a particularly foul humour, then she may well execute both thee and that lovely wench and baby over yonder. And I am certain thee would not wish that to befall, would thee?"

Apex stared at the pompous man, taking in the detail of his magnificent clothing and the elegant feathers that protruded from his black leather cap. He was clearly a man of power, but something didn't feel right. From his experience so far it seemed as though no one was trustworthy in this time zone. He'd even had his doubts about Sarah and she wasn't asking him to kill someone. And anyway, he wasn't a murderer. It was ridiculous to even think about accepting the Earl's offer. He was just an average guy who'd been landed with the task of saving the planet. He was the good guy. He wasn't someone who killed people when they hadn't done anything to him.

About to hurl abuse at the Earl, he stopped himself when he noticed an embroidered image of a woman on the lapel of his jacket. She had red hair on top of which sat a crown and was wearing a luxurious robe.

"Hold on, is that the Queen on your clothes?"

"Aye, 'tis standard for a noble to showeth his devotion to the Queen. I would liketh that to change, mind thee. I wanteth not to be forced to show devotion to such an unstable wench."

"OK, you have a deal. But, I want to travel without you guys following me; you lot really piss me off. Plus, I'm taking my girl and her baby with me. I don't trust any of you, so she comes or you've got no deal."

"I can agree to the girl and the baby, but I can alloweth thee not to travel alone. I needeth to know thou art a gent of thy word. Mine soldiers must escort thee to the Queen's residence. They will cause thee nay trouble."

"Alright, but if they piss me off or even think about touching Sarah and her baby, I will kill them all, you got that?"

The Earl nodded in agreement and then bellowed loudly to his men, "We hast come to an agreement. This gent hath agreed to meet with the Queen. I need some men to escort them. Do I hath any volunteers?"

There was an awkward silence. They were all too frightened by the prospect of spending time alone with this witch. Who knows what he might do to them. The Earl gave a disappointed sigh and yet again removed his pistol and began cleaning it with a piece of rag. "I repeat, do I hath any volunteers?"

The soldiers looked at each other, hoping and praying that someone would raise their hand and take the pressure off of everybody else. Eventually, a soldier stepped forward, which triggered several others to do the same.

"Good. Ten of thee shall suffice. We will meet thee at the Palace, where I expect thee to hath done the deed. Men, give the servant, I mean Apex, two horses. We can alloweth them not to travel by foot."

The Earl mounted his horse and looked down at Apex, grinning like an excited child. He straightened his back and pointed to the barracks with his pistol, signalling for the small army to follow him. Apex watched as they trotted off through the long, dry grass. The soldiers that were left stood frozen to the spot. Now that their leader had gone, they were terrified about what Apex might do. But Apex was in no mood to play games, he needed to make sure there were some rules in place before they left.

"OK guys, there's a few rules you need to know before we leave: don't piss me off, don't talk to me and if any of you even think about touching Sarah, then I will kill you all. Is that understood? Oh yeah and one more thing, don't call me a fucking servant, OK?"

A deep rumbling sound echoed in the distance. Apex and Sarah froze. They didn't know what the noise was, but it didn't sound good. And it was getting louder. Instinctively, everyone turned to look in the direction of the noise. There was a huge black mass spread across the length and width of two of the large fields. It looked like a dark pulsating blanket covering the land and it was swiftly moving towards the group. As the sound grew louder and the mass drew nearer, panic set in among the ranks. Apex screwed his eyes up to try and make out what it was and he saw what looked like thousands upon thousands of rats. He blinked and squinted again. It wasn't just rats, there were millions of animals; wild boar, stags, dogs, all weaving in and out of each other. The townspeople had raced to their doors to see what was going on, but the unfortunate ones who lived at the far end of town had no chance. The tide of creatures washed over them, swallowing everything in its path. Men, women and children screamed in horror as they tried to shake off the rats, which were scratching and biting at their eyes. Bodies disappeared beneath the swarm and the only evidence of human life were the jets of blood and flesh that burst out like volcanic fissures.

Sarah looked in horror as the hideous scene played out in front of her. Her brain refused to accept what her eyes were seeing. She screamed hysterically. Grabbing her by the shoulders, Apex looked deep into her eyes and said,

"Sarah, you need to get out of here. Get on the horse and go. I will find you, I promise. Now take Jake and go!"

"But Apex…" she protested.

"JUST FUCKING GO!"

Clutching Jake to her chest, she hoisted herself up onto the horse and grabbed the reins. She galloped off, glancing back at Apex as she did so.

The soldiers were still glued to the spot in shock. There was no way they'd be able to out run the animals and just like that the battalion of beasts was upon them. Dogs jumped up, digging their claws deep within the flesh of their victims, and the rats sunk their sharp teeth into their eyeballs and ripped off their ears with one vicious bite. Agonising screams filled the air, as the men sunk to the ground in pain. Their minds became filled with a deranged and deafening high-pitched voice that said,

"Tell us your name, tell us where he is."

Apex sprinted away as fast as he could. Sweat dripped off of him and his whole body shook with fear. Adrenaline was kicking in. It was fight or flight. He'd done it before, with Sarah's master, so he knew he had it in him. But that was just one man. This was way bigger.

He just had to concentrate…

OK this is for you Rose and John. Bring it on you motherfuckers!

Apex visualised the remnants of a collapsed building that lay in a pile next to him. Lifting the beams, the brickwork and the hundreds of tiny solid fragments, he used his force to effortlessly levitate them in a long horizontal line, aiming them at the massive stampede that faced him. He flung the objects as hard as he could, each missile hitting and smashing its target into smithereens. Rats flew up into the air like fireworks, creating a black mist in the sky as they exploded. Deer, horses and dogs detonated like bombs as each piece of debris struck

them. Their heads and body parts blew apart and landed in bloodied
splatters on the ground. But it wasn't enough. There were far too many
animals for Apex to control. The black blanket of rats swarmed over
him, consuming his body and face. He let out a muffled scream, but it
was no use, there was no one there to help him. As the air around him
grew thinner, he struggled to breathe. Fighting off his panic, he tried to
focus. This was his only hope of getting free. He imagined the rats being
thrown from him, opening up tiny gaps and allowing the air to flood
back into his lungs. But the rats were strong and just as the air hole had
opened, it closed over again, suffocating him once more beneath the
rampaging rats. A deep searing pain penetrated the sides of his head
and his chest began to cave in from the pressure. He thought of Sarah
and how beautiful she was. He pictured her beautiful face and her
piercing green eyes. He made the image of her so strikingly vivid in his
mind.

It was time.

Take me to her now…

Everything around him stood still, as though time and space had
suddenly stopped. The load bearing down on him eased slightly and his
breathing became more regulated. The screams and scratching noises
had reduced to an eerie silence and the creatures started to drift apart,
slowly increasing in speed, gathering momentum. Now he was free of
them and he was rushing past trees and fields, the sweet rush of air
pushing him forward, taking him to Sarah.

And then he saw her, galloping ahead on her horse, fleeing for her
life. As if sensing his presence, she looked at him and then shook her
head, unwilling to believe that he was really there. She pulled hard on

the reigns and the horse skidded to a halt. Gazing in wonder at Apex, she couldn't understand how it was possible. How had a man managed to out run a horse? Her bewilderment quickly turned to joy and dismounting the horse she ran over to embrace him.

"What is happening master? Why were those rats attacking? And how didst thou findeth me?" she gushed.

"It's the Greys, they are able to possess any living organism. Well, that's what I was told anyway." He held her hands and looked into her eyes. "I told you I would come for you," he said softly. "Now listen, I have an idea. Calcus told me, he's some invisible dude from another time zone by the way, that I can manipulate matter. I know it's difficult for you to understand, but basically it means I can travel through space and take you with me."

"I hast nay mind what thee mean?"

"Don't worry about it for now, I'll explain when it's all over. Just keep holding my hands, don't let go whatever happens, and trust me. I'm beginning to get good at this shit."

Apex took a deep breath and closed his eyes. He imagined the Queen's face; that same face he had seen on the Earl's jacket. He pictured her as vividly as he could, from her stern gaunt expression to her beautiful pearled, diamond earrings Once he had captured her image as accurately as he could, he turned his focus to Sarah and Jake, visualising them travelling alongside him. Again the trees whizzed past them, and then buildings and people too, all silently rushing past. Sarah couldn't believe what she was experiencing. It was somehow terrifying and yet relaxing at the same time, like an intense euphoria.

Apex opened his eyes and quickly looked over to Sarah. She looked back at him, her eyes filled with shock and admiration.

"Thou truly art the saviour," she gasped breathlessly, leaning in to give him a hug.

A loud booming voice interrupted their embrace.

"Who art thee, how hast thee appeared before me like this? Thee art the witch, thee art the one!"

Apex stepped forward and asked,

"Are you the Queen?"

"Oh mine lord, 'tis a most exciting time! Whither hast thee travelled from? How didst thee receiveth hither? I hast so many questions for thee; I knoweth not from whence to begin?" the Queen giggled nervously, like a shy schoolgirl.

"Look lady…" Apex began, but then he stopped, wincing in pain as Sarah poked him in the ribs and muttered, "Thy majesty, thou hast to sayeth majesty!"

"Oh right, yes of course, soz your majesty. Well look, some shit is going down that you need to know about, and I mean some seriously bad shit. Your land is currently under attack by this group of grey aliens. I need your help to find a guy called Ema so that we can try and put a stop to this. Can you help me?"

The Queen stepped from out of the shadows and drew closer to Apex. She stared in wonderment at the man, woman and baby who had magically appeared before her.

What strange language thou speaketh; 'tis like English, but different."

"I live in a country called America, in a place called South Detroit, so it's an English American accent. I'm from the future, the year twenty two hundred to be precise."

The Queen started walking round him, looking him up and down.

"How didst thee receiveth hither? I hath never seen a witch doth that before!"

"Look your majesty, I'm not a witch. I was sent here from my future time zone to find a guy called Ema. I need you to help me find him."

"Please taketh a seat, I wilt receiveth thee some refreshments, thee must be thirsty. We canst talk more about finding this…"she hesitated, "my most humble of apologies, what didst thou sayeth his name was?"

"Ema. His name's Ema, and apparently he's a God; he created our universe. I need to find him before the Greys get to him. Seriously your majesty, we're completely screwed unless we find this God dude."

"My dear servant thither is only one God," the Queen laughed, "our lord Jesus Christ."

She sat down in her chair and marked the sign of the cross with her left hand, before closing her eyes and muttering a short prayer.

Apex sighed, he didn't have time to go over this again, "Right I've had enough, you people need to start listening to me. The Greys are on their way and I have no clue as to how far it is from there to here, which means we need to find this Ema now!"

"Thou must speaketh not to the Queen like that!" Sarah said quietly, giving him another nudge in the ribs.

She looked at the tired, old lady sitting in the chair.

"Mine most humble apologies thy majesty, mine friend hither is not like this of norm, he hath been through a torrid time. His lady friend hath kicked the bucket and his other friend hath disappeared."

"'Tis fine, thee needeth not to apologise," replied the Queen nonchalantly.

Her face winced with pain as she tried to shift her body into a more comfortable position in the chair.

"Mine wretched back. Mine pain hath becometh a living hell for me," she groaned. "Thankfully I hast some wonderful servants who helpeth me and some most amazing healing herbs."

She picked up an ornate bell from the side table and gave it a gentle shake.

Almost immediately a man entered the room, his head was held high and his back straight. His face was a pasty white, livened up by his bright red cheeks and a small ginger beard. It looked as if his features had been painted on by a child. He was wearing a smart burgundy uniform, which had an elegantly embroidered sash hanging from his shoulders. He approached the Queen and bowed gracefully.

"Aye thy majesty?"

He did a double take when he noticed the Queen was not alone. How had these people got in without his knowledge? The baby started to cry and Sarah tried to calm him down, but he was hungry and nothing else would pacify him.

"Thou may retire in the next bedroom and rest with the little man. I shalt talketh with this special person alone."

Sarah curtsied and carried Jake through to the adjoining room.

"Henry I needeth thee to writeth a message and sendeth t out to each and every person in the kingdom. I needeth thee to asketh whither they knoweth of a gent called... " she hesitated and looked at Apex.

"Ema, a guy called Ema your majesty," Apex answered for her.

"Thy majesty, art thee certain thee art well with this gentleman?"

"Of course I am Henry, now please leaveth us in peace."

"Aye thy majesty."

Henry looked at Apex suspiciously and then took several steps backwards before turning to exit the room as instructed.

"I am most curious as to how thee didst findeth me, Apex?"

"I have this power that allows me to travel through time and space. All I have to do is imagine the place or person and I can travel there. I've only just learnt it really. My friends are much better at it, well they were," he said sadly. "Seriously though, it's fucking awesome. I can walk through objects too. Do you want to see?"

"Aye, aye most definitely!" the Queen shrieked, clapping her hands together excitedly.

"OK, well what do you want me to do?"

"Dost thou spy mine pipe over thither on the mantel, above the fire. Passeth me t without thee moving from that chair."

Apex looked at the Hath. He focused on the image of the roaring fire with its flickering flames and intense white, hot core. He pictured the walls and pictures that hung on each side of the fireplace, concentrating on every tiny little detail. Using all his mind power, he imagined the small clay pipe levitating and then slowly moving towards him.

Apex opened his eyes, expecting the Queen to be clapping her hands in admiration of his magic.

But she wasn't.

She looked disappointed.

"Perhaps I hast been wasting mine time with thee Apex, for this is nay magic. Maybe 'tis time thee and thy friend leaveth."

"Look lady, this shit is real and it does work. I just need to feel it, you know, like I have to fear for my life or something. I'm not so good at doing it on request. I need to be really angry or scared or something."

"Thou art a time waster and I am too old for timewasters mine boy. Mine guards shalt escort thee off mine premises. GUAR...."

"Stop, look I just need to be in the right frame of mind OK. Anyway, you shouldn't smoke that shit, tobacco's well bad for you."

"I wilt not beest spoken to in that tone! I smoke cannabis to helpeth with mine pains. 'Tis not tobacco; tobacco is for the commoners"

"Shit, really? Oh my God, why didn't you say so!" Apex said excitedly.

He rubbed his hands together. *Man I could do with a smoke,* he thought. His mind wandered back to the times he'd spent smoking with Chaz, dreaming about living in a better world; a world of acceptance and filled with healthy people. But it was the smoke, the weed he missed the most.

As his mind became consumed with the intensity of addiction and his deep-rooted need for weed, he began visualising the Queen's pipe lifting up from its platform and hovering in the air. It moved forward ever so slightly before rushing at Apex and falling into his lap.

"What the fuck!" shouted Apex jerking back in surprise.

The Queen's jaw dropped in amazement.

"Oh mine, hath mine eyes deceiveth me? How didst that befall?"

"See, I told you I could do it," Apex said triumphantly. "I can do almost anything when my mind is in the right place."

"Thou must stayeth the night. Thou and thy lady friend shalt hath mine finest room and stayeth as long as thou wish."

"OK, but you gotta give me some of that cannabis to smoke."

"Of course, 'twould be mine pleasure."

She opened a silver box and took out some of the green leafy substance contained within. She passed it to Apex, who sniffed it with delight and exclaimed, "Man that shit stinks to high heaven!" If he was going to be killed by the Greys then he would at least go out on a high.

Chapter 36

The Roe Buck Inn, Richmond

The sign on the Roe Buck Inn swung gently in the warm breeze, its rusty hinges squeaking with each small gust that caught it. Directly below the sign was a solid oak door that was adorned with four impressive looking locks and a huge metal knocker that was hanging below a small window. It was quiet inside. Most of the citizens were either dead or had left because of the threat of more earthquakes. The Roe Buck was one of only a handful of buildings that had survived, a true testament to the solid structure of the building. In the far corner of the dark and dingy room sat Robert, Paul and Captain Peters. The Earl looked most concerned. He was constantly standing and pacing around before sitting back down again.

"Where is that gent, that gent should beest hither by now?" he shouted loudly to the others, his voice tinged with frustration and impatience.

He knocked his drink back and then slammed his mug down violently onto the table. The contents splashed out covering both the walls and his companions.

"I am certain he wilt beest hither soon sir. The deed is not a simple one," Paul replied wiping the wine from his cheeks.

"Perhaps thine spy hast been murdered by that witch?" said Captain Peters, who was casually puffing away on his clay pipe.

"If't be true that witch fails me, I shalt take that wench he is so fond of and shalt cutteth her into little pieces and spread her body parts in each corner of this country."

"Indeed sir, but what maketh thee bethink this witch is a gent of his word? Hath thee ever known a witch to be worthy of trust? And he is a black servant. To bethink an honourable sir as yourself negotiating with a black servant! Thou shouldst hath killed that gent thither and then."

Robert frowned at the Captain. He should know better than to argue with him. Under normal circumstances he would have taken his gun out there and then, but he needed all the support he could get right now.

A noise came from the door and he glanced over to see it opening.

"Ah that gent is hither now, where hast thee been fool, we hast been waiting for thee too long."

The Queens servant, Henry, walked in, apologising profusely for his tardiness,

"Mine most humble of apologies sir, 'tis not easy to receiveth hence unnoticed."

"Thou art hither now, telleth me man, hath the witch done t?"

"Nay sir, the witch and the Queen art forming a valorous bond sir."

Enraged by this news, the Earl stood up and grabbed Henry by his collar.

"I didst know I could nay more rely on thee than I couldst the Queen herself."

"Ha, I didst telleth thee so," Captain Peters muttered, a smug grin forming on his face.

Robert growled menacingly at the Captain and bellowed loudly,

"I am going to hast to killeth the Queen myself. There art plenty of men out thither to seize her palace and thee art coming with me Henry. Thou art to square by mine side."

"But sir, I am merely a servant of the Queen, I am nay soldier!"

"Thou art a soldier today Henry. Now sitteth and joineth me in a flagon of wine."

He pulled Henry down next to him and placed his arm around his shoulders. Nothing would get in the way of his plan.

Nothing.

Chapter 37

Richmond Palace

T he cannabis was amazing. Apex had never experienced such a weightless, floating sensation from smoking before. It was exquisite weed; clean, pure and with no harsh oils or chemicals. He slumped back in the chair, melting into the seat, becoming a part of the furniture. He felt exhausted and was very, very stoned. The Queen had been fascinated by Apex's stories of his future time zone and how the world had changed and developed so much. Yet frustratingly, despite being intrigued by this so-called invasion, he still couldn't convince her that there was something capable of penetrating the great kingdom that was England.

Apex wobbled to his feet, clutching at the arms of the chair to steady himself. As much as he could think of nothing better than staying there all day smoking weed with the Queen, he knew that time was against them. It would only be a matter of hours, perhaps even minutes, before the Greys got there. The weed could wait. Plus, Sarah and Jake were depending upon him, they wouldn't survive without him being there to save them. Trying to convince the Queen that the world was about to end was proving incredibly difficult and he was starting to wonder whether his trip to the palace had been worth it. And then there was this God that no one seemed to know anything about. How on earth was he meant to find him? Nevertheless, he needed to look at the positives; he was still alive and as long as he was still alive, he would fight to the death. With this new sense of defiance, he looked the Queen square in the eyes and put his fist out to her,

"Give me some cookie Queenie."

"I understandeth not,' she replied with confusion.

"Just touch my fist, it's a sign of respect in my time zone."

The Queen put her fist out with a little giggle, enjoying this unusual cultural difference. She was beginning to like this boy and his funny ways. He'd make the perfect companion for her in her last few years of life. To signal her fondness for the boy, she offered Apex the pipe again.

He shook his head and said,

"I'm getting pretty tired and I seriously haven't been this stoned for years! I tell you something Queenie, I think your time zone generally sucks ass, but man you guys seriously know your weed. This stuff is amazing!"

He paused and then asked,

"Do you have a bath I could use and perhaps some clothes that might fit me properly? I absolutely stink and these tight trousers are cutting off my manhood, if you get where I'm coming from!"

"Aye, I wilt sendeth the maids to fill the tub for thee and wilt maketh sure thee receiveth some fine robes anon."

"Thanks your highness."

He was rather fond of the old dear. If she was forty years younger and lived in the year 2200 he could imagine hanging around with her. There was no way he was going to mention his assigned assassination to her, let alone carry out the deadly deed.

He followed the maid through to an adjoining room, keen to get out of the tight clothes. The thought of a bath, to be clean again, was the closest thing he'd got to a wet dream in a long time. The room was breathtakingly beautiful. Its decadent gold walls were lined with grand paintings and woven tapestries each one telling a story of the people who had lived there. But the most beautiful sight of all was that of Sarah lying on the large four-poster bed next to her sleeping baby. She was absolutely stunning. Seeing Apex, her face lit up with an infectious smile. Ever since Apex had rescued her, she had become infatuated with him. She had never met someone with such heroic, God like qualities. He was her saviour, her knight in shining armour. Apex smiled back at her.

Several maids entered and started filling a large tub with water. When the bath was deep enough, the maids left the room and Apex started to undress. He winced in pain as he struggled to ease the tight sleeves over the painful scratches from the rats. Sarah got up from the bed and walked over to help.

"Here, alloweth me to helpeth thee. 'Tis a little tight but if thee raiseth thy arms a little more I can taketh t off thee," she said gently.

Apex did as instructed and raised his arms with a groan. After several tugs and more groans of pain, Sarah lifted the garment over his head. Apex immediately felt the relief of finally being free.

"Ah man, that's the best feeling ever!" he said, swinging his arms around in joy.

"Jake is asleep for now. Would thee mind if I bathe with thee, sir? I have not hadst a bath for some months, 'tis quite the luxury," Sarah said shyly.

Apex blushed and replied in jest, "Eurgh, a few months?" He playfully flicked some of the water from the bath so that it splashed Sarah in the face.

She laughed. "I am but a simple maid. We maids do not oft receiveth a chance to bathe. Only the wealthy hast that privilege."

She slowly started taking off her clothing and as her dress dropped to the floor it revealed her beautiful slim figure. Apex stared in wonder, taking in every inch of her body. He noticed the deep scars that ran down the length of her back and looked away. It maddened that anyone could have harmed this girl in such a way. Holding onto the sides of the bath he eased himself into the hot steaming water and closed his eyes, breathing out all of the stress that had built up over the last few days. Sarah followed suit and stepped delicately into the other end of the tub. There was clearly not enough room for the two of them, but they made do and she placed her legs over his. This level of intimacy was new to Apex, he'd never bathed with a girl before, not without having a different agenda anyway. He could feel himself falling for her, perhaps now was a good time to find out more about her.

"So Sarah, tell me about you. You never did tell me about Jake's father."

"Oh, 'tis a little hard for me to speaketh about such matters," she choked, her eyes welling up with tears. "Mine master wast a horrid sir. That gent would beat me everyday. I hadst to maketh sure I putteth not a foot out of place. When thee arriveth, I did not wanteth to invite thee all in, for fear the master would find out. But I bethought it would be mine only chance of salvation and thankfully thee saved me and mine little knave."

She glanced over at Jake on the bed and smiled. She had never spoken a word to anyone about how her master had treated her, but she felt at ease with Apex, like she could tell him almost anything.

"There wast one time that gent cameth home and saw that I hadst not cleaned the floor to his liking. That gent beat me with his belt and then… " she sobbed loudly, "and then that gent didst hath his evil way with me."

"That fucker!" exclaimed Apex, banging his fist down on the side of the bath in anger.

"After that it becameth a daily thing, that gent wouldst rape me whenever he could. I was soon with child. Mine master never cared for Jake, he was a reminder of his wrongdoing and he didst oft threaten to taketh mine baby and throweth him in the river. I wast frightened every day; afraid for me, afraid for Jake."

"Shit man, no wonder you didn't want to tell me, that's harsh. I'm so sorry."

He looked at her sadly and leant over to brush the tears from her cheeks.

"Well, you don't need to worry about him anymore, he's dead. Although, well yeah, he will be reborn of course, so he hasn't really gone forever," mused Apex.

"What doth thee mean, reborn?"

"Well apparently we die, but then we're reborn as the same person, and live our lives in exactly the same way each time. So we're never aware that we're caught up in this loop of dying and being reborn, it's fucked up!"

"Art thou saying thither is nay heaven or hell, we art just reborn again?"

"Well yeah I guess, that's what I was told anyway. Things have all gone a bit crazy. I was just getting to the end of my college course and somehow I end up here, in the fucking sixteenth century, so if I'm honest I'm not entirely sure what to believe anymore. All I do know is that I'm the only one who can try and stop these fucking Greys and that I'm meant to find a God called Ema."

"Dost thou mean the Christian God?"

"No, I don't think so. The God I'm looking for is the creator of everything and is the reason for everything we say and do."

"That sounds like mine God for he is the creator and maker of everything, thee must mean that gent! Oh mine, I wonder what that gent doth look like? Wilt I receiveth to meeteth that gent, oh I doth desire so, Apex."

"Well maybe it's your God, who knows, but what I do know is that if I don't find him then it could mean the end of everything. The end of you, the end of me, the end of every single time zone ever."

"Thou wilt findeth that gent Apex, I hath faith in thee. Thee hath saved me and Jake, thou must findeth him and save us all."

Apex knew deep down that there wasn't much hope of that. How could he take on such a massive quest on his own. But he didn't have the heart to disappoint her, not when he could see that she clearly idolised him. He was getting rather used to the attention. If it really was the end of everything, then the best he could hope for was that the end would be quick.

They relaxed in comfortable silence for a few minutes more and then climbed out of the tub and helped each other to dry off. Under any other circumstances, Apex would have used the opportunity to charm this girl into bed, but this wasn't a normal circumstance, and although they would be sharing a bed tonight Apex had absolutely no intentions of doing anything with her. He was far too tired. He lay down next to Sarah and held her tightly. She flinched at his touch, but relaxed as she realised his arms around her made her feel safe. It wasn't so much lust that made Apex reach out for her, but more because he was terrified, absolutely petrified of what was to come. She was all he had now and he needed to be strong for her. He closed his eyes and drifted off into a fitful slumber, dreaming of the darkness.

Chapter 38

The Roe Buck Inn, Richmond

Robert stood outside the inn, tapping his foot restlessly against the ground. He was eager to get to the palace and make his attack when it wasn't heavily guarded. As a close confidante to the Queen, he knew not only the best days to attack, but also the best times. And considering he had all of Captain Peters' men at his side, he knew the odds were stacked highly in his favour.

"We wilt beest travelling through several hamlets on our way and I wanteth those people to unite with us," the Earl instructed the men. "The more we recruit, the stronger we wilt becometh. I am most certain that folk art becoming tired of this ruling wench."

One of the soldiers pointed and shouted,

"Sir, we may needeth not to recruit, look! "

"What art thee talking about thou ignorant buffoon, how dare thee interrupt me!"

"But sir, behind thee, in the distance, on the hills, behold there art a thousand folk or more. Those gents hath heard of thy attack and wanteth to join us!"

The soldiers cheered at the thought of re-enforcements, their objectives would be much more achievable with this many people fighting alongside them. Robert withdrew a primitive looking telescope from his pocket and peered through it to take a closer look. There was something unusual about the crowd, it was too chaotic, their movements too rushed. Something wasn't right. And there weren't just people in the group, there appeared to be animals too.

"Men, this is not re-enforcement, this is an attack. The Queen must have heard of our plans and hath sent her own army to attack!"

"Sir what dost thou mean?" asked Paul. "How can thou be sure? What is happening?"

"I hast never seen an army like this, hither must beest thousands of those folk! Make haste, we must defend ourselves. By mine honour I wilt not retreat again!"

"But sir, we art outnumbered. We cannot defend ourselves against such an army," protested Captain Peters.

Ignoring him, the Earl turned to his small army of men and ordered, "Defensive formation, receiveth into position!"

The soldiers grouped together, forming a long line of Arquebus at the front and ten rows of archers behind. There was a line of ramshackle houses on their right and with the inn on their left they had managed to create a bottleneck within the road. This would give them a good defensive position, anything coming towards them would struggle to get past. The soldiers nervously prepared their weapons, waiting in anticipation of what was coming. The ground began to tremble and the sound of stampeding hooves vibrated through the earth. In the distance there came an ear splitting screech. The men instinctively covered their ears and their weapons dropped to the ground. Unarmed and defenceless, the men began to panic.

Robert however, seemed unaffected by the noise. He was furious that his army had weakened so easily. Although he had no way of knowing for certain where this army had suddenly come from, he suspected it was witchcraft. And only one person sprung to mind.

Apex.

"Men, 'tis nay ordinary army. 'Tis the worketh of the devil himself! We must pray to God to help us defeat this evil that walketh our lands. Beest stout men and fire on mine command."

The screaming grew louder and the soldiers squealed in pain. The braver ones withstood the agony, their faces contorted in anguish, but they remained armed and ready to aim. However, not one of them could have prepared themselves for what they were about to see. Men, women and children advanced upon the group, falling over each other and groaning. As the soldiers looked closer they saw that each one was missing their eyes and ears. In their place were large gaping wounds dripping with fresh blood.

In among the mutilated people were thousands of rats and feral cats. They were pouncing on them, biting at the open wounds and screeching manically.

It was time to defend.

"ARCHERS TAKE AIM... AND FIRE!" roared the Earl.

The archers stretched their bows and released a fleet of arrows. The projectiles flew through the air with a haunting whistle, the sharp points piercing the air and then penetrating the heads and bodies of the possessed posse below. Some of them instantly dropped to the ground, a dark inky liquid rising out of them. The liquid gathered form, hovering in the air before shooting up into the sky and out of sight. Unperturbed, the archers fired another round of arrows at the advancing group. They were now only metres from the soldiers, a signal for the Arquebus's to aim and fire their weapons. The guns boomed with an almighty explosion, sending a sea of deadly bullets into the masses. Flesh tore off of their damaged bodies and mists of blood sprayed into the air, sending showers of crimson down onto the men. But they were still coming and before the Arquebus could reload, they pounded the front line. Robert's horse reared in fright, throwing him from his saddle right into the thick of the crowd.

In the chaos, Captain Peters, Paul and Henry had conveniently positioned themselves at the back of the soldiers, but even so there was little chance of escape. The zombie army was just too powerful. The frontline had already been swallowed up and the rest of the soldiers had broken away, running for their lives. The three men turned on their heels and galloped off on their horses to the only place left that they knew would be safe.

Richmond Palace.

Chapter 39

W hat the fuck, where the fuck am I? Shit, I've seen this place
before!" Apex looked across the snow filled park, it was
filled with cars, cars that he'd only ever seen in books. A
van was on fire, the flames crackling and popping, sending electrical
sparks onto the grass. He could feel the heat on his skin. It was a
pleasant sensation that helped drown out the bitterly cold wind.
Something inside the van caught his eye. It was a person. "Oh shit!
There's someone in it! Don't worry bro, I'm coming." He ran towards
the blazing inferno and tried to kick out the window, but the heat was
too intense.

"Man, it's too hot. I can't get you out! Shit, the glass won't break!

He watched in horror as the burning man screamed in agony. The
flames engulfed him and Apex watched his flesh melt away, the fat
dripping from his face like candle wax. "Man, I'm sorry. I can't get you
out. I'm so sorry," Apex wept.

Suddenly, the horrifying vision changed and he could see someone,
someone he knew.

It was Rose.

"Rose! Rose you're alive! It's me, Apex. I'm here with you, don't worry.

She silently stretched her arm out into the darkness.

"No, don't just point your finger, talk to me Rose. Tell me where you are!"

"Waketh up Apex, waketh up! Can thou heareth that outside?" Sarah said, shaking him gently.

"What? What are you talking about? What? Where am I? Where's Rose gone?" Apex mumbled, rubbing his head in confusion and looking at Sarah with bleary eyes.

Sarah beckoned for him to follow her to the window and pointed down to the courtyard.

"Apex, behold, behold outside!

Looking over her shoulder, Apex glanced down and saw thousands of strange looking people rattling at the gates. They looked as if they didn't have any eyes and they were moaning as though in pain. The guards looked petrified and clearly didn't know what to do. They'd never seen such a sight as this before and all they could think to do was to retreat back in to the Palace. Apex was dumbfounded by the sheer number of zombies that filled up every crevice of the streets. The palace was completely surrounded.

"Apex, doth something!" screamed Sarah. She held Jake in her arms, tears spilling down onto the baby's head. "Doth something Master, doth something!"

He had always known the time would come, but he wasn't expecting it to happen so soon. He'd had no time to plan.

Sensing his panic, Sarah took hold of his shoulders and begged,

"Apex thou hast to doth something. They art breaking the gates. Those gents wilt soon receiveth to us!"

"Sarah... I... I don't think I can help," said Apex helplessly.

"Apex, we hast to receiveth to the Queen. The lady is in most serious danger!"

Sarah was right. He couldn't give up the fight so easily. If he could just buy a bit more time to try and work out what to do.

"Yeah you're right, but I can't go out there butt naked. I need some clothes. And I'm not wearing those other ones I had. I can barely walk in them let alone run."

Sarah opened a nearby chest and threw Apex the first thing she could find. It was a very frilly, very lacy dress.

Apex spluttered.

"I knoweth 'tis for ladies, but thee hast not a choice."

"Are you fucking serious? I'm not wearing that. There's got to be some armour or something knocking around here somewhere."

He frantically opened up all of the drawers of the chest, tossing the clothes out onto the floor.

"Shit, there has to be something half decent in here! The Queen said she was going to get me some 'fine' clothes, where the fuck are they?"

"Apex, the gates art buckling and look those folk art climbing over each other. Make haste, it matters not what thee wear, we hast to wend!"

"Oh for fucks sake!"

He hastily put the dress over his head and shoved his arms through the puffy sleeves. The dress came down to his knees and although it made him cringe thinking about how ridiculous he must look, he had to admit it was a damned sight more comfortable than the clothes he'd had before. In the grand scheme of things it really didn't matter what he was wearing, after all death seemed inevitable if the scene outside was anything to go by.

Sarah strapped Jake onto her back and followed Apex to the Queen's door. They knocked out of courtesy, but then entered without waiting for an answer. The Queen was sat in her chair looking disapprovingly at a group of frightened looking men. Apex spotted Captain Peters, Paul, and Henry among the soldiers. Henry was crouched on his knees, begging the Queen for forgiveness.

"I would hast expected this from Robert, but Henry! How could thee betray me?"

"My most humble apologies thy majesty," Henry grovelled, "I wast frightened. The Earl threatened mine family and madeth me square with him."

The Queen turned to address Apex,

"This sir hither hath betrayed me. Mine own trusted servant hath plotted to killeth me and giveth power to that dimwit, Robert."

"But where is he?" asked Apex

"He is dead. He hath becometh one of those frightful cretins thou see outside," replied Paul.

"Most of mine men hath been killed too thy Majesty," added Captain Peters. "They hadst nay chance, their army tore through us with such ease. And now the rest of us art hither and those gents art outside breaking thy walls down."

"Twas that gent, that witch thither, that didst t!" Paul shouted, pointing at Apex accusingly. "He is the one who hath caused this. He is the one who plotted to killeth thee thy Majesty. That gent didst make an agreement with mine friend, mine friend who is now dead! That gent must beest ceased, he must beest rid of so that this sorcery ceases too."

Fuelled by grief, Paul withdrew his dagger and ran at Apex.

Apex felt a surge of emotion course its way through his veins. Anxiety took over his body entire body and his heart started to race uncontrollably. Rage rose up from deep within him. He couldn't hold it back any longer. Closing his eyes, he brought an image of the ornaments, the silver cups and plates, the paintings on the walls and the furniture into his mind. The objects began to shift, violently falling to the ground and smashing on contact. He imagined Paul being taken over by that powerful invisible force, his body helplessly rising up and levitating, controlled as if he were a puppet. Apex visualised him twisting like a corkscrew, his head and torso twisting one way, his legs twisting the other. Paul screamed as his body contorted, but Apex carried on. His spine gave an uncanny creak, before snapping entirely and the man fell to the ground, dead.

Apex opened his eyes and saw Paul lying facedown on the floor. The Queen and the rest of the men looked aghast. But Sarah had seen Apex do this before and knew he needed to refocus on what was going on. She grabbed his hands and said,

"Apex I can heareth them, they must hath broken through. What shall we doth?"

"Shhh, try and keep Jake quiet," whispered Apex. He walked over to the window, stepping over Paul, and peered out across the courtyard. The gates had been penetrated and thousands of people and animals were hitting and biting one another. Some were using sharp objects to stab and cut with and there was blood spraying everywhere, covering the faces and clothing of all that were fighting. The noise was terrifying, a mixture of screaming rage and pain, echoes of despair, unnatural sounds that were not of this Earth. Apex listened out and realised the sounds weren't just coming from outside, they seemed far closer than that. He ran to the doorway and put his head out to listen. The sounds were coming from the lower corridors.

Time was running out.

Apex saw movement at the end of the corridor and it only took him a few seconds to make out the shape of rats. He screamed with all his might,

"Close the fucking doors now!"

Captain Peters jumped to attention, but before he was able to close the door fully a rat jumped through the gap and ran across the floor, up onto the bed. It leapt on top of the Queen and started clawing at her face. She screamed, waving her hands around manically, trying to get the beast off of her. Apex ran to help. He grabbed the rat and squeezed it in his hands until the life drained out of it. Blood trickled out from its mouth and ears, before the strange black substance flew out and into the Queen's open mouth. She grabbed her throat and started to choke. Whatever it was that had entered her was clearly not good, but at the moment Apex's main priority was to barricade the door and stop any more of them getting into the room. The Queen would have to wait. He threw the dead rat onto the floor and shouted at the men to help him.

"Right you lot, help me with this chest, we have to stop them getting in. Oi, you lot, fucking help will you! Don't just stand there, help me move this chest!"

"I understandeth not what is happening," shouted Henry above the noise.

"It's the fucking Greys, they're coming and they're going to kill us all, unless you help me move this chest," cried Apex, trying to push the heavy wooden chest. Captain Peters rushed to his aid.

Henry and the rest of the soldiers jumped to action and between them they managed to drag the chest inch by inch across the wooden floor. Sarah watched them, clutching Jake protectively to her chest.

Suddenly there was a loud bang and the door began to shake.

"Quick, tip it over!" Apex shouted.

The men heaved as hard as they could, rocking the chest until it slowly gained momentum and started to tip. Giving one final burst of energy, they pushed in unison and the chest toppled over. It hit the floor with a thunderous crash in front of the door, blockading it from the nightmare that lay beyond.

"I don't know how long it will hold out, but it will buy us some time at least," Apex shouted above the screams that were coming from the corridor. The door began to shudder as the creatures pushed their weight against the barricaded door. Everyone instinctively started to back up against the far wall, getting as far away from the door as possible. Sarah held firmly onto Apex's arm and pulled him back with her. The Queen meanwhile said nothing. She simply stood there staring, trance-like into nothingness.

A small fault line opened up in the door and started to spread across the surface. With an almighty crack a bloodied fist smashed its way through. It immediately disappeared, but then smashed through again and again until a small jagged hole had been made. A featureless face thrust through the gap, groaning and twisting itself, trying to squeeze through into the room.

"Telleth us thy name, telleth us whither that gent is?" it screamed in an unearthly voice.

Captain Peters pulled out his wheel-lock pistol and fired a shot at the zombie's head. Fragments of brain and splashes of cranial fluid erupted over the walls as the bullet made contact. Then just as it had with the rat, a black watery substance rose from out of the corpse. It seeped through the ceiling, until all of it had completely disappeared, leaving no trace of its existence. Another head peered through the hole and without hesitating Captain Peters unsheathed his sword. He swung the weapon down hard, slicing through the monsters neck. Its head fell to the floor with a thud and Captain Peters stepped back, his hands shaking from the adrenaline that was pumping through his body. But it was no good, they just kept coming and the door shook violently as the growing mass of frenzied beings pushed forcefully against it. The soldiers sat with their backs against the chest and Apex piled up as many heavy objects as he could find, hoping that it would help to hamper the Greys attack.

An unnerving scream, like the sound of a pig being dragged to slaughter, came from within the room. It was the Queen. Apex stopped what he was doing and stared at her in concern.

"Art thou fine thy Majesty?" asked the Captain. He went over to her and tried lifting her onto the blood soaked bed.

She stood silently, an empty look on her face.

"Majesty, art thou good?" he asked again.

She twitched suddenly and screamed a harrowing cry, before proceeding to gouge at her eyes. Digging her nails deeply into the sockets, the blood poured down her cheeks, covering her clothing and saturating the bed linen. Slowly, she moved her bloodied hand towards the bedside table, fumbling with the objects, before grabbing an empty wine glass that she had been drinking from the previous evening. She smashed it hard against the side of the bed, keeping hold of the sharpest fragment in her hand.

No one had ever seen their Queen behave in such a manner before and they looked over to Apex for instruction.

But he wasn't sure what to do either. He'd dealt with some pretty gruesome things in his time, but this was on another level.

The Queen raised the jagged fragment to her head and began to viciously hack at her nose and ears. Without warning, Henry started sliding ever so slowly across the room. He looked around helplessly, his arms and legs held forcefully together, until he came to a stop at the foot of the Queen's bed.

Through her mutilated face, the Queen spoke.

"Tell me thy name."

"What, what is happening to me? Helpeth me, I can not moveth!"

"TELL ME THY NAME!" the Queen screamed again.

"M-m-mine name is Henry, thy Highness. 'Tis I, Henry, thy servant."

"But thou art not that gent, art thou?"

The Queen stared at Henry with hollow eyes and her body slowly started to levitate from the bed. The bed covers slid off of her and she stretched her arm out, pointing the shard of glass at Henry. She gently glided towards the paralysed man, stopping when the jagged edge was perfectly positioned in front of his eye.

"Tell me whither that gent is, whither is Ema?"

"Thy majesty, I knoweth not what thou art saying? Nor do I know who this gent is thou speaketh of."

Puppet-like, the Queen retracted her arm and lashed out at Henry's face, stabbing the glass repeatedly into his eyeball. Henry screamed in pain, writhing in the invisible restraints, trying to escape. Captain Peters ran from the room, but was stopped at the door by an invisible force, which thrust him back and slammed him against the wall. The doors gave a sudden bang and the makeshift barricade began to buckle. Furniture wobbled and fell from the defensive barrier and then the doors smashed open revealing an army of gruesome creatures.

Apex had to do something. He closed his eyes, feeling the familiar rush of anxious energy that he had increasingly got used to. That enormous surge of adrenaline as the images came so easily to him. He imagined grabbing the hoard of possessed beings and slamming their rigid bodies left and right against the corridor walls. The paintings shattering as the bodies crushed down to a pulp from the pressure of the force he was inflicting upon them.

Captain Peters and his men cowered behind Apex, shielding their faces from the horror that faced them.

"Please sir, saveth us from this witchcraft!" Captain Peters screamed.

Apex imagined a rippling, transparent force field encircling himself, Sarah and Jake. The zombies were now in the room with them, stabbing and hitting each other and they were screaming out for Ema. Some of them broke away from the group and charged at Apex, but the shield he had created was strong and they rebounded from the energy that was being emitted from it. Sarah screamed as each zombie bounced off of the liquid casing. She didn't understand how something as seemingly clear and delicate as a bubble could protect them. Bodies slammed into the other zombies, hitting the walls and smashing the furniture. But it

324

was getting too much for Apex, he couldn't hold this level of force for much longer, his energy was rapidly weakening. He fell to the ground in complete exhaustion.

"Apex, please helpeth me. Receiveth up, keepeth those folk hence. Apex!" Sarah screamed hysterically.

"I can't, I'm too weak, there's too many of them!" he groaned.

In sheer desperation, he gathered up what last remaining bit of strength he had and took possession of Captain Peters and his men. He snatched them up into the air and hurled them at the army of possessed zombies.

They watched as the zombies tore the helpless men apart. Apex pulled Sarah protectively to his chest. The force field had disappeared and while the zombies were distracted Apex took the opportunity to drag Sarah and Jake over towards the bedchamber they had stayed in the night before. Slamming the door behind him, he quickly dragged a chest over to block up the door. He knew it was pointless, but it was better than nothing.

"What art we to doth now, Apex?" asked Sarah.

"I have no fucking idea, there's no way out of here, we're trapped," Apex raged.

Once again, the door began to shake as the zombies relentlessly pushed and banged against it.

Apex was done.

This was it.

The end.

He embraced Sarah and Jake and waited for their inevitable fate.

"Sarah look at me, this isn't the end, OK? Even if I lose you now, there's still a chance you'll survive, Jake too. If I die here with you then maybe, just maybe, John is still alive somewhere and he'll find Ema. We've got to stay positive Sarah, you hear me?"

The door smashed open and the army of evil beings barged in. Apex tried pushing them back with his mind, but it was useless, he had no energy left in him. Sarah and Jake began levitating across the room towards the monstrous beings.

"Apex, helpeth me, please. Taketh Jake, thou must saveth him!" Sarah screamed.

Apex desperately tried to reach for her, but she was too far from him and he screamed her name out in despair.

He screamed louder, feverishly attempting to grab hold of Sarah with his mind. And for a moment he had her. He started to haul her in, dragging her back towards him, but the Greys were fighting back. He strained against their power, the two energies pulling on either side of Sarah. He gave one final pull, falling backwards from the force. The vision of the room took on the appearance of a rippling liquid and the zombies became distorted shapes, blurs in the distance. The light sucked away, fading, until there was nothing but silence and complete darkness.

Chapter 40

Unknown location

Darkness everywhere.
Not a shimmer of light.
Anywhere.

Just darkness.

And the smell, that distinct metallic scent he had smelt before.

Apex felt confused and disorientated, his mind absorbed with thoughts of Sarah's terrified face as the Greys had pulled her away from him. He'd tried his best to save her, he really had, but it hadn't been enough and he blamed himself for what had happened. "Oh man, that poor girl. I'm so sorry Sarah, I'm so sorry I couldn't help you and Jake," he sobbed to himself, falling to his knees and placing his head into his hands. Everything he had fought for was gone, it had all been for nothing. He felt like such a failure, a useless idiot, just like he'd felt back when he was at college.

"I can't take this shit anymore!" he shouted despairingly into the darkness. "I hate this life, I hate it! Just let me die, please. I give in!"

As if in response to his pleas, the lights flickered on. Apex blinked, looking around at the familiar dome where this had all begun.

"Great, I'm back in this fucking place again. Well that was worth it, wasn't it," he said sarcastically.

"Ah Apex, I'm so pleased to see you made it! I see your swearing hasn't improved much though," Calcus chided. "Anyway, how was your time in the sixteenth century? I see you have found something other than that dressing gown to wear, a dress looks rather fetching on you I must say."

Apex stared furiously in the direction of the voice.

"It's all I could fucking find if you must know. Funnily enough I had more important things to be dealing with than what I was wearing. And if you really want to fucking know how it was, I'll tell you. I've been chased, tortured, attacked, and insulted. And the people, don't get me fucking started on the people. They've got a cheek calling themselves human, treating people the way they do, in fact I'm starting to wonder who's worse, the assholes living there or the fucking Greys."

"Calm down Apex, I understand how hard this has been for you. However, I can assure you that your arduous journey has not been totally in vain. I can see just how powerful you have become and I am impressed Apex. But most important of all, we now know that the God is not in John's time zone."

"Well I guess that's some good news," Apex muttered. "Where the fuck is John anyway? He vanished and left me on my own, I've not seen him since. And Rose, have you seen what's happened to her? She's dead, I saw her die right in front of me."

"I'm sorry Apex, she should not have died, her death was never part of the plan. Unfortunately, it does complicate things somewhat. I will

have to run the termination process to get her back, bear with me it shouldn't take too long."

"I need some fucking answers, you owe me that much. How do you know all this shit and how come you know so much about these Greys anyway?"

"My dear Apex I understand your anger and yes perhaps I haven't been a hundred percent truthful with you, but before I explain let me get John."

"John? What, you mean he's here?"

A slight humming sound came from the far end of the room and a blue circular light appeared. John walked out of the centre of the light. He looked shaken. "What is happening, whither am I?" he slurred. As he staggered towards Apex, a wave of excitement and relief washed over him.

"Apex, Apex is that thee? 'Tis so valorous to see thee," he said giving Apex a heartfelt hug. "But, what robes art thee wearing? Is that a dress?" he said, playfully tugging at the dress.

"Shit man, calm the fuck down! I'll tell you about the dress later, I wanna know what happened to you. Where the fuck have you been, John? I needed you back there bro."

"Mine most humble apologies Apex, I wast visiting mine family. But those gents did not knoweth me, they sayeth they hadst nay son," he cried.

"Ah yes, I am sincerely sorry about that John," interrupted Calcus. "It never once crossed my mind that you would visit your family. I understand why you did, and I admit that I should have perhaps warned you about the consequences of seeing your loved ones. You see John, when you are taken out of your time zone, you cannot be in two places

329

at once. It's impossible to be their son when you are here, as they were reborn without you and they will continue to do so until you are ready to be reborn with them. Does that make sense?"

"Aye, 't maketh more sense. Whither is Rose?" he said, looking around the dome for her.

"John I'm sorry to tell you this, but Rose is dead."

"Rose is dead?" said John, his face turning pale from shock. A sudden feeling of guilt swept through him as he realised his actions had played a part in her death. "But how, how could that sweet lady hath died?"

"She got shot man, by that Sarah's master. I watched her die. Maybe if you'd been there, you could have helped us," Apex said crossly.

"Oh Rose nay, I hath done thee wrong. Mine most humble apology, oh Rose!" John wailed.

"It's OK John I'm trying to get her back. If you'll just be patient the termination process is nearly done. Wait… I think I may have her… just one more minute…"

The lights suddenly faded and a deep boom echoed around the domed ceiling. It was like there was a power cut, or the batteries had run out, everything had shut off, powered down.

They stood in darkness.

"What the fuck's going on now? Why's it gone dark? Calcus man, what's happening?"

"This is most unusual, it has never happened before. It seems my attempt to get Rose back has failed. The energy constraint appears to have reached its capacity. I don't understand, it doesn't make sense…"

Calcus trailed off and the lights switched back on. A low humming sound indicated that everything had powered back up. Apex glared angrily at John and continued with his tirade.

"It's no use you crying about Rose bro, you weren't there. You didn't see what I saw. Shit, I should be the one crying!"

"Blaming this on John is unfair Apex. He has a strong attachment towards his family, which made him curious and his emotions got the better of him. We cannot always seek to blame others in situations where it is highly likely we would ourselves act in the very same way. John, you don't need to blame…"

Calcus paused and then said,

"Who is that behind you Apex?"

Apex spun around, fearing a Grey had somehow managed to follow him back. But it wasn't. There on the floor was a person curled up in the foetal position clutching something beneath them.

Is it? No it can't be. It can't possibly be Sarah and Jake. Can it? thought Apex and he rushed over to look.

"Sarah! You're alive, you're alive! But how? I don't understand."

"This is most unusual. It's not possible," said Calcus.

"Are you OK Sarah, is Jake OK? I thought they'd got you, I thought you were dead!" Apex gushed, giving her his hand.

Sarah took his hand and eased herself up, clutching Jake closely to her chest. Apex pulled her into his body and held her tightly. He would never let go of her again.

"Aye, we art both fine master but…" she paused and looked in wonder at the large domed structure. "Whither art we? And whither is that voice coming from, I see nay man?"

"That's Calcus, he's the guy I was telling you about before. You know, the one that told me about the God, the one that made up all those lies. He doesn't have a body, just a voice. I reckon it's because he's too scared to show himself."

"I heard that Apex," Calcus called out. "Anyway back to the matter in hand. My theory is that you must have formed such a strong emotional bond with Sarah that it allowed you to exit the time zone with her. The amalgamation of imagination and intense emotion was enough to bring her here. This really is quite incredible!"

Calcus paused, mulling things over, before shouting loudly,

"But of course, that would explain the energy drain and why I couldn't get Rose back. Why didn't I think of that before? There is only a limited amount of energy for you all, Sarah must have used up Rose's share of the energy. There is only one other way to do this…"

"Enough of this bullshit, I want answers now! Who are you really and what is this place?"

"Apex, the reason I haven't told you the complete truth so far is because I knew that if I did, you would not have trusted me. Strange as it sounds, it was the only way I could get you to fight the Greys. It doesn't really matter who or what I am, that is insignificant. We are here because this is the only place the Greys cannot reach us. They come from a dimension called the 'Amygdala', an area known as the negative universe, a place that no one would ever want to travel to. It's like hell, but far worse, and anyone who was even remotely capable of traveling there, would never return. Those who do go there are subjected to a life of terror, torment and torture. Believe me, I know."

"OK, so where are we now?" asked Apex

"We all live in a 'Para-verse' and the domed structure that you're standing in now is set deep inside this Para-verse. This particular region of the Para-verse is what we call the 'Affirmative Cortex'. And for some reason that we have not yet managed to work out, the Greys cannot get to us here. However, the Cortex lacks the energy we need to pull you in and out of time zones. We can only achieve short bursts of energy after a lengthy charge and this would explain why Rose has travelled back to her time zone without my knowledge. To put it simply, this constraint of energy means I am not always able to see what you are doing."

John looked baffled, it was far more than his primitive mind could handle, but Apex understood and he still wasn't satisfied.

"Right OK, so that explains some of it, but who the fuck are you?"

"Like I said, it's really not significant, but if it makes you happy I will tell you," said Calcus patiently. *"I was once a human just like you. It was the year twelve hundred AD and I was a blacksmith. I loved my job and I loved my family. Life was good. Better than good, life was perfect, until it happened..."*

"What happened?" asked John curiously.

There was a pause. Whatever had happened had obviously been traumatic.

He coughed before recommencing with his story,

"...I was abducted. It was just an ordinary day, I was smelting the finest swords in the land, minding my own business, when I was snatched by a group of grey aliens. They came at me like a rushing tidal wave of liquid, screaming in a language I had not heard before. I was caught off guard and was unable to defend myself against them. They took me to their dimension and experimented on me. They took my

*genetic makeup and combined it with their own, which resulted in me
losing my physical form entirely. I became a hybrid consciousness of
both human and grey intelligence. I can use telepathy just like the Greys
can, but I have retained some human emotions. They never anticipated I
would still have these basic emotions and when I discovered their plans
to invade your time zones I had too much empathy left within me to
allow it to happen. My emotional attachment to the Para-verse is
stronger than they thought and that meant I was a problem to them. So I
deserted the Greys and came to the Affirmative Cortex.*

"Shit man, that's some story. So how did you come to find out about
this Ema dude then?"

*"The Greys trusted me at the beginning and they told me all about
Ema, about him being the creator of the Para-verse. As far as they knew
I was one of them, so they explained their entire plan to me about
finding and taking control of this God. They told me that the only
person who could stand in their way was you, so I made it my mission to
find you before they did."*

"So they're after you as well?" asked Apex.

*"Yes they are, but they are far more interested in finding Ema. Once
they find him, they will come after me."*

"Excuse me sir, but if't be true the Greys cannot receiveth us hither,
then how can thee beest hither?" asked John.

*"As I said, I have human in me, and whatever it is that the Greys
fear inside this dome, it doesn't appear to affect me. I believe that the
Cortex is made up of the purest of positive emotions. It is a vast energy
that breathes positivity, hope and love, a zone that protects us from
virtually every negative energy in existence. The Greys are scared of
this, as they have no understanding of what emotion feels like. For*

334

years I have had to hide my emotions from the Greys, pretending to be completely emotionless, so that they wouldn't suspect I was different to them."

"Hang on a minute Calcus, if you're saying the Greys can't feel emotion then how come they get scared. Fear is an emotion, right?" said Apex smugly.

"Yes you're right Apex and well done I'm impressed with your logical thinking. However, just because the Greys do not understand emotion, does not mean that they are unable to experience it. Like humans, the Greys have an organic primitive mechanism, but it is something they do not understand nor can they control. They don't see it as emotion, but rather an erroneous irritation and this is why they are irritated by you all."

Apex and John looked at each other in confusion. These claims seemed insane. How could a human exist as consciousness alone, and if Calcus was part Grey then was it really that wise to trust him?

"OK it sounds like you've been through a lot, I get that and I suppose I should be thanking you for trying to save us. But what really gets me, and what I really can't figure out is why these fucking Greys are so Goddamn brutal. I mean why the fuck are they taking people's eyes out and cutting their nose and ears off, it's fucking sick man!"

"It is part of their selection process. The God cannot function without his senses, so by removing the eyes, ears, tongue and nose of anyone that they suspect may be the God, it helps narrow down their search. They believe that once the God has been made mute, deaf, blind and is unable to sense, they will be able to capture him and experiment on him. Ultimately, they want to artificially replicate the senses so as to be able to control the God that gives us eternal life."

"Man that's fucked up, but I guess it does kind of make sense, in a sick and twisted alien way," said Apex pulling a face. "What about Sarah and Jake, what will happen to them? Can they stay here?"

"Sarah, I am so sorry that you have got involved in all of this, it shouldn't have been this way. Fortunately for you and your baby it gave you a means of escape, you're one of the lucky few shall we say. But I am sorry, we simply do not have the energy to keep you here and I am afraid that means you will have to leave. Apex, you must take her with you. You brought her here, she is now your responsibility"

"Excuse me sir, but doth thee mean I wilt beest going to the future?" Sarah said excitedly, looking up towards the voice.

"My dear Sarah, there is no future or past, just a time zone that is more advanced than yours. It will be very different for you all, but I assure you that the people in this time zone are… well how can I put this… more accepting of differences, more approachable shall we say."

"But how shall we get Rose back?" asked John.

"You need to go to her time zone, find her and make her remember. I must warn you though, it won't be easy. Her memory has been erased and she will not know who any of you are. It is up to you to convince her of her purpose and her gift."

Apex rolled his eyes and said, "And what if we can't, then what?"

"There are no what ifs Apex, you must find her and you must find Ema, there is no other option. Ema has to be in Rose's time zone and the Greys know this, so you must be on your guard at all times. You are much stronger as a threesome, which is why you need Rose, but we do not have much time, so stick together and don't do anything foolish."

"OK, OK we'll find her, but listen can you at least send us to the right location this time, I don't fancy walking aimlessly around the country again."

"I will do my best Apex, you forget how difficult this is for me. The Greys will be regrouping and I don't know how long it will be before they reach Rose's time zone, you must hurry. Find Rose and find Ema, that's all you need to remember. Now go!"

The wall began to shimmer and a black hole opened up before them. John went first, taking slow, cautious steps towards the hole before the vacuum sucked him in.

Apex looked over at Sarah and Jake. He poured all of his love, all of his emotional attachment to them into his imagination, allowing his mind to hold them, support them and take them with him. He visualised them travelling by his side, hand in hand, the three of them... together.

Chapter 41

Somewhere in Bristol, England

John opened his eyes and looked around. "'Tis so cold," he shivered. He wrapped his arms around his torso and explored the building in more detail. Looking at the impressive stained glass windows looming majestically up before him, he picked out the image of Christ within the intricate detail of the richly coloured glass. He immediately dropped to one knee and made the sign of the cross. "We art in a cathedral!" he gasped in awe. "But it confuses me greatly, for it doth not look like a future time zone. Why doth t feel like I am home hither." Rising up from his knees, he walked over to the front of the cathedral and gazed in wonder at the gold chalices and crosses, the sumptuous leather seats and the deep pile red carpet that lead up to the neatly organised altar. Residing over this was a magnificently painted ceiling depicting scenes of plump cherubs and heavenly angels. It was supported by a framework of aged beams, which stretched across the entire width of the building.

"Where the fuck are we?" said Apex, breaking the tranquil atmosphere of the cathedral. "Are we seriously in the twenty-first century? Man, it sure doesn't look like it, it looks like we're still in John's time zone." He brushed away the dust that had settled on his clothes, his nose wrinkling in disgust, and then looked around to make sure Sarah and Jake were there. Sarah was sat at one of the pews quietly nursing her baby, her eyes wide with shock. Apex breathed a sigh of relief. They'd made it.

Apex watched as Sarah placed Jake gently down on the seat and then crouched down onto her left knee, making the sign of the cross with her right hand. She mumbled a short prayer before standing and checking on Jake. He was sleeping peacefully now that he'd had his milk. She kissed him gently on the top of his head and then walked over to join Apex.

"I feeleth at home hither Apex, for it doth feeleth as if I hast never left mine own time." She smiled at him warmly.

Apex smiled back at her and reached for her hand. He led her past the rows of benches and up to the altar where John stood.

"What do you think we should do John?"

"I knoweth not Apex, but perhaps it beest a good start to wend outside?"

"Yeah, but we don't know what's out there do we? There might be killer zombies out there for all we know, or there might be dudes out there who mistake me for a woman. I look pretty hot in this dress, they might do all kinds of nasty things to me," said Apex, only half in jest.

"Apex, Calcus didst say that the gents art nice in this time zone, we must trust him."

"Yeah but he lied to us before didn't he, what if he's actually on side with the Greys and this is a trap. What if he's evil just like those other fuckers?"

"What else art we to believeth Apex? I know he hath told us one falsehood, but I receiveth not a bad feeling about that gent, he doth seemeth friendly enough," replied John.

"You wilt not leaveth me wilt thee Apex?" Sarah said quietly. "Promise me thou wilt not leaveth me. I am most frightened of what doth wait for us out yonder."

"Don't worry Sarah, I won't leave you, I promise," Apex reassured her. He took both of her hands in his and looked deep into her eyes, "I won't ever let anything happen to you."

They couldn't put it off any longer, they had to focus on the important task at hand and that meant going outside. Sarah strapped Jake securely onto her back and the three of them headed towards the large wooden doors at the front of the cathedral. Apex grabbed the handle and they braced themselves, expecting to see a world of devastation, a world full of strange creatures and unfamiliar landscapes. But as the doors creaked open a loud rhythmic, musical beat filled their ears. Crowds of people staggered around the streets and the air was filled with the sounds of laughter and shouts of joy.

John stepped back in fright, "Wherefore art there so many folk? What is this I see before me?"

"Oh man this is fucking awesome, now this is my kind of time zone!" Apex shouted above the noise of the revellers. "Look over there, night clubs, bars and loads of liquor! I've read about this in books, people go out, get drunk and dance, man this is epic! Quick let's move on, I need me a drink and it's about time we had a bit of fun!"

Apex led the way through the crowds. John and Sarah trailed behind him looking in bewilderment at the people stumbling around them, who were pointing at them and laughing. They needed to find somewhere safe to hide so that they could work out their next course of action. Ignoring the catcalls and pointing fingers they continued to push their way through the throng of people. Suddenly, three men staggered towards them and started prodding at their clothes.

"Oi-oi! Love the dress mate. You been to a fancy dress party?" one of them slurred. "Man you all look great, love the old fashioned clothing!"

Apex gave a wry smile.

"Yeah bro, been partying, you know how it is, just going for a few beers now."

"American hey, welcome to England! Whereabouts in America you from buddy?"

"Thanks, yeah it's great to be here in England. I'm from Southfield in Detroit."

"I recognise you from somewhere," said the man, leaning in to get a good look at Apex's face, "but I can't figure out where from?"

Apex flinched as the strong smell of alcohol on the man's breath hit his nostrils. "I doubt it bro, you don't look familiar to me. I've never been to England before, how would you know me?"

"I'm not sure, but I swear I've seen you somewhere before, maybe on TV…" He tapped the side of his forehead as if it would help him recall where he'd seen Apex before. "Ah well, never mind. Hey you guys have a good Christmas yeah, and enjoy Bristol!"

Apex smiled politely and grabbed Sarah's hand, eager to get as far away from these men as possible. But then he stopped abruptly and turned back towards the man.

"Hey guys before you go, I don't suppose you know a girl called Rose do you?"

"Rose? Na, don't think so. Guys do you know anyone called Rose?" he shouted to his mates. They both shrugged their shoulders.

"OK, no worries. What about someone called Ema?"

"Ema? I know an Emma, but not an Ema? Sorry buddy, I hope you find them."

Apex thanked them and the three of them continued walking past the stretch of terraced houses.

"Mine eyes can believeth not that this is Bristol," Sarah said. "I hath been hither before, but it hath never looked this way."

"Sarah, you hast to recall that we art not in our time zone. This time zone is far more advanced than our own, 'tis hundreds of years ahead" said John.

"What is that over yonder?" Sarah said excitedly, pointing at a car that was parked on the side of the road, "Why 'tis a carriage without horses!"

"Oh that's just a car. They were built like hundreds of years ago, pretty shitty if you ask me. The government blamed them for all the environmental damage that happened, loads of people died from the toxic shit that comes out of them. They replaced them with battery-powered cars for a while, but turns out they caused cancer or something like that. I think they got banned about a hundred years ago, well that's what they taught us in college anyway."

They continued further up the road until they came across a dark, secluded spot where they would be able to hide from sight. There was just enough streetlight for them to make each other out. John and Sarah looked at the lights in bemusement, flinching nervously every time they heard a noise from out on the street. The humming of engines and the raucous shouting and noisy laughter of passers by were noises that were new to them and it made them feel anxious. From the corner of his eye John noticed an old lady sitting in a wheelchair. She was dressed from head to toe in brown and had a pair of large rectangular glasses perched on the end of her nose. She was rocking back and forth in the chair, muttering to herself,

"The time has come. There is no escape. There is no escape. THERE IS NO ESCAPE!"

"I hath seen that lady and heard talk like that before," John whispered to Apex.

"How could you recognise her John, you've never been here before," Apex scoffed.

"I knoweth not, but I vow to mine own God that I hath seen that lady in mine time zone. She wast not in that chair with wheels, she was floating, for the lady hadst nay legs. I recall talking to that lady and all that she sayeth wast that thither is no escape."

He inched closer to the old lady as though mesmerised by her and he stared into her crazed eyes. She gave him an unnerving grin, revealing a set of yellow teeth. John shook himself from his trance and headed back to the others. As he turned his back on the old lady she pointed up to the sky and cackled, "Nobody lives. Nobody lives. We all die. WE ALL DIE!"

Racing to get away from this insane woman, the three of them ducked in and out of side streets, looking out for anything that would make do as some kind of shelter for the night. This time zone felt unsafe. It was busy and noisy and every single one of them felt out of place here. But no matter how scared they felt, Apex and John knew that this was nothing in comparison to what it would be like when they had to face up to the Greys. The pressure was mounting and time was rapidly running out, they had to stay strong and focus on finding Rose and looking out for any clues as to where they might be able to find the elusive Ema. First things first, shelter.

It wasn't long before they came across a small building with a large sign hanging outside that was swinging in the breeze of the night. On the sign there was a picture of an old house next to which stood a large man wearing round spectacles.

"It doth look to me like an inn," said John. "Maybe we can stayeth here for a while?"

A large man in a black suit stopped them as they approached the door. He grinned at them, looking them up and down in bemusement.

"Good evening folks. We don't normally let men in with dresses, but as it's Christmas I'll make an exception," chuckled the bouncer. "Anyone under 16 will have to leave by 9pm though, OK?"

"Sure, no problem," replied Apex self-consciously.

The bouncer opened the door for them and they walked into a small, empty bar. The yellowing nicotine stained walls were covered with pictures and whimsical ornaments and the low ceilings were criss-crossed with supportive wooden beams. There was a strong smell of beer mixed in with a slight musty scent that seemed to cling in the air. On the far side of the bar was a roaring fire and after the harsh coldness from outside, the three of them migrated over to the welcoming heat. Finding a seat was easy and they chose a table close to the fireplace. Sarah took Jake from her back and cradled him in her arms to help warm him up. She looked at Apex with concern.

"Dost thou bethink that lady in the chair wast telling the truth? Dost thou believeth we art all going to kicketh the bucket, is there nay hope for us all?"

"Nah don't you worry, she was just some nut job," said Apex reassuringly.

But deep down Apex was worried. The way things had been going lately, it wouldn't surprise him in the slightest if the old hag was telling the truth. This was their final chance to find Ema and the thought of the Greys returning filled him with utter dread. He'd already experienced just how powerful they were and he knew that there was virtually nothing they could do to stop them. But they had to at least try. He smiled at Sarah. He was her saviour, her God; he couldn't let her down.

"Honestly Sarah, please don't worry, we'll be fine. I promise."

He stretched his hands out towards the flames to warm up his numb fingers, groaning with pleasure as the feeling gradually started to come back into them. Yet despite the comforting warmth, he still couldn't help but feel awkward and uncomfortable dressed in female attire.

Behind the bar stood a man dressed in a checked shirt and a flat cap, he nodded his head in acknowledgement of his unusual punters and said, "Evening."

Apex nodded back with a strained smile, trying to act as normal as possible, knowing that all three of them looked anything but normal.

"Man, this is the most embarrassing thing that's ever happened to me. I need to get out of these fucking clothes," Apex muttered under his breath.

Neither John nor Sarah were listening however, as they were far too busy staring at the photographs on the walls.

"Mine lord, what is that up thither? It doth hath people living in a box, how can that befall?" said John in amazement. Sarah got up to have a closer look and they both peered at the strange rectangular object in the picture. "How art thither people in t?"

The bar man called over, "I can change the channel if you want?"

"No you're alright man," Apex hastily replied and then hissed,

"John, Sarah, sit down will you. I'll tell you what it is, but just come back here and sit down, stop drawing attention to yourselves."

They both started backing away from the TV, their eyes still fixed on the screen, fascinated by this strange moving photo. Eventually John sat down, still looking at the screen. The sound of Jake crying brought Sarah from out of her trance. She unbuttoned the front of her dress, preparing herself to feed Jake, when the bar man called over and pointed his finger in the direction of a doorway.

"Ladies toilets are that way love. You'll have more privacy in there."

Sarah nodded timidly and clutching Jake she blushed as she bustled past him to the toilets.

"You guys not drinking?" the barman asked Apex and John.

"We've just arrived from the States, I'm still getting my bearings and haven't got around to getting any money sorted yet," Apex lied.

The barman walked over to them with a friendly smile.

"Oh, nice one, I love the States! Here, let me give you some drinks on the house."

"On the house?"

"Yeah it's Christmas, this round's on me. What'll it be?"

"Oh well thank you, that's very kind of you man. Do you have any cider?" Apex asked.

"Yeah, we've got plenty of that here, this is the West Country after all!"

Apex got up and wandered over to the bar to take a look at the vast selection of ciders on offer.

"This one looks good, I'll have the White Stark please," Apex said confidently, as if he knew what he was talking about.

"Good choice mate," said the barman with a little wink and then leaning in closer to Apex he whispered,

"My friend I've got to give you credit, you're so brave coming out in public like that. Showing the world it's OK to wear women's clothes. If you don't mind me asking, where did you get your dress from? Because, between you and me, I'm quite partial to wearing a dress myself from time to time and I rather like this vintage look you're pulling off."

Apex stared at the barman, unsure of how best to reply. He cleared his throat and murmured,

"Well these aren't actually my clothes. I borrowed them from a mate to wear to this party we're going to."

"Ha ha alright mate, I believe you, millions wouldn't," chuckled the barman. He gave him another wink and passed him his pint of cider.

"Cola for the lad then is it?"

"Yeah and the girl too please bro," replied Apex. Despite knowing how bad cola was, he was keen to get away from this dress-loving weirdo as quickly as possible. In his time zone cola had been banned from every country, except his own of course. In fact, the U.S. had positively encouraged the consumption of cola, even adding in twice as much sugar as any other country had, before they'd banned it. One glass wouldn't hurt them. He thanked the barman and was just about to head back to the table with the drinks when he stopped and asked,

"Hey, I don't suppose you happen to know a guy called Ema do you?"

"Ema? No, not that I can think of mate. That's a pretty unusual name, I reckon I would know if I'd heard it before."

"Ok, thanks. What about Rose, do you know a girl called Rose?"

"Yes, I know a couple of Rose's as it happens."

Apex's eyes lit up with excitement.

"I've got a cousin called Rose and my grandmother was called Rose too."

"Ah shit, no worries, it doesn't matter," Apex said, turning to leave.

"Hold on though, now I come to think of it there is another girl called Rose. Hang on, you'll have to let me think for a minute, I'll get back to you on that one."

"Thanks bro, it's probably not the same girl I'm thinking of, but thanks anyway."

He smiled appreciatively, his previous judgements about the man having now disappeared thanks to this kindness. Although they'd only been in this time zone for a short while, he liked it way more than John's one.

"Man this place is awesome, everyone's so friendly, I could seriously get used to this," he said to John, passing him the cold glass of cola.

"Aye 'tis true, but we cannot receiveth too comfortable Apex, we hast to findeth Rose remember."

He took the glass from Apex and immediately returned his gaze to the TV. Apex sighed,

"It's a television John. People use cameras and the image gets projected onto this screen. These ones are so old it's a joke. In my time zone they're way more advanced. We use holograms and extremely high tech computers. It really isn't anything to get excited about. Hey, John, are you listening to me? John, earth to John, are you there?" said Apex waving his hand in front of John's face.

"How can thee beest on the box, when thou art here beside me?"

"What you talking about bro?"

John pointed up towards the television.

"Up thither on that box, how canst thee be thither and hither at the same time?"

Apex looked at the TV screen. His jaw dropped as he realised what he was seeing. John was right, it was him.

"What the fuck, that's… that's me…!" He watched for a couple more seconds before shouting to the barman, "Hey bro, can you turn the volume up please?"

The barman pointed the remote control at the TV and the sound blared out across the pub.

"After reviewing the CCTV footage we have found what appears to be another person present, a black male, approximately six foot two

inches, wearing only his underwear. The man, believed to be in his
early twenties, is seen behaving erratically and is clearly in a lot of
distress. As of yet we do not know who this individual is and we urgently
request that if anyone knows this person, or if you believe you may have
seen him in the area, to please contact the Avon and Somerset
Constabulary, or to contact Crime Stoppers."

"Wherefore art thee on that box, Apex?"

"It's my dream, it's my fucking dream man. I dreamt about that man dying. I saw him burning in that van. I tried to get him out, but I couldn't break the window, it was too hot. It's always the same, I dream about him dying and then I dream about Rose and after that, well that's when the Greys come. But I don't understand, how can I be on camera? It was a dream, just a dream, it doesn't make any sense."

Sarah walked back into the bar with Jake asleep on her chest.

"Those garderobes art so luxurious and thither wast this liquid slime, t'was all green and sticky, but t smelt wonderful. And thither wast this strange box that blew out hot air, it didst frighten the life out of me and poor Jake. And…" she paused, noticing the concern on Apex's face. "Art thee alright Apex? T looks like thee hath seen a ghost."

"I was on the TV, Sarah. I'm wanted for murder."

"TV? What doth thee mean, TV?"

"Never mind about that now, it's too complicated to explain, all you need to know is that there's going to be a hell of a lot more people after me now. Shit, it's the same old fucking story… hold on, what did you say Sarah?"

"I didst say what doth thee mean, TV?"

"No, no, before that, you know when you first came over?"

"That thee doth look like thee hath seen a ghost, thee behold a pale face."

"Yes, that's it! It must be!"

"What Apex, I understandeth not what thee art talking about?" said John.

"Ghosts. Remember what Calcus said? He said that we can be seen in other time zones as ghosts. He said that you can see people that don't match your time zone, so when I saw that guy burning in the van and then when I see Rose, it must mean that I'm in her time zone. And when I travelled to Rose's time zone I must have got been caught on the television cameras as a ghost!"

"But thou hast done nowt wrong Apex, thee hath not murdered anyone hither. It must be a mistake," Sarah said reassuringly. "And I am most certain thee art no ghost!" she giggled, playfully pinching his arm to prove his existence.

"I know, but that's not what it looks like on TV. Man, this shit just gets worse and worse. I tell you, when I meet this fucking Ema he's going to wish he'd never created me. How can this so-called 'God' be such an asshole? If he really is the creator of everything and determines what we do, then how come he allows such shit to happen?"

They sat in silence, each one bearing the brunt of Apex's anger as the negative tension filled the atmosphere. Apex sat with his arms folded, a deep frown on his face. John and Sarah looked on helplessly.

The barman came up to the table with a cloth in one hand and a glass in the other. The friendliness he had displayed earlier had disappeared and he now seemed reserved, apprehensive somehow.

"Hey that Rose girl you were asking about, well it might be the daughter of Michelle Herkes. She lives not far from here, and I'm fairly certain she works down at Trudy's fashion shop. Michelle's boyfriend Shaun has been in here a few times to drink and he plays darts for the Winterbourne pub team. Do you reckon that could be the Rose you're looking for?"

"Yes, that sounds like our Rose."

"I'll see if I can find out where she lives for you. But listen, I should probably tell you that there are some rumours going round that it was Shaun McCombie who was in that van at the Winterbourne. You know, the van that was mysteriously set on fire? Everyone's talking about it. So how comes you know them then?"

John and Sarah looked to Apex, who quickly invented a story.

"Um, she met me when she was on a trip in the States. I'm a friend of the family. Shit, I'm sorry to hear about Shaun, that's a proper bad way to go out." He nervously cleared his throat and continued, "But yeah, that would be great if you could find out where she lives for us please."

"I'll see what I can do," said the barman.

He walked back to the bar and then out through a door at the rear. Apex swallowed hard. What if the barman had seen him on TV? He thought back to the three men they'd encountered earlier. That must be why one of them had recognised him!

Unaware of Apex's concerns, John sat peering at the unusual brown liquid in his glass. He sniffed it and then took a tiny sip. As soon as the liquid touched his tongue he excitedly exclaimed,

"Mine lord, this doth taste most delicious! I hast never tasted anything quite like this!" He gulped down the entire glassful and gave a satisfied sigh as he placed the empty glass back on the table. Seeing how much John had enjoyed this new drink, Sarah followed suit, her

352

eyes also widening with delight at the taste. It made a welcome change from all the cider she'd had recently.

With his thoughts still firmly focused on the news broadcast, Apex asked,

"John, do you think he knows anything? Do you think he recognises me from the television?"

"Who?"

"The barman, he gave me a strange look when he came over."

"Worry not Apex, let us keepeth drinking. He willt beest back anon and that gent might findeth Rose for us. If thee doth recall, they art friendly hither."

"I guess," replied Apex.

"But of course," exclaimed John suddenly, jumping up and spilling Apex's drink.

"Woah easy bro, what's up?"

"That gent didst say that Rose's mother hath worked at this Trudy's shop."

"Right and...?" said Apex, unsure where John was going with this.

"Rose hath said that this lady, Trudy, didst killeth Shaun, like on that box up thither, like in thine dream Apex. And dost thou recall, Rose said that she didst killeth that lady," said John excitedly.

"Right, and what's your point?"

"If we can findeth Trudy's shop before the late morrow, we wilt findeth Rose; that lady wilt leadeth us to Rose!"

"Man that is absolute genius! Well done bro, give me some cookie!" said Apex putting his fist out to John.

Now there was the huge task of working out how they were going to convince her of their story once they found her. It was unlikely she would remember them, or anything that had happened to her in a previous time, and it seemed virtually impossible that she would believe anything coming from a man in a dress and two people that spoke Middle English. Then there was the small matter of the world ending because of an alien invasion. Of course she would think they were crazy, Apex didn't even quite believe it himself and he very much could remember!

The door of the pub creaked open and in walked two people. Hearing the noise, Apex turned to see who it was and wasn't at all surprised to see two men in navy blue uniforms. The policemen removed their hats and placed them under their arms, acknowledging the barman, who nodded in Apex's direction. They turned to look at the three unusually dressed people sat sheepishly in the corner.

"Hello you lot, are you having a good evening?" asked one of the officers.

"Yes thanks, we're loving Bristol officer, everyone's so friendly," replied Apex.

"On holiday are you? I see you're not from around here, that's an American accent if I'm not mistaken. What are your names?"

"Yep sure is, my name's Apex and I'm from Southfield, Detroit. I'm here on vacation with my friends, this is John and Sarah and that's Jake, her baby."

"I see, so where are you all staying then?"

"With friends," replied Apex, nervously rubbing his hands together.

"Right, and where do they live?"

"Oh, out of the city, they're from… err."

John cut in,

"Bath sir, from Bath."

"Now look, I can tell when I'm being lied to," said the officer with a frown. "We believe that you may have some information on the death of a man whose body was found in a van at the Winterbourne pub. The CCTV footage shows a person matching your description at the scene. Can I have your surname please Apex?"

"Sure, it's Mensah."

The police officer stared at them, making a mental note of their unusual clothing and dirty appearance. He lifted his hand to his mouth and spoke into his walkie-talkie.

"Can I have a background check on an Apex Mensah, recently arrived here from America. May also need to check immigration and inform the US embassy."

The other officer approached Apex and started reading him his rights.

"Apex Mensah I am placing you under arrest on the suspicion of murder, you do not have to say anything, but it may harm your defence if you do not mention when questioned something which you later rely on in court. Anything you do say may be given in evidence. Do you have any questions?"

"Look guys, I haven't done anything wrong, there's an explanation for this, honest. I've been sent here to save the planet and if you take me away we'll all be in serious danger. You've got to believe me. You all seem really friendly here and I don't want to hurt anyone. Just let me go and I can find Rose and get this sorted. Please, you really don't want to make me angry," said Apex desperately.

Ignoring his pleas, the officer said, "I'm afraid you will all have to come with us to the station so that we can interview you properly. Can you stand please Mr Mensah, we need to handcuff you."

Apex stood and placed his hands out in front of him. The officer slipped the cuffs over his wrists and locked them into place. As he was being escorted away he turned his head to John and Sarah and said,

"I'll go with them and tell them everything. I'll warn them about the Greys and tell them they need to get people as far away from built up areas as possible. Then they'll release us and we can concentrate on finding Rose."

"Aye, but recall we hast to beest out before the late morrow, otherwise 'tis no use," said John.

Apex nodded before being pushed into the back of one of the police cars. John and Sarah were escorted into the other vehicle.

As the police cars sped off, the skies darkened and a deep, ominous rumble reverberated across the land. Something was coming.

Chapter 42

Patchway Police Centre, Bristol

Apex sat at the small table, his cuffed hands resting in front of him. Glancing around at the bare white walls, his gaze came to rest on the large mirrored screen to his right. He stared at the reflection looking back at him and gave an embarrassed shake of his head as he took in the state of his balding head and the ridiculous dress hanging loosely from his muscular frame. Two smartly dressed, stern looking women were sat in the room with him.

"The date is December 22nd 2018. Interview time is 10:30pm. In the room we have Inspector Salima Cherrad and myself, Inspector Caroline Taylor. Also present in the room is the suspect, Mr Apex Mensah. Mr Mensah, could you confirm your name for the purpose of the recording please?"

Apex smiled at the Inspector.

"You all seem so calm here, it's so refreshing. You dress nicely too, that's a top notch set of suits you've got there." He looked admiringly at their smart, grey clothing. One of the officers had an almost exotic appearance; golden tanned skin and beautiful features. The other had a much paler complexion, her face was framed by long brown hair and she was wearing glasses. Both were attractive in their own way.

"Your name please!" shouted the officer with glasses.

"Sure, my name is Apex Mensah," said Apex blinking.

"And for the purpose of the recording could you confirm that you were offered legal aid, but you refused it."

"Yes, I have refused legal aid."

"Thank you Mr Mensah. Now, can you please tell us your reason for being in the UK?"

"Sure, but before I tell you I should probably warn you that you're probably going to find it difficult to understand. You're probably going to think I'm crazy, but please hear me out, because it's vital that you listen and believe everything I say."

The police inspectors looked at one another with raised eyebrows and then nodded at Apex to continue.

"OK here goes, I'm from Southfield Detroit in America, from the year 2200. I live in a future time zone and I was sent here to find someone, someone who is going to help save our world. I came to your time zone with John and Sarah. Are they OK by the way?"

"Yes they're fine, don't worry about them. They are with Sergeant Fitch in the other interview room. So let me get this straight, you're saying that you have travelled from the future Mr Mensah, is that correct?"

"Yes, that's right. I was sent here to save the world."

Inspector Cherrad coughed in disbelief, a smile forming at the edges of her lips. Inspector Taylor gave her a stern look. She took a sip of water before composing herself. Changing her line of questioning, Inspector Taylor asked,

"Do you normally go around wearing dresses Mr Mensah?"

"Look, I can explain that later, it's really not important right now," replied Apex, feeling frustrated at how much time was being wasted.

"Mr Mensah, you are in no position to decide what is and is not important right now, that's our job. Be aware however, that we are quite happy to sit here and wait for as long as it takes to get what we need from you. Can you tell me why you were seen around the van at the time of the incident? Why were you at the Winterbourne pub and do you know who that person was in the van?"

"I don't know him as such, but he's been in my dreams. I've seen that burning van more times than I can remember. One time in particular stands out, because I was staying over at the Queen's palace and that's not something you forget in a hurry. I remember the dream so vividly from that night, because I was trying really hard to get him out of the van, but I couldn't break the window. It was too hot and I couldn't get him out in time." He paused. "And then the dream changes and Rose is there, crying. That's when I see the fucking Greys. I'm telling you those fuckers are coming and if you don't let me do something about it, they're going to kill us all!"

Inspector Taylor sighed, she had no time for this kind of nonsense. She took off her glasses and rubbed the sides of the top of her nose, a habit she always did when feeling frustrated by a difficult suspect.

"So Mr Mensah to confirm, you are stating on record that you were at the site of the crime in your dreams? And that you were staying with the Queen in the 16th century at the same time?"

"That's right. Man, I know it sounds crazy, but seriously it wasn't me that killed him. It was Rose, she did it with her mind."

"Do you honestly expect us to believe this Mr Mensah?" asked Inspector Cherrad.

"You have to believe me, it's our only chance."

Inspector Taylor twiddled her pen, deep in thought on how to proceed with the interview. Putting her glasses back on, she stared into Apex's eyes, as if trying to find the truth hidden in them. Apex stared back. Unfazed by this, Inspector Taylor continued to stare while positioning her laptop in front of Apex so that he could see the screen clearly.

"We are about to show Mr Mensah the CCTV footage in order to help us identify exactly what happened on the night the victim died. Mr Mensah is clearly shown in this section of the recording. Mr Mensah can you talk us through this please."

"Sure, that's me there and I'm looking over at the van, but you can't see it because it's off screen at the moment. I'm running over to it. Look, the camera's following me, you can see it now. I'm trying to kick the window in, but I can't do it. It was awful watching him burn like that, I saw him die. And the screams, oh man, I've never heard anything like it before. It still haunts me now just thinking about it. And that's when I see Rose in my dream, but obviously you can't see…" he broke off as the recording began to distort. "Hang on, wait. Rewind that bit a second. Yes, that's it there, now pause it. Can you zoom in on that window in the background?"

Inspector Taylor pressed the pause button on the laptop and zoomed in on the window.

"Zoom in more. Now sharpen it. Yes, that's it. Do you see her? Do you see Rose?"

"I suppose it does look as though there's something there yes, but it's very blurry," said Inspector Taylor, squinting at the screen.

"Look closer, it's Rose, you can see her in the window, clear as day!"

"I agree, there is a girl, but it's certainly not clear enough to distinguish whether this is the girl you are referring to. Her hands are covering her face, it could be anyone."

"It's Rose I tell you. Go forward a bit more, that's it, right there, look!"

Apex's heart skipped a beat as he realised what he was seeing on the screen.

"There, can you see it?" he said shakily, pointing at the image.

"Mr Mensah, what are you talking about?"

"In the background, next to Rose. It's the eyes. I can see the eyes. They're like metallic silver, you must be able to see them." Apex shook with fear as he stared at the evil vision on the laptop screen.

"Mr Mensah I can see what you are claiming as 'eyes', but it is just a trick of the light, a reflection, nothing more."

"No, no you're wrong, it's a sign. It's the Greys, they're coming."

He jumped out of his chair. They were getting closer, he had to get out of this place.

"Mr Mensah, calm yourself. Please sit back down."

Apex took a deep breath, trying to compose himself. He didn't have time for their questions, but he did need their help and if he had any chance of getting it, he would have to co-operate. First things first, he needed to make them believe him.

"OK, I'm sorry Inspector." He sat down and continued calmly, "Listen, you have to warn people about the Greys. You need to get everyone out of the city to some place safe. I really need to find a guy called Ema, so I need you to use all of your inVestigative power, all of your manpower to help me find him. Tell your officers to ask around, speak to everyone, find me a camera crew, let me talk to the country. Someone, somewhere must know who Ema is. We're running out of time!"

"Tell me, who is this Ema you keep referring to Mr Mensah?"

"He's a God, the creator of the Para-verse - our universe. If the Greys find him before us, they will destroy every single one of us. Our world as we know it will be destroyed and the entire human race will be wiped out."

"Mr Mensah, I sincerely hope that this is not some lame attempt at pleading insanity, because if it is then I highly recommend you seek the advice of a solicitor."

"For fucks sake man," shouted Apex, slamming his shackled hands on the table. "Open your rigid fucking minds for just one minute. You see these cuffs you've put me in, well I can get out of these easily. I could have got out of here ages ago if I'd really wanted to, but no I came with you because I thought this time zone was cool, that the people here were nice. Man, I even thought you guys were nice. I mean for starters you haven't tried to kill me, which is a vast improvement on the last place. I came with you because I need your help, but you're not listening to me. I didn't want to have to do this, but you've left me no choice. Watch…"

Apex closed his eyes and visualised his wrists, concentrating on the red marks caused by the tightly secured cuffs. He imagined the

362

mechanical locks turning, the pressure of the cuffs easing, loosening
before falling effortlessly to the ground.

The two women blinked, unable to comprehend what they had just witnessed.

"How did you do that?" Inspector Taylor finally managed to utter.

"It's a lot easier than it looks, I've got better at it now. When I first tried it out it was really difficult to control, I had to be angry or afraid, you know have a really extreme emotion attached to it or something. But I seem to have mastered it now that I've learnt to control it. It's hard to explain, but I kind of imagine it deep inside me, a bit like when a kettle starts boiling. When I need it I just sort of let it go."

Now that he had their full attention, Apex started showing off.

"Look, watch this."

He closed his eyes again, this time imagining the pen nestled in the
top pocket of Inspector Cherrad's jacket. He visualised it slowly rising
up out of the pocket and then levitating in mid-air before floating
gracefully across the room and landing on the table in front of him.

The Inspectors looked at one another in bewilderment.

"Inspector Taylor, I think we need to speak to the Governor about this. We have it on camera don't we?" said Inspector Cherrad shakily.

Inspector Taylor nodded. Her face had gone pale and she looked visibly shaken. She stood up and placed her hand on the back of the chair to steady herself. Looking at Apex she said,

"We will return shortly Mr Mensah."

"Hey, can I go yet? I need to get out of here."

"Mr Mensah, we can detain you for up to twenty four hours before we decide to charge you. You might as well make yourself comfortable as you may be here for some time."

"You do realise I can just walk out of here anytime I like, right? You just saw what I'm capable of."

"I would strongly advise you not to Mr Mensah, we don't want to use excessive force unless we have to"

"Ha don't make me laugh, *excessive force*, you guys are so funny!"

Apex slid down into the seat of the chair and gave a sigh of frustration. The Inspectors left the room.

"I don't feel too well Salima, did you see what he did in there?"

"No, I don't feel too good either, how did he manage to get those cuffs off, they were on so tight, I checked them myself. He's got to be a magician or an escapologist, or something. It's the only logical explanation."

"Your pen levitated from your pocket though, there's no way he could have done that, I mean it's supernatural or something."

"So what? Do you believe what he's saying then?"

"I don't know Salima, my brain refuses to accept it, but something in my gut tells me there's more to this."

Sergeant Fitch entered the room. He also looked shaken and a little unsettled. Trying to compose himself he tucked his loose stripy shirt into his trousers and tightened his belt. He walked over to the women and plonked himself down on one of the chairs, exhaling loudly.

"So what did they tell you Sergeant?" asked Inspector Taylor.

"Inspector, I have never seen anything like it in the entire time I've been in the Force. They're claiming to be from the sixteenth century. Yes their clothes look old, but to actually say you're from another century, well that's madness!"

"Actors maybe, perhaps there's an acting school nearby, or maybe they're part of one of those historical re-enactment groups?"

"But Inspector, they speak in Elizabethan, the boy speaks full on Shakespearean. It's bizarre, really bizarre."

"Well, most actors I know take their art very seriously. I've got friends who are actors and they're always going on about how important it is to stay in character. Bristol's known for its period dramas, perhaps that's what it is?"

"I hear what you're saying Inspector, but no these are not actors. They speak fluently, as if it's their first language and they were looking at everything as though seeing it for the very first time. They were in there studying the walls and the chairs, and you should have seen them with my laptop; they were absolutely mesmerised by it."

Inspector Taylor leaned forward and placed her head in her hands. She gave a big sigh and then looked up at the Sergeant.

"Yes OK, that is a little weird. Could you understand what they were saying?"

"Just about yes, they mentioned time zones and some kind of invasion. Oh and they kept going on about this girl called Rose and someone called Ema."

"Right, let's take these recordings to the Guv and see what he makes of it. There's definitely something strange going on."

Chapter 43

Apex brought the image of John's face into his mind; his scruffy hair and that charming, almost naïve expression of his. The walls of the interview room turned to liquid, like rippling transparent walls of water. This enabled Apex to see through to the room next door and he watched the busy office staff rushing around answering telephone calls and sorting through stacks of paperwork. He allowed his mind to navigate around the building, passing through the myriad of doors and windows in the network of corridors until he found them. He extended his arm and imagined touching John on the shoulder. Chuckling to himself he repeatedly tapped, enjoying watching John flinch with every movement.

"John it's me," laughed Apex.

"Apex, what art thou doing here?"

"I think we have a way of finding Ema, but we all need to be on board with it. I reckon if I can get the media on my side then we can use them to help us ask the nation to find Ema. At the same time I can help

366

alert people to stay away from the Greys, to warn them of the danger and to get them to safety. It's up to us to save this planet and the people on it and the only way we're going to do that is by making it as hard as possible for the Greys. If people can spread out then it will take the Greys much longer to find Ema. And at the moment we need as much extra time as we can get."

"What is this media thou speaketh of?"

"For Gods sake John, it's like the newspapers, television that kind of thing."

"Ah that box thing we didst see at the inn, will every folk see it?"

"Yes. Look, I'll come and get you soon. How are Sarah and Jake doing?"

"They art well, the lady is sat by mine side. I can believeth not what mine eyes hath seen Apex, 'tis amazing. I hath seen short quills that can write and a box that maketh noises and pictures and doth alloweth thee to send letters. Never didst I think a future time zone would beest so exciting!"

"John, seriously man, that's nothing. Most of that tech is shit, anyway enough about that, we've got a lot to get on with. Concentrate on the reason we're here, OK?"

"Aye, oh and Apex, giveth me some cookie," said John putting his imagined fist out.

Apex smiled and imagined his fist touching John's.

"Cookie bro."

Chapter 44

A pex opened his eyes, the muffled sounds that sounded very much like his name alerting him.

"Mr Mensah, can you hear me?" Inspector Taylor called. "Mr Mensah, wake up?"

He felt dizzy and slightly disorientated. Inhaling a deep lungful of air he regained control of his body and smiled smugly at the Inspectors. For the first time since this had all started he felt as though he finally had the upper hand. He was the one in the position of power for once.

"So, can I go now?" he asked.

"Mr Mensah, you mentioned an invasion, where are you getting your information from? We have advised the counter-terrorist organisation and they will be here shortly."

"Man, we haven't got time for any of this, I'm not a fucking terrorist! You'll know when they're coming. It'll start with the ground shaking, like an earthquake. Your stupid scientists will probably say it's the earth's plates moving and that it's all completely natural, but it's not. When the quakes get stronger, you'll know. You'll just know."

"And how do *you* know all of this Mr Mensah?" asked Inspector Cherrad.

"Because it's already happened in my fucking time zone that's how. The Greys exert immense gravitational force on the earth, which causes the tremors. And yeah I admit I have absolutely no idea how they do it, I'm no fucking scientist, but I do know that the quakes are an indicator they're close. My time zone fucked up, they knew there was a strange energy out there but passed it off as a rare natural occurrence, don't make the same mistake. This is your chance to help, to save your planet, to be the hero. You must help me find Ema. Let me talk to the media. I need to talk to them now!"

"I am afraid we can't allow that Mr Mensah," Inspector Taylor said shaking her head.

They'd had enough chances, it was time to take matters into his own hands. Slowly Apex stood and turned to face the wall behind him. Taking small steps, he gradually drew closer to the wall until his nose was resting lightly on the smooth surface.

"Mr Mensah, what are you doing?" said Inspector Taylor nervously. "Sit back down and we can talk about this."

Apex ignored her and took another step, the wall becoming fluid and he moved effortlessly through it, disappearing through to the other side. The Inspectors quickly ran out to the corridor, barging their way through startled admin staff and into the adjoining office. Apex was stood there, a triumphant smile on his face.

"What will it take to convince you, hey? I've shown you the cuffs coming off, pens flying and now this. Is that enough for you, or do you

369

need more? Because I've got more. Or shall we stop wasting both our time and perhaps you can start listening to me now. What do you reckon?"

"Mr Mensah, I don't know how you did that, but let's just say we do decide to trust you, we can't tell the world we're about to be invaded, there would be mass panic."

The building suddenly started to gently shake. Coffee sloshed against the sides of mugs, spilling liquid over documents. Office workers stopped what they were doing and held onto their desks in alarm. Pictures shuddered and fell from the walls, smashing glass into tiny fragments across the tiled floor and as the shaking intensified, the office windows shattered. Cracks began spreading out like a network of arteries across the walls, splitting the plaster until the pressure became so great that the brickwork imploded, blasting out thick clouds of dust into the room.

"Quick! Everybody out! Now!" an authoritative voice commanded through the mist. "Form an orderly line please, no pushing. Leave all your belongings behind, it's not worth the risk."

Inspector Taylor turned to face Apex who was still stood behind her.

"Come on Mr Mensah let's go, I'll talk to you outside." She placed her arms around his shoulders to usher him through the rubble.

"No not yet, I have to find the others, make sure they're safe. Don't worry about me, you just get yourself out of here," he shouted, shrugging her hands away.

"But it's not safe in here, you'll be killed!" yelled the Inspector.

The building gave another almighty shudder. Inspector Cherrad grabbed her arm and yelled, "Leave him Nic, it's not worth it. Come on, we need to go." The Inspectors ran across the office towards the fire exit, casting one last look at Apex, but he remained steadfast. He wasn't going to leave without his friends. Picking his way over upturned desks, he made his way unsteadily out into the corridor.

"Sarah! John! Where are you? Call out to me," he shouted, his voice echoing through the deserted rooms.

He shielded his eyes from the dust, coughing as the tiny particles of plaster filled his lungs and tore the flesh at the back of his throat.

As a last-ditch attempt, he closed his eyes and imagined John standing before him, picturing him in as much detail as he could manage, before attempting to make contact.

"John, where are you?"

"Apex, I am outside. I hath Sarah and Jake with me, we art safe. Thou must make haste, come quick," replied John.

"Cool, I was worried for a minute there bro. I'm on my way."

Apex focussed on John's position outside. He could see the tall buildings towering over the chaos below and the flashing lights of emergency vehicles as they rushed to assist. He imagined he was right there with John and Sarah.

He opened his eyes and smiled.

"Ha thou art slow Apex," laughed John.

"I didn't realise we were competing John. I'll get better, just you wait and see, then we'll see who's slow," said Apex giving John a playful punch on the arm.

Sarah rushed over to Apex and embraced him tightly.

"I missed thee Apex, I am most glad thou art safe."

Apex hugged her back, inhaling the smell of her, feeling the warming rush of love from deep within.

"Ah Mr Mensah, I'm glad I've found you," a voice called out. Inspector Taylor emerged from the crowd. She was covered in dust, but still looked as if she meant business. OK, I believe you. There is absolutely no way you could have made the earth shake like that, and we have never had earthquakes of that intensity in the UK before. I cannot even begin to understand any of this, but I'm ready to accept that what you have told me is true. What do you need me to do?"

"Get the national news here, I need to address the country. I have to warn them."

"Let me make a few phone calls and I'll arrange a press conference. Just try not to scare people too much alright, the last thing we need is to panic the entire country!"

"I wouldn't worry about that right now Inspector. Trust me, when those Greys get here, that's when you'll know the true meaning of panic."

"Mr Mensah, please understand that I am putting my career on the line for this. I'm trusting you with this, so for both our sakes please make sure you do this right."

Inspector Taylor withdrew her mobile from her pocket and shakily tapped the buttons. She turned away, mumbling something into the speaker and then paused to listen to the response. She nodded as she talked, her blonde hair bouncing wildly as her voice became louder and her tone more aggressive.

"I don't care! Just get here now!" she shouted down the phone, before turning back to face Apex. "Right, most reporters are already out on jobs; it seems as though this has hit large areas of the UK and Europe. I've managed to find someone and they're on their way now.

Make sure you're prepared and that you know exactly what you're going to say, OK?"

Apex nodded.

"Believe me Inspector, I have never been more prepared in my life. Except maybe for the dress... I don't suppose you could get me some new clothes, could you?"

Chapter 45

Patchway Police Centre forecourt.
Several hours later.

The streets of Bristol were awash with panic. The UK had never experienced an earthquake of this magnitude before and people were scared. The flashing lights from the emergency services lit up the cloudless night sky, creating an eerie glow across the city. Paramedics and police officers were attempting to keep people calm, but even they looked fearful and confused by what was happening. Only Apex, John and Sarah remained calm. If they were to stand any hope of defeating the Greys they had to remain level headed, strong and most importantly work together. Their main goal was to find Ema and with the arrival of the reporter and camera crew Apex prepared himself to stand and address the nation. He glanced at his reflection in one of the windows of the police centre, straightening his shirt collar and smoothing down the suit that had been donated to him. It fitted him perfectly, as if it had been tailor made especially for him.

Sarah smiled admiringly at him. She'd never seen clothing like this before, but she recognised quality when she saw it and it made Apex look even more handsome.

"Thou doth appear most smart Apex, those robes doth suit thee greatly! Thou art most handsome," she blushed.

"Why thanks Sarah, anything's got to be better than that dress! Do you realise how long it's been since I actually wore something half decent? Man, I look pretty awesome in this suit, don't I? Not sure about the colour mind you, grey ain't exactly my favourite colour. I much prefer gold or some other shit like that, but hey beggars can't be choosers." Filled with confidence, he took another quick glance at himself and then turned back to Sarah. He closed his eyes and leaned forward, finally giving in to the overwhelming urge to kiss her. As he did so a harassed looking reporter barged in,

"Mr Mensah, are you ready? I had to travel through a lot of crap to get here, so this better be good."

Apex stumbled and opened his eyes, embarrassed that his amorous advances had been disturbed.

"Just do what you have to do and point the camera at me when you're good to go."

The reporter nodded and faced the camera,

"This is Robert Hammond reporting from outside Patchway Police Centre. We are still unsure as to what has caused the disturbance in the Earth's plates, but I am joined with someone who might just be able to help us understand. Mr Mensah what can you tell us about the unusual earthquake activity we've been experiencing?"

"Turn the camera so it's more on me," demanded Apex. "Yeah that's it, that's great." The reporter began to protest, absolutely mortified that his broadcast was being ruined, but Apex ignored him and stared deep into the camera lens. 'OK, all you people out there listen very carefully. My name is Apex Mensah and I've been sent here from the year 2200 to save your lives and the lives of future generations. These earthquakes are not being caused by any natural reason, they've been happening because of a massive gravitational force from outside of our solar system. This planet is going to be attacked within the next few hours, a day at most…'

Inspector Taylor and Inspector Cherrad stood off camera, cringing at Apex's choice of words. This would most definitely lead to mass panic; the Governor would be furious. Trying to regain control of his interview, the red-faced reporter positioned himself between Apex and the camera.

"Well I think that's enough, thank you Mr Mensah."

But Apex was having none of it; he hadn't gone through everything he'd been through to be silenced at this most crucial of moments. The Inspectors furiously waved their arms around trying to get Apex's attention to prevent him from causing even more damage, but it was no use.

"Hey bro, I haven't finished yet! Get out of my fucking way!" he shouted angrily. 'The Greys are coming and they're going to destroy us all. You must hide, hide wherever you can, wherever's safe. Avoid large groups of people, stay close to your loved ones and find refuge. Get out of the cities, head to the countryside and hide anywhere that is isolated. Stock up on rations and gather together anything that will serve as a weapon. Although weapons won't help you against the Greys, you'll need them to fight and, if need be, kill those people who have already been possessed. The Greys cannot be reasoned with, they don't care and will not listen to you, so don't attempt to communicate with them. Finally, I need to find a guy called Ema. He is the only one that can help us, so please if you know him or if you have heard the name Ema, contact the police immediately."

"Right that's enough!" shouted the reporter. "Are you trying to destroy my career? What the hell was that all about?"

He grabbed his belongings and ushered the camera crew away, cursing to himself as he walked off.

Apex walked over to Sarah, keen to ask her what she'd thought of his speech, when an angry voice boomed out in the distance, stopping him in his tracks. A large man waddled sluggishly towards them.

"What the hell was that on the news? Apparently people are leaving the city in droves, they've caused massive traffic jams in the city and if that wasn't bad enough, there are reports that the country roads are now blocked as well! What the hell have you done Inspector Taylor? You were meant to wait for the counter-terrorist organisation. And why are these lot not in cuffs?"

"Sorry Guv, I know this hasn't been handled in the best way, but you've always told us to go with our gut and as far fetched as it sounds I just can't help but feel they're telling the truth. Inspector Cherrad and Sergeant Fitch will back me up sir."

"OK, but if this ends up making my force look bad Inspector I will hold you personally responsible."

"Hey guys sorry to butt in on your conversation, but we need to go. We have to find Rose," interrupted Apex.

"What, you're letting them go? Inspector explain yourself."

"I can't stop them Guv, no one can."

"What are you on about, we're the police of course we can stop them. This is entirely unorthodox behaviour Inspector Taylor, I simply cannot condone this. I am shocked, this is completely out of character for you. I will expect to receive your letter of resignation on my desk first thing in the morning."

"Look Guv I know how it looks, but I'm asking you to trust me. I've witnessed things today that are way beyond my understanding and there is not a shadow of a doubt that something is happening. If we are faced with a potential threat, then it isn't something we should ignore. I'm asking for 24 hours Guv, that's all."

The Governor thought for a moment.

"Alright Inspector Taylor, you've got 24 hours. However, if all of this does somehow miraculously turn out to be true, I want it handed over to the military. Keep me informed."

"Yes Guv, and thank you."

Apex coughed sharply to get Inspector Taylor's attention.

"Inspector, we need a headquarters, a base, somewhere we can hide out and be protected. We also need to get hold of the military, make sure they're on board with this; they can protect the city while we find Rose. As I said in my speech, weapons won't help against the Greys - they attack through close contact, get into your mind and destroy you that way - but being armed will certainly help defend us against those who are already possessed and will buy us a bit more time."

"Mr Mensah come on now, this is England, I can't just go and pick up a load of machine guns down the local shop. Sure the armed units have guns, but they are very highly protected, they're not going to simply hand them all over because we've asked them to."

"I think you'll find they will. You're forgetting what I can do aren't you?" grinned Apex. "Gather your people together and go to the armed unit section. Get as many weapons as you can carry then meet me back here. We can use the police station as a base. You'll need to make sure it's as impenetrable as possible."

"Mr Mensah you're not listening, this is not possible. How am I going to convince everyone that this is the correct course of action? I need evidence Apex, proof that something serious is going to happen. Most people want a logical explanation and you've got to admit it does all sound a little far fetched?"

"For fucks sake, just do what you can OK? You're a person of authority so make them damn well listen! And look, there'll be more earthquakes. If you notice anyone acting strangely, more specifically if their movements are rigid and well basically if they look like a zombie, shoot them and get the fuck out of there. Got it?"

Sarah had stayed quiet up until now, the servant in her was used to being seen and not heard, but something had been playing on her mind for a while now. She tapped John on the shoulder and said,

"John dost thou bethink we should asketh the lady about the shop that Rose's mother didst worketh?"

"Aye of course, Sarah thou art more than a pretty face!" John smiled "Inspector, can thee findeth wherefore art the shop that is called 'Trudy's Fashion' is?"

"Yes, I believe it's on Gloucester Road, but I'm not sure exactly where it is. I'll find out and let you know, do you have a phone I can contact you on?"

"A phone?" asked John curiously.

"I'll explain later John," said Apex. "No, we don't have a phone Inspector."

"Here take mine, I have another in my car. I will contact you when I get any updates. Inspector Cherrad and Sergeant Fitch are going to help me; between the three of us we'll do whatever we can to get military back up. Head straight in that direction, that's the way to Gloucester Road. By the time you get there, I'll have found out the exact location of the shop. I'll be in touch."

She gave them an anxious smile and then turned and headed back to her colleagues. Apex, John and Sarah headed off in the direction the Inspector had pointed. The earthquakes would be coming again soon, so they would need to hurry. The risk of death was increasing with every single second that passed.

It was do or die time.

No choice.

If they died it was game over... the extinction of humankind.

Chapter 46

Patchway Police Centre Car Park

Inspector Taylor rested her hands on the steering wheel and took a deep breath. She suffered from episodes of anxiety every now and then, usually triggered by particularly distressing cases. Needless to say, this case was far more distressing than any she had ever encountered before. She had dealt with enough time wasters to know what signs to look out for, but Apex and his friends were displaying signs of genuine concern and that wasn't something she could ignore. The idea of time travel and aliens was ridiculous though; maybe all her years in the police force had finally taken its toll on her mental state. But Inspector Cherrad and Sergeant Fitch had seen it too, so she couldn't be going crazy. Even so, it didn't stop her from asking them again.

"Do you think we're doing the right thing? I mean what if this is all a hoax or just some crazy coincidence? We could all lose our jobs over this, not to mention looking completely stupid in the process."

"Inspector, you're never wrong. That's why you've won so many awards. You've solved some of the toughest crimes out there. I trust you and I'm sure Inspector Cherrad does too," said Sergeant Fitch looking at Inspector Cherrad for back up.

Inspector Cherrad nodded and placed her hand on her colleague's shoulder.

"What if they are right and we don't help them," she said. "What if this isn't some crazy coincidence? What then? We could have a lot of blood on our hands if we don't do anything. You're doing the right thing. Call Mr Mensah and let him know where that shop is and we'll take it one step at a time."

Inspector Taylor hesitated. Her mind was riddled with doubt, but she felt encouraged by her colleagues' positive words. She took out her phone and dialled the number to reach Apex.

"Mr Mensah, I've found out where 'Trudy's Fashion' shop is for you. It's on the corner of Gloucester Road; keep walking to the end and it should be there on your left."

"Thanks Inspector that's great. Is there any news on Ema, have you heard anything?"

"No nothing yet."

"For fucks sake man! OK, where are you now? Have you managed to get a base sorted, what about weapons?"

"I'm working on it Mr Mensah. I'm trying to gain access to the armed unit, but I need a good reason to be in there. You have to understand that there is a protocol to these kind of things."

"Fuck protocol! Here's a fucking excuse for you, a million grey aliens are going be here soon and they do not have any fucking excuse to kill us all. Now, you go into that armed unit and tell them that unless they let you in and give you access to their guns, then we're all going to die, do you get me?"

"I'm going to speak to General Leonard. It's a bit of a long shot, but if I can get him on side, we're laughing. I will get back to you shortly with any updates. Good luck in finding Rose, let me know if you find her."

"Oh we will find her Inspector, don't you worry about that. Catch you later."

Inspector Taylor hung up the phone and placed it back into her jacket pocket.

"How are we going to convince the General? It all sounds so absurd, what do you both think?"

Sergeant Fitch looked at Inspector Taylor, deep in thought. "We've got audio and visual evidence, surely that's enough proof that this isn't your average case? Plus, when was the last time the UK had an earthquake measuring four on the Richter scale?"

"Yes I know, but he'll want logical answers, logical answers we don't have," said Inspector Taylor..

"What choice do we have?" muttered Sergeant Fitch. "If we can't convince the General then we will have to break in to the armed unit and get the weapons ourselves. We have to at least try, because whatever happens we'll either be out of a job or dead."

"You're right Sergeant, come on let's go,"replied Inspector Taylor.

The roads were blocked with people desperately trying to flee the city and Inspector Taylor struggled to manoeuvre the police car in and out of the traffic. Panicked pedestrians were manically rushing up and down the street, stocking up on rations as they had been instructed to. Inspector Taylor had never seen anything like it; people were genuinely frightened. Men and women were wandering about yielding rolling pins and other household items as weapons. Shops were being looted and people ran out clutching televisions and other expensive electrical items. Eventually, they arrived at the front of the Military Conference Hall and she pulled into a space. They got out of the car and walked apprehensively towards the large building. A pair of Union Jack flags hung from each side of the heavy wooden doors and a serious looking armed guard stood at the entrance. He glared at them, asking their intentions, and then stepped aside after checking their identification.

The forecourt was taken up with several military statues. On the wall to their left was a plaque entitled 'The brave soldiers that fought heroically in the trenches' followed by a long alphabetical list of names, and on the right a memorial marked the lives that had been lost during the Second World War. Sidestepping their way through the statues they made their way over to a door on the far side of the forecourt and tentatively opened it. The room inside was filled with people, all of whom were sat listening intently to a speaker at the front.

"As noted by Professor Darren Fox in his recent report, we can see that the Earth's plates have indeed shifted, creating the unusual earthquakes that have occurred in and around the UK over the last few days. Professor Fox theorises that this rare occurrence was last documented over several hundred years ago. He has stressed that this is not something we should be concerned about, as having researched the history of global earthquakes he has noticed a direct correlation between environmental damage and a change in climate along with the natural formations found beneath the Earth's crust. He also states that in his opinion although military presence may benefit the morale of the people, he feels it would be a waste of valuable resources. We have had no reports of any casualties and we should therefore be focussing on repairing any damage. In addition, we will advise people to return to their homes, in order to start clearing the roads thus allowing emergency vehicles better access to those in need. Are there any questions?"

Inspector Taylor stepped forward and climbed the steps that led up to the speaking platform. The General hesitated slightly upon seeing her and then turned to his audience and said,

"Please excuse me a moment ladies and gentlemen, I will answer your questions in a few minutes."

He walked over to Inspector Taylor and guided her over to the side of the stage. It had been several years since they had seen each other; the last time had been when the General's daughter had gone missing. The case had gone cold after numerous attempts to find her had failed, but when Inspector Taylor took over the case she had managed to solve it within the space of a fortnight. His daughter's remains had been found in an area of woodland 50 miles from the family home. It turned out she had been murdered by one of the worst serial killers of the last 20 years. And because of this, he had an enormous amount respect for Inspector Taylor.

"Inspector Taylor it's so good to see you. What can I do for you?"

"You too General, I just wish it was under better circumstances. I have been passed information, which strongly suggests that we will be under mass attack within the next day or so. I have video evidence to back this up. I need your help to get the military out on the streets, armed and ready to attack."

"Inspector Taylor, we have one of the best intelligence services in the world, if there was any kind of threat to this country, we would know about it."

"But General, this is not an average attack. We're talking about an intergalactic attack from extra-terrestrial beings. Our technology isn't capable of picking up such an attack."

"What are you talking about? Don't tell me you were involved in this morning's scare mongering?"

"Well yes, I admit it hasn't been handled in the best way, but my source is genuine. I have proof that something strange is happening, will you please just take a look?"

"Inspector, we have been friends for many years and I cherish our friendship I really do, so please don't ruin it. I admire you and I have great respect for you, you have solved some of the most difficult of cases, including my Hannah's, but you cannot seriously expect me to believe any of this."

"Please General, all I'm asking is that you upload this to the projector and listen to the tape recordings. If after watching and listening to it you still don't believe me then I'll leave, I promise."

"OK, you have five minutes, but I warn you if this turns out to be rubbish I will have no choice but to contact your superiors and take further action."

"I'm prepared to take that risk, thank you General."

Inspector Taylor approached the stand and looked out over the sea of heads in front of her. She took a deep breath and spoke,

"Can I have your attention please? EVERYONE CAN I HAVE SILENCE!"

A hushed silence fell over the room.

"I am Inspector Taylor from the Avon and Somerset constabulary. At approximately 7pm yesterday a man was arrested as a suspect in a murder enquiry. The man had been recognised by a local barman who had seen him on the CCTV footage that was released earlier that day. During his interview the suspect claimed to have been sent from the future, accompanied by others who had come from the past. The suspect also stated that our planet is under imminent attack from what he described as the Greys, grey mind-altering aliens."

She was met with an awkward silence, before a massive roar of laughter bellowed around the room.

"CAN I HAVE YOUR ATTENTION, PLEASE?" she shouted. "I have the recordings from the interview here along with video evidence of the man in question. Watch and you will see things that cannot be logically explained."

Inspector Taylor turned and nodded to the General to start playing the recording.

The crowd sat with smirks on their faces; some shouted out obscenities and several walked out of the room. Feeling flustered and frustrated, Inspector Taylor looked back at the General and stammered,

"Can you play the video now please?"

She cleared her throat and continued,

"Can I have your attention please? As you can see from the video you are now watching, the suspect can be seen removing his handcuffs without a key. The handcuffs were securely locked and can only be opened using the key I had on my person."

"What does that prove?" shouted a woman in the crowd.

Inspector Taylor pushed her glasses back onto the bridge of her nose and ignoring the question she carried on. "After a minute or two, we can see that the pen from Inspector Cherrad's left breast pocket appears to levitate in the air before landing on the table."

A gasp ran around the round and people began to chatter excitedly. She continued,

"But wait it gets stranger still. Even though we had removed our own cameras, the standard CCTV footage continued to film. Watch what happens next."

Inspector Taylor hadn't actually had a chance to look through the video footage herself yet. She had watched Apex pass through an impenetrable wall, but she hadn't witnessed it from his perspective. The screen showed Apex sitting quietly, looking around the room. He closed his eyes and leant back against the chair. All of a sudden a glowing light appeared to float from out of his body and drift over to the wall. Inspector Taylor gasped, it was as much a surprise to her as it was to the other people in the room.

"That's just a trick of the light," a male voice called out.

"Well yes maybe, but can you explain what happens next? Watch what happens when my colleagues and I enter. Watch him walk towards the wall, can you see? Now look what he does."

The crowd watched in amazement as Apex passed through the wall.

"It's camera trickery!" someone shouted. "It's a hoax, it's got to be!"

"I was there, so was Inspector Cherrad! We both witnessed this event with our own eyes! What would I possibly gain from staging something like this?"

The General marched up to the front of the stage his arms raised in a bid to draw calm over the room. Inspector Taylor continued,

"There will be more earthquakes and they will get stronger."

"Inspector, what do you think is causing the earthquakes," asked a member of the audience.

"I am by no means claiming to be an expert on seismology, but what I do know is that the earthquakes we have been experiencing are not natural. The suspect told us that a massive fleet of aliens are approaching Earth. The vehicle or ship they are travelling in is creating a huge gravitational pull and this would explain these unusual earthquakes. When these beings get here, and I use the word when not if, they will destroy anyone or anything that gets in their path. We are talking worldwide destruction with the distinct possibility of human extinction."

"So how do you propose we stop this?" called another voice.

"I'm not sure I really know the answer to that, you have to remember this is all as much of a shock to me as it is to you. Until we have further information on how to deal with them, we are taking a defensive stance. From what we have been told, the Greys cannot be killed, however anyone who has been possessed by them can. The advice we have been given is that if you notice anyone acting strange you must run away as fast and as far away as you can."

"Do you know what they want?" asked the same voice.

"They are looking for someone called Ema. So far, we have not been able to trace anyone with this name, but we are continuing our search."

Suddenly, the entrance doors swung open and a man came rushing in. He passed through the startled audience, up the steps and onto the stage. Inspector Taylor recognised him as one of the research experts she had met during a brief visit to the cosmological agency. He had a cleft pallet and an old-fashioned hairstyle; he wasn't someone you forgot in a hurry. The man quickly glanced at Inspector Taylor in acknowledgment and then stood in front of the General, gasping to get his words out as he struggled to catch his breath.

"Sir... I have... had contact... with the BSA... and NASA. They have discovered some strange... activity in our solar system and... though they are unsure as to what it is, their computers show an anomaly approximately 500 million kilometres from the Earth. It is massive, almost as big as the sun, and it is travelling at enormous speed sir."

"Thank you," said the General a slight tremor in his voice. He turned to Inspector Taylor. "What do you need Inspector?"

"You have access to the military headquarters, so you can monitor the skies, I'll use the Police Centre as a base to monitor the ground. I need you to instruct your men to encircle the city and keep out the possessed. I will also need protection for the police station, so I'll need access to weapons."

"OK, I will see what I can do. I will need to inform the hierarchy first, but considering the circumstances I am certain they will pass it over to us."

"Can you grant me access to the police armed unit please?"

"Yes, I will call them now and make sure we get you in there."

Inspector Taylor thanked him and made her way out with Inspector Cherrad and Sergeant Fitch following behind. They climbed into the car and without waiting for Sergeant Fitch to close the door, Inspector Taylor revved the engine and reversed out of the space and out onto the road.

"There's still too much traffic, even the sirens aren't helping. There's got to be a quicker way to get there," groaned Sergeant Fitch.

"Come on, let's run the rest of the way, it'll be quicker," said Inspector Taylor pulling the car over to the side of the road.

They dodged their way through startled people and stationary vehicles, sprinting until they were out of breath. Stopping for a short rest, Inspector Taylor jumped as the phone in her pocket began to vibrate.

"Mr Mensah, have you found Rose?

"No not yet. We're on Gloucester Road, but it goes on forever, are you sure it's here?"

"Yes. It is a very long road, keep going and you should see it soon."

"What's happening your end?"

"I have good news. The military are on board and they are in the process of locking down the city to keep it as safe as possible. We've also been given permission to use the Police Centre as a HQ. As soon as you've found Rose, we can meet back there and discuss how to find Ema."

"That's great, I knew you had it in you. And what about guns, do you have any?"

"We are at the unit now. We have been granted access and I'm just about to get the weapons. I will be back in touch when we get back to the station."

"OK, stay safe…" Apex broke off suddenly as the ground began to shake violently. "Fuck, did you feel that? They're getting closer!"

The officers stumbled as the ground swayed from side to side. They desperately tried to grab onto something, but there was nothing within reach and they fell to the ground. Sergeant Fitch crawled across the pavement to the two frightened women, clasping their hands and pulling them in protectively towards him. Cracks slowly started to form in the ground and they could hear sound of car alarms ringing out in the distance.

A loud cracking sound came from behind them and Sergeant Fitch shouted,

"Watch out, that tree's going to fall, quick move out of the way!"

They rolled away from the swaying tree as it came crashing down on top of a parked car. The tremors continued for a few more seconds and then stopped, leaving a haunting stillness in its wake.

"We have to hurry," shouted Inspector Taylor, pulling herself up from the ground. "Let's get in," she said pointing to a large building.

"Sorry, you can't enter," instructed a guard who was stood at the entrance. "We are evacuating the building."

"We have been granted access by General Leonard, he has authorised us to take whatever we need," said Inspector Taylor impatiently.

"I have been informed of that order, but I would strongly advise you not to go in until we are sure there will be no more earthquakes."

"We don't have any choice, move!"

They barged past the guard, elbowing their way through the hoards of terrified officers who were fleeing the building.

"I think we need to go this way, look there's the sign for the armed unit sector."

The armed unit sector was filled with lockers and racks of MP5 machine guns and Remington 870 pump action shotguns. On one of the walls there hung stab proof vests, Tasers and batons.

"We can only take what we can manage to carry by foot, it's not going to be enough!" exclaimed Sergeant Fitch.

"We'll take whatever we can," said Inspector Cherrad. "Those heavy-duty bags will hold a decent number of guns and those backpacks can hold the ammunition. Cram as much as you can in them, then we'll work out a way to get back."

They filled the bags with as many items as they could and lugged them back through the corridors and out towards the front of the building. Evacuated police officers sat on the edges of the pavement looking confused. Some were just about managing to keep it together and were attending to minor injuries, others were on their phones checking their families were OK.

"Listen up everyone, we need your help," shouted Inspector Taylor. "Take a gun from one of these bags, load it, and then follow me to the station. An attack is imminent and we need as many of you as possible to help prepare our defence."

Some of the officers instantly refused, frantically shaking their heads, too scared by what had already happened. But to Inspector Taylor's relief a handful of them agreed and they immediately rushed over to take a weapon.

Inspector Taylor's inspected her makeshift army.

They were as ready as they were ever going to be.

It was time to fight back.

Chapter 47

Gloucester Road

The sun peeked from over the horizon, spreading its golden rays across the landscape and casting a spotlight on the destruction in the city. Most of the buildings were still standing, however many had collapsed, forming giant piles of rubble and creating even more roadblocks for the people who were trying to escape. People queued spilling out of the doors of shops that were still open, spilling out onto the pavements and causing even more chaos. Food supplies were already running low and as the shelves emptied, people began frantically fighting each other to make sure they weren't the ones who left empty handed. It was survival of the fittest and no one wanted to lose.

Apex, John and Sarah watched as the local authorities stepped in to try and keep the peace, but it was becoming increasingly difficult and a riot seemed almost inevitable. In reality, it didn't matter how much food they had, there was no way they'd survive an attack from the Greys, none of these people had a chance. If they didn't find Ema soon then life itself would become nothing more than a black abyss. The pressure upon them was greater than ever.

Having found 'Trudy's Fashion Shop' they stood outside and peered through the window trying to work out who Trudy was. Sarah shivered, it was a cold morning and having been outside for so long she was really starting to feel it.

"Can thee see that lady Master Apex?" she said through stammering teeth.

"I don't know what she looks like, Rose never described her to me. The only way we're going to find out is if one of us goes in there and asks, so come on who's going in?"

Sarah and John looked at Apex expectantly.

"Woah hang on, why are you both looking at me? I've done most of the work already, surely it's about time one of you guys did something!"

"Thee doth behold most smart Apex, whereas we art still in our Elizabethan robes. Thee would beest best suited to wend in a shop that selleth robes. Say 'tis for thy beautiful lady," said Sarah smiling sweetly.

Apex sighed. He knew they were right; after all he was the only one who looked and spoke relatively normal. If either of them went in they would be sure to raise suspicion.

"OK I'll do it. Shit, give me a minute."

He straightened his suit and tweaked the collar of his shirt so that it sat neatly around his neck. Taking a deep breath, he strolled over and entered the shop. The door made a gentle tinkling sound as he opened it and feeling immediately awkward he pretended to search through the racks of dresses and coats. When he realised that no one was paying him any attention, Apex discretely popped his head up and scanned the shop for the owner. From what he could see there appeared to only be customers on the shop floor, but as he edged closer to the tills he heard a couple of female voices coming from a room at the back.

"I'm seriously going to fire that stupid woman, Dawn."

"I know, she's a liability, isn't she? I mean, I was meant to be on holiday until tomorrow and this is the third time she's made me come back. Do you know where she is? Have you tried calling her?"

"Of course I have," snapped the deep, authoritative voice, "but there's no answer. We'll just have to make do without her. Damned cheques, why do people still pay with these antiquated bits of paper? Dawn, I'll need you to look after the shop while I go to the post office; I'll leave about one, OK?"

"Of course Trudy."

Apex inched forward and holding onto the front counter he leaned at an awkward angle to try and see through the slither of gap between the frame and the door. Straining his neck, he pushed with his fingers to stretch his body out even further until he lost his balance and landed with a heavy thud on the floor. A woman rushed out of the room and peered over the top of the counter. Apex stared up at her with a sheepish look on his face.

"Hello sir, are you OK down there? Let me help you up," she said in a friendly voice.

"Thank you," he replied, giving her is hand and easing himself up to standing. He brushed down his suit and cleared his throat, "I wonder if you could help me please, I'm looking for a dress for my girlfriend; it's her birthday, you see."

396

"Yes of course sir, do you know her size?"

"Oh, um good question," Apex mumbled awkwardly. "Actually, I don't."

"That's OK sir, we get that a lot. It does of course help if you know the dress size you're buying for, but we do accept returns if it doesn't fit, so it's not the end of the world," she said with a little giggle.

Apex forced a smiled and thought, *if only she knew.* The woman was slim with short, blunt cut blonde hair and was obviously someone who took a great deal of time and care over her appearance. He caught a glimpse of the name badge she had pinned to her bold pink dress; it read, 'Dawn'.

"It's such a cold day out today, isn't it Dawn," said Apex, deliberately making small talk in order to get as much information as he could out of this woman. "Tell me, do you own this lovely shop?"

The lady chuckled and blushed, "Oh no, it belongs to Trudy, she's out the back at the moment. Did you not see the sign? It's called 'Trudy's Fashion Shop', not 'Dawn's Fashion Shop'" she said, smiling at her own joke.

"Oh yes of course, silly me. So, do you have many people working here then?"

"Well there's me, obviously, and there's Michelle, but she's not in today. You sound American, are you over here on holiday?"

"Yes, I'm just here for a couple of weeks. I go back to Detroit next week," Apex lied.

"Oh, how lovely, I've always wanted to go to America. I expect you're used to all these earthquakes we've been having then? I've never felt anything like it in my life. I always thought it would be pollution, or you know some other climate issue that would be the thing to wreck our planet, I never expected it to be something like earthquakes. Well certainly not in this country anyway. We were going to close the shop like a lot of the other businesses on the street, but we were told there was no need. Anyway, between you and me, Trudy can't afford to close at the moment; this is our busiest time of year."

Apex nodded politely.

"Anyway, I'm sorry I'm going on a bit aren't I… the dress, which one was it you wanted?"

"Hey no it's fine honestly, don't worry about the dress for now. I'll find out what size she is and come back another time."

"Are you absolutely sure sir, it's not a problem if you needed to exchange or return it at a later date," said Dawn, starting to worry she'd get in trouble with Trudy over the loss of a sale.

"Yeah, it's fine I'll leave it."

"OK sir, whatever you think's best, have good day."

Apex left the shop and crossed the road to meet with John and Sarah.

"Didst thou find her?" asked John.

"Kind of. I now know who Trudy isn't, if that makes sense. There are only two women working in there today and I've met the one who isn't Trudy. As long as we keep track of who's going in and out of the shop, we'll be able to work out who she is. Plus, I overheard that she'll be leaving to go to the post office at one." Apex pulled out the phone and checked the time. "So, we'll just have to wait."

John tentatively reached his hand out to touch the phone, his eyes filled with wonder.

"Can I holdeth t Apex, can I behold with mine own hands what magic it hath."

Apex passed the phone to John. "It's all done by satellites - a signal is sent up from the phone and bounces off the satellite back down towards the phone you're connecting with. It's basically the same process in my time zone, except we can do more things with our E-ties."

"E-ties, I understandeth not," said John looking confused.

Apex groaned. He was getting fed up with having to explain every little thing to John and even though he appreciated that John didn't have any of these things back in his own time zone, it was seriously doing his head in.

"Firstly, do you even know what a tie is John?" John looked at him blankly. Apex asked Sarah the same question, but she shrugged her shoulders and looked as equally blank.

"OK, see what that man's wearing over there?" Apex said pointing to a man further down the street. "That long thing hanging from his neck? Well that's a tie. Men usually wear them to look smart at special occasions or for work, but to be honest they're a right pain in the ass, especially when it dangles in your food. Anyway, the E-tie pretty much looks like that, except it's way more awesome. You can call people on it like a phone, you can use it to store data, you can even project movies from it, but we're not really supposed to use it for that, it belongs to the college you see. It does a whole heap of other stuff too, it's pretty fucking amazing if you think about it."

"What is this data thou speaketh of?" asked John inquisitively.

"Ah man, look don't worry about it for the moment, I'll tell you later. We need to concentrate on watching the shop front, if we miss her we're screwed." He took the phone from John and turned his attention back to the shop.

Time passed slowly and all three of them grew restless. It was hard just sitting around doing nothing, especially when they knew their time could be spent far more productively. But without Rose's help the Greys would be much more likely to fulfill their mission, and if they were going to find Rose they needed Trudy. Sarah impatiently paced up and down the pavement, rocking Jake in her arms to keep him warm. The day was cold and he was only wearing thin layers, plus it was only a matter of time before he would need another feed. Eventually 1pm arrived and exactly as planned a woman came out of the shop. It had to be her.

"Look, there, that must be Trudy!" Apex hissed excitedly to the others. "Quick, come on we need to follow her."

They crossed over to the other side of the road, squeezing their way through the long line of traffic and a large crowd of protestors holding placards that read 'Pollution = Apocalypse' and 'Greedy fat cats to kill off the human race.' Had they had more time Apex would've stopped and explained that it had absolutely nothing to do with pollution, but they had to keep their eyes on Trudy. They continued making their way up the street, trying to keep Trudy in sight but at the same time holding back so that she didn't spot them and get suspicious. However, the group of protesters was growing bigger and three of them became separated from each other. Apex turned round to look for Sarah and catching a glimpse of her hair he shouted back, "Keep up, we can't lose her. Come on she's getting away, we have to hurry." He quickened his pace, barging his way through the crowd.

"Apex please, sloweth down, 'tis too much. I cannot keepeth up with thee," Sarah cried, struggling to hold Jake and run at the same time.

"Oh for fucks sake!" screamed Apex in frustration. "We've fucking lost her!"

"I am most sorry Apex, I truly am," sobbed Sarah. "Jake was wriggling and crying, 'twas too hard for me to run and carry him. Please, I doth need to sit down and feed him."

Apex put his hands on his head and screamed. Every time it felt as if they might actually be getting somewhere, something would stop them. He paced around in circles, his mind consumed with anger and frustration. Sarah looked at him meekly, unsure how to go about calming him down. John looked at her as if to say, "Just leave him." She looked away and instead concentrated on feeding Jake. Several minutes passed and Apex had by now managed to compose himself. He stopped pacing and took several deep breaths, before walking back over to where Sarah and John were sat.

He sat down next to them in silence, still sulking about how they'd managed to lose track of Trudy. Suddenly the phone started vibrating in his pocket. It was the Inspector.

"Hey Inspector, I hope you're having more success than we are?"

"Hello Mr Mensah, I take it you haven't found Rose yet then?"

"No. We found Trudy and started to follow her, but there are so many people here, we lost her in the crowds."

"Never mind, look if it's any consolation I have the guns here and we've got plenty of police officers armed and ready. Most of the windows have been boarded up and there are three snipers already positioned on the roof. Don't worry about finding Rose for now, you need to get back. Just remember to be careful when you get here and make yourselves known. The last thing we need is to be dealing with cases of mistaken identities, not when there's guns involved."

Apex hung up and sighed.

He had one idea, it was probably hopeless, but what did he have to lose. It had to be worth a shot. He stood up and shouted at the top of his voice,

"ROSE! Are you out there? ROSE!" The likelihood of Rose being within earshot was about a million to one, if not more and he sat back down in a huff.

"Man, this is fucking pointless, it's like looking for a needle in a fucking hay stack," he muttered.

"Apex sitteth down. I am most certain we will findeth Rose, but we must bethink a different way to reacheth her," said Sarah in a calm voice.

Suddenly John leapt up in excitement,

"Oh mine lord! How couldst we beest such dunces?"

"What on earth are you going on about now John?" grumbled Apex.

"I can imagine her, like we hath done before."

"Shit, you're right! John, if you were a girl I'd kiss you. That's fucking brilliant, well done bro!"

John closed his eyes and imagined Rose, recalling her beautiful smile and sweet feminine scent. He pictured her petite frame and her blonde hair standing out from the crowds of people, concentrating on her and her alone. All other people faded into the background until there was just one person left.

Rose.

He opened his eyes.

"So, did you see her?" asked Apex eagerly.

"Aye, she is sat over thither on that bench behind us!"

Apex turned to look where John was pointing and was amazed to see Rose sitting on the bench exactly as John had described.

"Fuck man, this is awesome! John *you're* awesome! Come on, let's go and see her."

They walked over to Rose, hesitating when they noticed her sad expression and tearful eyes. She was wearing the clothes that Apex and John had last seen her in - blue denim jeans and a simple white t-shirt. Her hair was tied up, slightly messy from where she had ruffled it. Her sadness was the same as that which they had both witnessed in their dreams, back when they had first encountered her. It was the deep sadness of a lonely girl who had experienced great suffering. Despite her distress, neither of them could hide the excitement of seeing their friend once again. John rushed towards her, like a lost child who had just found his mother.

"Rose, 'tis thee. We hath found thee at last!"

Rose looked up, startled by this stranger rushing at her with open arms and a silly smile on his face.

"Um, hello... do I know you? I'm sorry I think you must be mistaking me for someone else."

"'Tis I, John. And Apex, thou must remember Apex. Wherefore art my manners, I hath forgot thee hast not really met this fair lady before. This is Sarah and Jake."

"OK, that's all very lovely," said Rose awkwardly, "but I still don't know who you are I'm afraid." She got up from the bench and started slowly inching away.

"Thou hast forgotten who we art. Upon thy death thou didst lose thy memory," explained John. "I am most sorry I was not able to saveth thee, can thou ever forgive me?"

"Look, I know you think you know me, but you don't. I have no idea what you're talking about. How can I have died; I'm here look," she said, pinching her arm to prove her existence. "And anyway, why are you speaking like that?"

John tried putting his arms around her, believing that this simple gesture would be enough to ignite a memory within her.

"Hey, what do you think you're doing? Get off me," she screamed, batting his arms away. "I'm sorry but this is too much, you've got the wrong person, now leave me alone."

She pushed John out of the way and hurriedly walked away, glancing over her shoulder in confusion.

"Rose wait, you've been having dreams, haven't you?" shouted Apex. "You dreamt about Shaun dying in that van. I know you have, because I've seen it too."

Rose stopped.

"Who are you?" she whispered, slowly turning around.

"Aye 'tis most true," added John. "Thou didst kill Trudy too, didst thou not?"

"No, you're wrong. I haven't killed Trudy, how could I have, I've just seen her. She's not dead."

She turned and started to walk off again. John reached out and grabbed her by the shoulder.

"Rose, please do not wend. We doth need thy help," he pleaded.

"I don't know who you are or what you want from me, but seriously you're freaking me out. I need to get back to Jackie's, she'll be worried about me, so will you please just leave me alone and let me go."

"Haven't you seen the news Rose?" Apex called out to her. "The invasion? The earthquakes? Haven't you been wondering about what's going on?"

"What invasion, what are you on about? There isn't an invasion and everyone knows earthquakes are a natural phenomenon. I don't watch the news; I've got way better things to be doing with my time. I only happened to see Shaun's van on TV because Jackie insisted on having it on. And I can tell you something for sure, I did *not* kill him. It was just… a coincidence. Hang on wait a minute, I know you from somewhere." She peered at Apex. "My God, it was you on the CCTV, wasn't it? You were on the news, it was you who killed Shaun! I've got to go. I need to tell the police it wasn't me, I can clear my name. It's you who should be blamed for this, not me!"

She was about to run off when a loud screech of tyres sounded just a few metres away from where they were standing. Instinctively they turned to see what was going on and saw a large group of pedestrians gathering in the road. There was a scream followed by lots of shouting.

Apex crossed his arms, a smug look on his face and said,

"See, you've just killed Trudy."

"What? How could I? I've been stood here with you."

"Apex is right Rose, that wast Trudy. The lady died as we bethought the lady wouldst. Answer me this, how couldst we knoweth about thy dreams Rose?"

Rose shook her head and John continued. "We knoweth because thee didst tell us thyself. I hath seen with mine own eyes what that evil sir hath done to hurt thy mother. That gent didst hurt her badly and that maketh thou most angry, so angry thou dost want that gent dead. Apex did not killeth Shaun, that gent wast there in thy dreams."

405

Rose shook her head in disbelief. Sarah calmly approached the petrified girl and gave her a warm smile.

"Rose, please sitteth thee down. I giveth thee mine word as a lady that we will not hurteth thee. I knoweth 'tis most strange for thee, but please thou hast to trusteth us. We needeth thy help. Behold mine baby, he is but a sweet boy is he not? Dost thou bethink I wouldst beest in the company of a murderer with mine own child? Thou hast to trusteth us Rose."

"No I don't believe you, you're liars, all of you!" she cried.

"OK Rose, fine let's make a deal, at least give us that. We'll walk over to that bus over there and if the woman lying dead on the ground *is* Trudy, then you have to agree to come with us so that we can explain more about what's going on. If it's not Trudy, I promise we'll leave you alone and this will be the last you'll ever see of us. Deal?"

Rose thought about Apex's proposal. The very idea or her being able to kill someone with her imagination was utterly ridiculous. There's no way it would be Trudy. She was confident that when they walked over to the accident, they'd see it wasn't her and then they'd finally leave her alone.

"Fine I'll humour you, but I can tell you now it's not Trudy."

She marched confidently ahead, the others trailing after her. Barging through the crowd, she gasped as she was met with the horrific sight of a large lady surrounded by a pool of blood. Her head had been completely crushed and sections of her skull lay scattered across the pavement and road. Even with her injuries, Rose could tell it was Trudy; she was wearing exactly the same clothes she had seen her in earlier. She clutched her mouth, feeling the warm rush of vomit rising up from her stomach. She bent over and sprayed the acidic substance out onto the pavement. How was this possible? She'd been nowhere near the scene of the crash. Sure, she'd had angry thoughts about killing Trudy, she deserved it the horrible old bag, but it didn't mean she could actually make it happen.

John held onto her shoulder and gently guided her away from the scene. The others followed and when they were far enough away from the commotion, Apex looked at Rose and said softly,

"Do you believe us now? I know it wasn't the nicest way to get you to remember, and I realise it's all very confusing, but you will start to remember again Rose. We will help you, you just need to let us. Come with us to the police station, you'll be safe with us I promise."

Rose sniffed, wiping the tears away from her eyes. It all felt so surreal, surely it was all just some terrible nightmare. She nodded slowly, reluctantly agreeing to what was being asked of her. What other choice did she have?

"Which police station are we going to?"

"Patchway Police Centre," Apex answered.

"But that's miles away! How are we going to get there? We can't walk, it would literally take hours, and have you seen the traffic, it's a nightmare!"

"Ha wait until you see this. We don't need to walk and the traffic isn't going to be a problem, not how we get about anyway. Watch this."

"Holdeth hands and closeth thine eyes," said John taking a deep breath.

They huddled together. Filled with doubt, Rose joined hands and before she could even think about pulling away, a rush of energy filled her entire body. Daring to open her eyes she saw everything speeding past her as though in fast forward. Yet strangely, she couldn't feel any movement herself, there was no rushing of air, no sound. Rose felt in awe of this beautiful moment and tried to relax and enjoy the experience, but she could feel something else too, something oppressive, dark, evil. She looked over to the others for reassurance but from the looks on their faces she knew there was something wrong. It was as if there was someone else with them; a presence. Apex and John had felt like this before and although they couldn't see anything, they knew the Grey's were following them. They must have somehow got through to Rose, latched onto her. This was it. It was time to defend their existence. The Grey's were here.

Chapter 48

Patchway Police Centre

Inspector Taylor wiped the perspiration from her forehead. She grabbed one end of the table and Sergeant Fitch took the other end. Together they lifted it up and shuffled along to the far end of the reception where they flipped it over and pushed it against one of the windows. They'd managed to barricade the glass panes so that it would hopefully give sufficient protection against any potential threat from outside. Gaps had been left to ensure they could see what was coming and to allow plenty of time to fire a shot if need be. There were thirty of them there in total, each of them busy defending the impromptu base. The army had stepped in and donated whatever they could, which meant weapons were plentiful. Inspector Cherrad looked over at everyone that was helping, trying to work out which defensive positions she should give them. She held a mobile tightly in her left hand, expectantly waiting for any contact from the outside world. Communication from the forces in other countries was vital in their quest for survival. Helpers rushed around the room like busy worker bees, barricading the doors with heavy metal lockers and chairs. Everyone could sense the strange presence among them, it was like electric currents crackling through the air. And then all of a sudden Apex, John, Sarah and Rose appeared before them.

"Woah, what the heck? That was incredible!" exclaimed Inspector Taylor excitedly. "I was expecting you to come on foot, but then I suppose when you can do what you lot can do why would you walk?"

The other officers who had witnessed this sudden arrival, stood glued to the spot, their mouths wide open in disbelief. However, shock soon turned to suspicion and several of the older officers pointed their weapons at these strange and uninvited strangers.

"It's alright everyone, lower your weapons. This is Apex, he's here to help us. He was the one who warned us about the invasion. Believe it or not, he's from the future," said Inspector Taylor with a grin.

Apex cleared his throat.

"Actually, I'm from a future time zone. There is no future, just as much as there is no past. They all exist at the same time, just within different plains, do you get me?"

She looked puzzled, but not wishing to appear ignorant in front of her colleagues she agreed with him anyway. "Yes, yes my mistake. Of course I meant to say future time zone," she said. "I'm impressed with what you can all do. The police force could really make use of your abilities to assist them in future. Well, that is if there is a future… Anyway, everyone this is John, Sarah and her baby, Jake. And you must be Rose? I'm so glad they managed to find you, I'm Inspector Taylor."

Inspector Taylor reached a hand out to Rose, but Rose just stared back at her blankly. She felt sick and everything felt so mixed up. She was still reeling from being told that it was her who had killed Trudy and Shaun. And then there were these strangers that seemed to know everything about her, not to mention the time travel and all this mind power business. It was all too much. She burst into tears. Inspector Taylor put her arm around her to try and offer some comfort. Rose glanced up to show her appreciation and realised she recognised the Inspector from the TV. This was her opportunity to plead her innocence.

"I didn't kill Shaun, please you've got believe me. I was at home when he died, there's no way I could have set his van on fire. Please don't arrest me."

She looked around the room at the other officers, who automatically avoided eye contact and busied themselves with what they were doing. In desperation she ran to the corner of the room and squeezed herself as far as she could against the wall. She slid down onto the floor, clutching her face in her hands and rocked back and forth. "This can't be happening, it's a dream. This can't be happening…" she whispered to herself. John and Sarah walked over and knelt beside her. They had to explain more to her, help her to try and understand, help her see sense. Inspector Taylor beckoned to Apex to follow her and when they were out of earshot she asked,

"She's in a pretty bad way, does she actually know who any of you are?"

"It's a long story Inspector, but basically she can't remember any of it. Apparently when we die we forget all about our past lives. I don't remember anything from my past life and therefore I couldn't even begin to tell you if it's true or not. But considering I saw Rose die in John's time zone and she's now alive here, well I guess it's got to be true. I'm sure she'll come around eventually and if not we'll have to carry on until she does, because without her on board we're screwed."

"Come with me," she said. "Let me show you what we've done so far." She led him over to the barricade and said, "As you can see we've blocked off the entrance with absolutely anything we could find - riot shields, metal sheeting, tables, lockers etcetera. We've also barricaded the windows from the inside, but you'll notice we've left gaps to enable us to shoot defensively if we have too. I've got thirty police officers to help us, it's the best I could do I'm afraid, all the others have left to be with their families. General Leonard has informed me they are keeping constant and very close inspection on the sky. So far they haven't detected anything, however the UK Space Agency and NASA have both concurred that there is an anomaly heading towards us that they are keeping a close watch on. They can't predict how long it will take to reach us, as it appears to be pulsating every few hours and our technology can't keep up with it. One moment it seems far away, but then it can gain speed quite dramatically and suddenly appears much closer. This pattern has continued for the past hour or so and the scientists think the pulsations explain why the earth isn't constantly shaking; it comes in waves. From what the data is telling us, the object is capable of almost slingshotting itself across space at speeds beyond our comprehension. When it pushes closer to Earth it creates a massive gravitational pull. Unfortunately, they can't explain what it is yet though."

"I'll tell you what is," replied Apex, "it's the fucking Greys, that's what."

"We have weapons and plenty of ammo and we're stocked up with enough food and water to keep us going for a while. Have I missed anything else?"

"Yes. What about Ema? We still haven't found him."

"We haven't had any leads yet I'm afraid. We're doing what we can, but I'm running out of ideas here Apex."

"For fucks sake, seriously? You're the police, isn't it your job to find missing people? And you'd think being some almighty fucking God you'd want people to know who you were. It's doing my head in!"

Sergeant Fitch walked over and Inspector Taylor looked at him, grateful for the interruption.

"Sorry to disturb you both. Inspector, where would you like me to put this machine gun?"

"Over there in that window," she said pointing to a window on the far side of the room. "We have a good range on both sides of the street from there. Anything coming down it will be torn to pieces." She turned back to talk to Apex, "The military have been great Apex, they gave us these weapons and we've even got grenades too."

An almighty rumble from deep below halted the conversation and suddenly large sections of the internal walls began to collapse. Huge clouds of dust exploded into the room and everyone immediately dropped to the floor, coughing and spluttering as they tried to crawl under tables for protection. They gripped on to each other in terror, praying that the room was strong enough to stay intact. The earthquake felt different this time. Only Apex and John had experienced an earthquake of this magnitude before. It was an earthquake that sent vibrations straight through to the very core of your body. This could mean only one thing - the Greys had arrived.

When the earthquake finally appeared to have stopped, everyone stood up and gathered together in the centre of the room. Inspector Taylor brushed herself down and looked at the group. Taking off her glasses, she carefully rubbed the lenses on the hem of her jacket.

"Is everyone OK?" she asked.

They all nodded.

She took out a walkie-talkie from her back pocket. It crackled slightly before she heard a muffled voice coming from the other end.

"Are you all OK? Over," she asked the snipers on the roof.

"All fine up here Inspector. Half of the building has collapsed, but it still seems fairly strong from where we are. A lot of the other buildings haven't fared quite so well though. Three high-rise flats have collapsed and the cathedral's gone down too. I can see people running around down below, but it also looks like some have been crushed. Wait, hang on there's something else… in the sky. Inspector, there's something strange happening in the sky. I suggest you take a look. Over."

Apex ran to the window and looked out across the street. People were running about in blind panic, tripping and falling over the piles of rubble from the collapsed buildings. Some were crouched, cowering in doorways, too scared to even move. He looked up at the sky and squinted his eyes against the bright light of the sun. The sky was distorting into ripples of transparent liquid, flowing out across the vast blue expanse.

"Shit, they're here! The Greys are here!"

"What? What do you mean they're here? How can you tell?"

"The sky has changed. Look, can you see the distortion?" He pointed to the rippling effects in the sky and then turned to John and said, "John quick get over here. Is this what you saw in your time zone?"

John rushed over to Apex and peering out of a different window, he looked up at the distorting sky. It was exactly as he had seen it in his own time zone.

"Aye Apex 'tis the exact same!"

Inspector Taylor walked over to John and placed her hands lightly on his shoulders. She looked him straight in the eye and asked in a trembling voice,

"John, how long after you saw the distortion did it take before the Greys got to you?"

"I knoweth not… 'twas perhaps a matter of minutes if I doth remember rightly."

The Inspector took out her phone and dialled the number for General Leonard. It was answered almost immediately.

"Yes Inspector, what's the latest?"

"They're here General, the Greys are here."

"What? But we haven't detected anything, they can't be."

"I don't mean to talk out of turn General, but has it crossed your mind that these beings might be ever so slightly more advanced than us? They've obviously got through our detectors."

"This makes no sen…" His voice cut off, distracted by something that was happening his end. There was a moment of silence before Inspector Taylor heard him call out to his men. *"What's going on men?"*

"They're running towards us sir!" called a voice in the background. *"What should we do?"*

"Shoot, God damn it."

"But sir, there's too many of them!"

"Just shoot you idiots, shoot them all!"

There was a thud as the General dropped the phone and Inspector Taylor heard the muffled sound of gunshots.

"General… General… are you there? General! Shit, he's gone. What now?"

Inspector Cherrad hurried over to where Apex and Inspector Taylor were stood. She'd spent the past half hour trying to make contact with some of the other forces in the UK as well as those from overseas. She took a deep breath and said,

"It's not good Inspector. I've managed to make contact with the French military base in Calais, they're monitoring our country for us."

"And what have they said?" asked Inspector Taylor.

"They say that all British forces have been wiped out in the area. The Army, Navy and Royal Air Force have all been destroyed. Nearly half a million military personnel were destroyed in minutes. They say… ," she swallowed hard, "they say the country has been devastated."

"What about reinforcements? Surely there's got to be some kind of back up?" asked Inspector Taylor desperately.

"The UN are attempting to make contact with the Greys to negotiate some kind of compromise, but so far they've been unable to get through to them."

"That's bullshit! You can't reason with the Greys, they don't care," Apex exploded in anger. "All they want is Ema and they're not going to stop until they get him."

Inspector Taylor pulled up a chair and sat down. When she'd signed up to the job of Inspector she certainly hadn't accounted for dealing with the threat of alien attack. This was not in her remit. She put her

416

head in her hands. The pressure had got too much, she couldn't do it anymore. Apex stepped forward. They were the ones that had been sent here to help. It was up to him to take charge now.

He bellowed loudly to the officers,

"OK everyone, get in positions. These fuckers will be here any minute now. Sergeant, you need to get on that heavy machine gun and Rose, you need to come here now."

Rose stood up and walked nervously over to Apex.

"Yes?" asked Rose.

"Do you remember anything? Anything at all?" said Apex.

"No, I don't think so."

" What about your powers? Do you know how to use them?"

"I don't know… but I could try. How do you do it?"

"Right OK, so just think of someone or something that makes you really angry or anxious, then imagine what you want to do to them," explained Apex. "Go on, have a go now Rose, try it out."

Rose closed her eyes.

She imagined Shaun's evil, twisted face and thought about him beating her mum. She thought about Trudy and all of the nasty things she'd said about her mum. She felt the burning rage brewing deep inside her. But something didn't feel right. None of this was right. She wasn't meant to be here. She should be with her mum.

She opened her eyes and cried,

"Why did you have to come and find me? I don't want to be here, I don't want any of this. I'd rather be dead and be with my mum than be here on my own with you lot. I feel so stupid for believing you, I should never have come. Please enough's enough now, let me go!"

"Rose I know it's scary, but we're relying on you and I'm afraid there's no easy way out of this. Please, you have to remember how to do it. Pull yourself together and try again," demanded Apex. "And listen, I promise that when all of this is over we will all get to be with our families again."

Rose sniffed and turned her back on him. Apex sighed, she would come around eventually. For now he needed to focus his attention on the officers, they were starting to get restless. He needed to show them his own strength of leadership in order to help the rest of them remain positive. They needed to know that death was not an option; not on his watch anyway. He clapped his hands to get their attention and shouted,

"Come on guys, let's get ready. We can do this."

The officers ran to their assigned positions and methodically checked over their weapons. Making sure the guns were fully loaded with ammo, they then took the safety catches off and aimed them through the small gaps in the barricade. It looked just like any other normal sunny day outside, but as they peered through their scopes they could see the rising panic. People were aimlessly running around, desperately trying to escape, fighting anyone who got in their way. And there were animals too; dogs and cats jumping and scratching at each other. A chorus of feral yowling and barking combined with petrified screams and shouts for help filled the air. It was chaos out there. Suddenly a loud crack of gunfire broke through the noise, followed by more rounds of shots, and the entire scene deteriorated into a war zone. Explosions shook the ground and large plumes of smoke rose up from behind the buildings.

"Multiple shots fired down the street Inspector!" screamed an officer and then taking another look he shouted, "My God, can you see it? There are hundreds of them. Inspector, Apex, quick come here."

Inspector Taylor and Apex ran over to the officer and looked out. People were attacking one other, manically punching and kicking, blindly clawing and tearing at skin and hair. Dogs were jumping up to join in, savagely ripping ears off and scratching at eyes until they burst from their sockets. Terrified children dropped to the ground, crying out for their parents and trying to crawl their way out of this madness. Every now and then one of them would jump up and try to run away, only to be immediately ravaged by the dogs. Inspector Taylor let out a shriek and turned from the window, retching in horror. Apex reached out and gently touched her on the shoulder.

She flinched and her body started to shake. "Oh my God, we're going to die, we're going to die, WE'RE GOING TO DIE!"

"No!" shouted Apex, grabbing hold of her and looking into her eyes. "We're not going to die Inspector, not like this. Not today, not ever! We've got this gift, so let's fucking use it. Right guys this is it, OK? I want half of you firing while the other half reload, that way we have a constant flow of shooting. If things get real bad, then you shoot at fucking will, you hear me?"

Sarah came hurtling towards him and threw her arms around him in embrace. He was the only man who had ever made her feel safe and when she was in his arms it felt as if everything would be alright.

Tears filled her eyes and she sobbed, "I wanteth not for them to kill us Apex. I wanteth not to become one of those... those... those beasts," she gasped. "I am most scared Apex, most scared for my Jake. What will becometh of him?"

419

Apex stroked her hair and calmly whispered, "Sarah, humans are emotionally intricate beings and it is our instincts and creative imaginations that will conquer the Greys. I will look after you and Jake I promise you, but I need you to be strong. We all have to remain united, trust in our instincts, and defend what is rightly ours. It's our only chance."

"They're coming this way!" shouted one of the lookouts.

Inspector Taylor called up to the snipers on her distorted walkie-talkie,

"Shoot now, do it now, FIRE!"

The three snipers immediately took aim, carefully scouting the group of deranged men, women and children within their gun sights, before pulling the trigger. The guns recoiled with explosive force, sending bullets flying through the air and striking the heads of their chosen targets. Each one fell to the ground with an ear-piercing scream and that same strange black liquid rose up, out of their chests, hovering above them, before shooting up and disappearing into the sky.

"My God, what's that coming out of them?" shouted one of the snipers to the others. "It's like a kind of black liquid, look. Look there it is. Did you see it?"

The snipers continued shooting, but it wasn't enough. As fast as the zombies were going down, more and more healthy people were becoming infected. Thousands of possessed people and mutilated animals swarmed towards the station.

From inside, everyone could see just what little impact the snipers were having on the crowd and tension was growing among the troops. For every zombie that was killed another ten would appear. It seemed utterly hopeless, but they had to at least try. With the possessed army now in range Apex shouted,

"OK, get ready... FIRE!"

The room exploded in a deafening blast as guns fired in all directions. Rotten body parts littered the streets and a chilling cacophony of screams filled the air. But the maimed zombies continued their plight, crawling with relentless determination towards the police station.

"Don't stop!" shouted Apex, "Just keep shooting!"

"They're getting closer Inspector Taylor, I'm not sure how much longer we can hold them off for," yelled Sergeant Fitch above the roar of gunfire. "There's too many of them!" Struggling to reload the heavy machine gun, he took aim and fired, the bullets penetrating a pack of dogs, their bodies exploding on impact.

"Apex, John, Rose, please thou must do something!" shouted Sarah.

Apex and John looked at one other and then at Rose, who was still sat rocking in the corner. She still hadn't got her head around any of this and was convinced she'd wake up at any moment from whatever this strange nightmare was.

They would have to try it without her. Shrugging his shoulders, Apex said,

"You ready John?"

"Aye, let us putteth a stop to this."

Closing their eyes they pictured the vast number of men, women and children outside. They saw zombies in military uniform hobbling towards the building, their eyes, ears and noses removed. They imagined them being forcefully grabbed and pulled apart limb from limb, the blood spraying out in a crimson mist. John pushed as hard as he could, out to the front line of the possessed, slowing them down to give the officers an easier target. But they kept pushing and pushing until it became too much for John to bear.

"Rose we needeth thy help. Thou must believeth in thyself, I know thou can doth t!" John called out in his mind.

But Rose wasn't listening. She rocked herself back and forth, blocking out what was going on around her. She uncurled herself and crawled unnoticed past Sarah, who was clutching Jake and sobbing loudly.

John tried again.

'What art thou doing Rose, thee cannot receiveth hence. Surely though thinketh not of leaving us to fend for ourselves. Rose, return at once!'

'Leave her alone,' interrupted Apex, 'we have to deal with these fuckers first.'

They continued using their combined mental forces to fight off the frenzied zombies. The guns were helping to buy them some time, but the sheer number of zombies made it impossible to see how they would ever get out of this alive.

While all this was going on Rose had managed to find a small opening between the lockers and tables that were blocking up the entrance. She prised the doors open just enough for her to get out and escape. However, as soon as she was out in the open air she instantly began to regret her decision. Sensing her presence, the army of possessed beings immediately started surrounding her. She stood still, frozen to the spot as she felt the oppressive sensation of their energy draining her body. Her eyes began to close and she felt her body start to shut down. The sounds of screaming and gunfire became distant, as if she was travelling further and further away from the earth, until there was nothing but complete silence.

Chapter 49

Unknown location

L ight penetrated her pupils and as consciousness began to come back to her, Rose unwittingly opened her eyes. She was lying on a hard flat platform and as her eyes grew more accustomed to the light she saw that she was in a room made of some kind of transparent liquid, a pulsating black tar-like material passing through them. Her ears felt strange; hollow and muffled as if she were underwater. She tried to shake her head to see if that would help unblock them, but it was being restrained by something; locked into position. The viscous black magma oozed its way from out of the walls and hovered over her, suspended in the air like a dark rain cloud. Rose watched as the shape began to take on a more human-like form, its thin arms stretching out to the ground and its long facial features and wide, hauntingly hollow silvery eyes staring down at her. She gasped in terror and went to open her mouth to beg for mercy, to plead with whatever these beings were to let her go, but she couldn't. Her lips had been sealed tightly together by a thick sticky substance. She moaned helplessly, her voice unheard, locked in the prison of her mouth. Accepting defeat, she turned her eyes back to the creatures above her. One of the beings hovered over her and positioned a needle in front of her left eye. The metallic point glinted in the light of the creature's eyes and Rose shuddered as she watched it slowly draw closer. The needle pierced through the thick rubbery membrane of her eyeball. Tiny eruptions of aqueous humour ran down her cheeks mixing in with her tears and she whimpered in pain. She felt nauseous and as the needle dug deeper into her retina and up into her brain, she began to hear the voices of these terrifying beings in her mind.

"Where is Ema?"

"Please, please let me go! I have no idea what you're talking about?"

With a jolt, Rose could suddenly see what they were doing inside her head. It was as if they were searching through her memories, scrolling through a vast database of events that had happened in her past, flicking through the faces of people she had encountered throughout her life. There was her mum waving goodbye to Jackie after collecting Rose from her house after work. And then just as quickly, the image distorted and she was back at home with her mum. She saw Shaun returning home and beating her mum all over again and then she watched herself run to the bathroom to phone the police. The memory blurred and shifted again. Now she saw her mum in hospital, the monitoring equipment beeping and Jackie was sat next to her. And then again the memory changed. She was in the library looking at some random book she had picked out. And then shifting to the moment she saw Trudy die. Fast forward to that first meeting with Calcus, when she learnt about *time zones and the quest to find Ema. Further forward to being chased by men in old fashioned uniforms, Apex and John running alongside her and then the vision of Apex being tortured on the rack. The memories were coming back to her with such clarity.*

She remembered everything.

Suddenly the images in her head started to rewind and then paused on a familiar image. The beings had found what they were looking for. She was back in the library, holding that seemingly random book, but when she saw the title she realised she had to stop them.

She called out to them in her mind. "Let me go, please let me go," pleading with them desperately.

But the Greys ignored her and carried on talking among themselves in their strange unearthly language. It seemed as though they had agreed on something and even though Rose couldn't understand what they were saying, she could sense they were about to do something terrible. She felt a tiny object pass through the needle into her eye and then attach itself onto the inside of her head. They were taking control of her brain, stopping her from using her memory, blocking her thoughts.

This was too much, how dare these creatures get inside her head like this, Rose fumed. Now was the perfect time to practice her gift. She imagined she was back at the police station, watching as Apex and John forced back the relentless stream of possessed beings. She saw Sarah cowering in the corner, her arms protectively clutching her baby, trying to shield him from the horror around her. And there was Inspector Taylor and Inspector Cherrad wildly shooting at as many targets as they could. She imagined she was there, right there stood next to Apex and John, fighting alongside them.

Praying it had worked, Rose slowly opened her eyes only to be met with the sight of the dark beings looming over her. Screaming silently, she struggled to breathe through her nose whilst crying out in her mind, *Please John, bring me back! I'm here. Apex, help me. Help me!*

Chapter 50

Zombies came at them and Apex and John furiously grabbed them with their minds, thrusting them back into the hordes. Both men were weakening, the immense strain on their mental state gradually slowing them down. A faint whisper echoed through Apex's mind. He tried to ignore it, pushing it away, but it grew persistently louder.

It was Rose.

"John, did you hear that? It was Rose, I heard her. She sounds as if she needs our help. Shit, John you need to imagine she's here, quick!"

"But there art too many Apex. Thou cannot defend by thineself"

"Don't worry about me man, I can handle myself. Just fucking hurry up and get Rose back here!"

John reluctantly left Apex to fight alone.

He closed his eyes and focussed on Rose.

"Rose, can thou hear me? 'Tis I, John, panic thee not. I will thinketh thee back with us. Thou hath my solemn word nay harm will becometh of thee."

John used his mind to search for Rose, sensing her fear and using it as a guide. There she was, lying on a high platform, a black substance pinning her down. Her mouth was covered by thick black tar, preventing her from screaming and he could see that she was struggling to breathe. There was no time to lose, he had to get her out of there. He imagined the black substance breaking apart into tiny particles, hovering weightlessly in the air. Now that she was free of her shackles, John grabbed hold of her tightly and watched as the shadows of the Greys approached. They screamed the high-pitched noise that had haunted every one of John's dreams and as they glided towards them he knew he had to act fast. He closed his eyes and pictured them both safely back at the station. The power surged through his body and suddenly they were travelling at high speed, away from the Greys. Their screams dwindled to a quiet hum, before transforming into the deafening roar of gunfire.

John collapsed on the ground. Rose lay next to him, mumbling in distress. Her limbs were free, but her mouth was still clogged up with tar and she frantically waved her hands to motion for help. John clawed at the thick tar, stretching and pulling it away, forcing an airway for her to breathe. She coughed and spluttered and then doubled over, regurgitating more of the black sludge. Gasping with relief, she sucked in giant lungful's of the fetid air around her.

"John, I need you man, get over here quick!" Apex shouted. He had struggled to keep the possessed beings at bay without John and although a large mound of rotten zombie pulp pulsated on the floor next to him, there didn't look as though there were any less of them.

"We have to try something else," screamed Inspector Taylor. "This isn't working. We won't be able to hold them off for much longer and the ammo's nearly run out. There's just too many of them Apex!"

"Right everyone listen up," bellowed Apex. "All of you back up against the far wall."

The officers backed against the wall as instructed, continuing to shoot at the zombies as they did so.

"Come on, get behind us. Quick, everyone get behind us!" shouted Apex. "Rose, hold mine and John's hands, we need to combine our energy. You've seen how powerful we are on our own, just imagine how strong we can be if we combine all of that power together."

They joined hands and closed their eyes in unison. Apex visualised a force stronger than he had ever conjured up before, sucking the energy from John and Rose and combining it with his own. An intense ball of glowing energy radiated out from the three of them, growing larger and brighter, spreading out and consuming the people behind them until, they too, were surrounded by this protective force. The officers cowered in fear as the possessed beings tried to penetrate the bubble of energy, but each time they came close they bounced off it and smashed against the walls, knocking their zombified comrades down like bowling pins.

"John, Rose, we need to keep the force field up, it seems to be working for the moment. But in a minute we're going to charge this bubble up and really let it rip baby. Keep charging, that's it, more… more… almost there... NOW!"

The force field began to wobble, as though it could collapse in on itself at any moment and the energy inside the bubble began to feel like static electricity. The ball of light grew increasingly brighter until it became so blinding everyone inside had no choice but to close their eyes. It grew brighter and brighter and then suddenly froze for a few seconds, before exploding with nuclear force. Shockwaves blasted through the walls of the station, travelling out for miles and miles, destroying thousands of the possessed beings and obliterating buildings as if they were nothing more than wooden dolls houses.

An eerie silence filled the space and the three of them opened their eyes to witness the damage.

"Woah man, that was fucking awesome! I reckon we must have killed off thousands, maybe millions, of those fucking zombies!" chuckled Apex. He looked behind him and asked, "Is everyone OK? Sarah, are you alright?"

"Aye I am well Apex, a little shaken if truth be told, but I am fine none the less," answered Sarah brushing herself down and settling Jake onto her lap.

"Well done you three, that was incredible!" said Inspector Taylor, patting Apex on the back.

Apex gave a slight smile and then turned to face Rose.

"What the hell were you thinking going off like that? You could have got yourself killed... again!"

"I'm so sorry, I just really wanted my mum and I panicked," Rose said meekly. "I really am sorry. I believe you now, I remember everything. The Greys took me and experimented on my brain, they searched through my memories. They found something Apex, they found something that I think might be useful to us!"

"What?" asked Apex, his anger subsiding.

"I think I know where Ema might be."

"What the hell! How? Where?"

"They stopped my memory at a time when I was in Patchway library. I was looking at the front of a book I'd just randomly taken down from the shelves. I didn't even read the book, but I noticed it said the name Ema on the front cover."

"Shit, we need to get to that library. Do you reckon you can remember the library well enough to take us there Rose?"

"I don't know Apex, I've never travelled like that before, not when I've been in control of it anyway. I'm not sure I can do it."

"Thou must try Rose," said John encouragingly.

Rose nodded.

They gathered together, joining hands to form a circle.

Closing their eyes, each of them hoped and prayed that this would save them.

Rose thought of the library, picturing the institutional white walls and standard issue blue doors. She saw the yellow partitions and the tables and bookshelves arranged neatly around the large room. She imagined everyone travelling with her, flying past buildings, trees, abandoned vehicles and piles of possessed corpses. And then a wall, a brick wall towering up in front of her, preventing her from going any further.

She opened her eyes.

"I can't do it Apex. I think the Greys have implanted something in my brain to block me. I can still remember that moment, but I can't fully imagine it any more." Rose sighed, feeling as if she had let them all down again. "I'm so sorry."

"It's OK Rose," said Apex, "it's not your fault. We'll just have to get there on foot. How far do you think it is?"

"About a mile away," Inspector Taylor piped up, "so not far, but we'll need to take weapons and be on our guard. Let's just hope that almighty explosion you lot brewed up hasn't destroyed it." She picked up her own MP5 and ordered, "Everyone grab your weapons, we're heading out to the library. It's approximately one mile from here and as you all know it's not safe out there. I want you all to keep your eyes peeled and your ears open. It's going to be a rough ride."

Apex turned to Sarah, who was carefully strapping Jake onto her back.

"You stay with me at all times OK? I'm not letting you out of my sight."

She smiled affectionately at him. For the very short time she'd known him she had fallen for his quirky behaviour and strange way of talking. No one had ever made her feel this way before and overcome with emotion she wrapped her arms around his shoulders and kissed him passionately on the lips. Shocked and a little flustered, Apex kissed her back before slowly pulling away and exclaiming,

"Man, I wasn't expecting that. But thanks, that was nice!"

"Alright you two," Inspector Cherrad joked, playfully prodding Apex with her elbow, "there's a time and place for that and now is most definitely not the time!"

Apex chuckled self-consciously and picked up the discarded weapons to hand out to the officers, his cheeks flushed with excitement.

"Rose, do you think the Greys know how to get to the library?" asked Inspector Taylor.

"I don't know for sure, but I wouldn't be surprised, they seem fairly intelligent. But there are at least fifteen libraries in Bristol, so it will take them a while before they figure out which one it is."

"Right everyone listen in," shouted Inspector Taylor. " I want you to check your ammo, load up and take as much as you can carry. We'll leave the heavy gun here; it will slow us down too much. Here, Sergeant Fitch, you take this shotgun," she said, throwing the weapon at him. "Remember to use your ammo sparingly, make every shot count, we don't want to be out there without anything left to shoot with. We've still got plenty of grenades, but again use them wisely as we may need them at a later time. OK, everyone, move out! We're going to head south down Gloucester Road, which will take us straight to Patchway library. It's a long road and we'll be exposed so we may have to divert if things get bad. Stick together and listen out for my orders."

Apex wandered over to John and Rose and said, "I'll stay at the front, Rose you take the middle and John you cover the rear. Sarah I want you and Jake up here with me."

They made their way to the front of the station and looked out at the mass of corpses littering the ground. Bodies of men, women and children lay lifeless, their disfigured limbs detached and grotesquely hanging like broken puppets. The group headed south, clambering over the bodies and holding their noses against the stench of rotten flesh.

"Inspector, I see movement up ahead," whispered Sergeant Fitch. "Look, over there."

Inspector Taylor turned to her comrades and silently motioned for them to crouch down. They did as instructed and Apex took a closer look.

Thousands of zombies were grouped together rhythmically bashing into one another. All of them were missing their facial features and their bodies looked deformed and disjointed.

Apex, John and Rose linked together and Apex shouted out,

"Sarah, you stay beside me. The rest of you, I want you to shoot at the ones on the left, just kill as many as you can. We'll take the ones on this side and that way we'll have less chance of destroying the library."

Apex's shouts had disturbed the zombies and they came rushing at them from all directions. They stumbled over the scattered corpses that lay on the ruined streets, picking themselves up and continuing their attack. The officers to the left lined up, forming a curved wall to protect the others. Taking aim, they awaited Inspector Taylor's orders and then released a barrage of gunfire on the approaching army of zombies.

Fountains of blood sprayed up into the air and ragged pieces of flesh splattered down to the ground. Some of the zombies fell and lay motionless, but others continued to crawl towards the terrified officers, moaning through the gaping hole where their lips had once been. Apex grabbed Rose and John by the hands, preparing them for another combined attack.

"Right guys, are you ready for this? Just like before, OK?"

But John had already begun to take control.

He imagined the large army of faceless zombies hobbling towards them. They were chanting the same thing over and over, "We know where he is. You will not succeed. You will die". Ignoring their threats he pictured the buildings that surrounded the Police Centre. He imagined the ground cracking and opening up into a vast fissure running through the centre of the pack. Several of the zombies fell into the chasm and as it widened the ground began to shake from the pressure. Buildings crumbled around them, crashing down on top of the remaining zombies.

"Woah John, what the fuck are you doing man?" Apex yelled out to him in his mind.

But John was too caught up in the moment and continued to gather as much energy as he could from Apex and Rose. He gave one last concentrated effort and the ground sank away into the hole, carrying thousands of screaming zombies along with it.

The chasm had formed the perfect wall of defence and much to the relief of Apex, John and Rose the threat of attack was now massively reduced on their side. However, the zombie army was still very much at large on the other side and the officers were struggling to keep them at bay.

"We can't hold them off!" shouted Sergeant Fitch. "Throw a grenade, quick!"

One of the officers pulled the pin out of the grenade he was holding and lobbed it into a group of advancing zombies. It exploded on impact, covering them in remnants of body parts. Seeing how much damage it had impacted, the other officers threw their grenades too. And for a moment it seemed to be working. However, when the mist of blood cleared there were still more of the mutilated monsters clawing their way towards them. Several of the officers were dragged away, screaming in abject terror, helplessly scrabbling at the ground, trying to break free from their deathly clutches.

"Do something Apex," Inspector Taylor screamed. "They're going to kill us all!"

John continued fighting off the few remaining zombies on their side while Apex and Rose closed their eyes.

Apex pictured the dead bodies rising up before him and levitating in mid-air to form a macabre wall that pushed its way into the advancing army. Like some strange form of crowd control, the wall of dead bodies

*encircled the zombies, squeezing them tightly together and forcing them
away from the officers.*

Apex called out to Rose in his mind.

*"Rose listen to me, I don't know how long I can hold them off for so
I need you to be quick. You see that passageway over there? There
should be just enough room for everyone to get in. I need you to get
them to safety, OK? Go on do it, do it now!"*

Rose called out to the police officers to get their attention and then
shouted to John.

"John, quick we have to move. We can make it over there, but only
if we're quick. Go!"

They ran as fast as they could over to the passageway. Sarah turned
back to look for Apex, but two of the officers pulled her away. She
screamed out for Apex to go with her.

"Apex please, thou must cometh!"

Ignoring her pleas, Apex opened his eyes and the wall of dead
bodies dropped to the ground. The zombies immediately began to
advance again, but he had no energy left to handle them on his own. He
quickly ran to the entrance of the passageway and using the last of his
energy he imagined another smaller wall of corpses blocking up the
entrance.

He stood gasping for breath, completely drained, and as he regained
his composure he realised the others were nowhere to be seen.

He called out to John in his mind.

*"I made it out John. I'm in once piece and I've stopped them for
now, but it's not going to hold them for long. Where are you guys?"*

*"We art hiding in a building. It hath the words 'Tobacco Factory'
inscribed upon its side. Quick Apex, make haste!"*

Apex staggered to his feet and forced himself onwards until he spotted the sign for the tobacco factory. Stumbling across the empty road he fell through the doors straight into Sarah's arms.

She cradled him tightly and sobbed, "Thou wast so brave Apex, I loveth thee so much. Praise be to God thou art fine and well."

A few of the officers rushed forward to help. Gently taking him from Sarah they carried him over to a corner of the room. They set him down on the hard concrete floor and tried to keep him alert and conscious. It was a cold room with three large windows that only let in a small amount of light from outside. The panes of glass had all been smashed and judging by the collection of coats, handbags and other personal belongings whoever had been here had left in a hurry. At the far end of the office was a large steel door with a sign that read 'Entrance to shop floor.'

"What were you doing back there John," muttered Apex weakly. "I was just about to wipe them all out if you'd have given me the chance. I'd have done a much cleaner job of it."

"Why 'tis not fair that thou receiveth all the glory Apex," John said with a wink.

"For fucks sake John, it's not a fucking competition. If they find Ema before us, you'll have no one to show off to anyway!"

"This makes no sense, I'm confused," interrupted Inspector Taylor rubbing the side of her head. "How can the tobacco factory be here? It's several miles in the other direction. Plus, it hasn't been used as a tobacco factory for years, it's a theatre now. This doesn't look like how I remember it at all."

Rose and the officers nodded their heads in agreement. Inspector Taylor was right, it wasn't how any of them remembered it either.

438

"It's the Greys, they must be trying to confuse us," said Rose.

Inspector Taylor gave an exhausted sigh and said,

"We need to work out how much ammo we've got left. Throw down what you've got and we'll share it out between us." She turned to Sergeant Fitch and asked, "How many officers have we lost?"

"Three, Inspector. They didn't stand a chance, none of us do. We might as well shoot ourselves now."

"Sergeant, take control of yourself please, that is not an option," said Inspector Taylor with a horrified look. "We cannot, will not, let the Greys win. We are going to fight until we are down to the very last bullet. Now stop with the defeatist attitude and help me work out how we're going to get to the library. How far have we got?"

"Not even a tenth of a mile," answered Inspector Cherrad. "And I'm not even sure where we are exactly. There's hardly any ammo left, we've got no back up and the military have been wiped out. It's not looking good."

Suddenly an officer screamed out,

"Inspector, I can see them, they're coming for us!" He shakily cocked his weapon and pointed down the street. "Look, there in the distance. There are thousands of them!"

"Line up at the windows everyone, we're going to take out as many as we can. Apex, I'm counting on you to think of a way out of this. We have got nowhere near enough ammo for them all, so you're going to have to think smart and fast. But whatever you do, don't nuke in that direction, OK? That's where the library is and if you destroy that we're done for."

"Inspector, we've been spotted, they're heading our way!" screamed another officer, pulling the trigger on his MP5 at the same time. The other officers followed suit and shot wildly at the advancing enemy.

Apex propped himself against the wall and wearily stood up, clutching on to Sarah for support.

"Those frickin' Greys just won't give up, will they? I haven't got enough energy to fight them yet; we need to buy ourselves some time. If we can get through this door we'll be able to get up onto the roof. John, help me open it."

John rushed over and pushed at the door with his shoulder, but it wouldn't budge. Rose ran to help, desperately kicking at the panels, but still nothing. They turned in unison, as the sound of Sergeant Fitch's shotgun reverberated round the room. Heads exploded like ghastly piñatas, sending down showers of brain, blood and cranial fluid like bodily confetti. Sergeant Fitch screamed as the mass of zombies became too much for him and he was grabbed by an invisible force, his body violently dragged towards the open window.

"Help me, I can't stop it. Please somebody help me!"

Two of the officers tried to grab him, but his legs slipped through their grasping hands and he continued to be dragged across the floor and up the wall. He clutched on to the window frame with his right hand and in a last ditch attempt grabbed a grenade in the other hand and pulled the pin out just as he disappeared in to the darkness. A few seconds passed and then the sound of the grenade blasted through the window. The two officers who had tried to save him, stood frozen with shock, before also falling prey to the same terrible fate. Screaming loudly, they tried holding on to something, but like Sergeant Fitch they were unable to withstand the force. Rising up the wall they vanished into the army of zombies.

John closed his eyes and imagined the latch of the sealed door turning.

The mechanical lock turned with a clunk and John shouted, "Tryeth the door now."

Apex and Rose pushed their weight against the door and it swung effortlessly open.

"Quick, everyone out!" shouted Inspector Taylor. "Move into the next room!"

Sarah and Jake were the first through the doorway, followed by Rose and the Inspectors and the few remaining officers who continued shooting as they reversed out of the room. Apex and John were the last ones through, slamming the door shut behind them and then holding their backs against it.

"Come on, help us!" yelled Apex. "We need to keep this door shut."

Inspector Taylor motioned to one of her officers. "You there, drive that forklift truck up to the door. That should do it."

The officer climbed up onto the seat and turned the ignition key. The engine spluttered to life and he pressed the accelerator down, revving it into gear. He slowly edged the truck forward, before it gave a sudden lurch and slammed against the metal door.

"Right then, we need to find a way up to the roof. The zombies seem to all be at ground level, so if we can get to higher ground it should give us a bit more time. Come on guys, let's move," urged Apex, clutching Sarah by her hand.

The group split up to search for an exit to the roof. The tobacco factory was a huge building and the room contained long conveyer belts lined up with numerous boxes of cigarettes. There were only so many logical places an exit would be located and it wasn't long before an officer shouted out,

"Over here, I've found a way."

They ran over and ascended the steep flight of stairs to a fire exit door at the top. Apex pushed the handle to release the door and as he did so a gust of wind carrying the smell of death rushed past them. Rose gulped in disgust, instinctively putting her hand to her nose. There was a distinct chill in the air and as they all walked out onto the rooftop the exhaustion began to set in. Inspector Taylor sat herself quietly down to one side, her eyes welling up. She began sobbing.

"What's happening? I can't believe Fitch has gone. What did he do? What have any of us done? So many good people lost... and for what?"

Apex looked over at her sadly. He knew exactly how she was feeling; they all did.

"Inspector, I know you feel really fucking crappy right now, I get it, I really do. But they'll all be reborn, every single one of them. Remember I told you that none of us die, not for good anyway. When we find Ema everyone you know will be reborn and you won't remember any of this."

"I understandeth not how this Ema gent doth not help us," said John sadly.

He stood up and walked over to the edge of the building. He'd had enough. He missed his family, especially Jane and he wept at the thought of never seeing them again. Wiping his eyes he stared absently at the horizon, blinking through the tears. The world was no longer a place he recognised.

He gave a mournful sigh and then turned back to join the others. They were his family now, he needed to be with them.

Some of the group sat hugging one another, seeking comfort, while others sat and prayed and a few checked their weapons. Rose noticed John looking downhearted and sensed that something was bothering him.

"Are you OK John?"

"No, I bethink thee shouldst all behold," said John pointing down at the streets below.

Everyone grabbed their guns and walked towards the edge of the roof. The crowd of zombies had grown bigger and the ground looked as if it was moving. Slow ripples of walking dead filled up every last inch of space. It was the most frightening view any of them had ever witnessed.

Apex groaned, dropping his head and whispering under his breath, "We are totally fucked."

Suddenly a dark shadow cast over the roof and the sky filled with a deafening sound as thousands of birds flocked above their heads.

"This is what didst happen in mine time zone!" exclaimed John. "We must findeth cover before they attack us."

The group gathered together, forming a protective huddle, crouching down and shielding their heads with their arms.

The birds hovered above them, biding their time before swooping down past the group towards the zombies. Apex looked up in confusion, watching as the birds swooped and swirled and then rose up above the group once more. As if taking instruction from the birds, the zombies started screaming manically and swarmed over to the base of the tobacco factory. Clambering on top of one another, Apex realised what they were doing. They were forming a tower, a huge pulsating zombie tower. They were coming for them.

The officers who had ammo left in their weapons fired at the ascending mound of bodies, sending avalanches of screaming zombies falling to the ground. This seemed to enrage the birds and they swooped down, viciously pecking at the eyes of those officers bearing arms. The officers swung their arms around in defence, batting the birds away and any officers who were able to shoot tried fending them off by wildly firing their guns. Birds and officers dropped to the ground, figures becoming entangled in the confusion. Large pools of blood washed over Apex's feet and he looked at the others with a knowing look.

The three of them closed their eyes and grabbed the flock of savage birds by their combined powerful forces. They pulled them from the officers, flinging them off of the side of the building like giant catapults, striking the zombies below.

"It's no use, we're going to have to go back inside," shouted Inspector Taylor who had been cowering at the edge of the rooftop. She ran to the fire exit and opened the door where she was confronted by a crowd of the possessed beings. Without warning, she was forcefully grabbed and dragged inside, screaming in terror. Inspector Cherrad desperately tried to pull her back, but it was to no avail.

She was gone.

"Inspector Taylor!" shouted Inspector Cherrad. She held her breath, accepting her own fate. This was it; her time was up. As she was grabbed from behind and dragged into the stairwell, she gave one last terrified scream before being consumed by zombies.

Not knowing what else to do, the two remaining officers threw down their weapons and took a running leap off of the building, hitting the ground and dying on impact. The zombies swarmed over their bodies like flies, tearing at their flesh and ravaging their faces.

"Enough's a fucking enough, all of you grab hands," ordered Apex. "Form a circle. We're getting out of here!"

John, Rose, Apex and Sarah joined hands and closed their eyes against the chaos around them. Apex imagined a dome shaped force field surrounding them, its liquid mass pulsating with intense vibrational energy. The birds and zombies tried to penetrate it, but bounced off on impact.

"Come on think of something!" screamed Apex. "John, do something man. Rose, you have a go, imagine us somewhere, anywhere other than here!"

Trembling, Rose thought of the one place that was familiar enough for her to imagine clearly, the one place she felt safe.

Home.

She pictured home.

That dark, dingy building she called home. With its old fashioned charity shop furniture and its tired, scruffy looking carpet. She thought of the living room, the place where she watched TV and chatted to her mum. She imagined her friends travelling with her, over the buildings, past vehicles, trees, and the monstrous mob below.

This was it.

This is what it felt like to finally be in control of her subconscious.

She'd done it.

She'd finally done it.

She was home.

Chapter 51

The window gently knocked against the frame. It was freezing outside and a bitterly cold breeze blew in through the gap, lifting the curtain with each icy blast. There was something damp on the carpet, not completely saturated, but the smell of moisture hung in the air and the ground felt boggy and squelchy underfoot. Sarah twisted and turned in her restless slumber. Something wasn't right and her fears played out in her subconscious. She sat up and rubbed her eyes looking around the room in confusion.

How had she got here?

She remembered being on the roof of the factory and witnessing all those terrible events; the birds pecking and attacking everyone, and those poor officers who had hurled themselves from off the top of the building. She was used to seeing certain levels of brutality in her own time, but nothing came close to the horror of what she had experienced up on that roof. The images would haunt her forever. She heard a faint moan coming from across the room. It sounded like Apex and eager to be with him, she carefully stood up, patting her back to see if Jake was still safely attached. To her relief Jake was still sleeping, his baby breaths slow and relaxed, as though nothing had happened.

She softly called out to the others,

"Waketh up thee three, we art alive! Waketh up!"

Wearily the three of them opened their eyes, they felt so tired. All of their energy had been drained and it felt as if they had nothing left to give.

"Wherefore art we?" John asked, standing weakly and holding onto a small wooden table for support. "Rose, where hast thee taken us?"

John reached his hand out to her. She took it and carefully lifted herself up. "Don't you recognise it? It's my home," she smiled, happy to be back in familiar surroundings. And then she noticed the blood stained carpet and the smashed ornaments and it brought back another memory; the memory of her mum being violently beaten.

Sarah rushed over and wrapped her arms around her, tearing her away from her thoughts.

"Thou didst save us Rose. Thou didst saveth us all and mine baby too, I am most grateful," Sarah gushed, squeezing Rose tightly and kissing her on the cheek.

Embarrassed, wriggled free of her grip and looked around for Apex. He was over on the other side of the room trying to get up, but he was still shaky on his feet and didn't look at all like the strong outspoken man they had become accustomed to. His face was pale and he looked broken, the vision of a man who had lost the will to live.

"How far are we from the library now?" he croaked.

"Umm well, I think we kind of might be further away," said Rose tentatively, knowing the news wouldn't go down well.

"SHIT!" he shouted, grabbing a picture frame from a shelf and throwing it against the wall.

"I can't fucking take this shit anymore!" he screamed.

They'd seen Apex get angry before, it was a fairly common occurrence, but they'd never seen him this desperate, this frustrated. Sarah's natural maternal instinct was to hold him tightly and calm him down, to speak to him as she would her own child.

"Calm down Apex, thou art scaring Jake," she ordered, wagging her finger at him like a schoolmistress and holding his shoulders to steady him.

"Oh really, so we've been attacked left, right and centre, almost fucking died and he managed to sleep through it all and now all of a sudden he's fucking scared of me?" he screamed sarcastically. "Man, what I would give to be that baby right now, all innocently tucked up without a fucking clue what's going on."

They looked at one another in silence, the tension unbearable.

"Look we can't just stand around waiting for the world to end can we, we've got to do something!"

"But it's too late Rose, we're as good as dead," Apex muttered in defeat.

John had remained quiet throughout Apex's tirade, but he'd had enough. He walked straight up to Apex and without any hesitation drew back his fist and punched him square in the face.

"Hey what the fuck did you do that for man? Are you crazy?" Apex shouted, clutching his nose and staring at John angrily.

"I wanteth thou never to speaketh like that again Apex. Behold, thou art scaring the womenfolk. We hath cometh too far to giveth up now and we can alloweth not for the Greys to findeth Ema before us."

Apex crossed his arms in a sulk and stared at his feet. He was fed up of everything, of the situation, of all of them, even Sarah.

Suddenly, the doors and windows began to vibrate, banging loudly. The glass cracked and then shattered across the room. They turned in shock and saw a ravaged fist swinging wildly through the frame. A wild scream rang out from outside and more arms burst through the hole.

"Quick upstairs," shouted Rose.

Everyone jumped to action and ran to the hallway, apart from Apex who slumped himself down into a chair, his face expressionless.

"Apex make haste, receiveth up, thou must not let them win!" screamed Sarah, desperately tugging at his sleeves. "Please Apex, I loveth thee, please stoppeth this. We hast to wend!"

"Just leave me Sarah. Go if you want, I won't stop you, but we don't stand a chance. It makes no difference whether you stay or go, either way we're done for."

He sat stubbornly rooted to the chair, devoid of emotion, numb to her pleas. Sarah screamed loudly as she was forcefully grabbed and pulled towards the window. Sensing his mother's fear, Jake cried out as he was dragged with her, both of their bodies made rigid by forces unknown. Apex jumped up, panicking at the thought of something happening to the woman that he did indeed love very dearly. He closed his eyes and imagined pulling her back towards him, tying invisible ropes around her and dragging her back to safety. But it was no use. He opened his eyes and watched in despair as she was dragged up the wall and out through the window into the abyss.

"Sarah! NO! Sarah, I'm so sorry!" cried Apex. "Jake! Come back! No! NO! What have I done?"

John had been waiting patiently in the hallway for Sarah to convince Apex to go upstairs with them, but when he heard Apex's hysterical screams he rushed into the room. Seeing what a state he was in, he dragged him away from the window.

"Apex, 'tis not the end, thee knoweth 'tis not. Make haste, we can still saveth her; the lady can be born once more, remember? We all hath a chance, but only if we art alive. Cometh Apex, make haste, follow me upstairs!"'

Apex reluctantly followed John out of the room and up the stairs into Rose's mum's bedroom. Rose slammed the door behind them and locked it. They edged back to the wall and cowered in the corner. Apex slumped down onto the carpeted floor and rested his head in his hands. He started sobbing loudly and then looked up at John and Rose with bloodshot eyes.

"I'm so sorry guys, I'm so sorry for being such a jerk. I could have saved her, what the fuck have I done?" His body shook with fitful sobbing.

"Hark, what is that hurtling?" exclaimed John.

"What do you mean, John?" said Rose. "I can't hear anything".

"Why 'tis some kind of humming sound, hark 'tis coming from that box over yonder," John said pointing at the desk.

"Oh that's just my mum's computer, she must have left it on. I'm surprised the power's not been cut off."

"Oh my God, shit what if... No it wouldn't work...," said Apex, jumping up excitedly and pacing around the room. "I wonder if... Oh my God, I think there's still a chance guys!"

"Explain thyself Apex, I understandeth not what thou art saying," said John looking at him in confusion.

"The computer. Is there still an Internet connection Rose?"

"I don't know, but I can certainly check. How is that going to help us though?"

"When I was in John's time zone I managed to travel with Sarah by looking at an image of the Queen. So I'm thinking if we search for the library we might just be able to imagine ourselves there."

Rose sat herself down at the computer and clicked the Internet tab. To her disappointment a message popped up on the screen, 'No Internet connection, please check all cables before contacting your service provider.'

"It's not working Apex, there's no connection."

"Fan-fucking-tastic, well that's that fucking plan out the window," moaned Apex. "Oh and by the way, in case you're interested, I can hear the zombies coming up the stairs. Looks like this is it guys, any last words before we're clawed to pieces?"

Grabbing each other's hands they awaited their impending fate, looking at one other sadly and reflecting on everything they had been through together. As a desperate last-ditch attempt, Rose bent down to pick up the router and noticed something.

"Wait, hang on," she shouted. "We didn't check the wires! Look, the router isn't switched on!"

"Oh my God Rose!" shouted Apex, "Quick switch it on and get it set up. John, you and me are going to hold off these fuckers."

John nodded and positioned himself next to Apex, preparing himself for the onslaught.

Rose pressed the small black button at the back of the router, eagerly watching the flashing lights, waiting for the green flash to become a solid block. The door started violently shaking and a series of deathly harrowing screams came from beyond.

"They're coming John, you ready? We've got this bro, OK?" Apex said, fondly patting his friend on the shoulder.

John smiled at Apex, his eye suddenly catching sight of a bowl of ornamental pebbles over his shoulder. Reaching past him, he grabbed the bowl and threw the pebbles up into the air. Apex winced, expecting them to crash down and hit him, but they hung suspended in mid air.

"What the hell are you doing John? There's no time for games, quit it," said Apex crossly.

"Waiteth, thou will see," replied John, a knowing look in his eyes.

The pebbles hovered perfectly still as John stood deep in thought. Apex shrugged his shoulders and turned to Rose,

"How's it going Rose, any luck?"

"The light's finally stabilised. I'm just going to check the connection now."

Loud banging noises came from the door and Apex turned to see the wood warping and bending from the pressure from behind. Slowly the wood started to splinter, before a fist penetrated through it sending shards of wood into the room.

"John stop your messing, let's fucking do this!"

As the door smashed open, John took a deep breath and aimed the suspended pebbles at the army of eyeless zombies. Each pebble fired its way forwards like a bullet from a gun, slicing through flesh and bones like a hot knife cutting through butter. Blood exploded from their bodies, smearing red entrails down the wall and collecting in puddles of gruesome gore on the floor. The pebbles continued to strike until all that was left was a pile of twitching bodies like some macabre funeral pyre.

"Woah, that was awesome John, respect! Shit there's more of them, brace yourselves! Rose come on will you, get a move on with that Internet connection!"

"I'm nearly there, it's loading now!"

The next wave of zombies rushed into the room, waving their arms maniacally and screaming from the gaping holes in their faces.

Apex and John closed their eyes.

They imagined the zombies lifting up from the ground, their heads puncturing the soft plaster on the ceiling. They slowly ripped their arms and legs away from their bodies, flinging the dismembered limbs through the doorway. Apex grasped the large stereo system with his mind and started dismantling its mechanical components. Bit by bit he broke down the mechanisms into tiny jagged pieces, each one twinkling in the air like a distant star constellation. Pushing as hard as he could, he launched the tiny projectiles at the zombies just as he had seen John do with the pebbles. They ripped through their targets like razor blades, but still they kept on coming.

"Rose seriously now, you've got to hurry. We're running out of energy here and I'm not sure either one of us is going to be able to hold them off for much longer. Hurry!" shouted Apex.

John grabbed the zombies as they came at him, swinging them around like rag dolls. Working as a team, Apex ripped them to pieces as John held them in his grip and added them to the growing pile. Yet still they kept coming, more and more of them, swarming up the stairs, pushing the rotting mountain of body parts towards them.

"We're going to fucking suffocate if this carries on," Apex yelled, turning his head to check how Rose was getting on.

"I've got it! Quick, I've got it!" shouted Rose.

"Let's move out John!" he screamed. He turned his mental focus to the large wooden bed frame and turning it on its side, he dragged it over to the doorway to form a barrier. "That should hold them off for a while."

The three of them gazed intently at an image of Patchway library that Rose had brought up on the screen.

"John you do it, you take us there. I'm not sure I've got the strength, I'm absolutely whacked," said Apex wearily.

Grabbing both of their hands, John closed his eyes and imagined the blue walls and pale wooden beams of the library. He visualised the neatly stacked shelves of books, row upon row stretching across the room, ending at the tidily arranged study area. He imagined the walls of Rose's house transforming into quivering liquid, rippling gently as the three of them passed effortlessly through its surface. Cars, buildings, trees, corpses and armies of zombies passed below them. And then, they were there.

"Man, is this the fucking library? It's a right mess! Look there are books everywhere!" said Apex looking disdainfully around the room. "Right then Rose, where's this book you had?"

"I can't remember exactly. I was sat over here," she said pointing to an upturned chair, "and I just sort of randomly picked a book out from this shelf." She ran her finger along the spines of the books, eliminating each one as she read their titles. "You'll have to help me look for it, or we'll be here for hours,"

The three of them set to business, scanning the shelves for the name Ema. All of a sudden that all too familiar wailing noise came from outside.

"Shit, they must have followed us!" shouted Apex. "Search faster, it has to be here somewhere."

"I've got it! I've got it!" shouted John excitedly, pulling a book from the shelves and waving it above his head.

Huddling together, they looked at the cover of the dusty leather bound book John was clutching.

"How to Find Your God. By Dr. E.M.A.," John read aloud.

"What the fuck? So all this time we've been hunting for a God and it turns out it's just some a book?"

"Open it John," said Rose eagerly.

John carefully opened the book and squinted at the print on the pages. He could barely read Middle English, let alone these unfamiliar futuristic words. He passed the book to Rose, hoping she'd be able to shed some light on it. She followed the words with her finger, scrolling through the text, looking for any information that may help them. Her finger paused on the page and she gave a sharp intake of breath.

"Oh my God. How is that possible?" she said.

"What do you mean, Rose? What does it say?"

"Look, it's me; it's me in the book. There's my name, it's telling my life story!"

Apex snatched the book from her and feverishly flicked through the pages. He stopped when he found John's name.

"Shit John, you're in it too. What the fuck!"

Apex continued turning each page until he arrived at his own story. "It's me, it's my life. I'm reading my fucking life!"

He turned more of the pages, skimming through the manuscript.

"My God look, it says exactly what's been happening to us, you know fighting those zombies… it's as if our actions are being narrated by this story. Our story has already been written! Woah, this is too fucking much, I don't get how this can be happening? We must be tripping."

"No me neither, it's crazy," said Rose. "Does it mention about when we get to the library?"

But, before Apex could turn the page to check, there was an almighty crash and the doors of the library smashed open revealing hundreds of zombies. Apex dropped the book and prepared himself for the final stand off.

"I can't believe these fuckers, they don't give up."

The zombies screamed as they hobbled towards them.

"We've found Ema and now we will destroy you all," Apex yelled at them.

"Hold them off!" shouted Rose. "I'll take the book." She picked it up and ran to the far end of the library, desperately trying to find the page, while John and Apex stood strong in their defensive stance. *They held hands and brought the combined image in their minds of thousands of books lifting and levitating in mid-air, before shooting across the room. Each book stacked on top of another, increasing in height to form a barrier against the manic zombies.*

Apex spoke to Rose in his mind.

"Rose, they're blocked for now, but you're going to need to hurry up and read that page."

"I'm going as fast as I can, just hold out a little longer."

Rose fumbled with the pages, her whole body shaking with adrenaline. She turned page after page, knowing she didn't have much time.

The blockade of books crashed to the ground as John and Apex's power weakened and the zombies surged forwards, stumbling over the pile of books. John and Apex retreated to the far end of the library where Rose was still painstakingly leafing through the pages of the book. She let out a panicked yelp as she felt herself being moved against her will, pulled by that invisible force, sucking her into the crowd, taking the book with her.

"Rose!" shouted John, reaching his arms out in despair.

John and Apex cowered together, their bodies stuck to the wall in terror. The group of zombies crept closer, using their grief to feed their energy. Life was over; they had done all they could do. Tears streamed down their faces and accepting defeat they allowed their bodies to go limp, submitting to the Greys' power.

They were mere seconds from being sucked in to oblivion when an almighty light appeared from out of nowhere, hovering above the group of zombies. It floated motionless in space and a deafening high-pitched sound screeched through the library. John and Apex covered their ears and felt the grip on them weaken. They stared in awe at the glowing orb, hypnotised by it like a moth attracted to a light bulb, until suddenly it exploded. The shockwave blasted through the zombies obliterating them entirely and John and Apex were thrown across the room.

Then everything went silent.

John stumbled to his feet a dazed look on his face as he glanced around at the devastation. Body parts and blood covered the floor, but through the sea of red he saw one person still standing.

Rose.

"Apex, recieveth up, 'tis Rose. The lady doth live and breathe!"

Apex got to his feet, shaking his head in an attempt to make sense of what had just happened. He looked beyond the pile of corpses and saw her. They clambered over the bodies, laughing hysterically, tears of joy streaming down their blood stained faces. Hugging her tightly Apex asked,

"That was fucking awesome, how did you do that?"

"I don't know how I did it," Rose gushed. "I just kind of panicked and was so desperate to get out. Then... well then that happened."

They separated from their embrace and continued looking for the page in the book, knowing their task was still incomplete.

Rose turned the pages, stopping at the point when they were in the library.

"I've found it," she said.

She scrolled down with her finger, past the moment of her escape and her embrace with Apex and John.

"So... what happens next?" said Apex impatiently.

Rose tentatively turned the page and as she did the library started to creak and groan as the wooden beams stretched and tightened around them. It created the illusion, like the distorted mirrors you see at a fairground, but on a much larger scale. Everything was bending and contorting out of shape and the walls seemed to be folding, collapsing in on them.

Until there was nothing left.

Nothing to see.

Nothing to hear.

Nothing to feel.

Chapter 52

Unknown location

They stood side by side, looking blindly into the black abyss. It was completely silent and the air was still. Even the temperature had settled to a bland comfortable nothingness. It felt as if they were in a kind of vacuum and the only thing left in existence was them.

Nothing more.

Nothing else.

Nothing.

Unable to see, yet sensing their presence, they felt for one another's hands; holding onto them for security, waiting for whatever was about to happen to them. Suddenly their surroundings filled with snapshots and moving clips of moments from their lives. They interspersed together, creating a scrapbook of memories. There was Rose with her mum. And then John appeared, followed by Apex; tiny glimpses into their past lives. Frightened and confused, the three of them stood and watched as their lives flashed before their eyes. No words were needed, but all of them were thinking the same… is this where Ema was hiding?

As if reading their minds, a voice called out to them.

"I'm so glad you have found me at last."

"Hey what the fuck, who said that?" said Apex with a start. "I suppose you're going to tell us you're some form of advanced Grey aren't you? Or that you're some fucking hybrid thing or some other shit like that, right?"

"You couldn't be further from the truth Apex. No, I am none of those things. I am a God. I am the maker and creator of your universe. Without me, you would not, nor ever, exist. I am the one that has given you life."

"But sir," interrupted John, "what kind of a life hast thou given us? We hast had nowt but terror and dry sorrow, 'tis a life for nay man."

"John, none of this is real," replied the voice wisely.

"What do you mean?" asked Rose

"You are merely a figment of imagination; my imagination for that matter. You exist in my world alone. It may feel as though this is real to you, that everything you have ever experienced is real, but to me it is nothing more than a collection of creative thoughts."

"Man I thought Calcus was full of shit, but you seriously take the fucking biscuit!" shouted Apex in frustration. "Quit the bullshit and tell us what's really going on here."

"So it was you doing all of this, you were the one who created all this destruction and death?" screamed Rose. "You're the reason I lost my mum. All of this, everything, is because of you?"

She dropped to her knees sobbing loudly. John knelt down beside her and took her into his arms. The thought that everything they had ever known was fake, that the world they lived in wasn't real, that they themselves weren't real, that they didn't exist was too much to comprehend. Not after everything they had been through to get here.

"Where are you? I'm going to fucking kill you!" Apex raged.

"Apex, calm down, you cannot kill me," chuckled the God. "I live in another dimension, in another world far from yours. I can see you and I can determine everything that happens to you. You can't see me however, and you have absolutely no control over what happens to you. There is no point in fighting it, it just is."

Rose lifted her head from John's shoulder, wiping the tears from her cheeks and said,

"What dimension do you live in?"

"I live in the 'real' dimension."

"So what you're basically saying is we're not real, and you are?" said Apex sarcastically. He turned to John and whispered, "This guy's got a fucking screw loose. Let's ask him a few more questions and then I say we try and get the hell out of here."

"So go on then, tell me all about this eternal life shit then, because I've had to go through a hell of a lot to find you and I want some fucking answers," said Apex.

"You should already know the answer Apex, you have seen it for yourself in the book. That book is you, it is all of you. It is all of your lives bound together over hundreds of pages."

"Excuse me sir, but art thou saying we art in a book?"

"Yes John, that is correct. And there are many copies of you. Hundreds, thousands, millions of parallel versions of you, each living the same life, in varying degrees, over and over. But what you must remember is that there is only one God and there is only ever one way

461

to find me. You three have done it. You discovered the book that sent you to me. And here we all are."

There was a short silence, broken only by the sound of Apex cursing under his breath.

"But Calcus told us to warn you about the Greys. If we aren't real, then does that mean they aren't real either? He said that they had found something in us, an eternal life, which they don't have. He said they needed to find you in order to change their destiny. I don't understand, how can we even begin to know what's real and what isn't any more?" Her voice broke at the end as she tried to stop herself from crying again.

"Oh those Greys, how they do try. Fortunately for us they are not as smart as they make out. They call me Ema, but that is not my name, it never has been. These primitive aliens can only understand a few words, their vocabulary is so limited that they only really have the ability to pick out letters."

"What the fuck are you talking about?" interrupted Apex. "This is utter bullshit! If you're a God, prove it. Go on, prove you are who you say you are."

"I can easily prove it to you, Apex. I can stop you swearing for a start."

"Oh really and how the muck are you going to do that exactly huh?"

Apex hesitated, carefully thinking through what he had just said.

"I said how the muck are you going to do that? Hey, what the muck have you done?"

Rose and John started sniggering. It was entirely inappropriate considering the seriousness of the situation, but hearing Apex talk nonsense was highly amusing to them both.

"So you think you can control my ducking thoughts, do you?" shouted Apex angrily. "This is all a load of bullhit! Well done, bonus points to the invisible God, give yourself a sucking pat on the back! What's your real name anyway? If it's not Ema, what the suck is it?"

"My real name is neither important nor relevant."

"What about mine family?" asked John.

"They are safe and you will all return to your families soon. When this is over, you will lose all memory of me and of everything that has happened."

"And what about Calcus, where is that gent? Is he real?" asked John.

"He is real to you, but to me he is just imagination."

"So let me get this straight," said Apex, "everything that has happened is just 'your imagination', none of it has actually happened? Because, excuse me but I'm finding it very difficult to get my head around all this. If we're in your mind and you're talking to us, then that means you're talking to yourself, which means you're crazy. You're a sucking schizophrenic!"

"Slightly crazy, perhaps. Schizophrenic? Questionable. Please allow me to explain. You see the real world is not as you might think. It is filled with destruction, hatred and death. Depression has become an epidemic here and many of us live a life of anxiety, despair and helplessness. We are plagued by demons that attack our every thought, our motivation and our will to live. But with the power of positivity we are able to fight off these evil creatures. We battle against them; sometimes we win, sometimes we don't. The three of you make up my intellectual mind, the part that breathes hope. You three have helped me to fight off the negative by the power of thought."

"So you're saying the Greys are the negative demons in your mind?" said Rose.

"Yes, that is correct. The Greys fight my intellectual mind constantly and without you I would no doubt have let them win. I know you might not think it, but you three are incredibly important to me."

"Come on now bro, this has got to stop. We're in your head? Ha I've heard it all now! Where are the Greys now then eh? In your stomach? In your bowels? Enough with the bullhit already. And will you quit sucking with my words!" Apex huffed.

"Yes sorry about that, I've proved my point, I'll stop. In answer to your question, the Greys are still there, they have just retreated back to the primitive mind. But make no mistake, they will attempt to come back; they always do."

Apex gave a frustrated sigh. Surely if John, Rose and himself were merely figments of this God's imagination, then something could be done to change how boring and repetitive his life was. He'd be willing to accept all of this if he knew that what he was going back to had some kind of hope.

"OK so look, if what you say is true, then can you put me back in Rose's time zone instead of my one, because I fucking hate mine. And can I have Sarah, Chaz and Olive with me too? Plus, I'd quite like to be rich, you know like super rich, with a big house and a nice car. Anything, just please don't send me back to my time zone," Apex pleaded.

"I'm afraid I cannot do that Apex, for it has already been written. Everything is pre-determined. But you do have the ability to forget, which means by the time you go home you will have no recollection of anything. So long as your story continues to be read, you will always

have eternal life. Your story will forever be told and you will never die. If it is any consolation, the life you have is rather an exciting one, wouldn't you admit?"

"So that's it then, all of this was for nothing. What happens now?" Apex's question was met with silence.

A small orb of light suddenly appeared between them, illuminating their faces with an ethereal glow. They gazed at it, completely mesmerised, watching as it moved hypnotically from side to side. As it gathered momentum, the orb began to soften at the edges and slowly it started to change shape. It moulded into the shape of the letter 'P' and was then followed by a reversed 'P', which slotted neatly alongside it. The shape hovered in the air before being linked together by a single ring.

The voice of the God echoed around the void.

"I want you all to look at this symbol. This symbol represents eternal life, the endless cycle of existence and the power of positivity. You must walk towards it and repeat these two simple words, 'The End'"

"You gotta be shitting me, I ain't doing or saying anything you tell me to."

But it was no use, Apex was merely an imaginative creation, a pawn in the God's mind game; they all were. Any words they spoke, their actions, their very existence was controlled by this God. He was their creator, the maker of their universe; he was the puppet master.

Taking control of their thoughts and possessing their very beings he said,

"Now repeat after me, 'The End.'"

Apex, John and Rose stood motionless, transfixed by the brightly lit symbol in front of them. They were barely recognisable, shadows of their former selves, empty expressionless vessels. They walked rigidly towards the symbol.

Unable to stop themselves.

Unable to protest.

Unable to do anything other than walk and repeat the words…

"THE END"

Epilogue

E lation. Yes, that's what I feel. It's taken me over two years to complete my novel and as I write the final sentence, tap the full stop key, I can't stop myself from smiling.

It's done.

Dusted.

Finito.

Now all I need is for it to be edited, but it feels great knowing the hard work is over. I raise my arms above my head, enjoying the tight stretch and release as they relax back down. I am filled with so much euphoria, a feeling I haven't ever experienced before and it feels great. "Give yourself a pat on the back Edward, you've done good," I say to myself with a grin.

Now to be honest, I'm not normally one to self-congratulate. But this is something big, something that not everyone is capable of achieving within their short existence in this world.

It was time to break the news to my darling wife, Anupreet, who has had to put up with me talking to myself and my constant daydreaming more times than I can keep track of.

"Who are you talking to?" she'd call out from the other room. And I'd reply with a chuckle, "No one babe, just talking to myself... again."

I'm not crazy.

Let me just make that clear.

But after reading and re-reading my manuscript you can certainly go a little crazy. Because when you are submerged into a world that is far from your own, it's enough to drive anyone mad.

I press save and switch off the computer. I haven't ever forgotten to save what I have written, but the fear still lurks in me that one day I may lose everything.

I rise from my chair and call out, "Anupreet?"

I can hear the pots noisily clunking away in the kitchen and I know there's no way she'll be able to hear me above that racket. I make my way down the hallway and stand there watching her for a moment. Cooking is her passion, it's her life, and I love watching her pottering about doing her thing. I pull up behind her and lovingly wrap my arms around her.

"It's done," I whisper softly into her ear, "I've finished it."

I was expecting a 'yippee!' or at least a 'well done!', but for once in her life Anupreet is speechless. Relief was written all over her face. She had her husband back. I felt slightly guilty about the amount of time I had spent writing my novel and although I had tried to give as much of my time to my family as possible, I hadn't always been there for them. As soon as one idea manifested, another would quickly pop into my head and I would drop everything and run to the computer to quickly

468

type it out. It annoyed Anupreet immensely, but I knew deep down she was incredibly proud of me.

"So what happens now?" she asked, ever the practical thinker.

"Well, I'm going to get in touch with Bex and see if she'll edit it for me. And I'll contact Russell to give him the good news. Plus, I'll need somewhere to launch the book. I was thinking the Tobacco factory would be perfect, what do you reckon babe?"

She tapped the handles of the pans, creating a tuneful metal symphony with her perfectly manicured nails. I knew deep down she was just as excited about this as me, but there was still an ingrained sorrow in her face that she was unable to disguise. I made a mental note to start dedicating more time to her again. To take her out on dates and give her the attention she had craved over these past couple of years.

I licked my fingers. I had just finished eating my favourite snack; cheese on toast by the way, for those of you that care, and taking a large sip of my coffee I slumped down onto the sofa and stared out of the window. I can quite literally see the whole world through this window, it's that big, but the downside is that anyone looking back can see what I'm doing too. It's 10:30 am and the weather is terrible. We've had non-stop rain for days now and the thunder and lightning is an almost daily occurrence. It means I'll get drenched when I have to go and pick up my daughter, Kierra, from nursery. You never know, the rain might have passed by then.

I'm not really sure why, but my tiredness has become more and more of a problem of late. I've put it down to all those late nights spent tinkering away at my book, but I daren't admit that to Anupreet. I wriggle into my favourite position; legs up and laid out flat, remote control in hand. I know I'll fall asleep, I always do and it's one of Anupreet's pet hates.

Every time I lie on the sofa I say to her,

"Don't worry, I won't fall asleep, I promise."

But of course, I always do.

The news flashes up on screen and a stern looking news reporter appears, describing the details of all of the destruction that has been caused by the bad weather. Apparently there have been some minor earthquake tremors too. I didn't feel anything, too busy sleeping I should imagine.

Anupreet walks over to the sofa and looks down at me accusingly. I know what she'll say, but I've made a concerted effort to keep my eyes as wide open as possible. I stare up at her with a cheeky grin that says, 'yes I am awake, look' and she smiles and rolls her eyes at me.

"Have you contacted Bex yet?" she asks.

"Yes, I sent her an email and she's replied saying she feels very honoured to be editing my book. I've sent over the first chapter and she reckons it will take about a week. Oh yeah and I forgot, Russ will be coming over soon, he wants to talk to me a bit about the book. He has some more ideas on how it should end."

She tutted and shook her head in a mock annoyed way. I knew she couldn't stay mad at me for long; she strongly believed that everyone should be allowed the chance to follow their dreams, and this was mine. She wandered back into the kitchen to follow her own dreams and I have to admit, whatever she was cooking smelt amazing!

I stirred from my slumber. I could hear my wife talking to me, gently nudging and shaking me awake. I'd done it again. I slowly opened my eyes.

I don't usually like being woken up, especially when there's no good reason, but on this occasion I knew she must need me for something, as normally she'd leave me to sleep and then lecture me about it the next day.

"I heard a knock, I think Russell must be here," Anupreet said gently.

I heard a knock at the door, so I stand and stretch out my legs, feeling the pleasant sensation of endorphins rushing through my body. I put on my slippers and walk groggily to the front door, stifling a yawn as I go past the kitchen. The front door is covered in pen and crayon marks, a sign that a child lives here. For a while it really bothered me, but you can't shout at a two year old for expressing their creativity can you. I unlock the latch and open the door. On the other side of the door is someone I don't recognise, a person wearing a jumper with a large baggy hood covering his face. He's looking at the ground and doesn't say a word.

Feeling a little unsettled, I ask them what they want.

"Hello, can I help you?"

No reaction.

He stands there, motionless.

It's starting to freak me out if I'm honest.

I repeat my question.

"Hello, are you OK?"

Something catches my eye and I look behind this strange figure. There are more of them, lots of figures all wearing identical clothing to the one in front of me. They are all stood, hoods up, staring at the ground.

OK, so now I'm really freaking out.

I start closing the door, but before it shuts fully the hooded figure pushes his weight against it and looks up at me. His face is dark and ominous, shadowed by the hood. I shiver and start to protest when a sound like nothing I have ever heard before comes from his mouth. It's like an eerie screech, a bit like nails being dragged down a chalkboard, and there are words in there, definitely words, but words I can't quite make sense of.

My heart starts beating frantically as it dawns on me.

It can't be.

No, I must be imagining it.

For a moment it sounded as if he said...

"Hello... EMA"

About the Author

Edward Attridge lives in Bristol with his wife and two children. He began his journey to become a novelist during his studies for a Psychology degree and Hypnotherapy diploma. His mind was crammed with creative ideas for the stories he wanted to write and he would often spend time making up stories for his daughter.

.

Printed in Great Britain
by Amazon